Dead

A Jonah Pen

Keith Nixon

Dead Money
Published by Gladius Press 2022
Copyright © Keith Nixon 2022
First Edition

Keith Nixon has asserted his right under the Copyright, Designs and Patents Act 1998 to be identified as the author of this work.

CONDITIONS OF SALE

All rights reserved. No part of this publication may be reproduced, stored in a retrieval system, or transmitted in any form or by any means, electronic, mechanical, photocopying, scanning, recording or otherwise, without the prior permission of the publisher.

This book has been sold subject to the condition that it shall not, by way of trade or otherwise, be lent, resold, hired out, or otherwise circulated without the publisher's prior consent in any form of binding or cover other than that in which it is published and without a similar condition including this condition being imposed on the subsequent purchaser.

All characters in this publication are fictitious and any resemblance to real persons, living or dead is purely coincidental.

Cover design by James Webber.

Dead Money (slang)

In finance:

Money invested not earning interest, dividends or capital gain.

In poker:

Cash left in the pot after a player has folded, *or*,

An inexpert player, unlikely to win.

One

Two Months Ago
5.55a.m.

Every morning was the same. Wake up just before the alarm. Stare at the ceiling, A.K.A. someone else's floor, invisible through the pitch black, while the day's tasks ahead buzzed like angry bees in her mind: roll out of bed, check email, get a shower, take the Tube to the office, answering emails en-route.

Today would be different.

The analogue clock on the bedside cabinet rattled an alarm. She reached out, flicked the button on the top and the hammer no longer struck the bell. Her fingers continued, creeping like a spider over the wood grain, found the switch for the bedside lamp, pressed it. The bulb's wattage was low, the illumination soft, pushing back the darkness a few feet.

She always rose early to ensure first use of the shared bathroom in the bedsit. Traffic noise on the road beneath the window was often quieter at this time, too. But never absent. The house stood near traffic lights on a main thoroughfare into the city. Easy access for work, cheap, impersonal. But mainly cheap.

As a heavy truck rumbled past, causing the walls to vibrate in motorised harmony, she picked up a large handset – almost tablet rather than mobile phone – from off a wireless charging dock. The truck changed gear, giving a brief respite. She sighed, flicked the phone's screen, bringing it to life. The charge was 100% and would just about endure until the evening.

A couple of updates had occurred in the hours she'd been asleep. Normal. And there were emails. There were *always* emails. They arrived liked drips from a leaking tap, steadily filling up the inbox. Often people asking stupid, basic questions about how to do the most basic of stupid stuff. She skimmed the list. There was rarely anything really worth full devotion. But that was work.

Then the header of one message snared their attention, like a fish to a brightly coloured lure. The note was the kind of unsubtle phishing scam adopted by Black Hats; illegal hackers. However, there was an obvious difference.

In the subject line was her password – in full.

Which was impossible.

She pushed back the covers, swung her legs around until their feet touched the thin carpet worn down by many shoes over the years, rough on the soles. She moved a thumb over the message and tapped.

The fish nibbling the bait to see if it was real or fake.

She raced through the message, felt lightheaded at the end. Then she remembered to breathe, let out a lungful. Did that several times to calm her fibrillating heart.

She started reading the message again, properly understanding the depth of the communication now.

First, the password. Definitely correct, absolutely current. She changed her password twice a week and this one had been generated less than twenty four hours ago. Always a complicated string of random letters, numbers and symbols designed to be impossible to guess.

DEAD MONEY

So someone clearly had access to her details.

That simple fact sent a chill through her. What else did the hacker possess? She was certain she'd been badly compromised and reversing that problem would be difficult and lengthy. And already too late.

The first words of the message read, '*Now I have your attention know one thing. This is not sport. This is real.*'

She totally believed whoever had typed the message. The shower started in the bathroom next door, a hiss of water through lime scaled nozzles.

'*I have all your data. Everything. From your birth right to this very moment. Your parents and how you were raised. Where you've lived, what schools you went to, what detentions you had. Your boyfriends, girlfriends and your actual friends.*'

She stood then paced the room, floorboards creaking, back and forth while she read, each word a tiny, sharp jab in the soul.

'*I know exactly what you've been up to. Believe me when I say I own irrefutable proof of your guilt. I know what dirty games you've been playing, and I know why. I know the identity of every person you've damaged.*

'*You need to be entirely aware that I'm not lying when I say those people are vengeful and they possess many artistic methods of retaliating. They have money (less now, thanks to you). They are desperate to own you. However, don't think of running. There's no purpose in packing a bag. Even if you totally dropped off the grid, I would eventually find you. Again.*

'*At this instant, there are only two people in the entire world with these facts in their hands. Us. And we can keep it that way. I am not going to tell our mutual friends with retri-*

bution in their hearts who and where you are. Not unless you make me. However, I'm sure you'll understand when I state there's a price to pay to keep yourself out of harm's way.

'I promise three things. First, you will never learn my identity. Second, the fee for your continued anonymity will be steep. But it is achievable. Third, once our business is concluded you will never hear from me again. You can carry on your merry way, hacking whomever you wish.

'Therefore, in language you will be able to understand... you now face two options: a time bound binary selection – a zero or a one, an on or an off. Click the uppermost link and further instructions will follow. Make the selection beneath and your data will immediately be shared with the parties you have attacked, and they will come for you. The choice is, of course, entirely yours.

'You should note, however, the previous use of the phrase 'time bound'. A fifteen-minute countdown started the instant you opened this email. Once this period has expired the default is number two and your data will be shared. So, to state the obvious, be quick!'

At the very foot of the message were the options:
Hold.
Twist.
Each was underlined and in a blue font, meaning a hyperlink had been embedded into the words.

Like the movie, *The Matrix*, but not. Because in the film the hero was able to select between a new, confusing reality or going back to their previous existence, totally unaware of the wider world. The latter was not available. Her life had irreversibly changed the moment she'd opened the email.

She sat down on the edge of the unmade bed. There was no need to re-read the message again and only minutes remained. The statements and implications were entirely clear. There was just a single practical solution: play the blackmailer's game. She hit 'Hold' and the fish swallowed the bait. Then, a new window popped up containing several pages of text; instructions on how to proceed.

She closed the page, flicked off the screen, put the phone back onto the charging dock, and headed out into the corridor where one of her housemates was waiting. As the bathroom's current occupant exited, she pushed past and entered, ignoring the shout from the person she'd queue jumped. At least one of them would get over the beginning of their morning. She stripped off, started the shower. While standing under the bitterly cold stream of water she thought through all the options. None of them were attractive, all had danger lurking.

People were going to lose. That was a certainty because this was a zero sum game. She just needed to ensure one of the casualties wasn't her.

And she had the skills to do so.

Two

Now

The uniform cop standing beneath the glass-fronted building's overhang behaved like he owned the pavement beneath his highly polished boots.

Arms crossed, back straight, he stared at everyone who passed by like a watchful owl, wide eyed and head rotating constantly. Because of the downpour, workers and tourists alike were focused on their destinations; hidden under umbrellas or waterproof jackets. So, other than Detective Chief Inspector Jonah Pennance, nobody paid the cop the slightest attention.

A Japanese couple, probably old enough to be the cop's grandparents, carrying a map and wearing plastic see-through ponchos, thin as cling film, paused beside the cop. He leaned away from the Japanese, glanced them up and down as if they were suspects in the murder case which, to Pennance's knowledge, was playing out seven floors above in the penthouse apartment. They must have asked for directions as the cop flung out a long, bare arm and pointed past Pennance. The Japanese bowed in thanks, but the cop ignored them, returning to vigilant duty.

The cop's attention switched to a shuffling, heavily bearded tramp pushing a tartan shopping cart. A large mongrel dog lagged behind the vagrant, stopping sniffing a stone pillar supporting the overhang, then began to squat. The cop made to say something until he noticed Pennance approaching from Petty Wales, a pedestrianised section on the bank of the Thames. That tended to happen a lot as Pennance was literally tall enough to stand out from the crowd. The cop spun slowly on the ball of one foot, ready for confrontation because Pennance was maintaining his path and it seemed the cop wanted the apartment entrance to remain clear.

Pennance was near enough now to see the legend 'City of London Police' emblazoned in red letters on the cop's stab vest, instead of the standard blue. He wore a short sleeve shirt despite the elements and the oversized custodian helmet typical of his unit, which Pennance thought looked several sizes too large.

Territorial forces were divided into Basic Command Units. Pennance couldn't remember exactly how many BCUs there were across the UK, but at least two hundred. London itself was divided into twelve BCUs, each managed by a Superintendent. The City of London was, officially, a county treated separately from the rest the capital and existed within its own enclave. Although City Police were the smallest force in the UK and despite being formed ten years after the Metropolitan City Police, they'd somehow managed to remain a distinct unit.

Everything City Police did seemed singular – including the cop's helmet which displayed the City Police coat of arms instead of the Brunswick Star in gold, rather than silver. Another unique City Police rule was minimum height which meant their intake had loftier people than the other London units.

Pennance had never enjoyed dealing with City Police. They reckoned they had complete control, even when they didn't. Like they were better than everyone else, even when they weren't.

So, City Police were literally used to looking down on others. Not this time, though. As Pennance got closer, the cop tilted his head back, keeping his eyes locked with Pennance's. Taller than the average British male, shorter than the average basketball player, Pennance loomed over the younger man. As he opened his mouth to deliver an order Pennance revealed his warrant card.

"DI Pennance with the NCA Major Crime Investigative Support Team."

Pennance received what seemed to be the cop's trademark up-and-down glance before he examined Pennance's warrant card. Pennance didn't dress like a typical police. No business attire for him. The suit and tie fashion were headed the manner of the hat and the waistcoat; soon to be consigned to history. Instead, Pennance wore chinos, a shirt open at the neck, Converse Chuck's and a lightweight waterproof jacket.

"NCA?" The cop rubbed the deep cleft in his chin.

"National Crime Agency." A government department in its own right – operationally independent of the Home Office – whose purpose was to fight serious and organised crime. Maybe the cop really was that fresh.

"I know what the NCA is, sir."

Maybe not, then. In an effort to be disarming Pennance smiled, the opposite of his expression on the ID photo, which was right up to date, taken on his first day of the new job, thirteen days ago.

"Thank you, sir." The cop handed back Pennance's warrant card.

Pennance lifted his jaw, nodding upwards to where apparently a body lay. "What's gone on in there?" A murder in highly unusual circumstances, that's all he'd been told.

When Pennance had risen for work less than two hours previously he hadn't expected his day to unfold like this. He'd reached the NCA HQ in Vauxhall well before the start of his shift and was the only person in the office when his new boss, Crime Team Manager Stephanie Meacham, had entered and sent Pennance to Lower Thames Street. She'd told him City Police had asked for Pennance by name.

"I've no idea, sir, I'm sorry." The cop shrugged. "I just stand here."

Pennance should have known better – perimeter guards rarely possessed even a shallow knowledge of an investigation. The cop twisted to look over one shoulder, raised a hand to signal someone inside. A metallic click was obvious before floor-to-ceiling double doors, of the same reflective glass which ran along the length of the building, silently rolled back. A large black gap appeared, like the opening to a mythic cave. However, the impression was ruined when Pennance noticed that, judging by his attire, an actual footman stood within the entrance. A coat hung low on his arms and well down his thighs, and his hat was pushed onto his forehead, flattening his ears.

There was movement beside the footman and another City PC, a tall female, emerged. She wore a flat, peaked cap instead of a helmet. "Sir," she beckoned with one pale hand, "If you'll follow me."

Pennance nodded at the footman as he passed. A highly polished brass badge pinned on his chest read, Matthew. The footman sighed, drooped his shoulders and stared onto the pavement, like he wanted to be out on his patch, meeting and greeting.

The female PC led Pennance across a silent lobby absent of staff, nobody present to pay attention to the needs of guests. Except for a lone man in a sharp suit and well managed hair stood in a nearby office doorway, watching Pennance as he progressed between sofas and chairs in a zebra striped fabric. The PC paused, pressed the up button between a pair of elevator doors.

"You want the top floor, sir," she said. "Just hit 'P'."

Pennance entered the lift. A camera lens, a fisheye with a wide aperture, was obvious at the top of the keypad.

The PC said, "Someone will be waiting for you." She turned and walked back the way she'd come. The besuited man eyeballed Pennance until the lift doors closed. The box rose slowly, forcing Pennance to listen to the muzak. Pennance tapped his foot and not in time to the tinny jingle.

When the ascent mercifully halted, the doors parted, revealing a crime scene investigator, obvious by her white evidence suit, waiting beside a huge vase of white fresh flowers. "DI Pennance?" Her skin was the colour of a latte coffee and she clutched a face visor in a nitrile glove clad hand.

"I'm Lydia Gough, the Crime Scene Manager of the Forensic Investigation Unit. We've been expecting you." She held out a plastic bag the size of a large envelope – a suit for Pennance. "You'll need to put this on before we proceed." Pennance split the wrapper, let the fabric unfurl. It seemed a little short for him. Clearly, Gough agreed. "That's the biggest we've got, sorry."

"It's not the first time, won't be the last." Once Pennance had shrugged on the suit Gough handed him a pair of clear plastic glasses and offered a box of gloves which proved a tight fit also, pinching the hairs on the back of his hand.

"All good?" asked Gough.

"It'll do." Pennance nodded. "Where's the body?"

Gough put her visor back on, said, "This way." She led Pennance along the corridor to a solid door of a pale wood where yet another City PC stood. Older than his other colleagues, he seemed to radiate world-weariness in a seen-it-all-before attitude. Gough paused, said, "I understand you like to take your time."

"I didn't realise my reputation had spread so wide."

Gough raised an eyebrow narrow enough that it had probably been drawn on with a make-up pencil. "Only as far as the person who rarely stops talking about you."

"Oh?"

Leaving his question unanswered, Gough twisted the handle and shouldered the door open, allowing Pennance to enter a kitchen diner reception space. The CSM let the door swing slowly, and silently, shut behind her. "All yours," she said.

To one side a Formica table with accompanying steel tube chairs. Beyond that a small electric cooker, hob, sink and some cupboards. Three huge cylindrical lamp shades, long enough to cope with the double height ceiling, of a bright red fabric hung down over the table – more for display than practicality.

The kitchen seemed as if it had never been used. Spotlessly clean, all the surfaces gleaming. A total absence of odours, too.

Pennance headed for the appliances. The quiet hum of the fridge cut out and a bulb flicked into life when he tugged opened the door. The interior was almost empty. Just a carton of milk and, Pennance pursed his lips, two bags of blended coffee from Harrods. Overpriced and incorrectly kept. In comparison, the floor-standing wine store was about the same size and filled almost to capacity, multiple racks of condensation-speckled green bottles, several champagne magnums on the lowest level. Pennance touched the nearest, the chill palpable even through the glove. The dishwasher, a Smeg, was empty except for a mug and a cafetière. The oven interior was untarnished.

"Not very impressive, is it?" said Gough. "Through here is more like it, though." She hiked a thumb at the living space beyond.

Curved glass walls afforded a view out onto an expansive terrace, decked in a dark wood, and over the Thames. Light flooded across a dining table and chairs positioned by the window, facing outwards; presumably to impress the guests. Pennance failed to see how it couldn't. Nearby stood two sofas in what looked to be aubergine-coloured felt, also positioned for the river. Several bright artworks hung on the back wall and Pennance paused beside one; a riot of shapes and colours.

"Modern art," said Gough. "I don't get it."
"Me either."

"Quarter of a million quid's worth of smeared oil and pigment."

Pennance pointed towards a corridor on his left. "What's down there?"

"Bedrooms, on this floor and above. However," Gough said, "the interesting stuff is this way." She indicated a doorway into an adjacent room.

Pennance's shoes squeaked on the parquet floor as he followed.

A trio of white suits worked the scene. Two paid no attention but the third stared at Pennance over his shoulder. Pennance ignored him while he took in the fact that the floorplan this side of the wall was a mirror image of the space they'd just exited.

Three more artworks were fixed to the back wall; precisely spaced. Pennance had to look twice because there appeared to be a pair of TVs positioned above one another at the far end. Until he realised the lower display was actually a fire; while the other was the actual television and at least 60 inches across.

A squashy sofa and matching armchairs faced each other. Behind stood a grand piano in a glossy black lacquer, the lid open to reveal the soundboard and strings. Beyond the piano was a vacuum cleaner, the old-fashioned type you drag around behind you.

Pennance was tempted to reach out and press a key to see if it was properly tuned but held back. He wondered how the hell the removal men would have got the piano upstairs.

"On a wheeled trolley, turned on its side, I'd bet," said Gough.

"Excuse me?" Pennance blinked.

"Or lifted by a crane." Gough pointed to the piano. "You were staring. Probably trying to figure out the way it was installed. I did too."

The guy in the suit stood, came over, frown obvious on his face, despite the hood and glasses. "We're trying to solve a murder here, Lydia, not discuss instrumental décor."

Gough took a pace back. "I'm on it, Chief Inspector."

"Thank you."

Gough retreated, her embarrassment evident through her stooped shoulders.

The man switched his attention fully onto Pennance. In Pennance's experience, ranking officers didn't take to being looked down upon; literally or metaphorically and Pennance stood a good foot taller than him.

"I'm DCI Leigh Fulton, and the senior investigating officer here." Fulton indelicately informing Pennance who was the boss.

"I'm just here to help, sir. I've no desire to take over."

"Oh, that won't be happening, *inspector*. I assure you." True to form, then. "I've never had the National Crime Agency wade into one of my cases before. Inevitable, I guess, as not a month seems to go by without some new announcement about your lot's expanding power and influence. What was it most recently? Border control?"

"I wouldn't say I'm wading in. Actually, I'm not even sure why I was asked to attend."

"Might being in MCIS be a reason?" Although the agency had divisions to tackle organised crime, the trafficking of people, drugs and weapons, cyber-crime and economic crime, the NCA could be tasked to investigate any criminality and MCIS often operated in the field. "How is life after Sapphire?"

"Still finding my feet."

"I guess you'd both finally had enough looking at pictures of kids in compromising positions as well?"

"What, sir?"

"He means, me, Jonah."

Pennance flicked his attention beyond Fulton to the corridor where another person in a white suit was framed. "Simone."

Detective Sergeant Simone Smithson had inhabited the desk facing Pennance when they'd worked in Sapphire, the specialist unit investigating crimes against minors, up until the time Simone had transferred and long after the pair of them had somehow battered their friendship into submission.

"Don't know how you guys ever handled that stuff," said Fulton. "Anyway, what have you been told, inspector?" Simone moved beside Fulton. She tucked a lock of blonde hair back under her hood before fixing Pennance with a flat eyed glare. Pennance had the almost overwhelming desire to step back, to put more distance between them. "Are you listening, Pennance?"

"Sorry, sir." Pennance broke away from Simone's glare. "I've no information on the victim. Only that he died in unusual circumstances."

"You can bloody well say that again." Fulton pointed towards the sofa. "The corpse is Grady Carnegie."

"The celebrity fund manager?"

"The very same. Made his clients millions and himself even more if this place is anything to go by. I saw him on TV a couple of nights ago, advising a couple on their investment plan. Seemed like he's never out of the newspapers. I couldn't stand the guy myself; I turned him off."

"Somebody else did, too," said Pennance.

Fulton standing over Carnegie's body now, snorted, perhaps in an approximation of humour, while Simone rolled her eyes. Pennance took his time to review the body.

Carnegie lay on his back. He wore waistcoat and trousers in a matching light grey and a red tie paired with a pastel blue shirt, brogues on his feet. His eyes were open, the pupils narrowed almost to pinpoints. As if Carnegie had watched his life disappear down a long tunnel. The little exposed skin was the colour of old matte paint. A sensationalist reporter might have typed 'deathly pale'. Carnegie was clearly well beyond the recall of science and had expired at least several hours ago.

However, Pennance's attention hauled towards what filled Carnegie's mouth to bursting point. His lips were curled back exposing chemically bleached teeth, reminding Pennance of the last time he'd sat in a dentist's chair, waiting for the drill to descend. "What's that?" Pennance pointed.

"Bread," said Simone. Pennance frowned.

"You heard right," said Fulton.

Chunks of various sizes lay on Carnegie's chest. Crumbs were caught in the stubble on his chin and more pieces were scattered on the floor. Even his nostrils were blocked.

"Carnegie's position is interesting," said Pennance. "It's as if he's been arranged for a wake." The ankles were pushed together, legs straight, arms folded across his chest, hairy, freckled hands (now encased in CSI evidence bags and zip-tied) placed on opposite shoulders.

"I had the same thought," said Fulton. "Maybe we'll find some convenient DNA under the fingernails." The DCI raised an eyebrow at Simone, like he didn't believe his own prediction. She responded with a flat smile.

Experience told Pennance they'd be highly unlikely to. There was something all too careful about the scene.

"He's laid out feet pointing to the East," said Simone. "Like for a Christian burial."

Pennance blinked. "Facing Jesus for his Second Coming."

"News to me," said Fulton. "I don't do religion."

"Sunday school when I was a kid," said Pennance; dubious of God's existence, even back then.

Pennance squatted, got his nose beside Carnegie's cheek and sniffed, deep and long. No smell of alcohol, no tobacco. So, Carnegie hadn't had an end of day drink. He picked at some of the bread, squished it between his fingers – dry and crumbly.

Carnegie's head was straight. Red veins threaded through the whites of his eyes. Burst blood vessels – Pennance had attended enough post-mortems to be alert to the signs.

Pennance straightened again, caught Fulton's twisted expression. "You're right, sergeant," said Fulton. "He is strange."

Simone glanced down at her feet.

Fulton continued, "Proudfoot, the forensic pathologist, speculated that cause of death could be choking."

"No shit." Pennance looked along the length of Carnegie's body once more. "Something about the tie seems wrong. The top button of his shirt is undone, but the knot is tight up to his neck and the collar is rucked."

"Maybe the shirt was too small for him," said Fulton. "When the wife shrinks one of mine, I wear a tie in the same way. Saves buying a new one."

"How much is this place worth?"

Fulton pursed his lips in thought. "Easily a couple of million. The rent on a similar penthouse property nearby is over sixty K a month. There's a gym, swimming pool and, of course, the views." Fulton sounded like an estate agent and a touch envious.

"And Carnegie has art on the wall, each worth hundreds of thousands."

Fulton shrugged. "Yes, and?"

"DI Pennance is obliquely making the point, sir, that Carnegie could afford a new shirt when he wanted," said Simone. "The collar will be the right size."

"And what does that mean?" asked Fulton.

"I've no idea," admitted Pennance. "It's an anomaly."

"Great." Fulton rolled his eyes. "Glad we've got the NCA's brightest and best." Fulton directed his sarcasm at Simone, not him. She turned her head away, colour dappling her cheekbones.

"Excuse me, DCI Fulton." Gough snagged Fulton's attention and Pennance took his opportunity. He picked up a morsel from off the floor and popped it into his mouth. Definitely bread, stale, but bread nonetheless.

"Jesus, Jonah!" hissed Simone.

"What's that?" Fulton glanced back to Pennance and Simone.

"Nothing, sir," said Simone.

Pennance stood, asked, "What about time of death?"

Simone glared at him, keeping her face turned so only Pennance could witness her gritted teeth. "Proudfoot wouldn't be exact," she said. "Not until he performs the PM, but at a push he ventured around twelve hours, so roughly after 11pm last night."

"Carnegie's PA, some guy called Metzler," said Fulton having finished with Gough, "raised the alarm earlier this morning when Carnegie didn't come in. Metzler started ringing around and couldn't find him. Unheard of for Carnegie not to be at his desk for 6am, apparently."

"Meaning Carnegie came home in the evening, was attacked and lay here overnight," said Pennance.

"Assuming time of death remains at half a day and there are no signs of Carnegie being moved, then yes." Fulton held out an evidence bag towards Pennance, a mobile inside. Pennance didn't bother to take it, no point. Fulton continued, "Seventeen missed calls, either from Metzler's mobile or the office landline number."

"Who found the body?"

"The cleaner. She comes in twice a week. All the services are provided in the rent. This was one of her days. She's downstairs with the facility manager, Cresswell, until we can take a proper statement."

"Where's Carnegie's office?" asked Pennance.

"The Heron Tower." Simone gave the original name for the building, the one used by locals. Recently it had been rebranded as Salesforce Tower. "The company is called Hussle. Beside Carnegie and Metzler there's just one other employee, Stefan Neumann."

"Exclusive real estate there, too," said Fulton. "Among some of the most expensive space in London."

"Money, money, money," said Pennance. "Every way you turn." He shook his head. "What about CCTV? There's a camera in the lift."

"I wasn't born yesterday, Inspector," said Fulton. "It's on the list to check."

"Can I have a look around the rest of the place?"

"There's not much to see." Fulton shrugged. "Just more pricey gear and spectacular views."

"I'd appreciate it."

"I'll show him," said Simone, a spike still in her tone sharp enough to stab Pennance and do him some damage.

"What's up with you today?" asked Fulton. Simone ignored his question. Fulton continued, "Let the man walk around by himself, sergeant. I need you here, not on some estate agent's grand tour."

"Yes, sir." Simone's glance made it clear she wasn't done with Pennance yet.

Pennance retreated into the passageway narrow enough that for two people to pass one would have to turn their shoulders. In the double bedroom Pennance was met with a view similar to the living room. The covers on the bed were folded down like in a hotel, the carpet thick and springy underfoot. Pennance glanced inside a wardrobe. Empty, not even dust motes. Then a tiny bathroom – simply a sink and a toilet.

Another bedroom occupied the whole upper floor area. A bed in the centre of the floor had 180-degree views of the river – the Tower of London, Tower Bridge spanning the river, City Hall where the Greater London Authority was based. Then HMS Belfast, London Bridge and, finally, the Shard, the tallest building in the city. It was one hell of a view. And it had stopped raining.

Inside a bank of cupboards along the rear wall hung formal work clothes – neatly pressed Savile Row suits, the trousers creased as sharply as a fold of paper, and crisp shirts with a monogrammed GC on each cuff. Highly polished shoes, some slip-on, some laced. Folded pants and balled socks in separate drawers. Rolled-up ties, paisley-patterned silk handkerchiefs and even a segment for cufflinks. Finally, a collection of expensive watches in a display cabinet. He counted three chunky Rolexes, an Omega and two Breitlings.

Downstairs, outside on the decked terrace Pennance leant over the balcony looking onto Petty Wales where he'd walked earlier. Pennance heard a footfall behind him, Simone making herself obvious.

She leant her back against the rail, arms crossed. "What the hell was all that about, eating evidence?" She meant the bread, of course.

"Beats waiting for the lab," said Pennance. "And it wasn't exactly in short supply. There's plenty for the techs to turn into croutons."

"That isn't funny. Carnegie could have spat it out."

"Unless it's poisoned, I'll be fine." Pennance shrugged.

Simone briefly put her head in her hands. "Jesus bloody Christ." In the recent past Simone would have been frustrated with Pennance's bending of the rules for sure, but not furious like she was now.

"How's the new job?" Pennance wanted to move Simone along.

"Fine, Fulton's a decent boss. Not Kelso, but he'll do." Devon Kelso had been their superintendent at Sapphire.

"City of London police, though, Simone."

"And?"

"The jurisdiction is only a mile in diameter."

"Strictly it's 1.12 square miles from Temple to the Tower of London."

"Hell of a difference."

"8,000 residents, 575,000 daily commuters and 10 million visitors. The City has its own government, pre-dating Parliament, own lord mayor and, of course, police force. So, not too shabby."

"We used to cover the whole of London. Beyond, if need be."

"And now you have a national role, Jonah. Are we in some kind of pissing contest? You've grown while I've shrunk, is that it?"

"No, I..."

"Look." Simone cut him off. "Its maternity cover, maybe it'll become permanent. Who knows? Even if it's just temporary at least it puts some space between me and investigating juvenile sex crimes. But you'd know all that if you'd bothered to get in touch."

"This isn't the time or the place to re-connect, Simone."

Simone rounded on Pennance. "Then when is? And where is? You never call, we can't see each other at the office anymore."

"If I remember right," said Pennance, "you left Sapphire first."

"That's a cheap shot," snapped Simone. Which it was, but also true. "For God's sake, Jonah. It's like you just stepped out of my life."

"And now your ex is back."

She'd divorced her husband, Lars Rasmussen, more than a year ago yet he was on the scene once more.

"Leave him out of this." She took a deep breath, released it slowly. "It was me who suggested to Fulton that the NCA and you should be involved here."

"Why?"

"You have an unusual way of looking at a case and this isn't someone punched in a drunken fight or a marital assault. This is weird, which is you all over."

"Thanks, I think."

"Just don't make me look an idiot. I pushed Fulton to make the call."

"Why would he listen to a new sergeant?"

"Fulton's not stupid. He's ambitious, the youngest DCI in the Met and going places. Getting the NCA in spreads the risk. That's what I told him, anyway."

"Meaning, I'm a political pawn?"

"Sergeant." Fulton, in the doorway, beckoning. "I need you back in here."

Simone raised a thumb and Fulton retreated inside.

"I got that iguana," said Pennance.

"What the hell are you talking about?" Simone stared at Pennance like he was babbling.

"You said I needed to learn how to look after something, so I bought an iguana."

"A pet, you chose a bloody *pet*. That's your solution?"

"Not just any pet. It has a tank and everything. The atmosphere needs to be maintained, there's a light, special food and so on."

"You think a *lizard* is going to teach you how to relate to people?"

"And Lars needs the right food, otherwise he'll die."

Simone was briefly silent. "You called the thing Lars?"

"When you see him, you'll understand why. He has these beady eyes which seem to point everywhere at once." Pennance raised both hands to his head, aimed fingers in different directions and rotated them.

"Just fuck off, Jonah." Simone pushed off the rail and crossed the terrace, her hands clenched.

"It was a joke!" Pennance called after Simone. "Only one of his eyes looks at me in the wrong way!"

Simone stopped dead, spun around, stalked back, like a mobile volcano about to erupt. She halted a foot away from Pennance, staring up at him but she appeared to tower twelve feet above, such was her fury. "You know what your problem is, Jonah? It's this." She jabbed him hard in the ribs with her fingers. "Nothing and no-one gets through to your heart." Then she disappeared inside.

Pennance turned to look at the view, cursing himself for trying to be funny. Then his mobile vibrated against his leg. He checked the notification on his smart watch. Meacham. His watch screen wouldn't respond to a gloved finger and by the time he'd peeled it off his boss had cut the connection. He'd return her call later.

In the living room Simone was with the corpse, her back to Pennance, while Fulton leant against the piano. He said, "Find anything during your walkabout?"

"Just lots of expensive stuff, as you said. Unless you need me, I think I'm done here."

"I assume you'll want to know the results of the PM?" asked Fulton.

"I'd prefer to be present, if possible."

"Unusual request."

"He's a dick like that," interjected Simone.

"If you leave your details," said Fulton, eyeing Simone. "I'll let you know when and where."

"Sergeant Smithson has them," said Pennance. Simone's shoulders visibly tightened beneath the suit, but she said nothing, didn't turn.

"In exchange I'd appreciated you keeping me appraised of any developments at the NCA."

"Sounds fair."

"Dump your evidence suit at the door, Gough will sort it out later." And Pennance was dismissed.

The jaded PC was still at the entrance to the flat when Pennance exited. "I'm to give this to you for the CSM," he said.

"No problem, sir." The PC made it sound just the opposite.

Pennance slid off his evidence suit and folded it up.

The PC held out a veiny hand. "Thanks." He dropped everything on the floor before kicking them up against the wall. He shrugged, as if to ask what Pennance was going to do about it.

In a rare example of opportunistic fate the lift was already waiting, doors open. Pennance was about to press for the lobby when spotted one marked 'G' for garage. Pennance hit that instead. Then Pennance realised he'd extended the period he'd have to suffer the irritating muzak.

When the doors parted Pennance was faced with a brightly lit underground car park half full of vehicles varying from high to top end – Porsche, Audi, Maserati. Even a yellow Lamborghini in one corner under a dust sheet which Pennance briefly peeked beneath. Their value was more than Pennance would earn in his career – before tax.

A few hundred yards away the car park access was obvious; a steep ramp up to pavement level, currently barred by a steel shutter. Pennance pushed at it; heavy and strong. Maybe each resident had an RFID tag to open up. Next to the entrance was a solid and locked door and a numbered keypad for pedestrian access.

Pennance took the lift back up to the lobby. Behind the reception desk a narrow corridor gave access to four doorways, two open, two closed. Inside the nearest Pennance found the blonde PC and Cresswell, the manager, facing a bank of monitors. When Pennance's shadow fell across one of the screens both Creswell and the PC turned.

"Sir," said the PC. "We haven't been introduced. I'm Omerod. We were just reviewing the CCTV."

"Have you found anything?" Pennance pointed to the monitors.

"We haven't been at it long," said Cresswell. "When I can re-open? I have guests and residents due in." The manager had a faint North-eastern twang. Newcastle or nearby, perhaps.

"Nobody's stopping them," said Pennance.

"You have an officer at the front door."

"I suggest you talk to DCI Fulton, it's his investigation." Pennance raised a hand to stop another comment from Creswell. "Fulton told me the cleaner was here," said Pennance.

"She's next door." Omerod stood, led Pennance into the adjacent office.

A woman sat in a wheeled chair, concentrating on her phone screen. She wore a baggy pink-ish sweatshirt, sleeves rolled up to the elbows, ripped jeans and white trainers.

"This is Mrs Edwards," said Omerod.

"Hello," said Edwards.

"I'd like to ask you a few questions," said Pennance. Omerod retreated.

"Okay."

"How long have you worked here?"

"Nearly two year." Her accent was Eastern European. Edwards linked her hands together in her lap and began rubbing a thumb over her wedding ring. "I am married to Englishman, I am legal."

Pennance didn't care. "Tell me what happened this morning."

"Today my day to clean Carnegie's flat." Edwards nodded. "I always start downstairs in bedroom on left then work round in circle – upper bedroom after, then back down to other bedroom, living rooms and kitchen last as easiest." Her face fell. "Not today."

"Because you discovered the body?" said Pennance. She nodded. "Where was he?"

"Near piano, I not see him at first. I had headphones in, listening to radio, vacuum on. Then..." She paused, like she was replaying the memory in her head.

"How did he look?"

"Dead."

"No, I mean how was he positioned?"

"Lying on back, arms crossed, like this." She repeated the pose as if she too was lying in state.

"Then what did you do?"

"I call Mr Metzler."

"At Hussle?" asked Pennance. Edwards nodded. "Not the police?" A shake of her head. "Why Metzler first?"

"That's what he tell me when he give me job."

"The apartments here don't employ you?"

"They do, but I pay by Hussle every week for extra work."

"What did Mr Metzler say?"

"He ask me to describe dead guy. He told me it Mr Carnegie."

"You didn't know it was him?"

Another shake of the head. "I never see him before, just clean up his little mess."

"Then what?"

"Mr Metzler, he tell me to ring police and stay here. That is all." She shrugged. "When can I go? For my children."

Pennance rose. "I'll check."

"Thank you."

Pennance returned next door. Cresswell and Omerod were still reviewing footage.

"I've a blank slate here, inspector," said Creswell. "The footage has been wiped for the last twelve hours."

"Show me."

"This is now." Creswell pointed to the uppermost screen, which displayed the entrance, the shirt sleeved PC and passers-by. Pennance checked his watch. The times matched. Creswell used a joystick to wind back time. The pedestrians reversed their path in rapid, jerky motions before suddenly the image changed to darkness. Creswell paused and rolled the tape at standard speed.

Car headlights moved slowly past. The time read 7.15pm. A man walked towards the entrance, paused briefly to speak with Matt, the footman. "That's Mr Carnegie," said Cresswell. Then Carnegie nodded at Matt and moved off camera.

Cresswell fast-forwarded to 8.59pm. At 9.01pm the footage jumped to the morning, eleven hours later. "It's the same for every camera. Somebody wiped the recordings."

"How could they do that?"

"I'm no IT expert." Creswell shrugged. "I was in last night until 8pm, I saw Mr Carnegie leave myself, so this happened after I left."

"Does anyone check the CCTV?"

"Not unless we need to. I only did so now as PC Omerod requested it."

"What time did Carnegie return after his night out?"

"We can ask Matt."

The footman appeared not to have moved since Pennance stepped out of the lift. He faced the glass doors, arms behind his back.

"Matt," said Creswell. Matt turned around. "Could you answer a couple of questions for the inspector?"

"Sure." Matt's eyes flicked from Creswell, to Omerod and finally to Pennance.

"Do you remember Mr Carnegie coming back last night?"

"Yes," said Matt.

Pennance waited, but Matt didn't continue. "What time did he arrive?"

"Same as always."

"Which is?"

"7.15pm."

"When does he usually come and go?"

"Leaves at 5.50am, gets back at 7.15pm. Then he goes out again at 8pm."

"Every day?"

Matt shook his head. "Mondays to Thursdays. He's away Friday to Sunday."

"Where is he then?" asked Pennance.

"Don't know."

"Did Mr Carnegie leave at 8pm last night?"

"No. He didn't come down again."

"What did you think to that?"

Matt frowned briefly. "Nothing really. I just work the pavement."

"Was there anyone who entered the building during the evening who you didn't recognise?"

"Yeah, lots of people," said Matt.

"As well as permanent residents," said Creswell, "We also have short term lets, overnight stays and so on. Customers are regularly passing through. We're not quite Piccadilly Station, but it's not far off."

"Piccadilly Station is a couple of miles west," said Matt, pointing past Pennance. "It isn't close by."

"No, I meant..." Creswell tailed off. "Never mind."

"Is there anything else you'd like to know?" asked Matt.

"Not for now, thanks." Pennance handed Creswell his business card. "If something comes to mind, my details are on there."

"If you've another one I can enter it into our weekly draw." Creswell pointed towards a Perspex box on the reception desk where a muddle of cards were held inside. "Maybe win a free weekend stay?"

"I live in London."

"We have a swimming pool."

"No, thanks."

"Your loss."

"I'm sure." Pennance turned to Omerod. "Mrs Edwards is asking when she can leave. She has kids."

"I'll talk to the chief inspector."

Pennance said to Matt. "Would you mind letting me out?"

The footman hit a large button on a panel and the doors slid open. "Have a good day, sir," he said before seeming to remember the solemnity of the morning and dropping his eyes.

As Pennance exited, a photographer stepped out from behind a nearby pillar, pointed his camera lens towards him and the entrance and, by the rapid clicking, fired off a barrage photos.

"Hey." The young City cop stepped forward, hand out in an attempt to cover the lens.

"Rack off, man." The photographer wore jeans, a white shirt open at the collar, revealing a necklace of sharp animal teeth on a piece of string. He lowered his camera before switching his attention to Pennance. "Anything you can tell me about the dead guy?"

"How did you hear about that?" asked Pennance.

The photographer shrugged, "People talk, right?"

Pennance wondered who. The cop took a couple more steps and this time the photographer backed away in tandem before he paused and grimaced. He lifted a foot, glanced down at it. "Ah, what mongrel left crap there?"

"You have my sympathy, sir." The cop winked at Pennance.

"Rather than hassling me, you should be tracking down whoever didn't pick up; it's illegal." The photographer pointed to a sign on a nearby post which threatened a £1,000 fine.

"Perhaps I will, sir," said the PC. And then in a much lower tone only Pennance could hear, said, "And give them a bloody medal." Pennance suppressed a grin.

The photographer scowled while scuffing his trainer on the edge of the pavement in an attempt to clean off the mess.

"See you later," said Pennance to cop and got a nod in return. Pennance turned away from the river and towards the busy dual carriageway section of Lower Thames Street, pulled out his mobile and dialled Meacham. She answered within a single tone. "Jonah." She spoke with a soft Scottish burr.

"Sorry about not being able to pick up earlier, ma'am," said Pennance. "I was all wrapped up in an evidence suit."

"What did you learn?"

"As you told me, very odd circumstances. Seems like the victim was suffocated. With bread."

"So, it's murder?" Meacham seemed unperturbed by the novelty of the revelation.

"Unless Carnegie committed suicide by pastry, I'd say yes."

"I'm not a fan of rubbish jokes, inspector. Not until we know each other a lot better. Or maybe even never."

"Understood ma'am." A van turned into the street and drove past Pennance, the BBC logo obvious on the side. "And the press is outside the building." Pennance paused, pivoted around to face the way he'd come.

"They've got wind of this already?"

"Seems so. A photographer was snapping away. Maybe one of the neighbours told the press."

"Rich people, they're the worst."

"I'll take your word on that, ma'am." The van drew to a halt. Two people spewed out from a side door, urgent and aggressive. A cameraman and reporter, judging by the equipment they carried.

"What are you doing next?" asked Meacham.

Pennance turned away, got moving again. "Heading to Carnegie's office to interview his two colleagues."

"After that, get yourself back here and we'll compare notes."

"Yes, ma'am." Pennance disconnected.

Three

If money did actually talk then Heron Tower at 110 Bishopsgate could be considered the pinnacle of evident prosperity; a sun-dappled 46-floor building.

Pennance had always considered Heron Tower uninspiring from the outside because that's all he'd ever seen – glass and metal towers of differing heights bunched together; entirely straight lines and hard edges. The nearby Gherkin, named for its elongated curved shape, was much more interesting. Although Pennance reckoned the Gherkin was more akin to a huge egg laid by a gigantic animal than a humble pickled cucumber.

The entrance to Heron Tower stood opposite the comparatively tiny St. Botolph's church. The two buildings were constructed several hundred years apart, both created for the purpose of worshipping deities out of the true reach of most people – God and extreme wealth.

Pennance slowed as he neared, his attention on a loose huddle of maybe ten people to one side of the huge portico, overhung by massive slab of glass suspended about thirty feet up, designed more for theatre than to actually protect anyone beneath from London's climactic elements. The gaggle were clearly press corps because off to one side a reporter held a microphone, recording a piece to camera with one of the revolving doors behind him.

Pennance aimed for the entrance furthest away from the group. A concierge clad in thigh-length grey formal jacket and a black bowler hat standing between the revolving doors, nodded, affording Pennance far more attention than the correspondents, which was fine by him.

As Pennance put out a hand the doors began to rotate by themselves, moved silently by a hidden motor, before depositing him into a lobby synonymous of the whole building – supersized space, glass and steel everywhere.

And a huge fish tank directly behind the reception desk. Pennance reckoned he could drop a double decker bus inside the tank and still have room to swim. Right now, two staff in overalls were working on the tank, one up on a ladder prodding around in the water with a net, the other cleaning the glass. Hundreds, maybe thousands, of fish meandered and darted around the underwater world, weaving between softly undulating plants.

At the reception desk an administrator wearing a jacket in identical fabric to the concierge, a crisp white shirt and a shiny silver badge that read 'Melody' switched her attention from PC screen to Pennance before he got within three feet of her. "How may I help, sir?" she asked. Seemingly, visitors weren't expected to wait to do business.

Pennance showed his warrant card. "I'd like to speak with Stefan Neumann or Casey Metzler of Hussle."

Melody nodded past Pennance. "So would most of that lot. They've been camped outside all morning. Security has had to move them away several times."

"When did they arrive?"

"About 10. I took a break just before. No-one was outside when I went off, then there were a couple when I returned, and the gathering gradually swelled from then on. It's like they're cells dividing. Glance away for a moment and another appears." She picked up a phone. "I'll call Casey; Mr Metzler, sorry. He's American." Melody smiled like this explained everything. "He handles all of Hussle's enquiries." She tapped a number into the keypad, waited. "Hey Casey, it's Melody down in the lobby." She paused. "Yes, the zombies are still here and so is a policeman." Another pause and another smile at Pennance. "Detective Inspector Pennance, from the National Crime Agency." She fell silent, listened. "Okay, I'll tell him." Returning the receiver to the handset she said, "Mr Metzler is on his way down. He asked if you could go to the lifts and wait for him there, if that's okay. He's no desire to come out into the lobby area."

"And avoid the zombies?"

"Mr Metzler's analogy. He reckons they're like brainless corpses pressing up against the windows, slavering, baying for blood."

"I prefer your description," said Pennance. "It makes them seem a lot less threatening."

By the time Pennance neared the door to one lift was opening. A man and two women exited, revealing a short guy pressed into one corner of the box. He was below average height, a shaved head, round tortoiseshell glasses and an eye-stabbingly bright yellow shirt under a waistcoat. Pennance recognised him from the Hussle website. If Metzler was trying to keep a low profile his attire would be an obvious hindrance.

Metzler leaned forward, stretched one hand, the other on a panel inside the doors, and beckoned Pennance with an urgent wave while remaining low. "Come on, man!"

Inside the lift Pennance faced back towards the entrance; it was entirely out of sight. Metzler pressed the button for the 44th floor, only then standing up to his full height.

As the lift rose, quickly enough to make Pennance's stomach lurch, Metzler exhaled. "I didn't expect this kind of freakin' day when I woke up this morning, I can tell ya."

Pennance had little experience of America or Americans beyond TV. Brash, outgoing characters and perfect dentistry were his uppermost impressions. Pennance was about to ask which state Metzler originated from when the lift began to slow hard, the deceleration pulling his stomach down through his legs and feet. He remembered from his physics classes at school that if he were standing on some scales right now he'd apparently weigh more when slowing down and less when speeding up – the laws of gravity being momentarily cheated.

Metzler grinned, revealing sharp white teeth. "Frickin' fast, eh?" He prodded a button for the doors to open before the lift had even properly stopped and, when they were barely halfway parted, stepped sideways into the corridor. Pennance followed after a second or two. Metzler turned, kept walking backwards at the same rapid pace, facing Pennance, who was struggling to keep up. "We're just down here." He cast a thumb over his shoulder and spun on his heel, still moving. Pennance already felt worn out by Metzler.

Pausing by a door, Metzler pushed it open and stood out of the way, allowing Pennance to enter a large open plan office which took up a corner of one of the steel towers. Two glass walls overlooked London back towards the Thames.

Waterloo Bridge crossing the river and the dome of St. Pauls Cathedral were obvious.

The office itself was exceptionally tidy. A thick carpet underfoot, three desks each with several large computer screens. On the rear wall were artworks in a similar style to those at Carnegie's house and just as incomprehensible. There were potted fauna, too. Pennance recognised a castor oil plant, the foliage a glossy green, which stretched higher than Pennance himself, wound around a substantial moss pole. Several items Pennance was used to seeing in an office – bookshelves and filing cabinets – weren't present.

"Stefan," shouted Metzler. "The fuzz are here." Metzler turned to Pennance, said, "That's right?" When Pennance didn't answer Metzler said, "Fuzz, I like that word."

A man emerged from behind a bank of monitors, to Pennance's left, put down the phone he'd been holding, and threaded his way over, hand extended to shake. Pennance recognised him from Hussle's website, too.

"Stefan Neumann." His grip was tight, efficient. He pumped Pennance's hand twice before letting go when a phone began to ring, as if he'd suffered an electric shock from Pennance's grasp. Neumann turned his head towards the chiming phone before it cut off. "The answer service got it," he explained, though Pennance didn't really need to know.

"Can I see your ID now?" asked Metzler. Pennance passed over his warrant card. "National Crime Agency." Metzler bobbed his head like he was impressed. "Your version of the FBI, though not quite as cool. Everything here is smaller than the US. And we all know: size is what counts."

"Not always." Pennance beckoned for the return of his card.

"Go big or go home. So they say. And Jonah, that's your Christian name?" Metzler held the ID between two fingers. "Bad luck follows you around, I guess?"

"Seriously, Casey." Neumann possessed an accent, too; sounding as Germanic as his name might suggest. His inflection was clipped; urgent though not harried. "Shut up now. I apologise for my colleague, inspector."

"No problem." Pennance put the card away into a pocket. Metzler grinned, seemingly entertained by Neumann's rebuke.

"How about a coffee? We have a rather decent machine."

"Sure," said Pennance.

"Casey, would you mind?"

"Double espressos all round, I reckon," said Metzler. "Not quite New York style, but good enough."

"Whatever comes," said Pennance.

"Cappuccino for me," said Neumann. "It's still morning."

"You Europeans," said Metzler.

"Not anymore here," said Pennance.

Metzler nodded, said, "Brexit." He moved away to work a stainless steel bean to cup unit standing on a cupboard near the door. The phone rang again.

"Our clients, they're pretty nervous right now," said Neumann.

"Because of your partner's death?"

"Of course." Neumann nodded.

"It's a frickin' dumpster fire," interjected Metzler. Pennance wasn't sure what he meant.

"Why don't you come through to the meeting room, inspector?" Neumann indicated the way with an out-swung arm. Over to one side was a space behind more glass with a table, also of glass, a conference telephone in the middle and more than enough wheeled leather chairs. A large black TV took up much of one wall.

Neumann sagged into a chair, his arms flopping down before he sighed and then, with obvious effort, leaned on the table top for support. Pennance settled opposite. Metzler entered moments later, placed a small cup and saucer in front of Pennance and a much larger cup capped with white foam next to Neumann.

"I'll leave you alone," said Metzler. "Our clients will be expecting us to ring back."

"I'd prefer to speak with both of you together," said Pennance. "It'll be more efficient."

"But the phones..."

"Will have to wait a few minutes. Let your service do the job."

Metzler glanced towards Neumann, who nodded slightly.

"I'll just grab my joe," said Metzler.

"He means his coffee," explained Neumann. "I'm always translating for him. It's my second role; like I need another." A phone rang, and soon another, the tones out of sync, forcing a grimace from Neumann. "So many this morning."

The grinding of the machine started up again in the office area.

"Even though there's been no official announcement about Mr Carnegie's death?"

"That's irrelevant, the media are all over it. You've seen the leeches outside."

Amoeba, zombies and now leeches. "Not a fan of the press like Mr Metzler?" asked Pennance.

"Everything in life should be about creating value and so enhancing life. What do journalists add beyond neuroses and paranoia? They're hardly contributing to the wellbeing of society." Neumann paused as Metzler entered, cradling another espresso cup.

"Amen, brother," said Metzler.

"Shut the door, Casey, then we can't hear that racket," said Neumann. Metzler pushed the door with a foot, nudged it closed with a hip before taking a seat next to Neumann and opposite Pennance. Neumann continued, "In our game worth, and therefore value, is based on acuity and at the moment the perception is, incorrectly, we're foundering. Our clients demand assurance, hence the contact."

"We can put them right," said Metzler. "Stop them spazzing out on us."

Neumann stretched out an arm across the table towards Metzler, stopped just short of touching his forearm with his fingertips. "Please, cut out the idioms, Casey."

"Okay, boss." Metzler tore open two packets of sugar.

Neumann withdrew his arm then asked, "What happened to Grady?" asked Neumann.

"How much have you been told?" said Pennance.

"Ah, shit," said Metzler; sugar grains scattered across the table.

Neumann's shoulders tensed before he rolled them briefly. "Virtually nothing. Grady's cleaner, Mrs Edwards, rang to say she'd found him dead. Unsurprisingly, she was in a state, crying her eyes out. It was hard to understand what she was saying."

"That's not easy at the best of times," said Metzler. "She's a Commie."

"Casey." Neumann raised a hand, palm up.

Metzler performed a dramatic shrug. "Tell me I'm wrong."

"She's Hungarian."

"They're all the same."

"Of course, we contacted the police immediately," said Neumann. "Then an hour or so later we had a call from a DS Smithson, she confirmed Grady had indeed passed. However, she wouldn't give me any further details."

"I'm sorry to say that Mr Carnegie was murdered."

"Murdered?" Neumann leaned across the table, knocking his coffee over in the process. He seemed unaware of the foamy liquid escaping the cup. "Are you certain?"

Metzler stood, grabbed some tissues out of a nearby cupboard and mopped up the spilled drink, pulling out more tissues as needed, each scraping on the lip of the box as Metzler yanked on them.

"A post-mortem will confirm for sure, but at this stage, yes it appears so."

"How?"

Metzler dropped the wet tissues into a bin, producing a loud thunk as the material hit the empty plastic. "When Satan's bell tolls, Stefan."

"We'll have to await the examination. That's really all the detail I can give you right now," said Pennance, eliciting a frown from Neumann. "This must be a difficult time."

"I've worked in pressured environments my whole life." Neumann sounded as if he was in a job interview. "I thrive on stress."

"We eat anxiety for breakfast," said Metzler. Neumann lifted an eyebrow, causing Metzler to raise his hands in surrender, then mime zipping his mouth shut.

"I understand you're in the wealth management business," said Pennance. Neumann nodded. "What does that mean?"

"Simply put, Inspector, we invest our clients' money in a range of asset classes, such as property, individual stocks, unit trusts, OEICs, commodities and so on, to generate a positive return on that investment."

"In other words," interrupted Metzler in his American drawl, "we make our rich clients richer, quick or slow depending on their preference." Clearly Metzler had trouble staying quiet for long.

"And why do affluent people choose you over others?" asked Pennance. "There must be plenty of companies like Hussle."

"Well, that's where you're wrong." Neumann smiled. "There's *no* firm quite like ours. We *guarantee* a minimum growth to be at least double the best bank savings rate and with zero risk – none of our clients have any dead money; that's when cash isn't earning a return, Inspector."

"Which is where our name, Hussle, comes from," said Metzler. "We push our clients' assets along."

Metzler and Neumann were like a double act, practiced in performance; a subtle hard sell. Yet Pennance wasn't buying. "Hussle is another word for con, isn't it?" Neumann raised an eyebrow at Pennance. "And what if I were to give you my savings?"

"Have you got a half mill going spare?" asked Metzler.

"Which is the minimum, Inspector," said Neumann.

"Way beyond my means, unfortunately," said Pennance.

"You're not bent fuzz, then." Metzler grinned.

"It's about economies of scale," said Neumann.

"As I told you earlier," said Metzler. "Go big or go home."

Pennance doubted he'd be doing either just yet. "How do you achieve zero risk?"

"Because of me," said Neumann. "You might think that's egotistical, inspector, but I assure you it's a fact. I'm a finance expert with a unique brain."

Metzler nodded. "There's nobody like our Stefan."

Neumann settled back in his chair and folded his hands together. "All investment processes can be plotted on a continuum with passive at one end and active at the other. Passive methods are relatively docile in their approach; they take a long-term view of profit with minimal trading activity and consequentially are low in cost because trades cost money. An example is a fund tracker. Your police pension is probably invested in one. They're slaves to whatever index they mimic. So, the FTSE100, you've heard of it?" Neumann didn't give Pennance chance to answer. "It's the 100 largest businesses listed on the UK stock market by market capitalisation – that's the number of shares in existence multiplied by the valuation of each share. Just to make the maths easy let's say the biggest of these comprises 10% of the total and you've £100 to invest. So, the fund spends £10 on that company. The next largest is 9% then it spends £9 and so on. Do you get my drift?"

"On a fundamental basis, yes," said Pennance.

"Those 100 companies don't generally move in sync. They may if there's a big shock to the system, like 9/11 when pretty much everything fell, but typically some rise and some fall but over time there's an overall upwards trajectory. The tracker just follows what the index does.

"Then at the other end of the scale are active investments managed by stock selectors. In other words, people who take bets on which individual shares will gain and put money into them at whatever level they see fit. A few pickers do well, most not so, a handful are dreadful. Ultimately, it's about how much risk the client is prepared to accept for a return. Active processes cost more, because there are more trades." Neumann leaned over again. "And that's where Hussle becomes brilliant. We offer a process that sits somewhere between active and passive. We make a reasonable number of trades, keep the cost comparatively low, but deliver shorter term and higher returns *without* the concomitant risk."

"How?"

"Big data, Inspector." Neumann waved a hand towards the office space beyond the meeting room. "We run an almost paperless office. All the information we utilise is stored digitally. We collect vast amounts of information, slice and dice it, analyse it and make investment decisions as a result."

"That all sounds very opaque, Mr Neumann."

"No offence, but it will be to you. In the most basic of terms, over several years I developed and refined an algorithm which evaluates the individual components of a given market and determines which aspects to invest in or withdraw from. And we find early opportunities before they become popular."

"Buy low, sell high?" asked Pennance.

"Quite." Neumann gave Pennance a razor blade smile.

"Like what?"

"Blockchain technology products such as Bitcoin or Ethereum. I found those years before the other investment houses."

"I've heard of Bitcoin. It's a cryptocurrency, right?"

"Correct.

"Bit fringe though, isn't it?"

"Not so, inspector, digital cash is going mainstream. 18% of all Americans purchased cryptocurrency in the last twelve months. Amazon[1] and Starbucks[2] allow customers to pay in Bitcoin and some of the banks are piling in, too. And that's part of the problem," said Neumann. "Legend has it that Joe Kennedy, that's JFK's father, got stock tips from his shoeshine boy one day. So, he sold everything – just ahead of the 1929 crash and the Great Depression. Once the average man on the street gets interested that's the time to back out. Weak market signals are something we track as part of the algorithm. NFTs seem to be going the same way." Neumann must

---

1. https://www.coindesk.com/you-can-now-shop-with-bitcoin-on-amazon-using-lightning

2. https://www.ccn.com/starbucks-will-accept-bitcoin-in-2020-thanks-to-wall-streets-bakkt/

have seen Pennance's puzzlement because he said, "Non-fungible tokens. An example is digital artwork, not like Grady's pictures because NFTs are only stored on computers, there's nothing physical about them."

"One item recently sold for $70 million," said Metzler. "That's more than a Titian. And you can't even hang it on your wall. That's even worse than shoving half a goat in a tank of formaldehyde." Metzler made a circular motion with a finger around his temple.

"It was a shark," said Neumann. "Not a goat."

"Whatever." Metzler shrugged. "Still dumb."

Neumann continued, "Of course, I made some mistakes at first, but in recent years it's never failed me. We generate a lot of money for our investors, taking a small slice for ourselves, of course."

"Sounds like you didn't need Mr Carnegie," said Pennance.

"Not at all. Grady deserved everything he earned, and more. He was vital to getting the company up and running. Without him my algorithm would still just be an idea. The same as there would have been no Facebook without Eduardo Saverin seeing the potential in Mark Zuckerberg's idea for a social network.

"I sat in front of many company boards of directors and offered my wares. Every single one rejected me. Fundamentally, I'm a classic introvert; I'd rather be behind my screen looking at numbers than talking to you or anyone else. Grady brought two aspects – the seed capital to work up the algorithm and the initial investors. Then he was the face of Hussle; the extrovert who brought in the big assets. And the more his visibility and renown grew, the more funds flowed in."

"A face always in the newspapers, that's good for you?" asked Pennance. Neumann shrugged again. "If it was you or Mr Metzler who'd died, would there be a crowd of reporters clamouring at your door?"

"I hardly think that's an appropriate question." Neumann's jaw clenched and some colour rose in his cheeks.

"I apologise if I was insensitive," said Pennance. It was the first time Neumann had displayed any emotion, beyond frustration with Metzler, since Pennance had stepped into Hussle's office. Neumann felt too composed. "How much of Hussle did Mr Carnegie own?"

"Grady held a controlling stake." Then before Pennance could ask, Neumann answered the obvious question. "It means over 50%."

"Controlling as in, he made all the decisions?"

"No, we ran as a team."

"But he could overrule you and so have the final say?"

"If he wanted, yes."

"That's how a majority stake works," said Metzler.

"How often did Mr Carnegie do so?" asked Pennance. "Cast the deciding vote, I mean."

"Rarely. There was no point in messing with a literally winning formula," said Neumann.

"And the rest of the company is yours?"

"Not quite, Casey retains a proportion, too."

"10% to be specific," said Metzler.

"Less than your colleagues?" asked Pennance.

"Still, very lucrative. And I joined the team last."

"How did you two meet?"

"Via Grady," said Neumann. "We didn't know each other before Hussle."

"Originally, I hail from rural Connecticut," said Metzler. "I slogged away on the New York stock exchange for a decade, trading futures for a multi-national bank before I got transferred over the Pond to work out of the UK branch. That's where I ran into Grady."

"How did you all end up working together?"

"Grady was a non-executive director for one of the companies to which I pitched my algorithm," said Neumann. "After his colleagues had thrown me out Grady caught up with me on the street. He said the directors of the company I'd just left were idiots and he was interested, very interested. He took me straight to a restaurant, and over lunch we shook on a deal."

"Just like that?"

"Grady had a formal contract drawn up by his lawyers, but basically, yes. However, if Grady had written out some clauses on a napkin in blood, I'd have signed there and then. Nobody else was offering. And we had a partially shared history. Grady and I used to work for the same Swiss bank."

"You moved there from Germany?"

"No, it's my birthplace. I'm Swiss."

"My apologies."

"Are you sorry for me being from Switzerland?"

"No, missing your accent."

"Ah." Neumann raised his hands, palms out. "German, Austrian and Swiss German all sound pretty similar."

"And Grady asked me to join Hussle to replace someone who got themselves fired after a particularly big screw-up," said Metzler.

"What happens to Mr Carnegie's 51% of the business now?" asked Pennance.

Neumann shifted in his seat. "It'll be split proportionally between me and Casey, based on our current shareholding."

"So, the company becomes largely yours?"

"Correct. What'll be left of it after this mess."

"It just seems to be one disaster after another at the moment," said Metzler. "The vultures will be circling, trying to pick us off."

Neumann flicked a glance at Metzler, the warning frown obvious.

"What else has happened?" asked Pennance.

"Where's the harm in telling him?" asked Metzler of Neumann.

"I guess," said Neumann. He turned back to Pennance. "We were attacked online about six months ago."

"Nightmare." Metzler put his head in his hands. "A total frickin' disaster."

"Initially there were just a handful of critical comments about Hussle, some posts on social media apparently from an anonymous client claiming that our move into cryptocurrency was costing him money. At first, we were oblivious, until an investor got in touch. The assertion was clearly unfounded and easy for us to prove incorrect. All our investors had to do was review their financial status online. The numbers speak for themselves. Next there were a few negative Google reviews. Even though that's not really how Hussle operates

– we're not Amazon traders – much of our new business comes through word of mouth and for sure everyone turns to the internet for research at some point.

"We started to get questions from potential clients and it became that bit more difficult to prove ourselves. Then the competition discovered the comments. Our opponents are the jealous type, they've been trying to bring Hussle down for years. In fact, I wouldn't be surprised if it was one of them who flagged our challenges to the newspapers. Reporters began to call, and stories got published. In this country successful people are built up simply to bring them low for the same reason."

"And that wasn't the worst bit," said Metzler.

"Someone got inside our system," said Neumann. "We were properly hacked, shut out of everything. We received a demand to pay a ransom or never be able to access our data, algorithm or our nominee accounts."

"That can't have been good."

"Considering everything we do is electronic, 'not good' is the understatement of the year, Inspector." Neumann rubbed his forehead.

"But you clearly came through. I mean, you're still here."

"We employed a specialist digital crisis team to manage the initial situation. They undertook SEO to bury all of the negative comments beneath an avalanche of positive ones. And implemented a process to get the search engines and social media platforms to either archive or remove false documents, going to court if necessary. Frankly, we've only just got ourselves out of that particular problem."

"What's the name of the company?"

"Sting, they're based in Shoreditch."

"I'd like to get their details," said Pennance.

"I can message you that," said Metzler.

"Thanks," said Pennance. "I assume Sting got your data back?"

"No," said Neumann, pursing his lips. "Not fast enough, anyway."

"We had to cough up," said Metzler.

"How much?"

"Enough." Neumann held up a hand. "Approaching seven figures."

"Did you report this to the police?"

"What was the point? There's no way anyone would be able to trace them."

"We could follow the money."

Neumann shook his head. "We transferred Bitcoin. Impossible to track. That's why blackmailers ask for it."

"Even so, a crime was committed."

"Not by us and we made a decision."

"As a team?" asked Pennance. "Or did Mr Carnegie make the call?"

"He did."

"But we fully supported him," cut in Metzler.

"Anyway, it's all over now," said Neumann.

"How did you find Sting?" asked Pennance.

"That was me," said Metzler. "As the general office gofer all that kinda stuff falls to me."

Neumann rolled his eyes. "Don't let Casey fool you. Officially he's the Company Secretary. His organisational skills are exceptional."

"Stop, you're embarrassing me," said Metzler who looked anything but self-conscious. "I manage all of the office specifics, the accounts and our diaries. Dealing with Grady's life was a big job, let me tell you." Metzler huffed theatrically.

"Why?" asked Pennance.

"Busy work life which could be sixteen hours a day, six or seven days a week from 6am, right through."

"People are late all the time, though. Maybe he was ill or hungover."

"Me, yeah. Or Stefan, occasionally. But not Grady, no sirree. His life was his work. I can't remember a single day when he hasn't been here on time."

"Me either," said Neumann. "And I've known Grady for a lot longer than Casey."

"He'd be up at 5 every weekday, checking the stock markets in Japan and China, emailing me and so on. Today, however, radio silence. I rang him like, twelve times," said Metzler.

"Seventeen," said Pennance. "We checked Mr Carnegie's phone."

"That many? Wowzers."

"What did you think when you couldn't reach him?"

"Shocked, it was so out of character. Then I thought maybe was at his weekend pad."

"Mr Carnegie has a second property?"

"Yeah, a huge pile in Bucking-ham-shire." Metzler pronounced the county as three separate words.

"Beaconsfield, specifically," said Neumann.

Pennance knew it as a high value commuter town only twenty minutes by train from Waterloo station.

"He went to his suburban pad every Friday at 3pm on the nose," said Metzler. "And would be back in the office 6 sharp on Monday morning. Here, look." Metzler got his phone out, tapped the screen several times before showing Pennance a photo of a white-painted, modern-looking sprawl of a property in the centre of a swathe of lush green grass. "We went there once for a party. Sprawling frickin' place, hidden behind a big hedge to keep the rabble out, like all the houses along his street. Worth millions." Metzler turned off the phone screen. "Made no sense for Grady to be in Beaconsfield during the week, though. Most of his meetings were in zone one." Metzler was referring to the sections of the underground map radiating out from one in the centre to five on the city's extremities. "I just couldn't think of any other reason. Certainly not dying on us."

"Why didn't you go over to Mr Carnegie's flat?"

"No key, so how would I have got in? The footman on the front door, dumb-ass looking guy by the name of Matt would remember me. Door Matt, I call him."

"Did Mr Carnegie have a partner?" asked Pennance.

"Only his work," said Neumann.

"Nobody at all?"

"Not that I'm aware of."

"Nor me," said Metzler.

"Was Mr Carnegie religious?"

Metzler burst out laughing. "Not in the slightest."

"Why do you ask?" said Neumann.

"Just following a line of enquiry," said Pennance. He wouldn't be telling Neumann and Metzler about how

Carnegie's body was arranged. "What was in his diary for last night?"

"It would have been a client meeting for sure." Metzler pulled out his phone again and flicked the screen. "Yep." He nodded. "Cocktails at The Connaught in Mayfair, then dinner at Petrus in Knightsbridge." Both were exclusive destinations; the restaurant possessed a Michelin star. Metzler continued, "He was due to leave at 10.30. I'd have expected him to stick meticulously to that schedule and not deviate. End of."

A phone began to ring again. Neumann glanced meaningfully beyond Pennance into the office. "Is that everything, inspector? Casey and I still have a mess to clean up and a mound of messages to answer."

"I'd like to get an NCA forensic analysis team to come in and look through your accounts."

"You gotta be kidding," said Metzler. "Why?"

"You were hacked and paid a bribe," said Pennance.

"It was a ransom." Neumann tutted. "And last I checked, not illegal."

"No, however the attack certainly was," said Pennance. "They might have left some traces behind, maybe stop them coming after you again. And perhaps there's a connection to Mr Carnegie's murder. Isn't that enough?"

Neumann turned to look at Metzler who gave a theatrical shrug. Neumann got to his feet, leant over, fingers spread on the table. "We'll gladly do what we can to help."

Pennance took out a business card, said, "These are my contact details and I'll be in touch soon to let you know who's coming in and when." Metzler stood now. "One last question, Mr Metzler," said Pennance.

"Shoot."

"Which client was Mr Carnegie seeing last night?"

Metzler went back to his phone, flicked a finger across the screen. "Lars Rasmussen."

Pennance's skin itched like he had spiders crawling underneath.

"Are you alright, Inspector?" asked Neumann.

"Fine," said Pennance and pushed himself upright. "I'll see myself out."

Neither Neumann nor Metzler said goodbye as Pennance left their office, accompanied by the harsh trill of several phones and an air of desperation. He paused beside the door, leaned against the wall and gathered himself for a few moments. Because what Metzler had told Pennance meant he wouldn't be going back to the NCA just yet.

Instead he'd be going to speak with Simone's ex-husband.

Four

Pennance approached One Canada Square via a block-paved restaurant plaza where smartly dressed customers sat at outside tables, probably colleagues catching a quick bite. There was the chatter of conversation and the clink of cutlery on plates and dishes. Time was clearly money judging by the six large analogue clocks erected on long poles spaced equidistantly through the court, reminding everyone life was ticking inexorably by.

A pair of sweeping concrete staircases led to the building's grand entrance. Pennance trotted up the steps, passed between a pair of huge burnished steel tubes. A smoker talked urgently on a phone amid fast drags on a cigarette. Finally, Pennance used a revolving door which deposited him into an expansive lobby which opened out either side of him. By the handful of low slung leather chairs scattered around and the small reception desk (which had nothing on the Heron Tower), waiting was not encouraged. This was a transit area, only – get in, get out, get on.

However, Pennance needed to pause. He wasn't sure which company employed Rasmussen. Rasmussen himself had told Pennance one time, when Simone had forced them to sit side by side at a dinner party in an attempt for the two to get to know each other. The effort, though, had proven a dismal failure. If ambition were an Olympic sport, then Rasmussen would be a medal contender for Denmark.

The pair had ended up in a heated debate over the fact that Rasmussen was paid an excessive wage yet, because of various loopholes, gave up very little income as tax – less, even, than Pennance. By the time dessert arrived Simone had separated the pair to opposite ends of the table where they'd sat glaring at each other. Most of what Rasmussen told Pennance, up until temperatures rose, had been utterly dull and showy, which Pennance filed in a mental recycling bin with an extra wide hole in the base. The only detail Pennance remembered was Rasmussen being a VP at a bank on Canary Wharf yet not having a corner office – which apparently meant something.

Pennance headed for the reception desk where a woman in maybe her 50s, sporting a pair of winged cat eye glasses, sat. Pennance pulled out his ID, said, "I'm here to see Lars Rasmussen." A shaven headed, suited man standing ten feet or so away, hands behind his back and chest pushed out, turned and watched.

"At American Global Securities?" she asked.

"There's only the one Lars Rasmussen, right?" Pennance faked a smile.

The receptionist simply stared at Pennance, her eyes somewhat enlarged by the lenses. She lifted a phone, said, "I'll just call to see if Mr Rasmussen is in."

"No need," said Pennance. "What floor is he on? I'll find him myself."

"I'm sorry, sir, the rules are I must ring ahead regarding unsolicited visitors. AGS insists."

The suited man began to walk over to the desk.

"I'm police, if you'd forgotten, and I'd prefer not to have Mr Rasmussen forewarned."

"Strevens, the floor manager here," said the suited man. "What seems to be the problem?" Strevens adjusted the bow tie at his neck with one hand, straightening it minutely.

"The officer wants to see Mr Rasmussen." The receptionist still held the phone.

Strevens held out his hand. "Can I see your identity, please?" Pennance passed over his warrant card. "National Crime Agency. Must be serious. What do you need to see Mr Rasmussen about?"

"I'm not at liberty to say."

Strevens returned Pennance's ID. "I think we can make an exception in this case."

***

The lift doors opened at floor 49 immediately opposite the entrance to American Global Securities. A woman wearing a patchwork cardigan was obviously awaiting him. Pennance's eye was drawn to a large, angry strawberry mark which covered half of her face. He tried not to stare.

"Detective Inspector Pennance?" She held her shoulders straight and her chin up in a way which made the birthmark entirely obvious.

"That's right."

"I'm Hillary Gillespie, Mr Rasmussen's PA. Unfortunately you've had a wasted journey as Mr Rasmussen isn't here right now. He's at a meeting in The City. He left about half an hour ago."

"I've just come from there."

"Perhaps you passed each other. Pity, if you'd called ahead, I'd have saved you the trip."

"Where is he, specifically?"

"He was having lunch with a client; they could have gone anywhere."

"When will he be back?"

"That I don't know either. He may return to the office, or he might go straight home if it's a long meeting."

"Can you contact him?"

"No, he turns his phone off."

"What if you sent him a message?"

"Again, his phone is off, Inspector."

Pennance rubbed the back of his neck before he said, "Where's his office? Through here?"

He made for the doors and pushed his way through into a large open plan office jam-packed with long lines of tables in rows where people sat like battery hens. There were maybe a hundred staff occupying the space filled with overlapping conversations that were hard to separate. All seemed focused on the job – either a computer screen full of incomprehensible information, or talking rapidly into a headset, or both. Around the outside of the space were individual offices where, Pennance assumed, management resided. Some doors were closed, others open. Pennance headed towards the nearest with Hillary trotting to keep up.

"Please don't do this, sir." Hillary's tone had gone up a notch and sounded shrill.

"Which is his?" asked Pennance. "This one?" he pointed.

"He's not here, I told you!" Pennance glanced inside each office as he walked by, almost entirely men occupying them. "Please." Hillary grabbed Pennance's arm, stopping him. Her face had gone pale, though the birthmark was brighter than ever. Her voice dropped to a whisper and was hard for Pennance to hear over the hubbub. "I'll show you, but then you must leave. You'll get me into trouble."

Pennance felt a twinge of regret. He wasn't aiming to cause a problem for her, just Rasmussen. "Okay."

"Here." She blinked with relief, pointed towards the furthest corner. Yet Rasmussen didn't have the grand space, the two-way view over the Thames towards Greenwich – that must be someone else's room because Hillary took Pennance next door. The large wooden desk faced towards the office and away from the window. The black leather chair was empty. "I told you," said Hillary.

Pennance wandered around the room. Hillary nibbled the inside of her lip and twisted a corner of her cardigan in her hands. He tried to open a drawer in the desk, but it was locked. Same with the filing cabinet, on top of which stood a photo of Smithson and Natalie, both gurning for the lens. Pennance reached out, laid the frame down.

"Who's this, Hillary?" A man wearing a golf shirt, chinos, and centre parted, slick hair obstructed the entrance to Rasmussen's office. His accent was strong, reminding Pennance of a cowboy. He was missing the ten gallon hat but had the boots. Behind him stood two further men, both in uniform and looking very much like security.

Hillary visibly sagged, her head bowed she slowly turned. "Mr Vallance, this is DI Pennance, NCA," she said.

"The inspector is seeking Mr Rasmussen." Vallance chewed while he listened.

Vallance raised his eyebrows. "For what purpose?"

"Police business," said Pennance.

Vallance spat a piece of yellow gum into a nearby bin. "Unless you can be specific or have a warrant, I strongly suggest you haul your ass out of here now. And if you feel brave enough for a second attempt, either make an appointment or bring a team of colleagues."

Pennance knew defeat when he stared it in the face. "As you wish."

"Good call." Vallance nodded over his shoulder. "My colleagues will show you out."

"Not going to throw me to the floor? Rough me up a bit first?"

"This ain't my first rodeo, Inspector. Yours either, I suspect."

"You'll need to let me past," said Pennance.

"Why is every Brit always so damned polite?" Vallance smirked, stepped out of the way, then flicked his gaze sideways. "Stay here, Hillary. I want a word."

"She tried to stop me," said Pennance but Vallance paid him no attention, his eyes fixed on Rasmussen's PA.

"After you, sir." One of the guards pointed and Pennance made his way back around the large office space, followed by the pair. The drones' chatter fell to a murmur while he was escorted past their desks. Pennance glanced over his shoulder as he went through into reception, saw Hillary being berated Vallance. She kept her head bowed, weathering the rebuke.

The guards followed Pennance all the way down, standing at either shoulder until the lift reached the ground floor. He stepped out, turned to the guards, said, "I can make it from here, thanks." The doors closed on them.

The manager, Strevens, was waiting for him. "Causing trouble, inspector?"

"Just asking questions people don't like."

Strevens chuckled. "I was told to ensure you left."

"Be my guest."

When Pennance stood beside the huge column outside, Strevens paused. "I expect I'll see you again?"

"Count on it."

After a brief grin Strevens retreated inside, away from the light.

***

As Pennance waited for a train his phone rang. Meacham again.

"Where the hell are you, Jonah? I was expecting you quite some time ago."

"Heading in now, ma'am. I was following up on a lead."

"In Canary Wharf?"

"That's right."

"Which explains the rather irate call I've just received from Director General Quant, who herself had a rather irate call from a senior manager at the institution you just left."

"Vallance from American Global Securities?"

"Don't know, don't care. Just get your arse back here. Come straight up to my office, no dawdling."

"Yes, ma'am." But Pennance was speaking to static, Meacham had cut the cord. Already Pennance had riled his boss. Record time, even for him.

Five

The nearest underground station to NCA headquarters was Vauxhall, just a stone's throw away from the Metropolitan Police HQ on Cobalt Square. He strode up the escalator, rising from the depths and the unique, fusty smell of the underground – hard to describe yet never forgotten.

Pennance continued moving, reached the entrance area and slapped his Oyster card onto the pad in order to get through the exit barrier. Outside it was raining once more so he paused under the awning a few feet away from a homeless man sleeping on the floor, a dirty blanket pulled over his legs and with a cardboard sign, asking for donations. Pennance added some coins to the small pile nearby.

He felt the nibble of the smartwatch on his wrist. An email from Metzler giving Pennance the contact details for Damian Mulcahy at Sting.

Pennance dialled the number. It rang twice before being answered. "Hello, Damian Mulcahy."

"Mr Mulcahy, this is Detective Inspector Jonah Pennance of the NCA, I've just come from an interview with your clients at Hussle and I hoped to talk with you about a previous breach they suffered."

"Sure, when are you thinking of?"

"Can we keep it flexible? Say, within the next couple of hours?"

"No problem, I'm in the office all day. We're based in one of the Shoreditch trains."

***

Pennance passed under a railway arch before reaching NCA HQ on the corner of Tinworth Street and Citadel Place. Pennance had looked up the definition of citadel after his first interview. The word had two alternative definitions, either the core of a walled settlement such as a fortress or castle. Or it could mean 'little city'. Pennance assumed the NCA's location was intended to deliver some kind of subtle message.

He took the stairs, heading for Meacham's office which overlooked the railway track and, beyond, the Thames. He lost his way twice in the process, the interior layout still unfamiliar to him. The building was quiet, like a library. And he barely recognised any of the faces. Each person he passed seemed anonymous.

Pennance glanced through a vertical glass window strip in the door. Meacham wore a headset, talking into her laptop. A desk lamp cast a pale hue. His phone pinged, a message from Kelso, his ex-boss at Sapphire. It said, 'I can't keep on saving your arse'.

'No idea what you mean', replied Pennance. He glanced up; Meacham was staring at him over her rimless glasses. His phone beeped again but Meacham was beckoning, so Pennance grabbed the handle and twisted.

Her office was arranged such that she sat facing away from the vista outside and contained the minimum of furniture within. The walls were painted a light yellow. Another train crawled by on the nearby tracks, typically running at several a minute, the noise barely reaching through the triple glazing.

Meacham took off her headset and eyed Pennance. "Ah, Jonah, good. Have a seat." She stood, placed her glasses carefully on the desk, nodded to the conference table between them. Pennance took one of the four chairs. "You've got some explaining to do about this Canary Wharf trip." She jabbed a sharp finger at him. "Quant has been onto me again, checking if I've had chance to burn you yet. Turns out she knows the boss at American Global Securities. Quant was most unhappy that one of my officers – she said *my* by the way – had stormed into AGS without due cause and begun searching for one of their presidents."

"Vice President," said Pennance.

"Don't interrupt me again, or you win a prize. My boot up your backside."

"Sorry, ma'am."

"Imagine my surprise when I heard. Because I had no idea you were going over to the Isle of Dogs. You told me you were coming here to give me an update. Am I right? That's what you did?"

"It is, ma'am."

"Which puts me in rather a difficult situation. Because, either I tell my superior that a member of my team is doing whatever he wants, or I state I'm totally aware of your actions. Either I look like an idiot or I lie. I don't like looking like an idiot and I only bullshit my superiors when I choose to."

"Understood, ma'am."

"Ultimately, I told Quant I was aware of your actions." Meacham held up a hand, palm out. "Don't go bloody thanking me, I might change my mind." Pennance hadn't been about to, but he kept his mouth shut. Meacham dropped her hand, said, "What were you doing there, anyway?"

"Following a lead. Rasmussen, the person I was trying to speak with, was supposed to have a meeting with Carnegie the evening he died."

"Understandable, however you were informed by Rasmussen's PA he wasn't there, correct?" Pennance nodded. "Yet you marched around the office like you owned the place, according to Quant."

"I wouldn't quite describe it that way ma'am. I wanted to reach Rasmussen before he sat down with a lawyer."

Meacham nodded slowly. "I called your previous boss, Kelso. We were speaking when you arrived."

"Okay." Maybe this would explain Kelso's text.

"He said you and a Detective Sergeant Smithson had a fraught relationship just prior to you leaving Sapphire and Rasmussen was part of the issue."

"I can be impartial, ma'am."

"That's exactly what Kelso said, too. In fact, he used the word 'scrupulous.'" Meacham considered Pennance through narrowed eyes for a long, long moment. "Jonah, you came to me highly recommended. Your liaison work with CEOP a couple of years ago was exemplary. I'm well aware you can be somewhat capricious and like to do things your way. However, I appreciate an officer who thinks and acts independently if it means getting the job finished. In fact, individualism is what I seek in my team. All of which means there's a higher than usual turnover in the people who report to me. The strapline here is FIFO, Inspector. Fit In or Fuck Off. You'll have to decide which it is for yourself."

"Understood, ma'am."

"Kelso and I go way back. I trust his judgement. So, your challenge is figuring out what I deem important enough to know about and what I don't so you're not running to me every five seconds flapping but neither are you leaving me out of the loop when it comes to critical elements. Am I being entirely clear?"

"Yes, ma'am."

"Then we can move on from Rasmussen for now." Meacham clapped her hands together once, like she'd just performed a magic trick. "Give me an update on Carnegie, but don't go repeating everything I already know. Just the new stuff, please. I haven't the time and my memory remains perfectly adequate. It's your first occasion reporting to me on an active case and I can appreciate the challenges of a different job and managerial structure." Pennance riffled through his recollections from the day, like flicking through flash memory cards. Meacham continued, "My preference is to ask questions as we go, this isn't a presentation."

Pennance nodded. "I interviewed Carnegie's two business partners at the Hussle office. The place was chaos, phones ringing and a phalanx of reporters outside, waiting for a story."

"More of them?"

He nodded. "Into double figures."

Meacham whistled through her teeth. "I know gossip moves fast in this town but even so..." She picked up her mobile, tapped the screen. "Carnegie's death is the top story at several online publications. Breaking news..." She showed Pennance. They were well-known newspapers with a wide circulation.

"The twenty-four-hour news cycles is a hungry beast which needs constantly feeding, ma'am."

"Very poetic, Inspector." Meacham raised an eyebrow at Pennance. "What were your impressions?"

"Of the company or the partners?"

"They're one and the same, aren't they?"

"I guess so. Neumann is the brains of the outfit, claims he's reserved but had no problem talking. Didn't seem particularly flustered by Carnegie's death. In fact he showed very little emotion throughout, except for when I asked who got Carnegie's shares, which is him."

"*There's* a potential motive."

"Neumann told me Hussle suffered some online abuse a few months back before being hacked, losing access to key systems and data."

"Don't tell me they coughed up the bloody ransom?"

"Yes, in Bitcoin."

"And didn't report it?" asked Meacham. Pennance shook his head. Meacham sat forward. "I've been shouting at anyone who'll listen that making a payoff should be illegal. Cut the source to blackmailers and they'll go elsewhere."

"Like putting a burglar alarm on your house so a neighbour gets robbed instead."

"By neighbour, if you mean France..." Meacham gave a Gallic shrug.

"I suggested to Neumann that we send in a forensic analysis team to track the ransom payment."

"That's a good idea. Did he agree?" Pennance nodded. "We have a department for that." Pennance wasn't surprised. The NCA seemed to have a department for everything. "Top dog is Alasdair Tremayne. I'll get him to contact you." Meacham folder her fingers together. "Next steps?"

"There's Carnegie's post-mortem to confirm cause of death and I've just received Sting's details; they're based in Shoreditch. Someone needs to visit them."

"Well, that someone is you." Meacham bared her teeth, revealing a gap in the centre. There was little warmth in her expression.

"Isn't Carnegie's case under the City police jurisdiction, ma'am? The SIO, DCI Fulton, seemed perfectly capable."

"I'm well aware of the situation, and Fulton's capabilities, Inspector. He excels at telling anyone who'll listen how good he is. However, I need you on the team, working the case."

"Why?"

"Because Quant says." Pennance wanted more detail but Meacham made it clear he had all the answers he was getting. Meacham appeared to soften a little. "Listen, Jonah. You should know that Fulton applied for a transfer into my team, in fact it was between the two of you for the job you now have."

"Why me, ma'am?"

"What did you think of Fulton? In a couple of words."

Pennance tilted his head, thought briefly, simmered down his impressions. "Self-assured, uptight."

"Everyone has hopes and fears. Fulton, you, me. I selected you ahead of him because your emotions are worn proudly on your sleeve."

"You make me sound neurotic, ma'am."

"Not in the slightest. I think that, more often than not, I'll be able to tell whether you believe in something or don't. And that your head and your heart will drive you to take the right action. DCI Fulton, however, buries his sentiments under an avalanche of hubris. I'd worry about his decision-making criteria, which is something I don't need in my team. We act fast and we act independently. Understand?"

"I think so, ma'am."

"Good." Meacham smiled again. "Get yourself to the post-mortem and Sting. When Tremayne makes contact, take him into Hussle."

"Ma'am."

Meacham stood. "Keep me informed every step of the way. And don't forget..."

"Fresh information only."

As Pennance reached out for the door Meacham said, "Don't prove me wrong, inspector."

"I won't."

"Then there's a decent chance we might get along."

Outside Meacham's office Pennance dug out his phone and called Kelso. "I owe you one," said Pennance when his old boss and friend answered.

"Bloody right you do. What were you thinking, prancing around Rasmussen's office?"

"I don't know. And I recall purposefully striding."

Kelso sighed. "How's it going over there?"

"Early days, but ... strange, if I'm honest. I miss the old team."

"What old team? There's not many of us left. In a few months, Sapphire will be history."

"A shame."

"Everything dies eventually, Jonah." Another sigh from Kelso. "Anyway, Marta has been asking when you're coming over for dinner. She wants to make sure you're being properly fed." Kelso chuckled.

"Any time, just let me know when suits."

"I'll talk to the boss and see when she prefers."

"Look forward to it."

The moment Pennance disconnected his phone rang again. "Inspector Pennance?" A woman's voice. "It's Hillary from AGS. I have Mr Rasmussen on the line for you. Please hold."

Before Pennance had the chance to reply she was gone, replaced by Rasmussen. "Jonah, good afternoon." Pennance gripped the phone tightly. "I understand you've been trying to reach me." Rasmussen's Scandinavian accent was quite pronounced. "There was no need to burst into my workplace. A message would have sufficed. As Hillary told you, I've been extremely busy."

Pennance got walking. "I need to see you, as soon as possible. I have to be somewhere else right now but I can make this afternoon."

"I hope this isn't about Simone."

"It has nothing to do with DS Smithson."

"That makes a change and I can't possibly meet with you. The rest of my day is packed out with consultations. And you haven't done me the courtesy of revealing what you want to discuss."

Pennance reached the stairs and began to trot down them. "You'll have to clear your diary."

"I can't do that. My appointments are extremely important."

"You had an engagement with Grady Carnegie who subsequently turned up dead. That makes you a potential witness. You were probably one of the last people to see him alive. I'd suggest you take that seriously."

"Grady didn't arrive. I waited half an hour and left. For the record I'm more than happy to provide any help I can in order to catch his killer. I liked him a lot. However, I think I'll be speaking to my lawyer. After which my office will contact you to fix an interview at an appropriate time. Until then, you're going to have to wait." Rasmussen cut the call.

Pennance swore. He'd manged to let Rasmussen push his buttons. As usual.

***

"Excuse me."

Pennance paused outside his office door. It took him a moment to realise a woman had been in the process of exiting as he pushed open the door. She wore dungarees with high turn-ups displaying bright red socks. Her t-shirt was Breton style, red and white horizontal stripes, and her an inch or two of her black hair was tipped in a maroon dye which contrasted with her pale, makeup-free skin.

"Sorry," said Pennance. "I was miles away." Pennance's mind had been on Simone, Rasmussen and Carnegie.

"You're standing right there," she said.

"No, I meant..." Pennance stopped when he realised the woman was grinning at him. She slid through the small gap between door and jamb, like a wriggling lizard, then held the handle for Pennance. They exchanged places, Pennance taking her place.

"See you around." She pushed her glasses up her nose. Pennance watched her head along the corridor until she reached the stairs. She descended, making for the basement; Pennance wasn't sure what was down there, maybe bats.

Meacham had offered Pennance a room of his own, however he'd had a long preference for working in an open plan arrangement with colleagues around him. As a person towards the extrovert end of the scale he'd never enjoyed four walls and a closed door. He preferred to interact with peers, particularly during a difficult case.

Pennance's new workplace, the MICS office, was small compared to the space he'd been used to at Sapphire. Inside was only enough space for five desks and a meeting table, which nobody seemed to use. Pennance had barely got to know most of the team, often they were out on cases. He seemed to share the space with ghosts, leaving behind half empty mugs, contents cold to the touch. The exception was the reed-thin Detective Sergeant Vance Hoskins, who was always at his desk.

Hoskins leaned back in his chair as Pennance entered, the scar on his top lip giving his face the air of permanent amusement. "You met our Ava, then?" The porkpie hat he wore out of the office lay on his desk.

"Who?" said Pennance.

"Ava McAleney, digital forensic specialist." Hoskins pointed at the door with a length of baguette. "She just left."

Pennance shrugged off his jacket, hung it over the back of his seat. Wiggling his mouse to wake his PC, Pennance dropped into email and found dozens had arrived in his in-box already this morning; mainly notices from other command units on the lookout for suspects. Pennance deleted them all. He didn't have the time to deal with somebody else's problem.

"I might ask her out on a date for dinner," continued Hoskins, as usual thinking about his next meal before he'd even finished the current one. Hoskins liked to eat. Many of the analogies he used were food related. A victim might have sausage fingers or hair like spaghetti. "What do you reckon?"

"How would I know, Vance?" Hoskins appeared completely oblivious to Pennance's not-so-subtle efforts to ignore him.

"She's an interesting person, plenty of stories to tell. Not that she has, I've found out for myself."

"Uh-huh."

"She's from a wealthy background, father was a multi-millionaire investment guru. Lost it all several years ago after he made a balls-up and got fired for it."

A WhatsApp message arrived then, from Fulton. 'Carnegie's PM been brought forward'. Pennance checked his watch; the procedure would be starting shortly.

"That's good," said Pennance.

"Getting fired is good?" asked Hoskins. "Are you even listening?"

"Sorry, Vance." Pennance grabbed his jacket. "Gotta go and watch someone get cut up."

"And that's better than speaking to me?"

Six

The last degradation of Grady Carnegie was already in progress when Pennance shouldered his way into the pathology suite. His breath fogged, the steady rush of exhausted air obvious as the atmosphere was constantly evacuated. And it was several degrees lower in temperature than outside; like stepping into a huge fridge.

As standard, the room was white tiles and steel, the conventional design to easily hose down the blood and gore after each procedure. The floor possessed a subtle slope, a feature to allow the waste water to sluice down a drain under the influence of gravity. A couple of fume cupboards stood side by side against one wall. The internal illumination came solely from powerful overhead LED bulbs, no windows. The brightness from all the reflective surfaces made Pennance's eyes hurt.

The double doors shut behind him, creating a seal – autopsy suites operated under negative pressure relative to the room outside where Pennance had scrubbed up. His intrusion drew the attention of the loosely organised group assembled around one of the three examination tables, garbed identically to Pennance – surgical scrub suit, cap, plastic glasses, nitrile gloves, shin-length wellington boots. Everyone present (and alive) turned towards Pennance in near perfect synchronicity. Pennance recognised Fulton, the others were new to him.

DI Pennance," he said. "Sorry I'm late."

"My fault," said a man a few inches shorter than Pennance. He wore a visor over the top of his lab glasses, which protected grey brows and pencil thin moustache sandwiching bright blue eyes. "Doctor Proudfoot, I had a slot open up and I firmly received the sense of urgency from DCI Fulton at the scene." He sounded like a Midlander, the kind of accent that was neither strong Southern nor Northern.

"Carnegie is as prominent in death as in life," said Fulton without sarcasm.

Proudfoot pointed at the others in turn. "My assistant, Dr De Souza." A short woman whose dark skin gave the appearance of a heritage from somewhere on the Indian continent. "Photographer, Miss Thripp." A middle aged woman with a pronounced mole above her top lip. "My stenographer, Mr Bray." A man, wider than he was tall, who sat a little distance away from the table at a desk with a laptop. Bray's role was to transcribe Proudfoot's comments as he worked which would eventually become part of the post-mortem report and a matter of record.

Proudfoot continued, "And of course, let's not forget our star turn here, the victim himself." The body lay on a burnished steel table with holes to allow the excess bodily fluids to conveniently drain away. "Why don't you stand beside DCI Fulton, Inspector? You'll have a grandstand view."

"Great, thanks." Pennance suffered mixed emotions on the post-mortem process; part fascinated, part repulsed by the turning inside out of a corpse.

Fulton took a sideways step, giving Pennance the space to squeeze in pretty much opposite Proudfoot and De Souza with Carnegie just inches away. A man he'd never met in life but would now know intimately in death. Carnegie's skin was the colour of chalk, bloodless lips, grey hair mussed. The bread was still evident inside Carnegie's mouth. However, the plastic evidence bags which had encased Carnegie's hands at the scene had been removed and Carnegie's arms now lay either side of his torso, rather than across his chest.

"It never ceases to amaze me," said Proudfoot. "We're vibrant and animated one moment, the next we're a limp husk waiting for someone like me to hollow us out." Proudfoot paused for a moment before gently patting Carnegie's arm. Then he visibly straightened, as if he'd readied himself, eyeing Fulton then Pennance. "For the benefit of the record I previously measured Mr Carnegie's height to be 1.78 metres and his weight at a shade over 79 kilos. In old money, that's five feet ten inches and 12 stone 7 pounds." Behind Pennance, Bray tapped away at the laptop keys, his fingers moving quickly. He'd have to be fast because Proudfoot didn't pause between his comments. "Given Mr Carnegie's age at 52, the victim immediately prior to death was borderline overweight with a BMI of 25, if you believe in that kind of thing. Dr De Souza took a blood sample earlier and sent it away for analysis. The lab technicians will check for any foreign DNA."

"I also took scrapings from under the fingernails," said De Souza, her voice strong and with a local inflection. "They were shipped with the blood."

"Thank you for that information, Dr De Souza. Now," Proudfoot grinned, like he was about to tell a joke. "For the police and the television watching public, time of the victim's demise."

"Like I've never heard that one before," said Fulton.

"We need our little amusements in situations like these, don't we, chief inspector?"

"I guess."

"No guessing here, I'm afraid."

"That's not what I meant." Fulton sounded a touch exasperated.

"I'm ribbing you." Proudfoot chuckled, either at Fulton's reaction or amusement at his own terrible pun, Pennance wasn't sure. Proudfoot continued, "Anyway, back to practicalities." He turned to De Souza. "Would you mind helping me roll the body onto its side?"

They levered Carnegie up as if shifting a heavy piece of wood – Carnegie remained stiff and immobile – until the corpse was suitably balanced. Fulton and Pennance moved around to see what they did. The flash of Bray's camera revealed the livid mottling which ran the full length of the body.

"Mr Bray," said Proudfoot. "Please note the presence of livor mortis. For the benefit of my audience, there are three stages of decomposition; livor, algor and rigor mortis. Livor mortis, also referred to as hypostasis, artfully means 'discoloration of death'. When the heart stops there's no longer a force pumping blood around the body and so gravity takes a grip instead. As a result the blood settles at the lowest point in the cadaver, distending and distorting the vessels there and lending the skin the angry appearance you now observe." The length of Carnegie's body possessed a bright pink colouration with a bluish tinge, like a well-developed bruise. "I'm unable to see hypostasis elsewhere on Mr Carnegie."

"So, Carnegie stayed lying on his back and wasn't moved," said Pennance.

"Correct, inspector." Proudfoot nodded, like a student had told him something unexpected. "If someone had relocated Mr Carnegie, say, if he'd lain on his side for a length of time, then we'd note the effects of the blood settling along the arm and leg. In addition, you'll note the lack of hypostasis on Mr Carnegie's forearms, because they were laid across his chest. Usually thirty minutes to four hours are required for livor mortis to be observed and increases until maximum lividity occurs at between eight to twelve hours, dependent on conditions, of course."

Proudfoot turned to his assistant. "Miss De Souza, let's reverse the process." The pathologists returned Carnegie into a prostrate position on the steel table surface.

"Algor mortis is the cooling of the body," said Proudfoot, "as it no longer internally produces heat and is lost to the environment. The speed at which this occurs depends upon the surface area to body mass ratio; in other words thin people and babies cool faster than the obese. In addition, local conditions have an impact – heat dissipates faster in a cold room and vice versa. I measured the ambient temperature at the scene to be 25.6 degrees Celsius, quite warm. I also used a rectal thermometer to assess the body's internal temperature.

"Last, but not least is rigor mortis, a stiffening of the joints and muscles from biochemical changes within the corpse. Usually, rigor occurs first in the hands and face within approximately two to four hours. Faster in hot, damp conditions; slower in the cold and dry. So the hands curl up into fists and the mouth appears to fall open. Then the major muscle groups tighten over maybe the next twelve hours, less if the victim had exercised strenuously beforehand."

"Carnegie doesn't look like the keep fit type," said Fulton.

"Sex would also raise the pulse somewhat, chief inspector," said Proudfoot, to which Fulton had no reply. "This variance in rigor onset is observed in animals – rigor sets extremely quickly in one that has been hunted down, within an hour or two. A well fed, relaxed beast such as a cow, takes nine to twelve hours. Like livor mortis we can sometimes assess the rigor to determine if the corpse has been repositioned post-mortem. However, this assessment is very much time dependant. A return to flaccidity on average requires up to thirty-six hours but can take ten days when the body is refrigerated. As you can see, Mr Carnegie's body remains in the grip of rigor. Now, with these three data points in mind Dr DeSouza and I conferred and I estimate time of death at around ten to twelve hours."

"I concur," said De Souza.

Proudfoot continued, "Before I start to slice open Mr Carnegie, I will perform an external examination of his corpse. Most obvious are the contusions on the victim's biceps." Proudfoot pointed towards some light discolouration. "Given the lack of development I'd say these are peri-mortem; that is before Mr Carnegie died."

Then Proudfoot bent over, got close to the body and made an inch by inch assessment of the skin from feet to head. De Souza tracked Proudfoot's movements, her eyes roving over the corpse, too. No-one spoke; allowing them to concentrate. After more than a minute of silence Proudfoot turned to his assistant. "What do you think of this, Dr De Souza?" Proudfoot pointed at two angry looking red marks, spaced maybe an inch apart on Carnegie's chest, over the heart.

"May I?" asked De Souza. Proudfoot shifted out of her way and she took his place, getting as near as she could to whatever had piqued Proudfoot's interest. "From their appearance peri-mortem, too." Her tone was careful, thoughtful.

"What do you think they were caused by?" asked Proudfoot.

"I've seen this kind of damage previously. I would suggest the source is a high-voltage electronic control device."

"I agree." Proudfoot turned to Thripp, said, "Would you mind?" The photographer took several photos, the click of the lens loud.

"You mean a taser?" said Pennance.

"A taser is merely one type of ECD," said Proudfoot. "If you care to look there are small round spots." Proudfoot held a finger over the exact position.

Pennance leaned in. "They appear to be burn holes." As if Carnegie had been jabbed with a hot, two-pronged carving fork.

"That's exactly what tasers do to the body. The high voltage scorches the skin. Damn painful, I'd imagine."

"Would this have killed him?" asked Fulton.

"On its own as a single factor, a taser applied in the ventral region of the thorax can cause cardiac arrest," said Proudfoot. "As his heart would have been hit very hard it might have stopped, but I won't know for sure until I complete the examination, including assessing the organ itself. There are two methods of applying the shock – holding the electrodes against the skin or firing barbs into the subject. Either way, a massive voltage is applied by the ECD. In the former, called drive stun mode, the victim suffers only pain." Proudfoot blinked. "I say *only* pain. It would sting like a bastard, I imagine."

"Is that a technical term?" said Pennance.

"Don't quote me." Proudfoot gave a brief grin. "Anyway, in the latter the target is subjected to almost simultaneous pain and skeletal muscle contractions which leads to immediate incapacitation and the person loses complete control over their actions. The voltage can be applied variably – a short or long initial burst or several bursts of differing strengths. Each of these, and the person's individual physiology, affects how the body subsequently responds. It's relatively clear from the puncture wounds on Mr Carnegie's chest that spikes were fired into him, meaning the ECD was used for the purpose of incapacitation. He'd have been immobile for maybe a few minutes."

"Enough time to stuff half a loaf of bread down his throat," said Fulton.

"More, if you wanted," shrugged Proudfoot. The pathologist bent over again, continued up from the chest to the head. "This is interesting. Petechial haemorrhages in the victim's eyes. They're collections of blood from the rupture of capillaries. I estimate them to be about a millimetre in length."

"From asphyxiation, right?" asked Fulton.

"Asphyxia as a description isn't often used in clinical medicine, given the lack of understanding of the pathophysiology. Asphyxia derives from the Greek word *asphuxía* which means 'without pulse'. However, in forensic medicine, asphyxia is a lack of oxygen in the body. Legally, because the processes varies so greatly, determining the cause of the asphyxia and the manner of death are the most important elements. Asphyxia can occur just in the part of the body where the oxygen was deprived – that's tissue necrosis – the signs can be determined in the whole body. The extremities can last a lot longer without oxygen before damage occurs compared to parts of the central nervous system – up to half an hour for the former and mere seconds for the latter.

"The commonest form is a physical obstruction between the external orifices and the alveoli. A compression of the neck or chest will lead to a dramatic increase in venous pressure within the head and therefore the rupture. However, the presence of *petechiae* is not always certain."

"That's a nice lesson, Doctor Proudfoot, but is this cause of death?"

Proudfoot sighed heavily and fixed the DCI with a glare. "Chief inspector, you and I have never worked together previously and other pathologists have different methods; therefore I'll give you the benefit of the doubt. At this stage Dr DeSouza and I are simply gathering data. I will not be assembling these facts into any form of a conclusion until I've completed the entire assessment and weighed up all the aspects. Therefore, please stop attempting to draw deductions out of me. Are we clear?"

"Very." Fulton, gone as stiff as Carnegie, clenched his fists. De Souza stifled a smile. Pennance felt slightly sorry for Fulton, he'd suffered this kind of dressing down himself in the past.

"Now we have that out of the way; Miss Thripp, if you would."

Thripp snapped off several more photos of Carnegie's face before Proudfoot lifted a pair of long tweezers from a tray of instruments. "Okay, let's see what's clogging Mr Carnegie's oral cavity."

"Bread, I imagine," said Fulton, receiving the briefest flicker of a glare from Proudfoot.

Using the tweezers, Proudfoot removed one chunk at a time, some were entirely white, while others had a light brown crust on one side. Proudfoot placed the pieces side by side in a metal dish. The pieces were flat but irregular in shape, like a roughly torn slice. "Appears to be the cheap stuff you can buy from anywhere," said Proudfoot. "My wife calls it plastic bread." Proudfoot carried on until Carnegie's mouth was empty and a surprisingly large pile had built up across several dishes.

Proudfoot pulled down an overhead spotlight on a thin, adjustable arm, shifting the beam until it shone how he wanted, and peered inside Carnegie's mouth like a dentist. "There are abrasions on the oral mucosa which indicate the bread was pushed in with force."

"Even though Carnegie was incapacitated?" asked Fulton.

"Right," said Proudfoot. "And I suspect the bruising on the biceps resulted from the killer."

"Holding down Carnegie while cramming in as bread much as possible," said Pennance.

"A reasonable supposition." The pathologist picked up a substantial knife from the tray, it possessed a broad blade, as yet unsullied with blood, and a wide handle which seemed to fit well into Proudfoot's grip. Pennance knew that beneath the pathologist's gloves would be a second pair, but made of stainless-steel mesh – cut-proof in case of any slips. Each instrument blade was kept very sharp, honed by a technician after every procedure, and no pathologist wanted to expose themselves to the bodily fluids of the deceased.

"So, are we all ready for this?" asked Proudfoot.

"No," replied Fulton. "And I never will be."

"Too late to back out now." Proudfoot hauled down a hose vent to deliver a more localised extraction and capture any stray particles from cutting into Carnegie, before hefting the knife. He placed the blade on the skin at the base of Carnegie's neck. Pennance shuffled further forward until his thighs touched the table and Carnegie was just inches away.

"Starting at the sternal notch and cutting down to the *pubis symphysis*, I'm going to perform a bloodless dissection of the column," said Proudfoot. "Thereafter I'll examine the victim's torso. I'll incise at the coronal plane, that's the line amid the front and the back of the body." Proudfoot pointed the tip of the knife in the centre of Carnegie's ribs halfway between chest and spine. "Between the mastoid processes." This time the pathologist tapped the base of the skull. "Then I'll connect this incision to a midline opening at the sternal notch, which is the dip you can feel at the tip of the ribcage that's about the depth of a fingertip."

Pennance resisted the impulse to place his hand on his own neck.

Proudfoot continued, "Next, I'll dissect the throat structures layer by layer, starting with the skin from the mandible, or the jaw as you know it. I'll removed the sternomastoid muscles, they run down either side of the neck and are used for rotation and flexing of the head. Next comes the hyoid muscles so I can examine them and the thyroid gland, larynx, hyoid bone and neck vessels for any visible injuries. Lastly, and not least, I'll remove and examine the tongue. Enough detail for you, inspector?"

"Plenty, thanks," said Pennance.

"Jesus," mumbled Fulton. He backed away, leaving Pennance, Proudfoot and DeSouza surrounding Carnegie. Thripp hovered nearby, ready for whenever Proudfoot wanted her.

Proudfoot began making the first cut around Carnegie's trunk, followed by a business-like stroke straight down the centre of the chest. The blade cut as easily as Proudfoot drawing a line with a pencil. "Mr Carnegie possesses a reasonably condensed layer of fat." Proudfoot pointed with the knife to a substantial layer the colour of butter immediately beneath the skin and above the muscle. "It appears he lived his life well."

With further skilful wielding of the blade Proudfoot revealed the bony grill of the rib cage, like he was filleting a fish, before laying down his tool. Without prompting De Souza moved in to help Proudfoot roll back Carnegie's skin which came off in one, limp piece, making a soft, sucking slurp as it did so. De Souza put the folded skin to one side on a nearby table. Next, Proudfoot removed the rib cage, lifting the bones up and out. They joined the skin. Now, Carnegie's internal organs were entirely exposed, their anatomical protection removed.

De Souza wheeled the table away and, with her back to Pennance, cleaned down the ribs with a tap sprinkler in a large sink, spraying pink water up against a stainless steel back plate which sounded like urgent rain. Proudfoot continued, making several incisions around Carnegie's gullet, severing each connection between the organs. He removed and weighed one tissue after another, examining and listing out the data for Bray who dutifully tapped away at his keyboard while Carnegie's blood dripped out and down through the holes in the table. Once Proudfoot had withdrawn Carnegie's lungs De Souza again carried out a separate analysis, taking a slice of the tissue and examining it under a microscope. They worked seamlessly as a team, barely a word between them, in a well-practiced routine.

Eventually, Proudfoot paused in his evisceration. The pathologist put the now-bloodied knife back onto the table and De Souza handed Proudfoot a small saw. "The vast majority of my visitors find this the worst part," said Proudfoot. "You may want to look away." Pennance stayed in place. Proudfoot eyed him, said, "Okay then."

The circular blade emitted a high-pitched whine when Proudfoot switched on the motor. The screech grated on Pennance but was nowhere near as bad as when the teeth actually ground into Carnegie's skull, spraying micro bone fragments captured by the well-positioned and powerful exhaust extraction.

Mercifully soon, Proudfoot switched the saw off and the howl died away as the wheel slowed and stopped. Proudfoot removed the top of Carnegie's skull, revealing the ribbed and folded grey matter of Carnegie's brain. The brain easily slipped out into a dish which De Souza relocated into one of the fume cupboards.

Carnegie's gore was splattered up the front of the pathologist's gown and along his arms, bright red on what had been pristine white, but Proudfoot took no notice while he and De Souza worked. They spent several minutes evaluating Carnegie's cleaned rib cage, conversing in a low tone and using technical language Pennance barely understood. Next the pathologists focused on the lung section and finally the brain until Proudfoot nodded at De Souza, straightened and turned to his audience.

"To share my findings so far," said Proudfoot, addressing Pennance and Fulton. "There's some bruising to the victim's anterior chest, that's the sternum and the abdominal wall which includes the skin and muscles surrounding the abdominal cavity. Comparatively, the ribs are normal, there's no fracturing evident. Neither are there any contusions or ruptures of the abdominal viscera – stomach, intestine, spleen, liver and so on. Kidney and liver were slightly overweight; a result of alcohol over the recommended minimum and the regular ingestion of fatty foods. Mr Carnegie's heart is distended and shows some wear. Not surprising with the extra body mass and, I imagine, stressful job.

"Onto the lungs. The veins are black, rather than a light pink to purple colour. There are two likely causes. First, the smog from the London traffic – frankly that'll be present in all of us. Second, it appears the victim was a smoker, probably casual given the lack of nicotine staining on his fingers. I also noted multiple petechial haemorrhagic spots, they're purple or red in colouration as a result of broken capillary blood vessels, and in the heart and the brain."

"What about the taser?" asked Fulton.

"I'm coming to that, chief inspector. Studies into death caused by ECDs are few and far between. As far as I'm aware no-one has drawn a definitive conclusion between ECD shock and sudden ventricular fibrillation or cardiac arrest. Now, it's a perfectly reasonable assumption that applying a large voltage to the chest area will cause an activation of the heart. After all, that's the purpose of defibrillators. A high energy electrical surge for a sustained period of upwards of thirty seconds would be sufficient to interrupt the heartbeat. Officially a taser should only be applied for five seconds. Although Mr Carnegie's heart does show some underlying disease to the ventricles, I suspect the ECD caused him to lose consciousness and resulted in a minor ventricular fibrillation. So, the ECD was not cause of death."

"What was then?" Fulton raised his arms in apparent frustration.

"Suffocation and strangulation involve several stages." Proudfoot held up his fingers, ticked off one by one. "Beginning with the dyspnoeic phase, the victim experiences raised respiration and *tachycardia* – Mr Carnegie would have felt his lungs pumping for air and his heart racing." Proudfoot put a hand over his chest, tapped it rapidly several times. "This could last for maybe a minute. If you see here," Proudfoot lifted Carnegie's hand. "At the end of the fingertips the skin has a blue tinge? That's cyanosis."

Now Proudfoot had pointed it out, the subtle colour difference was obvious to Pennance.

"Then," continued Proudfoot, "comes the convulsive phase where the victim effectively suffers fits and they thrash. Respiration reduces and the victim may begin to lose consciousness and the heart rate will slow while blood pressure rockets. Maybe the victim's vision begins to tunnel. This stage could last for one or two minutes.

"Next is the pre-terminal phase. The lungs and heart begin to fail, breathing and blood circulation falter yet the heart continues to hammer in the chest." Proudfoot pounded his fist into an open palm several times. "Again, occurring over perhaps a couple of minutes. And we're reaching the point of no return from hereon in. The gasping phase consists of respiratory reflexes as the body tries to keep the major organs alive along with a loss of movement and pupil dilation. The victim would suddenly stop moving. To the casual observer it could seem as if the light were fading in the victim's eyes. The final phase is terminal. Circulatory and brainstem function completely shut down and the body expires."

Proudfoot paused for a moment. The only sound was the rush of air through the exhaust vent. "Most reported asphyxia-related fatalities occur by strangulation. However, in this case I believe cause of death was an obstruction of the lower respiratory tract by extraneous material."

"He choked to death as a result of the bread," said Pennance.

"I believe the killer hit Mr Carnegie with the taser in the living room. Mr Carnegie collapsed onto the floor, incapacitated. The carpet would have cushioned his fall. The killer then straddled Mr Carnegie, knees both sides of his chest and pressing into the upper arms. He, or she, proceeded to force the bread into Mr Carnegie's throat until the material entered the larynx, occluding it completely, thereby preventing breathing, speech and coughing. A typical room consists of 21% oxygen. Impairment of cognitive and motor function usually occurs at a concentration of 10 to 15%, loss of consciousness at less than 10%, and death at less than 8%. Given Mr Carnegie's physiology I'd have expected him to pass out in maybe thirty to sixty seconds and be dead within two to three minutes."

"Doctor," said Fulton, "you said he or she when referring to the killer. Surely, it must be a man."

"Not necessarily." Proudfoot tilted his head to one side. "The taser could incapacitate Carnegie for several minutes, depending on the charge. So, they had that period of time to block his throat."

"And there's the bruising of Carnegie's arms, but without any rib fracturing," said Pennance.

"Correct," said Proudfoot. "A lack of pressure that indicates someone relatively light."

"Or they didn't apply their full weight," said Fulton.

"Also possible," said Proudfoot. "I expect analysis of Mr Carnegie's blood to show a high carbon dioxide level, red blood cells and a concentration of lactic acid which occurs as a by-product of anaerobic metabolism without oxygen. Once I receive the lab analysis, I'll get that sent to you both, along with my report, which I'll complete as quickly as I can. But these are my main conclusions." Proudfoot clapped his hands together once, an unnatural and sharp sound. "Now, Dr De Souza and I will be putting Mr Carnegie back together for returning to the family," said Proudfoot. "You're welcome to prolong your stay, Inspector Pennance."

"I think I have everything," said Pennance.

Fulton grimaced. "I couldn't agree more." He walked out of the examination room at speed and straight-armed the door before letting it flap shut behind him. Proudfoot gave Pennance an obvious wink.

Fulton, his sleeves rolled, was already scrubbing up at a nearby stainless-steel trough fixed to a wall when Pennance entered from the examination suite. Thripp, the photographer, stood beside him and Bray was already done, removing an umbrella from a nearby locker. Pennance shrugged off his gown, dropped it into a lidded medical waste bin then washed under a stream of hot water Thripp left running for him. Pennance reached out to a dispenser conveniently nearby and ejected plenty of liquid soap.

"I always need to take a shower to get the stink of this place off me," said Fulton as he dried his arms, yanking out one paper towel after another from a rack.

"I've never really noticed," said Pennance.

"Really?" Fulton turned his head and Pennance flashed back to Proudfoot cutting Carnegie's sternocleidoid muscles either side of his neck. "I can always tell when a colleague has been down to the mortuary. The stench follows them like a shroud."

"See you," said Thripp, giving the detectives a wave as she exited. Bray had left without a word.

Pennance turned off the water using an elbow to nudge the tap handle which was well over a foot long, designed so someone scrubbing up didn't need to use their hands to control the flow.

"I understand you're to remain on the case," said Fulton. It wasn't a question.

Pennance grabbed a small pile of the paper towels. "That's right." Pennance dried himself too. "Not my choice, to be honest."

"It rarely is." Fulton rolled down a sleeve and began to button up. "I'd appreciate it if we could co-ordinate."

"Of course, sir. You're still the SIO."

"Thank you. And it's Leigh." Fulton moved over to a locker and grabbed his jacket. "So, I can tell you that I had CCTV checked at Carnegie's."

"No co-ordination, no information on the footage?" Pennance's locker was next to Fulton's and he took his coat out, leaving the door wide open.

"You know how it works." Fulton raised a shoulder. "It's not me personally. It's the structure, relationships, mutual back scratching, rivalries." Fulton shrugged once more. "The list goes on."

"True."

"The cameras were fully functional." Fulton, followed by Pennance, entered the corridor, got walking. "The blank section Creswell found could only occur in two ways – either somebody inside wiped the recording or an external hacker got in. So, I've no idea when Carnegie arrived home or how the killer gained access to the building."

"What about the keypad?"

"Meaning?"

"There are keypads at the front entrance and a door in the garage. Someone would have to know the code to get in. Maybe the residents all have different pin numbers?"

Fulton raised an eyebrow at Pennance. "Good thinking, I'll have it checked out."

"And let me know?"

"That's the definition of collaboration, isn't it?"

Pennance's phone rang. "Excuse me."

It was Meacham. "Jonah, you need to get your arse to Greenwich, pronto. A body has been found." Pennance abruptly stopped. Fulton carried on for a pace or two before he turned, a frown on his face. Meacham continued, "With bread in his mouth."

Seven

A squad car had been dumped in the middle of Colomb Street, a narrow, one-way road, blocking access so acutely that a pedal bike would have difficulty squeezing through. A uniform cop, presumably the driver, watched Pennance with interest as he neared. Beyond, at the intersection of Colomb Street and Pelton Road, a second squad car was slewed across several lanes at an angle blocking off vehicular access in or out of the immediate area.

"DI Pennance." Pennance paused in the middle of the road a few feet away from the cop and showed his ID. As he did so, his watch vibrated, delivering a text from Fulton, which read, 'Don't forget to keep me up to date'. Greenwich was outside of City jurisdiction, so Fulton would have to get approval before attending the scene. However Pennance could wander at will. He didn't reply; he'd already told Fulton as much and it irritated him that the DCI felt the need to remind him.

"Everything okay, sir?" asked the uniform.

"Sure," said Pennance. "Just someone pulling rank."

"You want to be at my level, sir. *Everyone* pulls rank, even the missus and her dog." The PC grinned.

"I feel your pain." Pennance remembered what Fulton had said, 'You know how it works'.

"It's the place on the end, sir. Can't miss it, what with the CSI porch."

Pennance walked about another hundred yards to where all the action was. The house was distinctly non-traditional.

The outer walls curved, like the construction had been shaped to the thoroughfare and not the other way around. Sash windows overlooked both Colomb Street and Pelton Road. Directly opposite stood an obviously ecclesiastical building, given the arched windows, cross above the portico door and on either end of the pitched tile roof – St. Joseph's and Catholic in denomination, according to the sign. A killing had occurred in sight of God's house.

With the high street just a short walk away this would probably be a high traffic area on a normal day, but normal it certainly wasn't. Another uniform PC hovered nearby, one foot on the pavement, the other in the gutter; an eye on the road, the other on a small crowd gathered opposite, who stood whispering between themselves, discussing ongoing events for sure. Several neighbours leaned out of their respective windows watching the weird world of a murder case unfold right on their doorstep.

A third PC stood at the doorway to the house itself, actually just in front of a tent-like construction made of a yellow plastic material which had been erected and set against the wall; in effect a temporary entryway. Access was gained through a rectangular flap which could be closed using a zip. At present the zip was partly undone, up one vertical, so someone could slide in or out with a little effort.

The uniform cop acknowledged Pennance and he reached for his ID once more. Dark curly hair spilled out from under her flat cap, freckles on her cheekbones. She lifted a hand, palm out, said, "I know who you are." She tapped the radio on her shoulder. "Webster told me." Pennance assumed Webster was the cop by the car back down Colomb

Street. She continued, "I shouted up the stairs for CSI, but they must have their noses stuck in some blood spatter or whatever." She glanced into the darkened hallway then back to Pennance. "If they're not here in a minute I'll go and put a boot up someone's arse."

"Whose arse would that be, PC Kaplinski?" A man wearing an evidence suit emerged into the light. He kept his hood up and visor on, but his medical face mask was down off his chin, revealing pockmarked skin, stubble and a raised eyebrow. He reached up, pulled the zip halfway along the horizontal, widening the opening some more.

Kaplinski's lips moved but no sound emerged while some colour rose on her cheeks. She kept her back to the CSI.

"Mine," said Pennance. "I'm late."

The CSI's eyes flicked between Pennance and Kaplinski before he said, "I'm Bloomsbury, the CSM. And you must be Pennance."

"I am." Pennance could feel eyes on his back from the locals. And eyes above. He glanced over his shoulder at the crowd, then up, spotted two CCTV cameras fixed to the wall just below the uppermost windows – high enough to be unreachable without a ladder. Nearby was the orange yellow square of an alarm box. Pennance returned his attention to Kaplinski. "Has door-to-door been done?"

"Nobody requested it, sir."

"Who's the senior investigating officer?" asked Pennance.

"Apparently, you are," said Bloomsbury.

"That can't be right."

"DI Carver came out from Lewisham." Pennance knew the nearest station was in Greenwich itself, though it was small, primarily undertaking local policing matters, and didn't include a CID unit so no-one there would be capable of running a murder scene. Bloomsbury continued, "Carver had one of my evidence suits half on when she got a phone call straight after which she took herself off. The woman didn't even get a foot over the threshold. As she left she said something over her shoulder about you turning up and taking over." Bloomsbury shrugged. "She seemed relieved, frankly. Like she'd just avoided stepping in a large pile of something brown and smelly. Rather similar to the stench upstairs. The victim released his bowels when he died."

Pennance wrinkled his nose, asked, "Who rang Carver?"

"I'd guess her boss; Superintendent Ballard, she's in charge of SEABCU."

Bloomsbury meant the South East Area Basic Command Unit, which covered Greenwich.

"Someone must have spoken to Ballard," said Pennance.

"I wouldn't know." Bloomsbury shrugged. "Anyway, you're here and you're competent, right?"

"I used to be CID."

"There you go. This is a bloody weird one, so can you sort the politics out later and give us a hand now?" Bloomsbury stared at Pennance for a long moment.

"Where's the body?"

"Good man." Bloomsbury offered a white garment in plastic. "Your very own evidence suit." For the second time today Pennance split the flimsy wrapper. Kaplinski held out her hand for the discarded waste. "First floor bedroom," said

Bloomsbury. "Not difficult to find, it's a small two-up, two-down." Then Bloomsbury gave Pennance gloves and overshoes.

"I'll walk the downstairs first, get a feel for the place," said Pennance.

"Come find me when you're ready." Bloomsbury faded back into the gloom.

"Thanks for that," said Kaplinski in a low voice.

"No problem." Pennance pulled out one of his business cards from an inside pocket. "Can you do me a favour in return?"

"Of course."

"Get Carver on your radio, and ask her to call me on this number." Pennance handed over his card.

"Absolutely, sir. Least I can do."

Pennance tugged the suit, gloves and lab glasses on before heading inside. He heard the zip to the tent go behind him as Kaplinski sealed up the temporary porch.

He forgot her, Bloomsbury and the onlookers the moment he entered the hallway. Steps stretched upwards at a steep angle on his right. The curved walls were plain white, marred by scuff marks here and there. A coat hung on a hook, a couple of pairs of shoes haphazardly tucked beneath. It felt like the antechamber of a lighthouse, without the tang of salt or the irritating screech of seagulls. He couldn't see a keypad for controlling the alarm, though. Usually they were in the entrance – the last task before leaving, the first when entering. Perhaps the box outside was fake.

For now, Pennance ignored the stairs. Doors led off to his left and ahead. Pennance chose to go straight on and found himself in a small kitchen of pine cupboards, narrow work surfaces and the usual all-in-one appliances designed for single living – fridge freezer and washer dryer. A window above the sink gave the attractive panorama of a garden fence panel and a slice of grey sky. When Pennance opened the fridge the light failed to come on. He found some vegetables in the salad drawer, eggs on a shelf and a can of lager, the plastic binder of what would have been bought as a four pack still around the neck. The largely iced-up freezer was empty except for a pack of peas and a half-drunk bottle of supermarket branded vodka.

The kitchen wall must have been demolished in the past because Pennance was able to walk through into a reception area via a wide opening. Here was a dining room, evident by the large table and chairs which dominated the space. Pennance ran a gloved finger along the varnished surface, leaving a swipe in the dust.

A pair of white-painted wooden French windows, locked from the inside, gave Pennance access to the garden that would make the average prison cell feel huge. Underfoot lay a circle of AstroTurf he could step across with a single pace and a couple of plants in slender soil borders, attempting to clamber their way up a trellis towards the light, a lone tendril reaching out. A high brick wall kept the neighbours at bay. On tiptoes Pennance was able to glance over and into the neighbour's garden, which proved to be equally constricted. Again, above Pennance's head, a CCTV lens glared down at him. Pennance retreated indoors.

The space adjacent to the redundant dining room proved to be a lounge. The furnishings consisted of a sizeable and well-used armchair, cushions squashed into the shape of a person, beside which stood a coffee table, and facing a hi-fi stack and a coffee table to the left. Multiple speakers, large and small, were located around the room in an arrangement Pennance assumed would swamp the ether with bass and treble loaded surround sound. A wall was taken up with row upon row of vinyl records and another of books. No television, though.

Pennance pulled down a few of the albums and flicked through them. They'd been grouped by artist but that appeared to be the only structure. And the mix was eclectic – modern jazz, some blues, plenty of rock, a smattering of ambient.

The books were the same – organised by author and publication date and in whatever method the arranger deemed fit. There were thrillers, police procedurals and historical fiction mixed in with true crime and quite a large section on what would be most politely termed as conspiracy theories: Roswell, the Kennedy assassination, 9/11 and so on. Two books lay open on the coffee table, pages down and on top of each other, next to two-thirds of a bottle of cheap blended whisky and an empty glass.

The uppermost was a paperback – George Orwell's *1984*, which Pennance had never read. Using a fingertip, Pennance pushed the novel to one side. The hardback beneath appeared to be a history of the British banking system.

Pennance had seen enough. He headed through the remaining door, finding himself in the hall once more. So, the ground floor was organised in a loop. He waited at the foot of the stairs while a camera-carrying CSI descended, then exited through the make-shift porch. Pennance was about to take the narrow steps upwards when his phone rang. A mobile number he didn't recognise. Maybe this was Carver. Pennance followed the CSI technician outside and moved further down Pelton Road, out of Kaplinski's earshot. The other PC remained near the onlookers, literally kicking his heels. By the time Pennance had taken off a glove and unzipped his suit to reach his phone the connection was cut. Pennance called back.

"Carver." The tone sounded distracted, like she was reading email at the same time, or perhaps in the midst of a conversation.

"Inspector, I'm DI Pennance, NCA. I'm in Greenwich right now at a murder scene on Colomb Street. You know the place."

"Okay." Carver's voice remained unaltered, no apparent recognition of Pennance's location.

"What's your rank?"

"Excuse me?"

"You're a DI in CID, right?"

"What—?" spluttered Carver.

"I understand you were in attendance earlier before taking the opportunity to sod off as fast as you possibly could. I've just arrived and none of the basics are underway. There's no door-to-door happening, just three of your team hanging around on the cordon, and CSI working away, who tell me that I'm the SIO. Is this the kind of shambolic operation you typically run? Because I'm not impressed."

"Who the fuck are you?" Carver was sharp and snappy now. Pennance had her attention, finally.

"I told you, DI Pennance with the NCA."

"You're not senior to me, Pennance. I don't appreciate you speaking like I'm some lackey."

"And I don't appreciate being dumped into this situation by you. Frankly, Carver, it's poor."

"Now wait a minute—" Some of the anger had seeped out of Carver's tone.

"I'm being generous and giving you fifteen minutes to get yourself back here and take over the investigation or I'll be going all the way to DG Quant at the top of the NCA, who I'm sure will be speaking to your Superintendent and so on." Pennance wasn't sure at all. "Then, I suspect, you'll be facing stiff questions from someone well above our respective level. So, your call, DI Carver." Pennance waited. All he could hear down the line was fast, deep breathing. "Fourteen minutes. And my boss is called Meacham, if you want to complain. I can give you her number."

"No need," said Carver, like she was talking through gritted teeth. "I'm on my way."

"That's the right decision."

"Dick." Carver disconnected.

As Pennance headed back into the house he pulled up his hood once more. Kaplinski slid him a sideways look as he passed. He trotted up the bare wooden stairs, the smell of faeces strengthening as he rose. He switched to breathing through his mouth.

He emerged onto a landing flooded with natural light from a Velux window set into the roof above. As on the ground floor, doors led off in both directions. The most activity was in the space furthest away from him, where at least two further CSI's were at work. Pennance paused at the door and stared inside. He could see the legs of the victim, who was clearly lying on his back.

A bathroom was obvious to one side. He entered. Toilet, sink and, behind a curtain, a shower with an extractor fan cut into the wall – no bath; there wasn't the space – and no window. One towel hung over a rail within easy reaching distance of the shower.

On the sink stood a glass with toothpaste and a single toothbrush. Above the taps a cabinet with a mirrored door had been fixed to the wall at a height suitable for a tall-ish man shaving. Standing straight Pennance could only see his chin in the reflection. He opened the cabinet, found creams and tablets on the shelves for managing minor ailments such as dry skin and insect bites. A bottle of out-of-date sleeping pills was the strongest medication.

Returning to the landing, Pennance paused outside the next nearest room which proved to be an office. Like downstairs, a wall had been removed and replaced with double doors which, if open, Pennance would be able to see the corpse. A Formica desk sat beneath a sash window and a laptop with the lid up. There were more hi-fi speakers fixed into each corner just below the roofline and several picture frames on the wall.

Bloomsbury stepped onto the landing, said, "The cadaver is in here; in case you hadn't noticed." The CSM had his face mask up now, muffling his speech, like he was talking through cotton wool.

"So you know," said Pennance, "I poked the bear and Carver's on her way over to take back the case."

"Oh, well done. So are you staying or going?"

"Staying for now."

"It should be a good show when the two of you meet." Bloomsbury must have been grinning beneath the mask because the skin beside his eyes crinkled. "Well, we've made a full sweep of the upstairs already. The pathologist has been and gone. As I'm sure you've figured out, this is an office and the victim's bedroom is adjacent. Let me show you."

Bloomsbury's CSI partner was working near the corpse and obscured Pennance's full view.

"This is Heather," said Bloomsbury.

Heather glanced over her shoulder. She had her hood down and wore a net instead, covering a mass of grey hair, crow's feet and a mask over her mouth. She nodded at Pennance before returning to the task at hand.

"Who's the deceased?" asked Pennance.

"One Stan Thewlis," said Bloomsbury. "Girlfriend called it in."

"Where is she?"

"At her place, as far as I know. A few doors down the road. One of the constables will be able to tell you, I'm sure."

"It's pretty clear Thewlis lived alone," said Pennance.

"Yes, proper bachelor's pad. No kids running around, no cushions, dried flowers or chintzy curtains." Bloomsbury sighed.

Pennance raised an eyebrow at the CSM. "Sounds like you're talking from experience?"

"Wives." Bloomsbury snorted.

"That's a bit sexist," said Heather.

Bloomsbury held his hands up. "Just my little joke, Heather. Anyway shift out of the inspector's way. Give him a proper look." Heather did as she was told, standing and backing up a few feet. Thewlis had dark but greying hair and the beginnings of a beard, maybe several day's growth. He wore a jumper and jeans but was barefoot and his grubby soles faced Pennance. Light from the nearby window fell across the corpse in a wide slash.

The body had been arranged identically to Carnegie. On his back, arms crossed over the chest and eyes wide. Like Carnegie, Thewlis' mouth was open in an apparent scream and was crammed with something white. Lumps and crumbs lay on and around the corpse.

"Bread in his mouth," said Bloomsbury. "Damndest thing I've ever seen."

"Same here, until earlier this morning." Pennance pulled out his phone, tapped at the screen and pulled up a compass app. Thewlis also lay in an East – West direction.

Pennance moved up to his shoulder before squatting. The pungent smell of body odour, as if Thewlis hadn't washed or showered for a while, mingled with the reek of shit assaulting his nostrils. Like with Carnegie, the bread appeared to have been rammed in until there was no more space. Pieces were evident in Thewlis' facial hair. He looked like a squirrel who'd died part way through a feast. "You've fully recorded everything you need?"

"As I told you," said Bloomsbury, "we're done. Photos, swabs and so on."

"Give me a hand then." Pennance moved some more so he was at Thewlis' head.

"With what?"

"I want see at the victim's chest. I need to raise him so I can pull up his jumper." Pennance knelt down.

"Are you sure? Rigor's not broken." As Thewlis's arms and legs would be stiff and the corpse immobile Pennance would definitely need help.

"Until Carver arrives, I'm still the SIO, right?"

Bloomsbury shrugged. "I guess so."

"Then get yourself over here."

Bloomsbury didn't move. "Come on." The CSM blinked before he shrugged and got in place next to Pennance. Heather was staring at Pennance open-mouthed. "You too."

Heather switched her attention to Bloomsbury, who nodded. "Do as the inspector asks."

"Where do you want me?" asked Heather.

"When we lift," said Pennance, "You pull the jumper as far as possible."

"What about his arms?"

"You'll need to get the material underneath them," said Pennance. "Just be careful. The last thing we want is to damage the corpse and affect the post-mortem results."

"We, inspector?" said Bloomsbury.

"Ready?" asked Pennance. Bloomsbury then Heather nodded. "Go."

Between them they lifted Thewlis a few inches off the floor. Without further prompting, Heather grabbed Thewlis' jumper and tugged it up to his elbows, revealing a hairy stomach. "Get him higher," she said, all initial reluctance seemingly forgotten. Pennance and Bloomsbury responded, hefting Thewlis further. Heather shuffled the jumper up, then moved around to Thewlis' head and tugged the jumper at the shoulders, sliding the material from under Thewlis's forearms.

"That'll do," said Pennance. He and Bloomsbury lowered the corpse.

Pennance knelt near Heather, so he was beside Thewlis' torso. Heather stayed where she was, obviously curious as to what Pennance was doing. The B.O. and shit stench had raised a notch from moving the body. Pennance could see one of Thewlis' nipples, but a hand was in the way of the area above his heart.

"Jesus." Bloomsbury went to a nearby toolbox then offered Pennance a bottle of menthol vapour rub. "Want some?" A smear beneath the nostrils went part way to masking odours emanating from the corpse.

"No, thanks," said Pennance.

"Me either," said Heather.

Bloomsbury coated the skin between his nose and top lip before capping the jar again. "What are you looking for?"

Pennance ignored the CSM. Instead he pushed Thewlis' arm. There was a little give, but Thewlis shifted on the floor. "Brace the corpse, would you?"

This time neither CSI debated with him. Bloomsbury put some of his weight on Thewlis' feet, while Heather had the more awkward job of holding his shoulders. Pennance pushed again and this time the arm moved slightly, maybe just enough. "Okay, you can let go." Pennance brushed at the mat of thick hair on Thewlis' torso, then, using both hands, held the hairs back. There they were: two angry red pinpricks.

"What is it?" asked Heather.

Bloomsbury leaned over. "A taser. Right above the heart."

"You knew what you were looking for," said Heather.

"Suspected, at best," said Pennance.

"What does it mean?" she asked.

"That Thewlis suffered before he died."

"Shall we pull his jumper back down?" asked Bloomsbury.

"Not a lot of point." Heather stared past Pennance.

Pennance glanced over his shoulder. Two paramedics in green uniforms loitered on the landing. The nearest, a woman with her hair in bunches and a sewn-in name badge on her chest which read Newton, said, "We're here for the body."

"He's all yours." Pennance stood.

"Do you mind?" Newton made a sideways motion with her hand.

Pennance shifted right out of the way. The other paramedic, Asprey according to his tag, brought in a body bag and placed it next to Thewlis. The stairs were steep and narrow; a gurney or stretcher would be next to impossible to manoeuvre. Newton unzipped the bag.

"There's rigor," said Pennance.

"We know how to deal with that," said Newton. Between Newton and Asprey, they lifted Thewlis into the bag. While Asprey braced the corpse, Newton levered a leg, like wiggling the limb of a chicken, until there was a sickeningly loud crack. She'd broken the tendon which had tightened as the body cooled. Newton and Asprey reversed roles, her steadying, him levering. Another crack – worse this time as Pennance knew what was coming.

"Where are you taking him?"

"University Hospital, Lewisham," said Newton. She zipped the bag up, Thewlis's face the last part of him to disappear from view. Newton grabbed hold of the bag at the top, Asprey picking up the end where Thewlis' feet were, backed out of the room and then down the stairs, watching where he stepped over his shoulder. All that remained of Thewlis was a brown stain on the carpet and the odour in the air.

"Do you mind if I take more of a look around?" asked Pennance.

"Be my guest," said Bloomsbury. "There's just the electronic items to bag up."

"I can get those analysed back at the NCA," said Pennance.

"Fine by me. Heather will make a note in the crime scene log that you took them." Bloomsbury went back to his plastic box, returned with a fistful of clear plastic evidence bags. "You'll want these." He pressed the bags into Pennance's hand.

A laptop, a big and once expensive Mac Book, lay on the desk beneath the window. The lid was scratched and there were knocks on two of the corners, like it had been dropped a couple of times. Next to it was an Apple mobile phone, several generations old.

Four picture frames were mounted on the wall; two either side of the window. They could be easily seen when sitting in the chair pushed under the desk. All contained articles cut neatly out of magazines – close set type and some photos.

The laptop was connected to a monitor and an external hard drive. A button on the front of the computer monitor glowed a muted amber colour, meaning it was on and in standby mode. Pennance lifted the laptop lid then pressed a couple of the Mac's keys with a gloved finger, expecting the screen to light up and reveal a box in the centre for a password in the same way Pennance's PC did. However the display remained stubbornly black. Pennance shifted his attention to the phone. He tapped the screen though it too was dark. He tried to switch the phone on and off, but nothing happened.

He decided not to fiddle with the devices any further. He disconnected the power cable and the external drive, pushed the lid closed. Bloomsbury picked a suitably large evidence bag, slid the laptop and cable inside, sealed it and wrote a number on the outside in heavy black indelible pen with Heather noting the corresponding details on a pad. They repeated the process with the drive, which went into a second bag.

Pennance slid open the desk drawers, one after the other, glancing into each before running a hand through the contents – pens, a post-it note pad, some paper – the usual kind of stationery. Pennance discovered a thumb drive at the back of the middle drawer which he also itemised as evidence.

"Seems to be it," said Pennance, pushing the lowest drawer shut with a foot. "Thanks."

Bloomsbury waved his hand like it was no problem, turned to Heather, said, "Let's leave the inspector to it."

Once they'd departed, Pennance turned his attention to the picture frames. They contained an in-depth expose, apparently cut from a publication before mounting, and Thewlis's name was on the by-line of each. The one Pennance read was about data harvesting by the government and large online corporations.

Next, Pennance headed into the bedroom via the hallway, unwilling to open the doors in case he disturbed anything. The bedroom proved slightly smaller than the office and contained only a neatly made double bed facing the window which overlooked the church, and a wardrobe in a dark, heavily varnished wood. Pennance pulled open the wardrobe doors. Plastic and metal hangars arranged on a racks to one side of the inner space were mainly casual shirts and t-shirts and a few jumpers. Right at the back, a suit dangled. The shoulders were dusty, so it clearly hadn't been worn for a while. A couple of drawers on the other side held socks and pants separately. Several pairs of shoes lay on the base, tucked under the clothes above. Pennance shut the doors.

He knelt down, looked under the bed, and discovered plenty of dust and two lidded cardboard document style boxes. The dirt had been disturbed and very recently – drag marks where the boxes had been hauled out. Using handle holes cut into the cardboard Pennance drew both from under the bed and opened them. Inside were sheaves of paper in individual plastic folders racked up against one other, organised like a filing cabinet. Each possessed a white tab, running from left to right in a diagonal and alphabetically organised. Written on the tabs were descriptors such as Flatiron, Iceworm, MK-Ultra, Wirecard and so on. Pennance didn't recognise any of the names.

Sitting on the edge of the bed, Pennance and pulled a random folder, rested the file on his lap and flipped the cover open. Inside was sheet after sheet of statements from a bank in Munich Pennance hadn't heard of, listing payments in and out. Some had been circled, others had hand-written comments in the margin, which Pennance assumed were by Thewlis.

Pennance returned the dossier to its rightful place and picked out another. This one held several photos, groups of adults standing in front of a chain-link fence – they looked to be from the '80s, given the clothes they were wearing – dungarees, white t-shirts, colourful bandanas around the neck or in their hair. An inscription on the back revealed the people to be a ban the bomb group at an American Air Force base in Cambridgeshire. There were bios on each person, too. He placed this back into the box, also. He flicked through a few more in the second container and confirmed his assumption that this was Thewlis' old research. Then he paused, recalling the drag marks. Had someone searched Thewlis' house? Or was it just Thewlis going back to old work?

Pennance opened the drawers again, unsurprisingly found the same useless junk before returning to the office and switching his attention to the framed articles. When he had finished reading the last one, still none the wiser, something on the floor caught his attention. A sliver of yellow in the gap between the desk and the wall. Pennance moved the desk a few inches, got on his knees and reached into the space with gloved fingers to retrieve the small square of a post-it note.

Written on the paper was a $ sign, then a short arrow pointing towards a single word in block capitals – Blackthorn. Pennance stood and returned to the research files. No Blackthorn in the index. He moved to the section with statements from the German bank and compared the lettering between them and the post-it note. They appeared identical. Then he searched through the folders; none were titled Blackthorn.

Pennance took a photo on his phone before heading downstairs, found Bloomsbury and Heather in the living room. "Have you got another evidence bag?" He held out the post-it.

The note went into its own plastic wrapper and got given an individual number.

"What's Blackthorn?" asked Bloomsbury, peering down his nose at the word.

"It's a tree," said Heather. "Otherwise known as the sloe. Although the fruit is edible, the leaves and flowers are poisonous because they contain prussic acid. And the seeds, too because of the hydrocyanic acid. Plus the branches have spikes, sharp little buggers that easily draw blood. So you need to know what you're doing with blackthorn. Get it right, nice fruits and a decent steeped gin. Get it wrong." Heather made a harsh grating sound in the back of her throat and drew a finger across the skin.

"Very theatrical." Bloomsbury's eyes flicked upwards briefly. "This arrow seems to show dollars moving to whatever Blackthorn is."

"Maybe," said Pennance. "I'm going to interview the deceased's girlfriend. I'll leave my card with PC Kaplinski on the door. I'd appreciate if you send me your report when it's complete."

Inside the temporary porch, Pennance pushed back the hood before slipping off his evidence suit. He folded it up into an approximate rectangle with the overshoes and gloves inside and the glasses on top before heading out through the zip door where Kaplinski was still on duty.

"You off, sir?" she asked.

"I'm done for now." He held out his suit.

Kaplinski picked up a large plastic bag, neck open. "Just drop it inside, sir."

He did.

Kaplinsky closed the bag and rolled the top down.

Pennance continued, "Where's does the victim's girlfriend live?"

"Webster knows the address, sir."

"Okay." Pennance dug out a business card from an inside pocket. "And I'm to give you this."

"Are you asking me on a date, sir?" Kaplinski narrowed her eyebrows, her mouth a straight line.

Pennance felt his cheeks colour. "No, that's for Bloomsbury."

Kaplinski burst out laughing. "Sorry, sir. I was just joking." Kaplinski raised her hand, revealed a wedding band. "It gets boring standing out here all day. Don't worry, I'll pass your details onto the CSM."

As Pennance ambled along Colomb Street he dialled Meacham's number. When she answered Pennance said,

"The dead man is one Stan Thewlis, appears to be a reporter. And he seems to have been murdered in the same manner as Carnegie – tasered, then bread shoved down his throat."

"Is he connected to Carnegie?"

"Too early to be sure. There's some IT gear here, a laptop and a drive. And CCTV outside. Maybe the footage is stored on the internal memory."

"I'll send someone out to collect them," said Meacham. "We've a bright tech in the forensic digital department, Ava McAleney."

"I've met her briefly."

"Well, she can tear the equipment apart. If anyone is able to plumb the depths of electronics, it's her."

"There's also some paperwork in a couple of boxes, perhaps research for Thewlis; that could do with being brought back, too."

"Okay," said Meacham. "I'll get a car on the way. They can pick you up, as well."

"No need, I'm going to speak with Thewlis' girlfriend, see if she can tell me anything. And, in other news, I was SIO for a period of time."

"Excuse me?"

"When I arrived CSI were well underway but there were only uniform cops here. According to the CSM, DI Carver left within minutes of arriving after she had a call from her boss."

"Ballard."

"That's him."

"Cheeky bastards! I rang Ballard to request he give you the courtesy of being involved, that's all."

"Well, Carver and Ballard dumped Thewlis in my lap."

"Believe me, Jonah. As soon as we're finished, I'll be booting Ballard's backside. Better still, I'll get Quant onto this. She can hammer whoever Ballard reports to."

"I've already sorted it, ma'am. I called Carver, told her to get here or there would be phone calls and plenty of angst. She's on her way but made it pretty clear she's not happy with me."

"Tough shit," spat Meacham. "I'll be speaking with Quant, regardless. Well done putting a rocket up Carver. Now, I've got some pointy shoes to polish on a pair of starched trousers."

"Enjoy."

"Oh, I will, Jonah. I certainly will."

As Pennance neared Webster he finally saw the funny side of Kaplinski's joke and chuckled to himself.

"He's here now," said Webster into his Airwave. "Kaplinski tells me you want to know where Victoria Semple lives. She's at eighty two." Webster hiked a thumb behind him. Pennance had walked right past the house when he'd arrived. "Someone from the family liaison department was with her earlier. Not sure if she's still there."

"Okay, appreciate it."

Then, a car came along Colomb Street causing Webster to glance over his shoulder. "Who's this idiot?" He turned, held up both hands at head height, palms out. "Whoa, slow down!" The car, a black Audi, screeched to a halt. Sunlight reflected off the windscreen. The driver's door opened, but only a few inches because it knocked into the wing of a parked van. The Audi pushed forward another couple of feet, making Webster retreat the same distance. Webster stood, hands on hips, while the door opened fully. A middle-aged woman with tight-cropped sandy hair and the kind of skin which would burn under a 40 watt bulb squeezed out. She was stocky and filled out her striped suit. Not fat, but muscle.

"DI Carver," said Webster, dropping his hands off his hips.

"Is he Pennance?" Carver asked Webster, pointing. She switched her attention to Pennance as the PC opened his mouth to answer. "Are you Pennance?"

"Last time I looked," said Pennance.

Carver focused on Webster once more. "Get this idiot off my crime scene. Immediately." Carver slammed the Audi's door shut and headed directly for Pennance, like she was going to walk right through him. Pennance knew how the next few seconds were going to pan out. He spread his feet, planted his heels, ready for the inevitable shoulder barge. But at the last moment Carver checked right, cut between two parked vehicles and onto the pavement. Pennance relaxed, let out a breath.

"Looks like you've made a friend for life there," said Webster.

"One more in an ever-growing collection," said Pennance.

Webster grinned. "I'd better 'escort' you away, then, sir." He used fingers to make a brief air quote. "Perhaps as far as 82?"

"I guess you should, Constable."

Webster walked beside Pennance until he was a couple of houses away from Victoria Semple's. "That's you good and gone, sir."

"I've learnt my lesson."

Webster grinned, then returned the way he'd come.

Eight

Victoria Semple lived in one of the original terraced houses on Colomb Street, probably built around the turn of the 20th century. Thewlis' house was out of sight, though less than a minute's slow walk away. Like her partner's, the front door was right on the pavement, no front garden. However, large pots stood either side of the entrance. Climbing plants not yet in flower entwined their way up a pair of trellises to meet in a perennial embrace above the door. When Pennance rang the bell, a dog inside responded with a deep, sharp bark. While waiting, Pennance wondered if Victoria had had a hand in establishing Thewlis' back garden. Thewlis hadn't seemed the green-fingered type.

The door was opened by a middle aged and athletic looking PC. By the ID she wore, this was the family liaison officer. Pennance showed his warrant card, said, "I'm here to see Miss Semple." The dog poked its snout through the gap between the wall and the PC's leg, sniffing the air like a sommelier sampling the bouquet of an expensive wine.

"PC Horan, sir. Come in." Horan reached down, grabbed hold of the dog's collar. "Get out of the way, Boris." The dog was a stubby mass of yellow shaggy hair, no taller than Horan's knee. Boris wagged his bushy tail in welcome so hard his body swung in the opposite direction like a contradictory pendulum.

On the wall beside Horan, hooks had been fixed into the plaster where a couple of wax coats and a dog lead hung. Beyond were several picture frames. One was on the floor, leaning against the wall. Pennance pushed the door to, plunging the narrow hallway into gloom.

"Just on the right, sir." Horan pointed towards the first entryway, still bent over and holding back Boris. Pennance paused beside the fallen picture; a photo of a woman with her arm around Thewlis, both smiling, drinks in front of them on a table, the backdrop a beach and deep blue waters. The frame was cracked in one corner and the wood had parted, like it had fallen down.

The living room proved to be the polar opposite of Thewlis'; comfortably crowded, the space well utilised but not cloying. A sofa, matching footstool and armchairs, big enough for Pennance to wonder how they'd been carried in, took up most of the floor space. A window dominated one wall. A TV on a wooden box was large enough to occlude part of the view onto the pavement. Some daytime programme was on screen, although, in a small mercy, the sound was muted. Wooden shelves either side of the fireplace were so tightly filled with paperbacks Pennance doubted he'd be able to work as much as a fingernail between the spines.

A woman, a few years older than she appeared in the broken photo frame, sat in one of the armchairs, fixing Pennance with an interested stare.

"Miss Semple?" asked Pennance.

"That's right." Victoria picked up a remote control held together by Sellotape from down beside her, pointed it towards the TV and repeatedly pressed a red button. "Bloody remote's on the way out." Finally, the TV flickered off and the screen darkened.

Boris came bounding in, Horan close behind. Without being invited the dog leapt into Victoria's lap. "Sorry," said Horan. "He got away from me."

"Get down, Boris." Victoria none too gently pushed the dog off her legs. He landed nimbly, sat on his haunches and turned his wide, doleful eyes on his owner. After a couple of seconds ticked by, Victoria patted a thigh, said, "Come on then." Boris retook his place. Victoria switched her attention back to Pennance. "Dogs, they take the piss every chance they get. They're like bloody kids, or so I'm told."

"I wouldn't be able to judge on either count. I'm Detective Inspector Pennance, I wondered if I could ask you a few questions about Mr Thewlis?"

"Park your arse wherever you want, inspector. And please, call him Stan. I can't think of him as *Mr Thewlis*."

"Can I get either of you a drink?" asked Horan.

"I've only got instant coffee," said Victoria.

"It'll do," said Pennance.

"How do you take it, sir?" asked Horan.

"Plenty of milk," said Pennance.

Horan disappeared out of the room and Pennance sank into the fabric embrace of the remaining armchair. Boris leapt down and investigated Pennance by sniffing his shin.

"He's such a tart," said Victoria. Pennance stroked the dog's head. "He likes a good rub behind the ears." Pennance obliged for a few moments until Boris flopped to the floor, head between his legs. "That's him done for the day. He's getting on, nearly sixteen. He can't cope so well with long walks anymore. I've no idea what I'll do when he's gone."

"Get another dog?" offered Pennance.

"Easier than another partner, I guess."

"I didn't mean…"

Victoria raised a hand. "You've nothing to apologise for. We don't know each other. If it hadn't been for Stan dying, likely we'd have never met."

Pennance could apply that distinction to far too many people. He said, "I understand it was you who found his body?"

"That's right. As you can see, Stan and I didn't live together. We tried for a few months not long after we first met, but it didn't work for either of us. We both liked our own space and Stan worked odd hours – he preferred to be up late tapping away into the small hours whereas I'm an early riser. Otherwise we fitted well together. Stan was particularly difficult to be around when he was in the last throes of an article. Usually, I'd just leave him to it. When he knocked on my door we'd be friends again."

"He was a reporter?"

"Called himself a freelance investigator, always pushing his nose into other people's business. Should have been a cop." Victoria glanced up sharply at Pennance, eyebrows raised and teeth bared. "Ouch, now it's my turn to say sorry, I didn't mean that. Sometimes I blurt stuff out."

"I'm not offended in the slightest."

"Good."

"Was Stan always freelance?"

"No, he was gainfully employed by an actual newspaper for a while." Victoria gritted her teeth briefly. "Well, when I say actual newspaper, I may have been exaggerating; it was the *News of the World*." A sensationalist tabloid and a so-called red top because the title was printed in bold red at the top of the front page. You knew exactly what you were getting – gossip, innuendo and, often, bullshit. "He was with them from when they moved from Fleet Street to Wapping and right up to the end."

Horan returned with a mug in each hand. She passed the first to Victoria, the other to Pennance. "Do you need me for anything else?"

"Not right now, thanks," said Pennance. He put the mug down on a nearby table whereas Victoria sat her coffee on the arm of the chair.

"I'll be in the kitchen." Horan retreated.

Victoria continued, "Let me preface this by saying all I'm about to tell you happened before I met Stan, I only have his word for it, okay?"

"Sure."

Victoria shifted in her seat. "At the time the *News of the World* was the biggest-selling English-language newspaper globally. The reporters, including Stan, had a lot of leeway and plenty of resources to draw upon. They were the bad boy rock stars of the tabloid world. But with power and influence always comes hubris and, sometimes, disgrace. Do you remember the hacking scandal? Where employees of the paper were breaking into celebrities' phones, learning about their private lives and publishing the information as gossip?"

"Of course. There are still cases coming out, even now." Pennance had read only yesterday about a TV star receiving a settlement for being outed as gay.

"Well, the activity was going on for years until a piece about a member of the royal family was published, and the police got involved to find the source. Up until then, nobody in authority had been interested. After all, it was just stars getting hacked, right? However, once royalty got dragged in, then people sat up and listened!" Victoria rolled her eyes. "And the whole dirty secret unravelled. There were court cases, financial settlements and, eventually, the newspaper closed." Victoria took a sip of her coffee. "Stan told me that the majority of people still at the paper when it shut struggled to find work afterwards. For Stan it meant going solo."

"How did he feel about the end of his career in journalism?"

"Again, there was a few years between this all happening and us meeting," said Victoria. Pennance nodded, giving her permission to speculate. "There was a simmering anger beneath the surface, I'd say. He felt he'd been badly treated."

"Was he involved in the hacking?"

"I asked him once. He said no."

"And you believed him?"

"I'm not sure I did. Some of the things he told me before about how he'd hunt down a story, he had to have some kind of moral disassociation."

"The end justifies the means?" asked Pennance.

"Yes, kind of. Maybe it's a stereotype – like highly successful people must be bastards to get to the top; that kind of thing. My assumption was he didn't do the actual hacking, but he more than likely wrote articles using the results." Victoria considered her coffee mug for a moment. "Stan was a lovely man, but he was … unusual. And he fostered some strange habits in the last year or two."

"Like what?"

"He got into all sorts of conspiracy theories."

"Such as?"

"Mostly ones centred on the elites running the world. That the rest of us are just drones, acting unthinkingly under their direction. Very Big Brother."

Pennance thought back to the novel Thewlis had been reading, said, "*1984.*"

"That bloody book. I threatened to torch it, but that just set Stan off again. He reminded me the Nazis destroyed any works that didn't agree with their perspective. Ray Bradbury's *Fahrenheit 451* was another favourite of his."

"The temperature at which paper burns, firemen setting books ablaze, rather than putting them out."

Victoria nodded. "He wasn't peddling conspiracy theories by the way, he was just fascinated by them and the people who spread them. I mean, who the actual hell believes there are mini-computer chips in vaccines or that windmills cause cancer?"

"Far too many people." Pennance's watch vibrated on his wrist. He glanced briefly at the screen. Confirmation that the laptop and files had been picked up from Thewlis' house.

"There's one question I always see TV cops asking during interviews, inspector. Was the victim acting differently recently?"

"And would you like to answer it?"

She nodded. "Stan *had* changed." She leaned towards Pennance. "He was engaged, like a proper reporter, not working on something crap that was scant use of his talents. He was a good writer, inspector, very good. He could weave an intricate story and keep hold of all the threads right up to the end. It seemed as if he had something in his lap which meant a great deal. But I don't know what the subject was. He became incredibly secretive again."

"What do you mean, 'again'?"

"Stan didn't want his stories leaking or being picked up by competitors."

"He didn't even trust you?"

Victoria shifted in her seat, pursed her lips. "Not in the development phase, no. He'd always been cautious. Ever since one of his stories got stolen by a colleague. Before I met him. However, in the last few months he took his vigilance to the extreme. After he got attacked."

"Was he badly injured?"

"Only his pride." Victoria must have seen Pennance's puzzlement. "There was no actual violence. He got stalked online and somebody spread malicious rumours about him."

"Like what?"

"That he was a paedophile. Which would have been laughable if it wasn't so sick. Even the few business contacts he still had simply evaporated, people he'd known for years stopped answering emails or picking up the phone. All outlets, bar one, no longer published his work. Despite him being totally innocent. After the phone hacking, it was almost the end for him."

"How did Stan feel about that?"

"The same as anyone would, he was bloody furious. Ultimately all it did was feed the hungry beast that was his paranoia. He became even more focused on his plots and machinations. The number of people he was in contact with shrunk."

"He operated within an echo chamber," said Pennance.

"Bang on." Victoria's eyes narrowed. "You see, Stan figured that he'd only been hit because he was getting close to something."

"Close to what?"

"I've no idea. He wouldn't discuss it with me, said it was dangerous for my health. Well, he got that bloody wrong."

"You believe that's why he was murdered?"

"Inspector Pennance, it's the only thought in my mind. You saw the security cameras?" Pennance nodded. "He put them up immediately after the attack."

"Why? What was he concerned about?"

"He wouldn't be specific. He only said he was being watched."

"Did Stan mention Blackthorn?"

Victoria considered that for a moment. "No, sorry."

"When did you last see him?"

"Alive? Three days ago, just before I headed off to work." Victoria paused, rubbed at her eyes. "I'm a supply English teacher, so I go all over London. He answered the door looking typically dishevelled. He came in for a bit, we argued about how he was when he was working and I threw the TV remote at him." Victoria lifted the device to Pennance. "He stumbled, knocked a picture off the wall and it fell. A picture of us. Maybe it was an omen." Victoria briefly fell silent. "He said he was nearly finished and he'd call me. But he never did."

"Is that why you went around today?"

"Yes. Although that wasn't the first time." Victoria took a sip of her coffee. "Typically, Stan needed a final forty-eight hours of work straight through to shape his article. Before he sent it to his editor, he'd let me to read it. That was his way of involving me. I popped up the street, to see how he was doing. He didn't answer, I even waved at those bloody cameras, but nothing. I assumed he was either still working or asleep so I left."

"When was that?"

"Last night, just before 9, I'd say. And then again this morning. I wasn't in school today so I didn't rush over. I took my key to go in and tell him he was being an arsehole for ignoring me. That's when I found him dead." Victoria squeezed her eyes shut. "Sorry. I loved him, despite all his recent crazy."

"Do you have any idea who might have wanted to harm him?"

"Nobody and everybody."

"I don't know what that means," said Pennance.

Victoria sighed. "Stan had this knack of rubbing people up the wrong way. He didn't make many proper friends. He said that when you're a reporter it was impossible to be liked by people other than those you work with. His job was to get into people's business. Particularly those who wanted to keep their business in the dark."

"What is the publication he last worked for?"

"*Watchman*, it's a digital magazine owned by Scott Langridge. If you search the name, it'll pop up."

"Have you heard of Grady Carnegie?"

"The fund manager who died earlier? Sure. I do my own investing. Nothing major, only a self-select personal pension. So, yes, I know who he is. I listened to his podcasts and watched his YouTube channel. Bit of a star in the asset world."

"Did Stan have any form of connection with him?"

"Like what?"

"Such as had they met previously? Or did Stan ever talk about Carnegie?"

Victoria fell quiet while she considered Pennance's question, then shook her head. "I'd doubt it very much. Carnegie is the kind of person Stan would have loathed because Carnegie's obvious wealth gave him power and influence over others. Stan was against all of that. Powerful elites, and so on. Like the royals again. Do you think Carnegie's death and Stan's are connected?"

"I'm just following a line of investigation," said Pennance.

"How did Stan die?"

"Not well."

"Because when he knocked the picture off the wall, he banged his head."

"To my knowledge that had nothing to do with his passing, Miss Semple."

"Thank God." Victoria passed a hand across her face.

Pennance pulled a business card out from an inside pocket and held it out. "My details, in case anything else comes to mind." Victoria took the card and placed it on the arm of the chair.

Victoria grabbed Pennance's wrist as he stood up. Boris rose too. "I haven't cried yet, inspector." She lifted her eyes to stare at Pennance. "Is that bad of me?"

His mobile vibrated in a pocket. The number came up on his watch: the NCA. "Did you hate Stan?" asked Pennance.

She waited a heartbeat, said, "No."

"Then the grief will come, I'd say."

"When?"

Pennance didn't have a meaningful response for her. "I'll see myself out, Miss Semple." In the hall Pennance answered the call.

"Inspector Pennance, this is Alasdair Tremayne, I'm a senior financial investigator and I've been assigned to work with you at Hussle."

Pennance stepped out onto the pavement. "Great, what do you need?" He pulled the door closed.

"For you to meet me at Hussle and take me in."

"When?"

"How about soon as you can?"

"I'm in Greenwich, it'll take maybe half an hour to reach you."

"Excellent. Me and my team will be waiting for you in the lobby of Heron Tower."

"How will I recognise you?"

"I'll look different to everybody else in my field, inspector. See you shortly."

When Pennance cut the call, he felt eyes on him. He glanced over his shoulder, saw Victoria in her window, staring at him before she withdrew into the darkness.

Nine

Pennance dodged the gaggle of reporters still hanging around the entrance to 110 Bishopsgate. He paused on the edge of the lobby area and glanced about. There were maybe ten other people, beside Pennance, milling around the interior. Three were obvious Heron Building employees judging by their uniforms, the rest all wore suits. Which left a woman and a man standing side by side halfway across the lobby; casually dressed, verging on the scruffy, both with a rucksack over a shoulder, both intent on their phone screens. And a man standing facing the fish tank, peering into the depths. He clasped the handle of a backpack, bent over at the waist. He wore jeans and a t-shirt, his hair tied in a bunch with an elastic band.

"A whole world right behind this thin sheet. Incredible, when you think about it and not too dissimilar to the world of accounting." He stood upright, turned around. "Pleased to meet you, Inspector Pennance. I'm Alasdair Tremayne." He was right, he appeared nothing like a typical accountant.

"How are fish similar to numbers?"

Tremayne gave a thin smile. "There's bottom feeders, plankton, oxygenators, top feeders and so on. Co-existing, yet with their own objectives. It's the same in the financial world."

"Which of those are you?"

"I'm whatever is uppermost in the food chain, and everyone else's worst nightmare." Tremayne grinned and not pleasantly. "I'll immerse myself in Hussle's world and figure out their purpose in life. Numbers can be manipulated to tell different stories and it's my job to determine the right tale."

"I guess they're with you?" Pennance indicated the pair with the rucksacks who were still on their phones. The suits were giving them a wide berth.

"How did you guess?" Another humourless grin.

"The lift is this way," said Pennance.

"Before we proceed, what do you think I'm looking for?"

"How much are you aware of?"

"Assume I know nothing," said Tremayne.

"This morning the guy who ran Hussle, Grady Carnegie, was found dead. When I interviewed his two partners, they revealed they'd suffered a ransomware attack recently and were forced to pay up to release some key data they were no longer able to access. I'd like to trace that financial transaction."

"Sounds reasonable. Let's go."

"Before we do, can I ask you a couple of questions?"

"Sure."

"Do you know American Global Securities on Canary Wharf?"

"I most certainly do." Tremayne screwed up his face. "They're a shadow bank. Basically there are three banking structures. First is the central bank, like the Bank of England or the Federal Reserve in the US. They're a national authority that determines monetary policy and regulates the member banks, which are often your typical high street lenders – they're the second structure. Third are the shadow banks. They aren't subject to the same kind of risks, liquidity and so on as traditional banks because they're outside the jurisdiction of the central bank. So they can provide money to dubious customers yet don't have to hold as much money to protect themselves in case of a problem. If they go bust the shockwaves are significant. Shadow banks were a major factor in the expansion of housing credit up to the 2008 financial crisis – the Enron bankruptcy, a company with $63 billion in assets, was a direct result of oversight failures."

"AGS are a bank, but not a bank."

"I know, it's a weird description. The best way of thinking of them is like a loan shark."

"Dodgy then?"

Tremayne hissed air in through his teeth. "I wouldn't go that far, but AGS, and others like them, tend to take risks to win big. I'm a professional gambler, inspector. I play poker online, sometimes I head to Vegas. I'm good at reading people and I have an excellent memory, therefore I can often make an educated assessment of who is holding what cards and who the inexpert players are. I make money by playing the system and the people. In turn I pay some of my winnings as taxes. What I do is not illegal, I'm just smarter than my competitors and the government is there to take its cut too. That's exactly what AGS and shadow banks do, operate within the rules yet on the edge of them and it's allowed to happen because of the revenues they generate for the tax office. Does that help?"

"You've given me something to think about."

Tremayne clicked his fingers to get the attention of his colleagues and they fell in behind. "My compatriots, Jasper Keenan and Alison Zephyr." They nodded at Pennance before returning to their phones. "Jasper will assist me in the forensic financial review while Alison is a Blockchain Analyst and will investigate the source of the ransomware strain."

"Strain?" At the lift doors Pennance reached out, pressed the up button.

"There's two types of ransomware," said Zephyr, attention still on her screen. "'Crypto', which encrypts files on a device so they can't be accessed or 'Locker' which blocks the user from the device itself. Most attackers, we call them affiliates, rent the use of a strain from a developer, the original designer of the ransomware programme. In return the developer gets a cut of the profits."

"The profits being the payoff?"

"Right."

The lift arrived, empty for once. Pennance allowed the trio to enter first. "It's like borrowing a book from the library, then."

"A library with illegal books, though," said Zephyr. "The affiliates move between different developers and use different strains so they have a lifecycle which ebbs and flows. I can analyse the blockchain to identify the developers and affiliates."

"And blockchain itself?" asked Pennance.

"Just leave it at 'complicated'," said Tremayne.

"That's no fun," said Zephyr. "Blockchain uses computers all over the world to store information, rather than in a single location, like on a hard drive. So the long chain of data is broken into blocks and then each is placed onto different devices. Which makes the information very secure, like taking a 1,000 piece jigsaw puzzle and spreading the parts randomly all over the UK."

The lift jerked to a halt and Pennance took the lead when they entered the offices of Hussle. Metzler glanced up from his monitor before slowly rising. "Inspector Pennance, what are you doing here?" He looked past Pennance. "And who's that?"

"These are the forensic accountants we discussed." Pennance glanced around the office area. "Where's Mr Neumann?"

"Out." Metzler came round in front of his desk.

"Who's he?" Tremayne tilted his head towards the American.

"I'm Casey Metzler, Company Secretary. Stefan will be some time, so you'll have to wait."

Tremayne moved past Pennance and placed his rucksack on a desk, like he'd taken control now. "We're here to run our fingers through your accounts. Metaphorically speaking, of course."

"I don't frickin' think so." Metzler sat on the edge of his desk, crossed his arms.

"When we spoke earlier Mr Neumann was fine with the idea," said Pennance.

"Well, I'm not. I never was. And it's just me here right now."

"Isn't Mr Neumann the senior partner now?" asked Pennance.

"He is." Metzler's admission sounded grudging.

"Call him then, please."

"Why would I do that?"

Tremayne unzipped his rucksack. "If you help it'll go smoother and we'll be out of your hair that much faster." He removed a chunky laptop from his bag.

Metzler sighed, turned around, picked up the phone and dialled. "Stefan, its Casey. That cop, Pennance is here again, with some forensic accountants." He paused, listened then held the phone out to Pennance. "He wants to talk to you."

"Inspector Pennance," said Neumann. "You're back, and with some friends, Casey tells me."

"He's right."

"I think Casey is a little upset."

Pennance flicked his attention briefly towards Metzler, caught the narrow-eyed glare he was directing at the thick-skinned Tremayne. "Seems so."

"As we agreed during our meeting, I'm more than happy for anyone to review our systems. I'd be delighted if we can catch whoever hacked us and get our money back."

"Good to know, Mr Neumann."

"Now, if you could put Casey back on, I'll iron everything out."

Pennance passed the phone back to Metzler, who listened for a moment, nodded, said, "Sure."

Metzler slowly replaced the phone into its cradle. "Stefan says to proceed."

"Thank you," said Pennance.

"Can we use your meeting room?" asked Tremayne.

"Why not?" Metzler shrugged. "Coffee machine's off limits, though."

"I only drink boiled water, so that's fine."

"No kettle." Metzler gave Tremayne a thin smile.

Tremayne turned to his team, said, "Let's get started." Zephyr and Keenan headed into the meeting room, removing their own laptops, identical to Tremayne's, as they walked. Tremayne continued, "We'll need your passwords. And unfettered access to all your systems."

"Jesus."

"When I say need, I don't really. I can break into your set-up, given enough time. It simply means we'll be here longer." Tremayne gave Metzler a decent imitation of the same unamused smile he'd suffered moments ago.

Metzler waved a hand in obvious defeat before slumping into his seat. "Whatever."

"That's the optimum choice, Mr Metzler." Tremayne gave Pennance a conspiratorial wink, said, "Top of the food chain, remember." Then, "You can leave us to it, inspector. I'll call when we find anything."

"When?" said Metzler.

"There's always something hidden," said Tremayne.

Ten

Pennance placed the plastic-wrapped sandwich and Styrofoam coffee cup on the only unoccupied section of his desk.

"Those got left here earlier." Hoskins leant sideways around his two large monitors and aimed the stub of a well-chewed biro at the document boxes Pennance had removed from under Thewlis' bed.

Pennance hefted the boxes down and pushed them against the side of his desk so they were out of the way. He removed the lid from one, took out a handful of folders, placed them in the middle of his desk.

"What are they?" asked Hoskins.

"Past articles written by the reporter found dead earlier today. I'm going to catalogue the files. Probably a long shot but maybe there's a connection between Thewlis and Carnegie in here."

"The guy with bread in his mouth?"

"Meacham told you?"

"No, I haven't seen the DCI all day. Her Ladyship's too busy for the likes of me." Hoskins tapped the top of his computer screen. "It's on here."

"Show me." Pennance came around to Hoskins's side of the desk, knowing what he was going to find. He was right. A headline in an online newspaper, 'Investment Guru Found Dead In Bizarre Circumstances'.

"It mentions the bread in the first paragraph." Hoskins tapped a finger on the monitor.

Pennance skim read the article. "I'd better call Meacham."

Hoskins briefly pulled a face, pursing his lips like he was in pain, then said, "I can do the document analysis, if you want."

Meacham picked up so Pennance raised a hand at Hoskins, palm out. "Have you seen the news, ma'am?" He barged his way through the door and into the corridor, keen to be away from Hoskins's probing eyes.

"Just now. Quant brought it to my attention in a call." Meacham sighed heavily. "Carnegie's cause of death was supposed to be kept under wraps."

"Yes, ma'am."

"So, who the bloody hell leaked to the press?"

"Wish I could tell you."

"Whenever I find out, I'm going to rip his balls off."

Pennance thought of the cleaner, Edwards. "How do you know it was a man, ma'am?"

Meacham was silent for a long moment. "Good point."

"I didn't see any mention of Thewlis," said Pennance.

"Well, that's something." Meacham sounded mollified for now. "But we'll have to assume it'll get out at some point."

"Probably."

"Then you'd better move fast." Meacham cut the connection.

When Pennance re-entered the office, he found Hoskins standing by his desk, flicking through the Thewlis files like he was in a record shop searching for an LP. Hoskins nodded at Pennance's lunch. "Did you get that from the Corner Café?" Hoskins meant a place on Vauxhall Walk, a building surrounded by green space – a park and a noisy children's playground – just a few minutes' away from here, which Hoskins himself had introduced Pennance to on his first day.

"Uh-huh." Pennance flipped open the first folder.

"I told you it's best to eat inside the cafe, not at your desk." Hoskins waved his arms around. "Get away from here, pretend to be someone different."

"I prefer to go for a run."

"Who needs exercise?" Hoskins made a pffft sound. "What did you get?"

Pennance sighed, gave in. "The half club."

"That's a good one." Hoskins licked his lips. "What else was on the menu?"

"I didn't look," lied Pennance and peeled the lid off the cup. "I just went for the tried and trusted favourite."

"An amateur mistake."

"In your world." Pennance took a sip. The drink remained hot enough to almost scald his tongue. "Bloody hell."

"And there's another one." Hoskins snickered. "*Jonah.*" Hoskins returned to his seat.

Sucking air through puckered lips, Pennance carried on turning over the sheets from Thewlis' research folder. However, it was immediately clear the information would need a proper in-depth evaluation to determine if any of it could be connected to Carnegie and Thewlis' murders.

Pennance was hungry and wanted to unwrap the chicken, mature cheese and bacon, but Hoskins was still watching. "What's Ava McAleney's extension?" asked Pennance.

"3475," Hoskins responded immediately. Pennance picked up the phone, tapped in the numbers, waited for it to be answered. "Don't forget to mention me."

"Digital Forensics, McAleney."

"Ava, this is Jonah Pennance."

"Ah, inspector, a laptop and some drives got delivered to me with your name on them earlier."

"Call me Jonah, please."

"Like the prophet in the Hebrew bible?"

"I haven't been around that long."

McAleney laughed. "What are you looking for from the digital analysis? I'd appreciate some guidance." She sounded like Tremayne earlier.

A forensic examination of a victim's electronic equipment was always carried out, assessing the websites they visited, which pages they opened, what keywords the victims used while online how long they stayed on each site, any posts or messages in their social media accounts, who they connected with, and so on. It all contributed to building a picture of the victim's activities in last days and hours of their lives, what their mental state was, what their plans had been and so on.

"The victim was a reporter," said Pennance. "Apparently, he was working on an article before his death. I'd like to see if any documents exist and any websites he may have researched in the process. And there's several CCTV cameras outside his house. Hopefully footage of whoever attacked him exists."

"We can do better than hope!" McAleney laughed. "Given enough time I'm confident I can access the information, *Jonah*."

"How long will it take?"

"I'll be looking at the laptop myself. We're pretty busy right now and resources are tight so it might be a few days before I can schedule the social media assessment."

Speed was important in the earliest hours of a murder case – the so-called golden time.

"I'll take a quick look around myself then."

"You won't find as much as I can, Jonah. I wield a significantly sharper knife."

"I'm aware of that, but I want to move fast and I prefer to build my own picture, so I can shape them as a person in my mind, to put some life back into the corpse and understand who they were."

"Fair enough, we can compare notes."

"Great, please let me know as soon as you have something." Pennance disconnected.

He couldn't hold off any longer and unwrapped the sandwich. He bit into it as he opened a web browser. The granary bread was soft, the bacon salty and the cheese strong enough that the chicken was just further filling. Hoskins winked, like a proud father. Pennance tapped Thewlis' name into the search bar, hit enter and took another bite before wiggling a grain out from where it had got stuck between his teeth with his tongue.

"Christ, it's like watching a lizard eat," remarked Hoskins with a grimace, which was rich, coming from him. "Good job nothing puts me off my grub." Hoskins stood, pushed down his mat of unruly dark hair with a palm. "I'm off to the café, want anything else?" He grabbed a raincoat off the back of the chair and his porkpie hat from off the desk which he placed on his head at a raffish angle.

Pennance pointed to his sandwich. "I'm good, thanks."

"We burn enough calories in our jobs, right? Big brain." Hoskins tapped his temple before hefting his belt over his narrow waist and wandering off. Pennance shook his head, glad Hoskins had gone.

The link to Thewlis' website was towards the bottom of the first page of search results. A click of the mouse button and Pennance landed on a pretty standard design with selections such as 'About', 'Articles', 'Blog', 'Get in Contact', 'Archive' along an uppermost bar and a large photo of Thewlis, below. The image seemed to be old, in that Thewlis appeared young. Thewlis was clean-shaven, short hair swept back, no grey streaks, no worry lines marring his face. Even a smile played across his features, like the future was something to be welcomed, rather than feared, and the past not yet a ball and chain.

When Pennance clicked on 'About' he discovered the structure to be a roller blind –automatically scrolling down a short distance to the relevant area before pausing. The webpage was simply one long list – a spin of the mouse wheel would take Pennance where he needed.

The section proved to be short and initially difficult to read because the background was black, while the text was in a blood red, forcing Pennance to squint.

Stan Thewlis is a highly experienced investigative reporter with nearly thirty years in the industry. Stan's hard graft and tenacious attitude means he has broken many exclusives and continues to regularly do so. Stan has a unique nose for unearthing the buried facts and putting himself where others won't go. Stan is driven to uncover the truth, no matter where that leads him and no matter what the cost.

Pennance leaned back in his chair, briefly wondering whether Thewlis' inquiries had revealed something that meant he paid the ultimate price.

He returned to scrolling, pausing at the 'Articles' section, organised as a headline for each story with a brief description of one or two sentences beneath, along with an associated image to the side. The titles were all in a blue underlined text, which meant a hyperlink. Pennance counted six articles in all.

Uppermost was '*Big Pharma – Their Role in Your Death*'. A click jumped Pennance to Thewlis' blog. The opening paragraph read:

'Where *social media syndicates control our daily existence through information manipulation, pharmaceutical giants manage our death. How, you may ask? By determining when and at what cost life-saving treatments are delivered. Many, many billions of dollars have been spent on finding the cure for cancer, but where is it? Why has cancer not been eradicated? I can tell you that it* has. *It's simply that the big pharma companies are withholding the solution because profit and individual wealth for the very few is at the root of* everything.'

"Wow," mumbled Pennance. He read through to the end, but the opening statement proved to be the thrust of the argument – a small number of people were deliberately affecting world health for their personal gain. At the bottom of the page was a counter; the page had been opened 7,327 times.

Pennance remained on Thewlis' blog and kept searching. The pharma post wasn't the most recent. Above sat '*Dog Theft – A Pernicious Trend*' which discussed the recent development of people's pets being stolen. Thewlis had appropriated a picture of Victoria's dog, Boris, inserted part way down into the text, Pennance assumed for illustrative purposes as Boris was still very much at home. Thewlis had posted it a week ago and the counter was more than triple the pharma column.

Next was, '*CrowdStrike – A Threat to Democracy?*'

'*CrowdStrike is a cybersecurity business based in California, USA, hired to investigate the hacking of the Democratic National Committee (DNC) back in 2016 prior to the election of Donald Trump as President. The establishment stance remains that Russia was behind the raid. However, what if that is just a front? What if CrowdStrike, an* American *company, was integral in the attack and thereby affected the outcome of an election and the future of not just US citizens, but those across the globe? Could this happen in the UK? And, if it did, how would you or I even* know*?*'

Pennance dropped off the blog and typed 'CrowdStrike' into a search engine. Immediately he saw the accusations Thewlis had outlined were a widely debunked scheme. Returning to the blog, Pennance skimmed a handful of the other posts, which continued the same premise. Thewlis, while clearly intelligent and able to engage the reader, appeared somewhat divorced from reality. Victoria, he recalled, claimed Thewlis wasn't a conspiracy theorist himself, merely fascinated by them. Pennance wasn't convinced he agreed with her.

Then Pennance accessed the 'Articles' section on Thewlis' webpage. The next link took him to a Sunday magazine, one of the serious broadsheets with a wide readership. The story was an in-depth evaluation of insider trading at a London bank, which Pennance read from beginning to end. It was well written, compelling, loaded with evidence and led Pennance to draw his own conclusions, rather than what he was being told by Thewlis. There were no skewed personal theories, no judgements of the system, simply the facts. The publication date was three years ago. Pennance Googled the bank and found three junior traders (but nobody in management) had been fired and subsequently ended up in court with two receiving prison sentences (which they would still be serving) while the third had walked free.

The next link was another expose in the same Sunday magazine a few months previous, this time detailing arms sales from the UK to Saudi Arabia and making connections between government officials and a corrupt regime with a dreadful humanity record. Another web search showed a different outcome to the banking expose – the officials were moved sideways into new roles and the government denied the story.

If Pennance remembered correctly these were two of the framed articles in Thewlis' office. He pulled out his phone, checked the photo he'd taken. His recollection was correct.

Next, Pennance clicked on 'Archive' which delivered a long list of hyperlinked titles – no text, no photo – and appeared to be a dumping ground for everything Thewlis had written that was available online. Pennance randomly clicked on four hyperlinks, one after the other. Each took him onto a news website – *Watchman*; the online magazine Victoria had told him about. Pennance took a screen shot of owner and editor, Scott Langridge's contact details – an email, landline and a postal address in Soho. Pennance tapped Langridge's number into his mobile and placed a call. After five rings an answer-machine dropped in, a robotic voice stating, 'Leave a message'.

After an extended beep Pennance said, "Mr Langridge, this is DI Pennance at the National Crime Agency. I'd appreciate it if you could call me back on this number. I've some questions about Stan Thewlis."

He disconnected, put the phone on his desk and wrote a quick email to Langridge using similar language and sent that, too. Then he returned to the *Watchman* front page, clicked on a search bar at the top, typed '*Stan Thewlis*', hit enter. The response was a list of tightly spaced links that extended over two pages. There were maybe sixty in total, published through a three-year period up to around a couple of months ago.

Hoskins came back into the office then and said something but Pennance just waved at him and Hoskins sat at his desk, hidden behind his monitors.

Pennance thought for a moment before picking up a pen and paper and drew two lines from top to bottom, creating three columns. In Thewlis' blog once more, Pennance noted the dates and broad themes of the articles in the first column, then he flipped to *Watchman* and repeated the process in the next column, before dropping onto the archive on Thewlis' website and completing the list, having gone more than a decade into Thewlis' online past. There was more history in the Archive area, but Pennance had his conclusion now.

Furthest back in time Thewlis was writing exclusively for the *News of the World*, before operating across a number of magazines and newspapers of various sizes – when he went freelance after the *News of the World* shuttered.

Over the entire decade, Thewlis' had published to his blog on a regular weekly basis. However, distinct, periodic breaks punctuated the timeline, meaning every few months there weren't any posts at all for typically three weeks. Pennance reckoned Thewlis was developing and finalising his investigative pieces here.

Finally, Thewlis' time at *Watchman*. He'd started publishing there five years ago up until twelve weeks ago. He had blogged every other day, abruptly halting nineteen days ago. Perhaps Thewlis had paused relations with *Watchman* while working on the new expose which, according to Victoria, he was close to finishing.

On a far less analytical, softer evaluation, Thewlis' earliest stories, written for mainstream publications, felt deeper, better constructed, more compelling. And, frankly, more grounded in reality. Over time the blog articles veered away from well-thought-out posts, to the sensationalist or localised news – as if Thewlis' worldview had shrunk down to where he lived and what he read. His *Watchman* work was somewhere in between – decent enough, not to Thewlis' previous high standard, but not degraded into wild speculation. Maybe Langridge had refused to publish the strongest stuff?

Pennance stretched, realised he'd been sitting at his desk for over an hour. He headed to the canteen, getting lost only once on the way, which was an improvement, and brought a coffee back. Hoskins hadn't moved, barely glancing at Pennance when he entered, absorbed by something on his screen. Pennance re-opened his web browser before accessing the most popular social media platforms: Facebook, Instagram, Twitter, LinkedIn and, most recently (and annoyingly), TikTok – the style of posts grated on Pennance. He only logged onto social media when he needed to investigate other people's profiles. Pennance possessed multiple accounts on each with varying levels of personal detail, friends and history, depending on the kinds of people he was targeting.

The start point was always Facebook because of the platform's popularity with the general public. His go-to profile possessed only the most basic of information – no place or date of birth, a generic location of London and, of course, a different name – Jonah had become Joe, Pennance had become Peterson. Peterson had no friends and the personal photo was literally generic. One of his IT colleagues at Sapphire had used some Deepfake software to produce various facsimile images, both male and female, for Pennance to upload. Pennance wasn't about to steal anyone else's image and impersonate them. That was just plain wrong.

Pennance's objective was two-fold, first to hide who he really was and, second, to entice his targets into making friends and allowing him to read their posts and look around their connections. Pennance could appear to be an attractive teenager, or a good-looking guy in his 20s, he could be white, or black and so on. Pennance ensured his profile was as attractive a lure as possible to hook his prey because that's what they were and the kind of people he'd been after while at Sapphire were smart; many of them hidden in plain sight.

First, Pennance activated a Virtual Private Network, a piece of software which scrambled his location. More pretence; Pennance could be in the US or Iceland or Nepal. He certainly didn't want the people he was researching being able to track him to the NCA.

As usual there were several friend requests, all from users he didn't know. One was a knock-off sunglasses salesman by the look of their previous posts. Another was a Russian woman looking for companionship 'and maybe more'. Even Hoskins would be able to work out what she meant by that. Her bikini beach photo displayed plenty of skin, though not very much fabric. Pennance rejected them and afterwards Facebook kindly informed him that he had 'no friends'.

He dropped into the search bar and typed in 'Stan Thewlis'. Three others with the same name popped up – two were Stan, the other a Stanley – one in Canada, another in Australia, the last in Italy. Thewlis himself seemingly had zero personal presence on Facebook. Not even a business page, which Thewlis could have run adverts from.

However, there were multiple references to Thewlis' work. His blog showed up many times. The lost dog post had been shared regularly, spreading like a virus through the system by pet lovers warning others to the peril and to be on the lookout for thieves. In comparison, the scandalous articles barely appeared and when they did, there was a clear consistency of who shared them and where – all were similar thinkers to Thewlis.

Another page about halfway down, called NOW-Over, snagged Pennance's attention. Because it was a closed private group, all Pennance could read was the terse description: 'A place for embattled *News of the World* reporters to vent.' To learn more, he'd have to gain access, which meant signing up. Pennance clicked the button and was immediately presented with three questions:

'What year(s) did you work at *N.O.W.*?'

'Who was your editor or editors?'

'What was the name and breed of the office cat?'

Probably Pennance could search online and find sufficient information to answer. However, he decided honesty was the best approach so he wrote a direct message to the group, assuming it would be end up with to the administrator.

'I'm DI Pennance with the National Crime Agency. I'd like to talk to you about your ex-colleague, Stan Thewlis, who was found dead earlier today.' Pennance added his mobile number and pressed send. Pennance had the app on his phone so he'd know if and when he received a reply.

Searches on Instagram, Twitter, TikTok and even Pinterest returned the same response – no presence for Thewlis. Finally, Pennance went onto LinkedIn; it was like Facebook for business people to connect. Mainly, it seemed to be somewhere for job hunting or bleating about whatever boring industry the person happened to work in. Pennance hadn't bothered setting up his own account because LinkedIn allowed sufficiently detailed searches. But it proved to be a further waste of two minutes. Thewlis was absent there, too. It was a fair bet that the online abuse Thewlis suffered had driven him off social media entirely.

Carnegie, however, was an entirely different matter. He was *everywhere*.

A web search returned 343,000 responses. Pennance highly doubted the claim; too precise and surely nobody was that interesting. However, it appeared the media and the general public liked the look of Carnegie. His role at Hussle came high up the list. He had his own personal website which promoted his media appearances and public speaking duties. The enquiry section directed Pennance to Carnegie's agent.

And the media loved him too. Carnegie was the kind of beast they lapped up – a self-made man from a working-class background. Paid his taxes, spoke his mind. Three separate articles, including one in the *Financial Times*, consistently painted Carnegie as hard-working with adjectives like 'driven', 'results-focused' and 'value-chain-aligned', whatever that meant.

Pennance even found an interview in the glossy gossip magazine, *Hello*. The commentary was peppered with photographs of Carnegie in several locations – Pennance recognised the balcony view over the Thames; he and Simone had stood in pretty much the same spot. The journalist, however, had to work hard to build a narrative. There was information about Carnegie's upbringing (very similar to what Pennance had read before), then Carnegie's early successes (also nothing new) followed by his founding of Hussle, including a photo of Carnegie, jacket off and arms folded braced by Metzler and Neumann either side, both with their hands in their pockets in Hussle's office. Behind them the London vista stretched away. Further down, Carnegie was quoted directly. "There are no secrets for you to dig up on Grady Carnegie," he said. "There's nothing to sell on, nothing to manipulate me with. What you see is what you get." And another shot where Carnegie sat on an aubergine-coloured sofa with his arms wide open, like he was being expansive. Carnegie's mouth had later been stuffed with bread only yards away from that very piece of furniture.

Carnegie was extensively represented on the social media platforms, except TikTok. Quickly, Pennance got the impression someone other than Carnegie was posting the messages and photos, which were entirely focused on his media and business life. The missives felt displaced. And on each of the platforms the same post appeared, with the same statements and photos at the same time. The poster must have been using some form of app to do the work for them.

Pennance sat back in his seat, finished his coffee, dumped the cup in the bin and ate the last of the sandwich, screwed up the packaging and discarded it too. A thought occurred to him. He returned to Facebook and tapped Lars Rasmussen into the search bar. 'His' Rasmussen was second on the list. Pennance clicked on the picture – a grinning man wearing mirrored skiing sunglasses with the backdrop of snowy mountain peaks.

Rasmussen's feed was a stream of his material life – his holidays abroad, his Ferrari and his family. Pennance's chest tightened at a recent post right near the top; a photo of three people with their heads pressed together – Rasmussen, Simone and Natalie.

Simone was smiling. She appeared genuinely happy. He thought of the many, many times he'd listened to Simone complain about, cry about or say she loathed Rasmussen. The date on the post was three weeks before Simone had come around to his flat and told him she was getting back together with her ex-husband.

A message from McAleney interrupted Pennance's misery. 'I've accessed the laptop. Can you come to the lab so I can show you?'

So much for her needing a couple of days to get around to Thewlis.

Eleven

Pennance took the stairway down to the basement where McAleney and the NCA's digital forensics department was located.

As Pennance descended, the steps cut back on themselves twice before depositing him into a cramped vestibule. The way ahead was barred by oversized double doors, both with a glass insert, same as Meacham's, but frosted so Pennance couldn't peer in. To either side of Pennance were standard-sized doors, each with a plaque affixed to it – 'Gentlemen' and 'Ladies' respectively.

Ignored the toilets Pennance leaned on one of the double doors. Locked. He noticed a small black pad attached to the wall, an access control reader. He tried his ID, pressing it against the plastic, but the doors remained firmly secured both times.

"Excuse me." Pennance turned, a woman stood behind him, security pass in hand. She large, red framed glasses. "Can I help?"

"I'm due to meet Ava McAleney."

"No problem." She made a sideways movement with one hand. "If you'll let me through."

"Sorry." Pennance shifted so she could hold her pass to the pad. This time came the obvious metallic sound of a lock unbolting. Inside she pointed across the room. "Right over there." McAleney stood, waving expansively at Pennance to get his attention before beckoning him with an equally enthusiastic gesture. Pennance threaded his way between the desks where people sat behind multiple monitors, working on who knew what. Most wore headphones, none glanced in his direction.

To Pennance's eye, the light was different down here: cleaner, brighter. Maybe because of the overhead bulbs. And there was the subtle electric undercurrent of equipment operating, and he got the slight metallic tinge of ozone in the air, like sucking on a piece of aluminium.

He paused beside McAleney's desk, or more accurately, collection of desks. She had three, arranged in an inverted U. One held several computer screens, two keyboards, two mice (or was it mouses?), a desk phone and two mobiles. The next desk had pieces of anonymous electronics scattered across it. And on the third, Pennance recognised Thewlis' laptop, hooked up to a piece of kit and yet another monitor.

"Sorry, I should have been at the door to let you in." McAleney held out a hand for Pennance to shake.

Pennance indicated Thewlis' laptop. "What did you find on the hard drive?"

"Absolutely nothing."

"Excuse me?"

"The drive is blank, look." McAleney turned the monitor screen towards Pennance. It was a bright white. "When I say blank, I mean there's nothing – just the basic operating system. No software or apps, no files, no usage data. Absolutely zero. Every file, every piece of data, every line of code has been scraped off the hard drive and dumped. Then the bin was stomped on – meaning no place to recover information from. I can't do anything whatsoever with the laptop. The mobile and back-up drive was the same."

"This doesn't make any sense."

"It does if the owner used a logic bomb."

"You've lost me."

"It's a digital explosive; a piece of code written by someone to carry out an action when a set of fixed criteria are met. For example, if a password isn't received within a certain number of hours, or days, then the booby trap trips."

"And wipes everything out," said Pennance.

"Scours down to chip level. It's like cleaning off a chalkboard with a wet rag but there's not even a smear left behind afterwards."

"The laptop was powered up when I found it."

"There you go. Thewlis must have had a timer. He died, the clock ticked down, activated the logic bomb and killed all the on-board data."

"That's paranoid behaviour." Pennance thought back to what Victoria had told him.

"Which is one way of looking at it. I would call it defensive."

"What would anyone have that's so important?"

"Different things have different priorities to different people, Jonah."

"I guess." Pennance stared at the computer, like it was going to change its state. He knew it wouldn't.

"What about the thumb drive I found?"

"Empty."

"Logic bombed as well?"

"No, it's simply a storage device that had nothing actually stored on it."

"So, we're screwed then," said Pennance, rubbing his chin.

"Not entirely. First, Thewlis must have been backing up his information somewhere, in all likelihood to a cloud storage facility. I just have to find it. For this I can start with a packet sniff. Second, most people use email to communicate online. Unless the bomb wiped all the messages too, the host should still have them stored at their end. I can maybe gain access via a network analyser."

"What's a packet sniff?"

"Sorry. The technical term is Deep Packet Inspection. The internet works by slicing the information you send over it into chunks, or packets. Each packet then moves in a series of jumps – it's not a continuous flow like a river because the internet is a huge number of interconnected individual segments; a disparate network rather than a system."

"Okay," said Pennance. "This I understand."

"The first step consists of the user entering material onto the internet via their local ISP, or internet service provider."

"I've got one of those."

"Well done," said McAleney. Pennance wasn't sure if she was being sarcastic or not. He could understand why Hoskins liked her. She made Hoskins seem normal. McAleney continued, "Next, the data takes an extended trip, like a long haul flight on a cyberspace carrier airline. The airline, so to speak, uses what's called a Border Gateway Protocol to seek the most effective route. The data takes several more hops, each plotted out individually, before the packet arrives at its destination and is reassembled into its original form. The final stage is for the receiving party to ship a message back along the line to tell the original dispatcher that the data has been successfully received. Think of it like matter transportation in sci-fi programmes; break something up over here, send it in bits, reconstruct it over there."

"And the network thing?"

"Analyser. It's a piece of software which allows me to search for password traffic in various ways," said McAleney. "To capture POP3 data, for example, like an email password you can set up a filter and a trigger to search for the PASS command – that's a simple monitor which stores the password within an encrypted GPG file. Then, when the network analyser sees the PASS command in the packet, it captures that specific data.

"Network analysers require the capture data by two methods. Either on a hub partition of your network or via a monitor / mirror / span port on a switch. Otherwise I'd be unable to see the other person's data traversing the network, only my own."

"I didn't realise the internet was so complex."

"This is pretty basic, Jonah."

"I wouldn't like to see the difficult stuff."

"Do you know how your TV works? Or your car? Would the average person on the street be able to tell you how you go about your job?"

"Unlikely."

"It's essentially the same situation. We all specialise in one area and leave the rest to others. Humans are like a massive loosely connected hive. That's why the NCA employs me, to figure this kind of stuff out. Although some might argue, I'm the best in here." McAleney appeared perfectly serious.

"What's next?" asked Pennance.

"While I go through the network analysis, I'll need someone to place a RIPA request for me so I can gain access to Thewlis' internet connection record. Then I can evaluate Thewlis' web traffic in more detail and maybe determine where he was sending his data. Of course, if I find something suspicious, I'll have to get a warrant to obtain the actual information. All I can do is sniff, remember. I can't actually take a bite."

"I'll handle the RIPA," said Pennance. "Thanks for your help."

"I haven't done anything yet." McAleney shrugged. "There's a switch on the wall by those doors to let yourself out."

Pennance raised a thumb at McAleney before threading his way back through the desks. He pressed the switch, pushed through the doors and took the stairs back to his office. When Pennance entered Hoskins was nowhere to be seen. Maybe he'd needed to refill his digestive system. Pennance woke his computer to deal with the RIPA request.

The Regulation of Investigatory Powers Act forced ISPs to maintain a record of all internet connections made by users in the last twelve months and the police could request this digital information, including phone records, without needing to get a warrant. The process was automated but operated under seemingly strict guidelines. However, in reality, all that was required was for one officer, Pennance in this case, to give permission to another to gain access by filling in the required paperwork.

Back at his desk, Pennance pulled the form up on his laptop, entered the relevant data and fired it off to McAleney. As he did so he remembered her explanation of chopped-up packets. Before he got too far into wondering where in the ether all those bits and bytes were right now, his phone rang. "Inspector, its Hillary Gillespie." She sounded stiff, forced. "I'm Mr Rasmussen's PA." Hillary's tone lifted at the end of the sentence, like she was asking a question.

"I remember."

"That's nice, thank you. Mr Rasmussen said he's ready to meet, here at AGS."

"Just let me get my calendar up and we can fix a time."

"No, he means now. Like straight away." Hillary lowered her voice. "I'm sorry, he does this all the time. They all do, they're like a load of unruly, aggressive little boys pushing the boundaries. If you don't come to the office right away then I don't know when he'll make time next."

Pennance sighed. "Tell him I'm on my way."

Twelve

Lars Rasmussen wasn't alone when Hillary showed Pennance into a windowless, anonymous, basic meeting room, a floor below where Pennance had earlier wandered around the offices of American Global Securities at One Canada Square. Rasmussen was bracketed by two men in three of the five seats at a table. A yellow legal pad and pen lay in front of an empty space.

The person on Rasmussen's left was a dapper-looking young man wearing a black waistcoat with bright red buttons and crisp shirt but no tie. A matching jacket hung over the back of the nearest empty chair. His sweeping grey hair was at odds with his youthful, unlined face. Lawyer, reckoned Pennance.

Then Rasmussen; older than the legal guy for sure, though he didn't look it. His hair was suspiciously black, the skin around his forehead and eyes were curiously smooth. His eyes were very blue. Pennance knew Rasmussen's vision was such that he had to wear glasses or contacts; Simone had told him this and plenty more. Maybe the contacts were coloured. As a minimum, Pennance suspected hair dye and Botox – ageless maturity in one fake package.

The final guy was Vallance, the aggressive cowboy type who'd ensured Pennance was escorted out earlier in the day. Vallance's face was a bright red, and he chewed viciously on gum while he rattled nicotine-yellow fingers on the table. The nails were gnawed right down.

"Inspector Pennance," said Hillary by way of introduction. They were the first words she'd spoken from when she'd collected him in reception. She'd said nothing in the lift on the way up or as she led him to the room.

"Thank you for coming, inspector," said Rasmussen. All very formal and polite.

"Would you like a coffee?" Hillary asked Pennance. A silver pot and a single cup, inverted onto a saucer stood on a tray near Rasmussen's elbow. The others already had cups part-filled. All were black.

"Yes, thanks," said Pennance. "With milk."

"I'm afraid all we have is cream." Rasmussen flashed artificially bright teeth in a wholly insincere grin. Pennance felt like he was in some exclusive club where the rules were only known to the insiders. Rasmussen pointed at the empty chair nearest Pennance. "Take that seat."

Hillary leant over the table to reach the tray, she caught the edge with her fingertips and pulled it towards her. She flipped the cup and poured the coffee.

"Davenport is my lawyer," said Rasmussen, indicating his fake grey-haired associate.

"I suspected as much," said Pennance.

"Simone said you were a great detective." Rasmussen eyed Pennance as Hillary poured cream almost as white as Rasmussen's grin into the cup.

"If we're being formal, I'm Toby Davenport." The lawyer placed a business card on the table and used a single finger to flick it across to Pennance. "I'm the youngest partner at Flint, Foster and Davenport."

"I'm pleased for you," lied Pennance. He picked up the card, the paper was thick, the lettering raised and bold. His first name was actually Tobias. After his surname were several sets of grouped letters which indicated Davenport's qualifications and bar associations. The address was St. Mary Axe. "Your offices are in The Gherkin?" Which meant Flint, Foster and Davenport were just a very short distance from the Heron Building and Hussle.

"Well spotted, inspector," said Davenport.

"Told you." Rasmussen leant conspiratorially towards Davenport. "Top detective."

"Do you know Grady Carnegie?" asked Pennance. Hillary placed the cup next to Pennance.

"Doesn't everyone?" replied Davenport.

"You're aware he's dead?" asked Pennance.

"Of course." The lawyer shrugged. "I watch the news."

"Was he a client of yours?" Pennance lifted the cup to his lips, watched closely by Rasmussen. He could tell straight away the coffee was at best lukewarm. Pennance took a sip anyway.

"I'm not at liberty to reveal that information."

"Let's cut the crap." Vallance gave Davenport a sideways glance in a seeming notification he felt he was doing the lawyer's job for him. "And get to the real subject at hand.

"Quite," said Rasmussen. "I thought it wise to have legal representation, given you kindly informed me I was a potential suspect."

"And costing me a Goddamned fortune in the process," said Vallance.

"It's my budget, not yours," said Rasmussen, eliciting a scowl from Vallance. "Close the door, Hillary." She did so, before sitting down again in the last empty seat and lifting the pen from the pad. "Hillary is taking the minutes of our meeting. My employer is an American company. Any aspects which may include litigation are taken extremely seriously. There's a standing rule to always adopt legal advice and include Human Resources, hence Vallance's presence."

"I'm Vice President of HR," said Vallance. "What do you want with Rasmussen?"

"He was probably one of the last people to see Grady Carnegie alive," said Pennance.

"I highly doubt that." Rasmussen frowned deeply, or at least he attempted to, the Botox interfering with his ability to crease his forehead.

"According to Mr Metzler at Hussle you had drinks and dinner with Mr Carnegie the night he died."

"To be specific I was due to, yes. But Carnegie stood me up."

"How so?"

"We were supposed to meet at The Connaught for drinks at 8pm sharp, then go onto Petrus. But Carnegie didn't arrive. I found that highly unusual, Grady was a particularly punctual person."

"What did you think he was doing instead?"

"No idea. He could have met someone along the way. Carnegie seemed to know everybody. But there's no way he would have allowed anything to get in the way of profitable commerce."

"Yours was a professional rather than personal meeting?"

"Always, without exception. I don't think Carnegie could be anything other than business-like. However, we were mixing in some rather fine food all being paid for by Hussle."

"Did you call him when he was late?"

"No, I happily sat there all by myself." Rasmussen rolled his eyes to emphasise the sarcasm. He pushed his phone over to Pennance. "Of course I rang him, more than once." The call log was on screen. Three attempts within as many minutes to the same number.

"You'll find that's Mr Carnegie's mobile," interjected Davenport.

"Obviously," said Vallance. The muscles either side of the lawyer's jaw stood out as he clenched his teeth.

"What were you going to discuss?" asked Pennance.

"I can't see how it's relevant," said Rasmussen.

"In case you'd forgotten, Mr Carnegie was murdered," said Pennance. "What was the subject of your conversation?"

Davenport leaned in. "You don't have to answer, sir. This isn't a formal interview."

Vallance gave Rasmussen a nod so slight Pennance almost missed it.

"No, it's okay." Rasmussen stretched a forearm out across the table, cutting between him and Davenport. "The inspector is correct. He's investigating a heinous crime and, as an associate of Carnegie's, I feel duty bound to help as much as I can."

"I appreciate that," said Pennance.

"I hope you do," said Vallance. "Hillary, I'll have to ask you to step outside momentarily, please."

Hillary nodded, put the pen down and backed out.

Once the door was closed again Vallance shoved a piece of paper at Pennance.

"What's this?"

"A non-disclosure agreement."

Rasmussen said, "What we are about to discuss is highly confidential. Anything I tell you cannot leave this room."

"So you need to notarise it," said Vallance. He held out Hillary's pen.

"I'm not signing anything," said Pennance.

"Then we're not talking." Rasmussen crossed his arms and glanced away.

"Inspector Pennance," said Davenport. "I think my client has been exceptionally generous with this offer."

"If anything got out it would affect my employer's share price," said Vallance. "Maybe even the banking sector as a whole."

"I'll remind you all once more, this is a murder investigation, not some business venture," said Pennance.

"Here's the deal, son," said Vallance. His skin tone had reduced to something looking more normal and he spoke more quietly than previously. "Either sign the NDA or we walk."

"Mr Vallance, I couldn't give a toss about share valuations or anything else, only who murdered Grady Carnegie and that's why you'll be helping me, one way or the other."

"Your views have little bearing, boy." Vallance dragged the NDA back across the table and flipped it over. He picked up Hillary's pad before turning to Rasmussen. "We're done here."

"What a waste of everyone's time," said Rasmussen, shaking his head. "Simone said you couldn't see a good thing when it was right in front of your nose."

"Lars," said Vallance, one hand on the door handle, glancing over his shoulder, eyes narrowed in a not-so-subtle warning.

Rasmussen rose, said, "You're welcome to sit here and enjoy the coffee, inspector."

Pennance stood, caught Rasmussen's arm as he passed by, pressed his business card into his palm. "Call me if you think of anything."

Rasmussen raised his hand, crushed the card and dropped it onto the floor. "Unlikely."

Pennance said, "If you're involved in this, I'll find out, believe me."

"Fuck off, Pennance." Rasmussen shook off Pennance's grip and stalked out of the room past Vallance who remained at the entrance.

"I'll be contacting the NCA about your conduct here," said Davenport.

The threat was so hollow there was an echo. "Go ahead."

Davenport glared at Pennance briefly before grabbing his briefcase and jacket and following Rasmussen out of the door.

"I'll ask Hillary to escort you to the lobby," said Vallance, then disappeared himself.

Pennance wasn't about to wait for her. He could find his way back downstairs on his own. The corridor was empty when he stepped into it, but he paused because he could hear Rasmussen's tone, full of venom. Pennance turned in the opposite direction to the lift and Rasmussen's voice got louder. He glanced into what appeared to be a utility cupboard where Rasmussen, his back to the doorway, towered over Hillary, hand raised to her mouth, eyes wide. She spotted Pennance, gave a minute shake of her head. Reluctantly, Pennance drew back so he was out of sight, leant against the wall.

"What the hell were you thinking, you stupid bitch?" hissed Rasmussen. "Letting a cop wander around for fuck's sake? And him, of all people!"

"I'm sorry, I—"

"Shut the hell up. If it wasn't for the company's diversity quota I'd have kicked your bony backside out of here years ago."

"Excuse me?"

"You know companies have to employ people of a certain type – low IQ, women, transgender, cripples and so on. So, if I got rid of you then I'd be in trouble with HR, meaning we're stuck together, for now at least." A co-worker came towards Pennance along the corridor, reading something on a tablet. Pennance turned his back, leant against the wall, staring intently at his phone. Rasmussen continued, "But believe me, if you screw up at all from now on there will be significant consequences." The co-worker passed by a foot from Pennance, barely nodding in his direction. "Big, shitty consequences, Hillary."

"Sir."

"I know some nasty people, Hillary," said Rasmussen. "Extremely nasty." Pennance moved again so he could see into the cupboard. The banker had closed in on Hillary, was almost in her face. Hillary had turned her head away, facing the wall. Rasmussen continued, "So foul I'd personally jump out of my office window rather than confront them. And I'm not a weak woman, am I?"

"No, sir."

"Do we understand each other?"

"Yes, sir." Hillary's voice quavered.

"Good." After a moment Rasmussen stepped away. "Maybe there is a spark of intelligence in that dense skull after all." Pennance backed up. "Now, get that fucking idiot out of my building."

Pennance trotted back to the meeting room and waited just inside the entrance.

"Are you okay?" asked Pennance when Hillary entered. Her neck was red, yet her face pale. Even the strawberry mark seemed washed out.

"I'm fine."

"Rasmussen's behaviour was unacceptable."

"I don't know what you're talking about."

"If you want to complain, I'll back you up."

"Complain?" Pennance opened his mouth but Hillary cut him off with a chop of her hand. "*Please*," she said in barely a whisper then set her jaw. "It's my decision."

"Fair enough."

Hillary smoothed down an imaginary crease in her blouse. "I have to see you out of the building."

"Lead the way," said Pennance. Then Hillary spotted Pennance's screwed up card on the floor. She bent down. "Rasmussen ditched it," he said.

"Figures." She put the card into a pocket. "I'll give it to him later." She moved to across, indicated the door with a hand. "Would you mind?"

"Not at all." Pennance left the room.

Hillary walked a few paces behind him, paused at the lift and pressed a button. When they were inside and heading down Hillary said, "Thank you."

Pennance glanced over but Hillary kept her eyes fixed forward. "No problem."

When the doors opened on the ground floor Hillary stepped out and took him into the lobby. She paused, passing the baton, which was Pennance, to the manager, Strevens.

"You again," said Strevens.

"What can I say?" asked Pennance.

"Maybe, 'I won't come here anymore'?"

Pennance shrugged. "Don't bet on it."

Strevens left Pennance at the bottom of the sweeping concrete steps. "See you soon then," he said.

Pennance crossed the concrete plaza, One Canada Square towering above him. He wondered if Rasmussen was watching him leave, a small figure walking away.

It didn't matter. Pennance had other ways of getting to Rasmussen.

***

Soho wasn't exactly on a direct route from The Isle of Dogs back to Vauxhall but, according to the Transport for London website, it wasn't much of a detour either.

Scott Langridge published *Watchman* from an office on Berwick Street. Pennance liked Soho, named after a hunting cry, 'So Ho!' back in the 17th Century. It had been one of those kind of places ever since.

Many of the back streets were free of cars, though usually filled with pedestrians. The buildings, most of them old, loomed three or four stories over the narrow streets and gave the area a feeling of constriction, where residents lived a life on top of each other. Soho had largely moved beyond its seedy past; once *the* place to visit after prostitution was banned in the late 1950s, but there remained enough adult stores, strip clubs and dubious basement level bars to keep the district interesting.

Pennance walked up and down Berwick Street, cutting between market stalls, searching for the entrance to Langridge's office. Eventually, he found it down an alley next to a Chinese takeaway. The door was solid wood, painted a grimy white and scored with graffiti. Further on lurked a large orange dumpster bin on wheels. The alley itself stank of sweet and sour chicken – the sickly, glutinous meal so popular with Brits – a vent next to the door pumping out dense, hot air from the takeaway. Some shouting erupted, all sharp syllables, echoing through the aperture but Pennance didn't understand the language.

There wasn't a bell, so Pennance hammered hard on one of the panels with the side of his fist. A few moments later he tried again. No-one answered either appeal. He dug out his phone, found Langridge's number and dialled. The same five rings, the same robotic answer machine and the same message.

"Mr Langridge, this is DI Pennance, calling about Stan Thewlis once more. I'm outside your office right now. If you're there, please come down." Pennance paused for half a minute. No movement inside.

Pennance's phone rang then. But it wasn't Langridge.

"Where are you, Jonah?" asked Meacham.

"Soho."

"I've just had word that the PM on Thewlis is getting underway shortly and you're wanted there."

"Where?"

"Lewisham."

Which wasn't near Soho either.

"Is somebody doing this on purpose, ma'am?"

"Doubtful," said Meacham. "Call me afterwards."

Pennance headed back onto Berwick Street. He went to the far side, stood between two market stalls, one selling clothes, the other LPs, and scanned the two floors above the Chinese. The windows were blocked off – curtains or nets across most, a large piece of faded cardboard over another.

He called Langridge, wandered back into the alley as he waited for the robot to answer, said, "Mr Langridge, DI Pennance. Please contact me as soon as you get this so we can arrange to meet."

Pennance left his number again, cut the connection. He stood for a few moments, hands on hips before he kicked Langridge's door in frustration then got walking to the nearest Tube station.

Thirteen

Stan Thewlis' body lay in the hospital mortuary about three miles south from where he'd been murdered. Whoever designed the place had decided to go out rather than up. Consequently a sprawling construction filled a large section of low-lying ground between the Ravensbourne River to the rear and Lewisham High Street, a busy north-south cut through joining the A205 at Catford and the A20 which ran on into Deptford. On the opposite side of the road, high-rise flats loomed over the area.

Pennance had already scrubbed up and donned the requisite gown, mask, gloves, glasses and overshoes. He waited alone in the relative chill of the examination room, which was near identical to where Carnegie had been eviscerated – spotless, white, bright, easy to clean and antiseptic smelling. Clearly, Pennance had arrived first because not even the corpse was present. He wandered the room, wasting time, and paused beside the instrument table. He picked up a solid-looking knife, which sat well in his grip. The blade had been sharpened to a wicked edge. He put it back, then lifted what appeared to be large pliers that opened outwards in the opposite direction to the handles. Then the double doors popped unexpectedly. Hurriedly, Pennance returned the tool to its place.

"Ah, the guy who took my case," said Carver. "Then called my boss to complain I wasn't interested in said case."

"I'm just here to observe," said Pennance.

Carver looked Pennance up and down, mostly up. "You're a tall bastard."

"That's unlikely to change."

"Don't bet on it, mate. I like cutting people back to size." Carver took a step forward, the sole of her boots squeaking with each movement. "I really have no need of people like you cluttering up my investigation."

"The investigation you couldn't wait to drop and run."

Carver clenched her fists. "I was called off, believe me, I wasn't happy about it."

"You don't seem to be glad about much."

Carver took another step towards him. "I'll be overjoyed to smack you in the mouth."

"Want me to get a ladder?"

The examination room doors crashed open as a gurney being pushed by orderlies in green uniforms was shoved through like a battering ram taking down the gates of an ancient castle. A form, presumably Thewlis' corpse hidden by a thin paper sheet, lay on the gurney.

"'Scuse me." The orderly pared Pennance and Carver apart, paused beside the nearest examination table, pumped a foot on a lever to raise the gurney slightly so its height matched the table before sliding Thewlis over into his new resting place. The orderlies turned around, slid between Pennance and Carver once more like they weren't there, before busting through the doors, briefly revealing a group of people in scrubs.

As the doors swung back on their hinges yet again, four individuals entered in a line. The person on point said, "Good to see you, DI Pennance."

"And you, Doctor Proudfoot."

"We must stop meeting like this. You remember Doctor De Souza?" De Souza emerged into the lab.

"Of course," said Pennance. It had only been earlier today. The remainder of Proudfoot's team spread out across the space – Thripp the photographer, and Bray, the stenographer.

"You all know each other already." Carver stated the obvious. "I'm DI Christine Carver, by the way."

"With a name like that you should have been a pathologist," said Proudfoot.

"What?"

Proudfoot picked up the same knife Pennance had held earlier. "You know, Carver." Proudfoot waved the knife around like he was preparing vegetable. "Chop, chop."

"Not bloody likely," mumbled Carver.

"Or maybe a butcher." Proudfoot seemed not to have heard Carver's reply.

"Aren't they one and the same?" said Pennance.

Proudfoot chuckled. "DI Pennance attended an autopsy I performed earlier. The victim expired in seemingly similar circumstances, so I was asked to come over here and perform this process for continuity." He extended his arms from his body in a non-verbal apology. "Now, just give me a moment to familiarise myself with everything. These are not my usual surroundings."

Carver moved over to stand beside Pennance while Proudfoot briefly nudged around the tools and instruments, so they were easy to reach. Pennance's phone vibrated in his pocket. He read the face of his smart watch. A text from

Simone. 'Call me soon as you get this'. It wasn't difficult to guess what Simone wanted – to give him a hard time over Rasmussen. Maybe even to tell him to back off. Which wasn't going to happen.

"Who was the other victim?" asked Carver.

"Grady Carnegie," said Pennance.

Carver said nothing for a few moments, staring at Pennance while she processed the information. "That's the fund manager choked to death by bread, right?"

"Correct."

"Okay, that explains your interest in Thewlis."

"Apology accepted," said Pennance. Carver snorted like a rag and bone man's nag.

"Shall we begin?" asked Proudfoot, focusing on Carver then Pennance. DeSouza removed the covering, revealing Thewlis' corpse, which was as pale as the paper that had hidden it.

"Jesus," mumbled Carver.

Thewlis was a thin man, his ribs obvious beneath the skin, and naked. His clothes would be in evidence bags, ready for analysis at the labs, searching for any biological matter which may point towards Thewlis' killer. His eyes were closed, yet the mouth remained wide open and packed with bread.

"From notes made already on Mr Thewlis by the attendant pathologist which I reviewed earlier, his height was measured as 1.8 metres and his weight just shy of 59 kilos," said Proudfoot. "In other words, 5 feet 11 inches and 9 stone 4 pounds, slightly below the ideal ratio. I'm also aware a blood sample has been taken and sent away for analysis.

"In addition, the pathologist measured the victim's temperature, assessed the lividity and rigor subsequently estimating time of death at approximately eighteen to twenty-four hours prior to discovery."

"Meaning Thewlis died before Carnegie," said Pennance.

"That it would," said Proudfoot.

"I took a look at Thewlis' chest at the scene and I found what appears to be a taser mark above his heart, same as with Carnegie."

Carver raised eyebrows at this information. "Let me check." Proudfoot bent over to examine Thewlis' chest. Pennance had worked with other pathologists who'd have ranted at Pennance or treated him with disdain for telling them how to do their jobs. Proudfoot didn't seem bothered at all. "Yes, I think you're right, Inspector. For DI Carver's benefit, Mr Carnegie was incapacitated by a taser prior to his murder. The wounds on Mr Thewlis here appear identical."

"I'll need to see a copy of your report on Carnegie, Doctor Proudfoot," said Carver. "I feel like I'm way behind you guys here."

"I'll have it emailed it over to you when it's completed." Proudfoot addressed his assistant. "Miss De Souza, if you wouldn't mind?" The pair lifted Thewlis' corpse in co-ordinated movements, examined Thewlis' back before lowering him down. "Based on the observable lividity, Mr Thewlis also lay on his rear following death and was not moved." The pathologist repeated the procedure he'd followed previously, examining Thewlis closely from head to foot, tracked by De Souza. Eventually he said, "I can see no further wounds on the body, other than an abrasion on the forehead. I'd suggest Mr Thewlis struck his head with a glancing blow. However, this injury is several days old, so did not occur at time of death."

"His partner threw a TV remote control at him," said Pennance. "And he fell against a wall."

"That would do it."

"What about the bread?" asked Carver.

"Now we can move onto the occlusion in Mr Thewlis' throat," said Proudfoot.

"Finally," mumbled Carver.

Again, Proudfoot used tweezers to extract the blockage. "Same plastic white bread," said Proudfoot as he placed the sections side by side on a tray. "And as with Mr Carnegie, the material was pushed into the victim's mouth with a significant degree of force given the abrasions inside Mr Thewlis' mouth and throat."

Pennance's phone vibrated again. A quick flick of his wrist revealed another chaser from Simone for him to call her.

Proudfoot picked up the hefty knife from the tray. "Now," he said, "I'll be going inside Mr Thewlis."

"Jesus," said Carver.

Proudfoot undertook an identical procedure as with Carnegie; cutting through Thewlis' skin from the top of his collarbone down to where his pubic hair began, removing the rib cage then the organs which Proudfoot weighed one after the other, before cutting off the top of Thewlis' skull and removing the brain. De Souza examined the organs with a microscope. Neither Carver nor Pennance spoke through the process, leaving Proudfoot to concentrate.

"That's that," said Proudfoot eventually, placing down one of his blood-stained instruments.

Pennance received yet another message from Simone.

"The boss chasing you?" asked Carver.

"She can keep," said Pennance.

"The victim was reasonably healthy," said Proudfoot. "His organs were in an acceptable condition, with the exception of his liver and lungs. Its apparent Mr Thewlis was a regular drinker up to the time of his death. His liver was moderately fatty so I'd estimate Mr Thewlis was consuming ten or so units of alcohol a day – meaning several pints of beer or shots of spirits on a regular basis."

"There was alcohol in his house," said Pennance.

"Isn't there booze in most people's?" asked Carver.

Pennance's phone buzzed yet again. He sighed.

"Persistent," said Carver.

However, this time the message was from Tremayne, not Simone. It simply read, 'Call me'.

Proudfoot turned to De Souza. "What did your evaluation of the lungs reveal?"

"The victim was once a heavy smoker, under the microscope I observed a higher than average level of anthracnosis – black speckles of pollutants. There were also multiple petechial haemorrhagic spots."

"The same as Mr Carnegie, and a clear sign of hypoxia," said Proudfoot. "A follow-up examination by another pathologist on Mr Carnegie's brain and heart also revealed haemorrhagic spots. And I anticipate we will discover the same with Mr Thewlis. Likewise, I expect the analysis of Mr Thewlis' blood to show a high level of carbon dioxide and an elevated red blood cell count. In terms of cause of death I believe it to be identical to Mr Carnegie – choking as a result of the obstruction of the lower respiratory tract by extraneous material."

"Thank you, doctor," said Pennance.

"My report will be sent to you, DI Carver here and DCI Fulton shortly."

"Appreciate it," said Pennance.

He and Carver left Proudfoot and his team. After discarding their gowns and scrubbing up the pair walked back to reception and Pennance called Tremayne.

The analyst immediately answered. "I've found something," said Tremayne. "Best I show you, rather than explain. How soon can you be here?"

"Half an hour, maybe?"

"See you then." Tremayne disconnected.

Pennance ran a hand through his hair, suddenly feeling drained. Another rush trip across the capital.

"You okay?" asked Carver.

"I actually don't know," admitted Pennance.

"Can I give you a lift somewhere?"

"I'm heading to The City," said Pennance.

Carver grimaced. "That's a little out of my way, sorry. But I can drop you at the underground station." She stopped just outside the main doors, turned to Pennance. "Look, I'll keep you up to date with progress on Thewlis if you'll do me the same courtesy with anything you think is relevant on Carnegie."

"That case is being run by DCI Fulton out of Thames Valley."

"Never heard of him," said Carver. "But I know you now. And you know Fulton. You're the keystone, right? Without you the whole structure collapses."

"That's somewhat of an exaggeration."

Carver cocked her head, thought briefly. "Sort of describes the NCA." She held out a hand, business card between two fingers. "We help each other, okay?"

"Sure." Pennance took Carver's card, swapped it with his own.

"Doesn't mean to say I like you, though."

"Likewise."

Carver grinned, slid Pennance's card into a pocket. "I'm this way." Carver nodded in the opposite direction to where Pennance needed to go. Then she was striding away just as the rain began to fall.

Pennance re-considered the offer of a lift and ran after her.

Fourteen

Dodging the rain, which turned the pavement almost black, Pennance arrived at the Heron Tower on Bishopsgate for the third time today. The journalists were still outside, sheltering under the portico, though reduced in number. Pennance assumed something else shiny had got the attention of their editors. Or the reporters were in a pub.

The receptionist behind the lobby desk, Melody, recognised Pennance and nodded. He raised a hand in return and strode across the lobby to the lifts.

His phone rang. Simone again. Pennance sighed, he couldn't keep dodging her. He stopped beside a large pillar stretching upwards several floors. The block gave Pennance an odd feeling of protection in the exposed environment.

"You took your bloody time." A bite in Simone's tone.

"I've been in a post-mortem."

Simone grunted, maybe as an acknowledgement, maybe not. She said, "Why did you interview Lars?"

Here it came. "In connection with a case."

"Really?" The word was cold enough to chill a gin and tonic.

"Why else?" Pennance's response was deliberately brief. The less he said the less there was for her to latch onto.

"What case?"

"Ask Lars."

"He wouldn't tell me."

"There's a surprise."

"Arsehole."

"Who? Me or him?" Pennance winced as soon as the words came out.

"Christ's sake, Jonah; you've regressed to childhood."

"Actually, I was very quiet back then. Now I would be called withdrawn."

"It's Carnegie, isn't it? Is Lars a suspect?"

"He's not anything."

"You're doing this to get at me," said Simone.

"The only thing I'm *doing* is my job."

"I want you to back off."

"You know how this works. None of it's personal, I'm following leads. You'd be the same."

"You're just jealous of him," said Simone.

Pennance couldn't reply. He wanted to, but the words stuck in his throat and the silence between them stretched.

"I wish you were jealous," Simone whispered eventually. "Then at least I'd know you cared." She cut the connection.

Pennance rubbed a hand over his face. He wanted the pillar to absorb him, so he could disappear from sight.

***

Hussle's office was subtly different to the last time Pennance was here; no ringing of phones, no urgency in the air. Neumann spotted Pennance and bounded from behind his desk. Metzler glanced up only briefly from his computer screen then shrank into his seat as Neumann charged over like an angry bull.

"Are you trying to ruin me, Inspector Pennance?" Spittle flew from Neumann's mouth, making Pennance recoil. "Your people have been going through every iota of my business." Neumann threw an arm out towards the meeting room where Tremayne and his two colleagues remained at work behind a closed door. "It's extremely disruptive. And when we've barely begun mourning one of our own."

"There's no malice intended, Mr Neumann. Now, if you'll excuse me?" Pennance tried to pass but Neumann shifted, blocking Pennance's path.

"I need to know what's going on."

"I'm not aware myself yet, sir. That's why I'm here."

"I want to come in and listen."

"That's not possible."

"This is *my* company!"

"And this is my investigation, Mr Neumann. Into the murder of your business partner, which handed a controlling share of Hussle to *you*."

Neumann opened his mouth to continue the argument, before slowly closing it again and blinking.

"Just get out of the way and let the guy do his job, Stefan." Metzler slowly pushed himself to his feet. He sounded and looked tired, beaten almost.

"Fine, have it your way!" Neumann waved an angry arm before spinning on the ball of his foot and stalking back to his desk. Metzler raised an eyebrow at Pennance and shook his head while Neumann began battering away at his keyboard.

Pennance entered the meeting room. "That was fun."

"They're stressed out," said Tremayne. "Every time either one of us has gone into the office Neumann has been constantly at our shoulders like a mini devil, trying to figure out what we're up to."

"Have you found anything?"

"Zephyr is still working on the blockchain analysis but Hussle's accounts are interesting. On the surface the company appears successful – reasonable costs, very interesting profit margins, excellent debt ratio and a positive payment record. The business itself is divided up into several divisions, each undertaking different activities depending on the investment vehicle. There's one for the stock market, another for cryptocurrency, and so on. Each has a different name, get this, after Greek and Roman Gods like Ares, he's the God of bloodlust and is for shares; or Ceres, the goddess of grain and agriculture for commodities. It's only when you dive down to a forensic level that problems start to appear, specifically in Janus."

"He's the god with two faces, right?"

"That's the one."

"Janus was the god of doorways and entrances," said Zephyr. "Later writers connected him with deceit and hypocrisy."

"What's wrong with Janus?" asked Pennance.

"It's a not too clever fraud." Tremayne frowned. "You've heard of Ponzi schemes?"

"I know of them. But nothing specific."

"The most recent high profile example was Bernie Madoff in the US although they've been around since the 19th Century. Dickens included them in some of his novels, I believe."

"*Martin Chuzzlewit* and *Little Dorrit*," interjected Zephyr.

"You're the regular brain box," said Tremayne.

"I try."

"Basically, Ponzi's are a 'rob Peter to pay Paul' process. An investor makes a capital investment into a scheme which promises higher than average returns. They're encouraged not to withdraw any cash, often via a lock-in scheme. Usually they start as legitimate vehicles, like a hedge fund, but if they begin to lose money then the operators fabricate a better-than-reality business performance. As more investors are enticed in, their cash is used to pay what seems to be a profit to the early stakeholders and the cascade effect begins."

"More suckers are needed to keep the income flowing?" asked Pennance.

"Right," said Tremayne. "Theoretically, a Ponzi scheme can succeed – say a risky bet pays off for the operators, bringing in a profit. However, more often than not, the house of cards eventually comes crashing down."

"Cards don't crash," said Zephyr, interrupting once more. "They're varnished paper."

"Jesus, techies." Tremayne rolled his eyes. "It's just a phrase." Zephyr chuckled to herself. "Anyway, as I was saying," continued Tremayne, "the schemes fail for several reasons. Either the fraudster runs off with the proceeds. Or the company is unable to bring in new depositors and fresh funds, causing liquidity issues. Or an external market issue such as an index collapse rapidly devalues the investment and everyone loses their money. As yet Hussle is still liquid, though they're running pretty close to the line."

"What are we talking?"

"Hard to determine exactly how much money is actually tied up in Ponzi's without months of analysis. But, in the scheme of things, if you pardon the pun, not huge. I'd estimate a couple of million."

Pennance whistled. "Not huge?"

"Bernie Madoff's scam ran at $64.8 *billion*, Jonah."

"Maybe this explains why Neumann is so agitated." Pennance glanced out at him through the glass.

"He's the investment guru, right?" asked Tremayne. Pennance nodded. "Then he should have been aware of what was going on."

"Do you know that for sure?"

"Not yet, but one thing I am certain of. Those two need to be taken in for questioning."

"I'll handle that," said Pennance and pulled out his phone to dial Fulton.

***

City of London police station was literally just along the road from Heron Tower, at 182 Bishopsgate. Even with traffic the drive only took a minute to transport Metzler and Neumann. In comparison, the station was nowhere near as grand a building. From the outside it give the impression of being a four-storey concrete-rendered cake with a fifth, smaller tier, right at the top. The station was braced by two takeaways – a Starbucks one side and a KFC the other, and directly opposite stood the Broadgate shopping centre.

Fulton had turned up in a squad car and an accompanying van, parking at the Tower's delivery entrance, rather than out front where the reporters were. Neumann had threatened to sue the moment it became obvious he and Metzler were to be arrested. Metzler, however, remained quiet in Neumann's wrath.

Fulton himself handcuffed the pair, bundled them into the van and slammed the door. It was one of his sergeants who opened up outside the station before Neumann and Metzler were taken inside to be processed. Pennance watched them go from the rear seat of the squad car where he sat with Fulton.

"It'll be some time before I talk to them," said Fulton. "I'll give you a call when the interviews go ahead."

"Thanks, appreciate it."

"No, you should welcome the fact I have to do all the paperwork." Fulton grinned.

"What can I say?" asked Pennance.

"Thanks, maybe?"

Pennance's phone rang. "Sorry, got to take this."

"Inspector, Tommy Haas here." Traffic noise in the background.

Pennance searched his memory, and failed to come up with an answer. "Sorry, who are you?"

"I run the *News of the World* Facebook page. You sent me a message earlier. Wanted to talk about poor Stan. I read what happened to him. I'll do anything I can to help."

"Great, when can we meet?"

"How does now suit?"

Fifteen

Ye Olde Cheshire Cheese was located at 145 Fleet Street, in what was once Britain's beating heart of news, insinuation and hearsay. Pennance had only been into the pub itself a couple of times; Fleet Street was off his usual patch.

The unassuming exterior hid a large bar area and a warren of small rooms some would consider dingy, others quaint – both the result of no artificial light inside. Whatever illumination there was came through the small windows, except in winter when a blaze burned all season in the inglenook. The entrance was along a narrow side alley – Wine Office Court – off Fleet Street itself. Right above the doorway hung a large, circular sign and the legend, 'Rebuilt in 1667', one year after the Great Fire of London. To one side of the entrance a white-painted board fixed to the wall listed the name of every monarch who'd ruled England since then, starting with James the Second.

On the way over Pennance had carried out a quick social media search, immediately finding Tommy Haas, who was totally bald, not even eyebrows. The expression on his round face was one of forced humour, as if attempting to grin his way into, through and out of trouble.

Pennance found Haas in the alley, leant against brown wood panelling, drawing on a cigarette as if he was trying to suck the obstruction out of a blocked pipe. He caught sight of Pennance, left the cigarette stub hanging out of his mouth, held out a hand for Pennance to shake. "Inspector." Haas appeared slightly older than his photo, the wrinkles a little deeper, a darker shade to the circles under his eyes. He could be anywhere from 50 to 70 years old.

"Thanks for meeting me," said Pennance.

"No problem." Haas took one more draw on the cigarette before carefully knocking out the ember onto the pavement, placing the remaining third of the stick back into a packet and flipping the flap closed. "Come in."

Haas leaned on the door and allowed Pennance to go ahead of him. The process of entering was like a graduated gloom – the traffic noise and sunlight of Fleet Street, muffled and shrunken by Wine Office Court, then swallowed altogether by the pub as the door swung shut.

"We're over here." Haas pointed to a snug off the main bar. He already had a pint on the go, something amber coloured, a thin head typical of London beer. "I didn't know what you wanted."

"Just a coffee is fine, Mr Haas."

"Mister? Not many people have been so polite over the years." Haas went to the bar briefly before returning. "Park your bloody arse, inspector." He waved a hand towards a table. "God didn't mean for us to stand all day."

The chair creaked as Pennance sat. Haas took his space opposite, dropped the cigarette packet onto the table. "Before we talk about Stan let me give you some flavour first. You need to know the job to know the person."

"If you think that's necessary."

"I do." Haas settled back in his seat and started talking, no pause needed to gather his thoughts. "Every national paper and most regionals had an office within a half-mile radius of here. Fleet Street," Haas rapped knuckles on the table, "was where the majority people in the UK got their information, before the internet and social media. We directed thinking and opinion in Britain for decades. Print was a male-dominated, hard-drinking, 24-hour role. I was in a pub most days because that's how it worked. Almost all of those are shut now. And there was a café down the way, gone also, that stayed open 24 hours a day, in case a caffeine kick was needed. It was sexist, too. Hardly any women occupied senior roles; most were secretaries or reporters writing the most basic of stories and the pubs were pretty much off limits for them.

"All told, I've been walking the Street of Shame for over six decades. I started working when I was 14, selling *The Daily Standard*, then at 16 I got offered a printer's apprenticeship at *The Sun*. It was a letterpress process, and essentially the same as it had been for hundreds of years.

"The class system was much more overt than it is now, directing society and funnelling news. *The Sun* was a mess, 'til some brash Aussie turned up and bought it. Rupert Murdoch, of course. That was 1969, and I remember like it was yesterday. Back then he was an upstart, determined to kick the establishment's arse and kick its arse he did, turning the culture of journalism on its head, attacking what he saw as a prudish and patronising British establishment."

A barman turned up with a beer for Haas and a coffee for Pennance. Haas finished his first pint, handed the glass to the barman.

Haas continued, "Murdoch used to walk the shop floor every morning, to see how we were doing. He really connected with his employees. Then he brought in new printers –

offset – which meant a whole different process and re-training. It felt like a crossroads. Now *The Sun* was cheaper to manufacture and easier to carry and read on the Tube compared to the broadsheets. Turning the pages of one of the big dailies in a crowded carriage isn't a good idea and Murdoch capitalised on that. Next he insisted we start printing topless women. Jesus. Open the front page and there were boobs looking back at you. We thought it would be a disaster, but circulation rocketed pretty much overnight. He was right. Murdoch was always right."

Haas took a drink. "One morning when Murdoch was stalking the print floor, I flat out asked him for a reporting job. He pulled me off the press straight away and he brought me here, to this very table. The pub was where people got hired, fired, gossiped and sniped. I was scared as hell, my voice aquiver and my legs shaking. I needn't have worried because that was the easy part. Murdoch said okay and I started stringing the very next day."

"Stringing?" asked Pennance.

"Freelance, basically. Out in the field gathering stories for the paper. A stringer does everything in the process, takes photos, does interviews and so on. The components are then delivered back to the newspaper. Most times the stories were attributed to in-house reporters. I didn't care, though. It's a really important role; you have to be tenacious. Murdoch paid me in the old way – per line of text. It was a test, Murdoch wanted to see if I could survive in the role. I was only a printer after all, with ink under my fingernails. Stringing is tough. Up early, bed late – sometimes not at all. The pay was crap, I had to build all my own contacts, and in the end there was virtually zero visible credit for the work. However, it was the making of me and I lapped it up.

"Murdoch wasn't looking for your average story – it was sex that sold, hence the page-three girls. He and his editors demanded pieces on other people's problems while readers wanted to be entertained. And that's what I did – I wrote about celebrities and the Royals in gossip columns. *The Sun* was the first celebrity scandal paper, really. I was even an agony aunt for a while, answering reader's letters with 'advice'." Haas made air quotes. "All of that stuff I made up. Murdoch didn't care as long as the newspaper shifted copies."

"What about Stan?" asked Pennance. Haas had talked enough about himself.

"Huh, Stan." Haas drank some more. "I was an old hand by the time he joined, in maybe 1985. Gone were the days of me working the streets as a stringer. Now, other upstart kids did that for me. I was the in-house reporter. I'd moved over to another Murdoch publication, *The News of the World*, where I was a column writer, I even had a few front page articles in my time. Murdoch still walked the floor, though not much as he had in the beginning. We saw him maybe once a week. Anyway, one day I got lumbered with this new starter – that was Stan. God, he was green! I had to lead him around by the nose for months, but it was worth it because I could tell almost straight away he had a knack for the job."

"In what sense?"

"Some reporters can't see the heart of a story, but Stan, he was laser-focused, and fantastic at building rapport with people. They just trusted him. He opened them up like shucking an oyster with a sharp knife."

"What did he work on?"

"Initially, whatever he was told to. That's how it was." Haas gave Pennance a flat stare. "Before long, though, it was clear Stan shouldn't be doing cookery or gossip columns. He was simply too good. So, I pulled in a few favours, went to see Murdoch himself and Stan moved onto the Sunday publication."

"What was the difference to the daily?"

"Shorter deadlines for one." Haas chuckled. "The dailies were like a meat grinder. It was chew, chew, chew through the pieces. But the weekenders... there was time and there was word count. It was the perfect place to put Stan and the guy thrived. He broke some really great stories – one on Diana and Charles' combusting relationship, then another on the oil crisis in the Middle East. He was capable of handling the sprawling, wide-reaching stuff and distilling it down into a logical progression and readable package. He was bound for big things." Haas shook his head. "Such a pity."

"I was told the phone hacking scandal crashed his career."

"Not true, that was just the guillotine. He had problems well before then."

"Like what?"

Haas picked up the cigarette packet and began to twist it around in his hands. "Same as it was for most people in the industry. Booze. We all abused our livers. Stan, though, he took it to a new level. Managed it brilliantly, at first. He'd be called high functioning these days. Stan could get smashed one night, then be at work the next day, looking sharp. It couldn't last, unfortunately. After a couple of years of burning the candle at both ends and the middle he began to struggle. No field reporters, including Stan, kept standard office hours. Stan started to come into the office later and later, claiming he'd been working. Then he missed deadlines and the quality of his work dropped right off. He had several warnings, I know that for sure because I gave him one myself."

"Did he get fired?"

"He was about to, but in the end no, because I staged an intervention, told him he was out of chances. And to his credit he stopped drinking, cleaned himself up and started putting in the time on his work. Maybe I saved his life." Haas paused, remembered why he was here now. "For a while, I guess."

"Did Stan cut out the alcohol altogether?"

"Absolutely. I saw him a couple of years back, after Murdoch shuttered the *News of the World*. He was still sober, going to Alcoholics Anonymous and so on."

Pennance thought back to the booze in Stan's house and Proudfoot's assertion that Stan's liver displayed long-term alcohol use. "How easy was it to get a new job after the paper closed down?"

"It depended on the person and when they left. You know how it is. The good ones go early, the average ones next and finally there's just the typical dross."

"What about you?"

"I got out before the beginning. It was obvious what was coming." Haas smiled. "I moved to *The Mirror*. Stayed there until I retired. It wasn't the same, although it was a job."

"And Stan?"

"Stuck it out to the end. He wasn't dross, though. I offered him a role at *The Mirror* but he turned me down because he felt he owed the paper for not kicking him out when they could have."

"He went freelance afterwards, I understand."

"That's right. Still was when I met him. He seemed to be doing okay. Every now and again I came across some of his work, particularly in *Watchman* – I got him that position, by the way – it was decent enough, I could even see some shades of the old Stan underneath. After the being on the sauce for so long, though, his stories were never the same quality. Such a waste of a talent. Ultimately, I was just glad he was keeping himself busy because that's all you can do, really."

"So you know Scott Langridge at *Watchman*?"

"Of course."

"I've been trying to reach him."

"I assume he hasn't replied?"

"No."

"He's a decent guy and, equally, a flake. I'll have a word for you. Expect him to call."

"Appreciate it." Pennance drank some of his coffee, it was over-bitter so Pennance poured some milk into the cup. "And what about you?"

"I do alright. I come here most days. I'm still writing. At the moment I'm working on a history of Fleet Street. The first paper opened in 1702, *The Daily Courant*. The last closed down in 2016 – *The Daily Record*. There were just two reporters then. Now there are none. 314 years of history finally ended." Haas sighed. "Do you know what I see when I walk down Fleet Street? Spectres, legions of shadows. I hear the hubbub of printing presses and plenty of swearing, smell the cigarette smoke, the stale beer, not the clink of coffee cups and the rustle of sandwich plastic. I see lorries trundling down the street delivering huge rolls of paper, and string-bound piles of papers going into the back of a truck, rather than tourists and yummy mummies with their over-fed kids.

"There's me and another couple of old timers that pound the pavement, keeping the memories alive. However, I'm 74 next week and these things," Haas pointed to the cigarettes, "are chipping away at my remaining time, but I don't care. I live in a flat on my own. Never had the time for a wife or kids. All I've got is what's up here." Haas tapped his forehead. "And now Stan is a ghost, too." Haas shook his head then stood, grabbed his cigarette packet. "I need a smoke." He shoved on the door and went outside.

Pennance waited, finished his coffee which, thanks to the milk, had cooled to tepid. It had been a couple of minutes and Haas hadn't returned. Outside, the alley was empty. Haas wasn't on Fleet Street, either.

As Pennance went back into the pub to pay the bill his phone rang. "Inspector Pennance? This is Scott Langridge at *Watchman*, I understand from Tommy Haas that you've been trying to reach me."

Sixteen

Ordinarily, Pennance would have walked to Langridge's office. However, Pennance wanted to reach him quickly in case he changed his mind about talking, so Pennance took the tube.

When Pennance arrived the market was beginning to pack up for the day. Pennance headed down the alley beside the Chinese takeaway. Hot, sweet air still pumped from the vent outside the kitchen, blowing the rhythmic sound of chopping from the kitchen as a heavy blade thudded into wood. He reckoned more graffiti had appeared on Langridge's door since he was last here, a tag in red spray paint. Using the heel of his palm Pennance hammered on a panel for several seconds.

"Coming, I'm coming!" shouted someone from inside. A couple of locks clicked and turned before the door was dragged inwards. A man with thinning hair and full, flushed cheeks wearing a t-shirt and jean shorts but no shoes or socks, swore when the door stuck halfway, caught on some junk mail previously shoved through the letterbox. He leant over, tugged at the envelopes until they came free. He tossed the correspondence in the space behind the opening. "What do you want?" He spoke fast, licking his palm before smoothing his hair.

"Scott Langridge?" asked Pennance.

"Yes, yes. That's me."

"We spoke earlier." Pennance showed his ID and Langridge leaned back, like he was faced with a poisonous snake.

Pennance put away his card and Langridge blinked, as if recovering from being temporarily mesmerised. "Mr Langridge?"

"Ah, sorry, sorry!" Langridge's expression cleared and he stepped back out of the way. "Come in, Inspector, come in." Pennance found himself in a narrow stairway, magnolia-painted chipboard wallpaper, scuffed skirting and worn brown carpet on the steps. "Up you go." Langridge pointed towards the landing where a naked bulb hung from the ceiling and cast a plain, white light.

Pennance took the steep stairs and found himself on a narrow square with three routes off – one into a tiny kitchen, the other for an equally constricted bathroom, just a sink and toilet. Ahead was a more expansive space. The room ran along the width of the building. Where downstairs had been spartan, here was the opposite.

Fixed in the centre of the high ceiling was an ornate medallion, grand enough to likely once have had a chandelier suspended beneath. Now there was a strip of white cable, a lightbulb and a dusty shade. Three large rugs covered the stripped-wood flooring. Four equally spaced sash windows, pretty much skirting board-to-coving in height, allowed a flood of light to enter. The glass was maybe original because when Pennance looked through it the buildings opposite appeared slightly distorted. Beneath him pedestrians went about their business, the hum of their chatter and laughter obvious. Pennance had stood down there himself only hours ago.

Over at the far end of the room sat a large desk in front of unruly piles of books stacked sideways on shelves. Then a small cot bed, the covers turned back, and the pillow squashed. In between, a couple of armchairs faced towards the windows set far enough back that no-one from below could observe the observer. Suspended on the walls were several framed theatre posters, the show dates from over a hundred years ago, along with black and white photos of old London, well before the arrival of the skyscraper.

"Can I get you a drink?" asked Langridge.

"I'm fine, thanks."

Langridge sat behind his desk and pushed the keyboard to one side, the rubber feet juddering as he did so. Pennance glanced around, didn't see anything beside the armchairs.

"My apologies," said Langridge. "I don't have many visitors."

Pennance moved a biography of Churchill from an arm and perched uncomfortably in its place, balanced on the curve, feet on the floor, and resting his arms on his thighs like he was a fulcrum. "I tried to call you several times."

"Yes." Langridge's eyes flicked to a Bakelite phone beside an old tape machine on his desk, then back to Pennance. "And I apologise for not answering. It's simply, you know, I won't speak to someone I don't know." Langridge shifted around in his chair, like a bored child.

"I stated I was police."

"Anyone can say anything these days." Langridge shrugged. "However, Haas vouched for you and you're here now, inspector. So, ask your questions." Pennance was used to London bluntness. The majority of people who actually lived in the city moved fast, spoke fast and usually had somewhere to be yesterday. Langridge lifted a mug off his desk, drank from it, spat the contents back in. "Ugh, cold."

"You're a reporter, right?" asked Pennance. Langridge lowered the mug back onto his desk and stared at Pennance briefly with wide eyes. Pennance said, "Tell me about yourself."

"Where to begin?" Langridge tapped a paper opener onto the desk surface like a metronome. "I've been in the business since 1977 when I started working on a local publication in Macclesfield. That's where I'm from. It's near Manchester." As if Langridge had always had to explain the location. Pennance didn't sound northern. "I did the usual stuff, writing articles on village fetes, petty theft and old people's significant birthdays. What I really wanted to cover though was crime. Proper crime. So I got a job at the *Manchester Evening News* and moved to the city in the early '80s. Manchester was pretty run-down back then, and suffered lots of unrest, like the Moss Side Riots. Parts of the centre were piles of rubble, never rebuilt after the war. There was something vibrant about the place, however. Punk had briefly exploded and then imploded, leaving behind this flourishing independent music scene. Not that I gave a shit about the music; particularly when acid house hit in the late '80s and early '90s. But," Langridge wagged the opener at Pennance, "All those class A drugs brought problems. Not county lines like today, no, no, no. There were gangs in Manchester, with their own turf, their own network, rubbing up against each other and creating friction. I used to spend a lot of time at The Hacienda, on Whitworth Street, watching the sparks fly first hand."

"What's that?"

Langridge stared at Pennance like he was an idiot. "An iconic New York style nightclub, built in an abandoned yacht warehouse down a shitty street in a shitty neighbourhood. There was nothing like it. All gone now." Langridge sounded like Haas, living in the past. "All gone."

"I thought you said you didn't like the music."

"I didn't and don't. However, The Hacienda was the centre of the action, where anyone who was anyone could go. Famous, infamous or irrelevant. And so did I, to record what I saw."

"What, people dancing?"

"Not so basic, Inspector. The drugs were a key part of the social interaction. This was a microcosm of strife. Gunchester and Madchester, the city was known as for a while. But all empires come and go; The Hacienda was no different. The club got shut down a couple of times due to major trouble on the door as the gangs fought each other for control until, finally, the council and police had had enough and the company ran out of funds so the club closed for good. That's when I ended up in London. I'd been offered a couple of jobs and turned them all down as there was just too much happening in Manchester. However, once The Hacienda crashed and burned, I could see the city's raw edge was being blunted. It was going up-market." Langridge pulled a sour face. "So, I moved down here as the senior crime reporter for *The Standard* before I became a sub-editor. Then I went to the *News of the World* as an editor."

"That's a long bio, Mr Langridge."

"Hard to keep over forty years of work down to a few paragraphs."

"How did you know Mr Thewlis?"

"Stan and I worked on quite a few articles together. He was a natural as an investigative reporter and we made a good team. We broke some decent stories, even if I do say so myself. But unlike Stan, I could see the writing on the wall, if you excuse the cliché, for the *News of the World* and I didn't like the look of what was coming. Apparently, life goes in phases. Mine was a return to my roots. I didn't return to Macclesfield, my home was London by then. Before the hacking scandal properly exploded, I took an editing position covering several borough newspapers. It was pretty straightforward work. Like retiring wounded after fighting on the front lines for years, shots zinging over my head, bombs going off everywhere."

"I get the analogy, Mr Langridge."

"I did that right up until the borough papers went online and then merged. I still have a hand in them, but it's largely about advertising revenue now, not local, evocative stories. I mean, who has use for an actual physical paper these days? It's understandable when most people have access to 24-hour news channels and apps on your phone constantly dinging away with updates from all over the world."

"I can't remember the last time I picked one up," admitted Pennance. Not even the *London Evening Standard* which was handed out for free on many street corners. Even though they always seemed to be lying around on trains, Pennance had heard the circulation was plummeting. The owners couldn't even give the news away anymore.

"So, I set up my own magazine," said Langridge. "It's all online, of course, but it's designed in a digital format with pages which flip, glossy photos and so on. It doesn't fool anyone, how could it? And there has to be adverts because nobody actually buys the magazine itself. I get a small remuneration every time someone clicks through to the product." Langridge shrugged.

"And you continued your working relationship with Thewlis after the *News of the World* closed down?"

"Stan hit the ground hard when the paper closed and I felt sorry for him. Periodically he'd bring me articles he thought I could publish. I pay a flat fee per article rather than, say, per each hundred words. I find it keeps the writer more concise. Readers these days want brevity. However, he'd got a bit ... strange. Maybe it's better to say *stranger*."

"Meaning?" asked Pennance.

"He was the kind of guy who saw a narrative every place he went, every person he met. His knack was picking the right angle. The redtops became associated with crazy pieces, not alien-base-on-the-moon kind of stuff, but far-fetched at least. These days the law is much tougher when it comes to burden of proof. Back then we could get away with publishing stuff with only the most basic of verification. Stan was brilliant at rooting out information, but over time he focused his skill more on the sensational and paranoiac. He got dragged down that rabbit hole and never really returned to daylight."

"How many articles of his have you put out?"

"It would be a guess." Langridge paused, flipped his eyes to the ceiling for a few moments. "Upwards of fifty?"

"That's quite a lot."

"Not for someone of Stan's productivity and this is over several years."

"On what subjects?"

"All kinds. I try and appeal to a wide audience. As I mentioned earlier, ad revenue is key to staying afloat. I put as much time finding and keeping sponsors these days as I do with actual 'printing.'" Langridge used air quotes. "I'm lucky enough that I own this place outright from top to bottom. I had some property in central Manchester, which I sold when I came to the capital and bought here when prices were a lot lower than they are now. The takeaway downstairs rents from me and I get free food whenever I want. Thankfully, I don't need a lot of income from *Watchman*."

Pennance reckoned the building would be worth a million plus now, maybe more.

Langridge continued, "I have to say, though, I put out fewer and fewer of Stan's stories recently; they'd taken a marked step up in their extremity."

"I spoke to his partner earlier. She mentioned Mr Thewlis suffered online abuse?"

"Sadly, they're an occupational hazard. No matter what you write, someone somewhere has a deeply opposing view. Social media gives people the belief they can say what they want about anyone with no repercussions and, largely, they're right. Stan wrote something which set off the masses. His Twitter feed became particularly vitriolic. Eventually, he deleted his account and came off all other social media. All he maintained was his website."

"What was the article about?"

"The banking sector, which he blamed for the financial crash of 2008. I can find it, if you want."

"I'd appreciate that."

"I'll email the link over." Pennance passed Langridge his business card. Langridge tucked it under his keyboard, said, "Perhaps you can click on a few ad links as a thank you?"

"If I remember. Can you give me some examples of where Mr Thewlis' articles became more extreme?"

"Broadly, they fell into claims of a deep fake society, media manipulation led by unethical corporations allowed to go unchecked by self-interested politicians and law enforcement agencies. Which," Langridge pointed a finger at Pennance and chuckled, "would include you."

"As his commissioner, what do you think?"

"People's beliefs are more likely to be reinforced by the reactions they receive in response to an opinion than by logic or reasoning and scientific information. In practice, this means you end up in a loop. So, if you think you know a lot about a topic you're not very likely to explore further, because why would you? Trouble is, if you happen to be wrong, that you actually know very little on the topic, you'll never learn how big that gap is. Which was Stan all over. I couldn't reason with him, couldn't get him to see where he was going. The rabbit hole again. Ultimately, that's why I stopped taking his articles."

"How did Mr Thewlis react?"

"Probably how you would anticipate. He wasn't pleased at all. In fact, he accused me of becoming part of the establishment, part of the mechanism that needed to be fought against. He stormed out. Before that, he would be on at me weekly, popping ideas my way. I had mixed feelings about his withdrawal. On one hand it was great not dealing with the crazy. On the other, I missed the old Stan. I felt a bit crappy for cutting him off."

"Did you ever hear from him again?"

"Sure. Early one Sunday morning a couple of weeks ago he turned up, hammering at my door. I was still in bed. In my spare time I run a local historical society. A committee meeting had over-run and I was back late. I ignored the noise at first, then there was shouting in the street. I went over to the window and it was Stan, standing on the pavement, hollering up at me. I let him in so he'd shut up."

"What did he want?"

"He said he had something amazing for me. He was talking in a rush, tumbling over his words. He looked a little wasted, if I'm honest. Maybe he'd been drinking. His eyes were wide, his hair all over the place and he smelt like he hadn't washed for God knows how long." Langridge wrinkled his nose.

"Did he tell you what the article was about?"

"There's no way he would say. Not in any detail, anyway. Stan was freelance, he guarded his stories very tightly which was fair enough. I never saw or heard from him again. I emailed him a couple of times, though he didn't reply."

"Give me your best guess," said Pennance.

Langridge didn't need to think about it. "If I had to make a stab, the 'evidence' was probably related to his favourite theory: a deep fake government. Like the QAnon cult in the US he saw bad guys everywhere. He even reckoned the royal family were in on it. I mean, please." Langridge rolled his eyes. "The only word he said was Blackthorn."

"That was all, just Blackthorn?"

"Yes."

"Any idea what it means?"

Langridge shrugged. "Knowing Stan, probably a cover name for something. Look, it's getting late." He pointed outside; it was dark. "Is that all you need?"

"I think it'll do. Thanks for your help, Mr Langridge."

"No problem, I hope you find who killed Stan." He tapped Pennance's card with the tip of a finger. "I'll dig out that article and send it your way."

"If I have any more questions I'll be in touch."

"Sure and I'll pick up this time when you call."

Pennance's phone rang. It was Simone. Pennance let it ring, deciding whether to reject her call. "Is the takeaway downstairs any good?" he asked.

"Pretty decent," said Langridge. "If you go in, ask for Mr Hong and mention my name. The old boy will look after you." Pennance's phone was still ringing. Langridge said, "Are you going to answer that?"

Pennance noticed that Simone was using her work number, not her personal phone, so this could be official. "DI Pennance."

Simone didn't reply. All Pennance heard was laboured breathing, a rattle in her throat. "Simone, are you okay?" Pennance rose, pressed the phone tighter to his ear. Langridge stared.

"Jonah, help." She groaned. There was a clatter over the line. Maybe she had dropped the handset.

DEAD MONEY

"Simone!" No reply. "Where are you?" All Pennance heard was harsh coughing, then silence.

Pennance disconnected, speed dialled Hoskins in his office.

"Hey," said Hoskins. "How's my favourite boy?"

"Shut up and listen," said Pennance. "I need a location ping on a mobile number, and I need it now."

"Okay, shoot." All of Hoskins's jocularity disappeared, for which Pennance was grateful. He supplied Simone's details. Hoskins paused briefly. Pennance prayed for him to be fast. "Got it. Top of Whitehall." It was close, very close. Hoskins was talking again. "Need me to send anyone?"

"An ambulance." Pennance ran out of Langridge's flat.

Seventeen

Pennance dashed full pelt from Soho to Whitehall, passing through the edge of Leicester Square, Trafalgar Square and their tourist throngs. Nobody gave the tall man in jeans the barest of glances. Pennance was fit and a regular middle distance runner so he ate up the half mile or so in a handful of minutes. Normally Pennance would have barely broken a sweat, but his heart pounded and his breathing was short and sharp.

The entrance to 15A Whitehall, a tall, narrow building set between The Silver Cross pub and a mobile phone shop, was a varnished wooden door with a steel handle set back deep into shadowy porch of concrete. An acrid stench of urine belted Pennance's nostrils as he stepped inside. Maybe a drinker from next door having a smoke and relieving themselves at the same time, or a tramp's resting place in the small hours.

Pennance grabbed the handle and pushed – unlocked – finding himself in a dimly lit hallway. The door, on a badly adjusted spring, swung rapidly closed behind him with a bang which echoed through the building. To one side stood a rack of metal letterboxes fixed to the wall, maybe fifty of them, access gained by a small flap with a keyhole. Pieces of paper stuck out of the gaps in most.

He forced himself to pause, take a few extra seconds; despite his gut-twisting fear for Simone. All was silent inside, as silent as it ever could be in a city of millions of people. Pennance tried to block out the sounds of traffic from beyond, but all he could hear was the banging of his heart, as if a blacksmith were smashing a hammer onto an anvil, and the breath rushing in and out of his lungs as his body fought to replenish oxygen. A pair of pinpoints of light faced him on the floor, then another, before they blinked out and Pennance heard the scurry of claws.

Rats.

He pushed a nearby white plastic button. An overhead bulb on a timer flickered into life. Cobwebs stretched from the wire towards the ceiling. The hall was grimy, footprints all over the cracked linoleum floor, like no-one had cleaned it for months, scuff marks on what had once been white walls. A couple of doors were obvious along a narrow corridor and stairs stretched upwards. Pennance's brain told him to move and he snapped into action.

The first door had a half-frosted glass window and was locked, Pennance rattled the handle, but it didn't budge. It was dark within. He moved on, tried the other door; same result. The bulb flickered out then as the timer counted down to zero. Pennance fumbled his way back, smacked the button once more and began to climb the stairs, two steps at a time, the traffic noise receding as he rose. The banister felt flawlessly smooth.

On the next storey were three more doors, all the same as below and all locked. Pennance began to wonder if someone had been playing a joke on him, perhaps Rasmussen pulling his chain, but the dread that had smothered Simone's voice drove Pennance on. He struck the button again and moved to the floor above. This time when he reached the landing there was a difference – two of the doors stood open, the yawning darkness within barely penetrated by the dim illumination from the landing light.

Pennance entered the nearest room, felt for and found a switch, flicked it, but nothing. He tried again, same result. Pennance pulled out his phone, clicked on the torch app and swung it around. The broad beam revealed what seemed to be an office, with a desk and a filing cabinet. A shapeless hump lay up against the far wall, like a substantial pile of discarded rags, but Pennance was experienced enough to recognise it as a body. He ran over, knelt down, and shone the light onto the face.

Not Simone.

A young man, maybe in his 20s, who Pennance didn't recognise. His skin glinted under the shaft of light. Droplets of a liquid, like he'd just dunked his head in a sink full of water. The man had been arranged exactly as Carnegie and Thewlis – on his back, arms crossed over, eyes open. He was dressed smartly in a three-piece suit and blue tie, wore cufflinks and a paisley handkerchief in his jacket top pocket. Pennance pressed two fingers into his neck, searching for a pulse. The skin was clammy and slightly warm to the touch. Pennance couldn't feel the repetitive thrust of flowing blood underneath. He pushed his fingers in harder. Then he got something. A nudge under the tips. The guy was alive, but barely.

Pennance dialled 999, put the phone to his ear.

The call connected quickly. "999, what's your emergency?" A woman.

"This is Detective Inspector Jonah Pennance of the NCA." He rattled off his badge number. "I'm at 15A Whitehall. I've a critically ill person here. An ambulance is supposed to be on the way. Where the hell is it?"

"One moment, let me check." The seconds ticked by while Pennance waited. He forced himself to be calm. He still hadn't found Simone. "It's en-route, sir. Just a few minutes."

"Tell them to hurry up!" Pennance disconnected.

Pennance took a fast photo of the man before he moved him into the recovery position; on his side, legs drawn up in an effort to keep his airway free. Unconscious people choked to death if they vomited. Pennance tugged off his jacket, pushed it into a rough pillow before placing under the guy's head. There was nothing more he could do. He had to leave; he still didn't know where Simone was.

A slight retching cough caught Pennance's attention. He whipped his head around, went back into the corridor then to the other darkened room. He entered, swayed the beam around once more, revealing piles of boxes of varying height and size. He headed deeper inside, keeping the beam on where he was putting his feet as he took a pace, before pausing briefly, swinging the torch.

Where the hell was she?

He froze when he heard another soft groan. Nearer now.

Then the beam lit an irregular shape. Two long strides and he was next to her. Simone lay partially on her side, torso twisted, one arm on the floor, her hand gripping a mobile. A pool of vomit stained the carpet.

"Simone!" said Pennance. He knelt down. Like the other guy, she was wet, although her pulse was strong and vivid. Ignoring the stench of puke Pennance sat on the floor beside her before cradling her in his arms. A plastic bottle rolled away, some liquid sloshing around inside, and the phone slipped out of her grasp, clattering on the floorboards.

"I'm sorry," she said in a tiny voice. A couple of tears leaked from her eyes.

"There's nothing to apologise for," replied Pennance. He faked a smile, bent his neck and kissed her on the cheekbone. Her skin felt chilled and he got a powerful taste of salt. "It's okay." She groaned and dry retched. Her eyes rolled back in her head and she lost consciousness again.

"Don't you die," said Pennance as he held her close and wondered where the hell the ambulance was. He felt utterly powerless. Simone could die in his arms and there was no nothing he could do to prevent it. Pennance willed her to keep breathing. Even praying to a God he didn't believe in. Any God would do, as long as they listened.

Then Pennance heard the scrape of a shoe sole on the floor. "Hello? Ambulance!" The paramedics. Powerful torches shone out. Pennance felt an almost overwhelming surge of relief. "Anyone there?"

Pennance carefully laid Simone down, stood, the shape of a person silhouetted in the open doorway. Pennance shouted, "Over here!" He flicked on his torch app so they could see where he was. A second silhouette joined the first. "There's a man in the other office and a woman here. Both need urgent attention."

The paramedics separated, one came inside while the other disappeared back along the hallway. The paramedic who'd chosen to attend Simone proved to be a young and short woman, carrying a large medical bag. She knelt beside Simone and said, "What do you know?"

"She's been sick and is barely conscious."

"Move out the way and let me take a look."

Pennance stepped back while the paramedic inspected Simone, taking her pulse and lifting her eyelids to shine a torch into her pupils. Simone didn't respond. The paramedic turned to Pennance over her shoulder, said, "Did she ingest anything?"

"I'm not sure. I found a bottle of liquid near her. I've no idea what's in it." Pennance didn't know much of anything. "Is she going to be okay?"

"We need to get your friend to hospital, immediately. Stay here with her while I get a gurney."

The paramedic went back onto the landing. Pennance squatted, held Simone's hand and willed her to be alright. More footsteps on the stairs and then the paramedic returned with a colleague, wheeling a trolley. Between them they neatly lifted Simone onto the bed, and moved her onto the landing.

Pennance followed. "Where are you taking her?"

"University College Hospital." On Euston Road, a couple of miles away. "There's been a multi-car pile-up on the A2, lots going on tonight and we're pretty stretched." Which explained the delay in getting the ambulance here.

Pennance paused outside the other office. Two more medical staff worked on the unconscious young man under torchlight. One pushed a syringe into a vein. Simone's gurney reached the stairs and the paramedics began to descend. Pennance followed, his feet heavy as lead.

Outside, on Whitehall, a pair of ambulances were parked in the bus stop directly in front of the pub. A crowd of maybe ten loosely arranged people had assembled – some were drinkers, plastic glasses and cigarettes in hand, others were tourists wearing backpacks – most had their phones out and were filming. Simone was taken to the rear of the nearest ambulance, its doors already wide open. Then the trolley was inside, the legs collapsing underneath, neat and smooth. The female paramedic climbed up and began hooking up instruments while her colleague got into the cab.

"Can I come with you?" asked Pennance.

"It's best you follow on, sir," said the paramedic, her tone firm. She reached out, closed a door as the engine started. Smoke spewed from the exhaust in Pennance's direction. "I need to work on her as we go and you'll just get in the way. If you want the best for your friend, you'll leave us to it." She shut the other door to ram her point home. Moments later the ambulance pulled away. Then the driver lit the blues and the sirens blared as the ambulance swung around in a 180-degree arc to head in the opposite direction and skip past the traffic and out of sight.

Pennance dialled Hoskins's number. "Vance, I need your help again."

"Sure, what's up?" Sounded like he was eating.

"Can you go to the University College Hospital? One of my friends, Simone Smithson, is being taken in. I need to know she's okay."

Just then the young man was brought past on a gurney, too. One paramedic pushing, another holding a drip high. A tube ran into the victim's exposed arm. They loaded him onto a second ambulance.

"I'm on it," said Hoskins."

"Another thing – can you take your laptop?"

"Why?"

"I found a man with her. When I find out who he is, I want to start digging."

"Just let me know and I'll start."

"Thanks, I owe you." Pennance disconnected.

Once the ambulance siren had faded into the distance, there was no outward sign that anything had happened here and the crowd, bored now, began to disperse. Pennance trotted over, getting himself between the pub entrance and the men making their way back. They seemed to be in a group; younger guys, on the town together. Pennance held up his warrant card. "Did any of you see a man or a woman enter that property earlier?"

All shook their heads. Pennance got a photo of Simone he'd taken last year up on the screen of his mobile. "Her."

A man with a well-trimmed ginger beard said, "Nope, never. There's people everywhere here, pal. Sorry."

The group filed back inside, leaving Pennance alone on the pavement. Pennance shook himself. He needed a clear head and Simone would have to be compartmentalised for the moment. Pennance made several calls. First to her boss. "DCI Fulton," he said.

"Sir, its Jonah Pennance. I'm outside 15A Whitehall. Just now I found DS Smithson and an unidentified man injured. Both have been taken to hospital."

"Injured how?"

"Sir! There isn't time to explain. Just trust me. I need CSI here, soon as."

"Whitehall is outside my jurisdiction."

"I know, but DS Smithson is part of your team and I thought you'd know who to rattle to get things moving fast."

"I do."

"Then please call them. I'll explain as soon as you're here."

"I'm on it." Fulton disconnected.

Next, Pennance called Meacham.

"Jonah, it's late. What's up?"

"Ma'am, I'm not sure." Pennance then explained Simone's call and what he'd found on his arrival.

"Is she okay?" she asked.

"Last I saw her she was unconscious in the back of an ambulance."

"Hopefully she'll be fine. What do you need from me?"

"Nothing right now. DCI Fulton is organising CSI. I'm keeping you in the loop, ma'am. I'm unclear what authority I have here."

"We'll sort that out later. Best to act with haste right now."

A squad car drove at speed along Whitehall and pulled in at an angle across the bus stop.

"Ma'am, I've got to go," said Pennance. "Uniform has arrived. I'll need to direct them until Fulton turns up."

"Contact me if you need anything." Meacham disconnected.

Two uniform stepped out of the car, both placing flat caps on their heads before slamming the doors like double-tap gun shots. Pennance walked over.

"Who are you?" asked the nearest cop, a medium-height dark haired man with small, close-set eyes.

"DI Pennance, NCA." Pennance showed his ID once more. "What's your name?"

"Renfrew." He nodded across the squad car to his colleague. "She's Gaskill."

"Okay, I want a cordon setting up across 15A. Nobody goes in or out under any circumstances until CSI arrive, okay?"

"Yes, sir." Gaskill popped the boot, took out a roll of blue and white barrier tape.

Pennance turned away. He had one more call to make. Kelso picked up quickly. "Jonah, to what do I owe this pleasure?" His voice was deep and booming down the line, some jazz in the background and the clink of cutlery on ceramic.

"I have to be quick, Devon. I wanted to let you know, Simone is in hospital. I found her unconscious in a building on Whitehall."

"Where are you?"

"Outside a pub, The Silver Cross."

"I'm on my way over."

"You don't have to, everything is in hand."

"Try and stop me." Then Drexler was gone.

Renfrew and Gaskill were unreeling the tape across the building's entrance.

"Have you got a torch in the car?" asked Pennance

"Check the glove compartment, sir," said Renfrew.

"I'm heading back inside to ensure there's no-one else."

"Sure." Renfrew shrugged, his expression blank.

Pennance leant into the squad car. The glove compartment held a bag of sweets, a box of nitrile gloves and the black, round metal barrel of a flashlight. Pennance grabbed the torch and a pair of gloves. He flicked the switch on and off a couple of times before heading back to the cops. "Stay out here by the doorway," he said to Renfrew.

Once Pennance was in the hallway he pulled on the gloves, pressed the white plastic button, illuminating the space once more. He headed upstairs and managed to make it onto the second floor this time before the bulb clicked off.

Outside the office where he'd found Simone, he turned on the torch and entered. The beam cut a narrow slice in the darkness. He played the light around, checking his immediate surroundings. He made deliberately slow progress, watching where he placed his feet to avoid compromising any evidence. All the room contained were the piles of boxes he'd seen first time. Inside them were large quantities of stationery – ream upon ream of paper, pens, pencils, sharpeners and so on. Enough to equip hundreds and hundreds of other offices like this.

Then, the shaft of light fell on the spot where Simone had lain, obvious because of the stain on the floor. Pennance shifted the torch until the beam reflected off the bottle he'd seen previously, lying on its side. He squatted down next to it.

The bottle was clear plastic, maybe one-litre capacity, the kind you'd buy from a supermarket. The label had been torn off, and the plastic was thick and strong when he prodded it.

Inside, a small amount of a densely clouded liquid remained. Some had drained onto the floor, creating a dark pool. Pennance picked up the bottle carefully; two fingers on the narrow lip just beneath the thread, one finger of his other hand in the centre of the base. Pennance placed a fingertip over the spout and tipped, wetting the glove. Carefully, he placed the bottle exactly back where it had been before he lifted the wet digit to his mouth. He pushed any thought of the potential risk to one side and licked. He got the rubbery taste of the nitrile, but the other flavour was abundantly clear.

Salt. Highly concentrated, overpowering, even. First bread and now salt.

Pennance wanted to spit to clear his mouth. Instead he wiped his tongue on a sleeve.

Next, he entered the adjacent room where he'd found the young man. A chair, wrapped in a clear plastic film, used to protect items during transportation, stood in the middle of the room, back to the door, covered in dust. The desk drawers were all empty and nothing hung on the walls. No internal phone, either.

He headed to where the man had lain. Another bottle on its side, six feet or so off, identical to the one next to Simone, except this one was empty. Pennance was about to retrace his steps downstairs when light flashed off something on the chair. A mobile.

The phone was propped up and faced directly towards the man's position. The arrangement must be deliberate. He squatted down recognising the case immediately; it belonged to Simone. This was her personal handset. It felt all wrong, being there like that. Pennance picked up the mobile and shoved it into a pocket before retreating onto the landing.

Downstairs, he paused in the hallway, looked over the metal post boxes fixed to the wall. There were lots of individual cases, way more than there were actual rooms in the building. He slid his fingers inside the slot of the nearest and tugged. It held firm though there was some wiggle; the casing was quite thin. He noticed labels were fixed to most of the flaps, a small typeface, located behind a plastic cover. Some were faded, others more recent. Pennance read the words one after the other. Keystone Composites Ltd, Craven Capital LLC, Firestar Partners.

Pennance almost missed it, the writing nearly faded away.

Blackthorn.

He worked his fingers into the gap and yanked hard. The lock bent but didn't give immediately. Two more tugs and the flap came away. Pennance directed the beam inside, but there was just a spider's web. He pushed the door closed again, making sure it looked reasonably straight before making his way back outside, ducking under the tape now fixed across the doorway as two CSI vans drew up beside the squad car – and DCI Fulton in a silver BMW 5 Series. Gough, the Crime Scene Manager who'd handled the Carnegie investigation, spilled out of the nearest vehicle. She nodded when she spotted Pennance.

"I've just checked inside," said Pennance, "Nobody else is there."

"Okay," said Gough. "I'll take it from here." She strode away and began to direct her team once she'd told Renfrew and Gaskill to set up a wider perimeter covering the whole of the pavement around 15A.

"Want to tell me what you've found so far?" asked Fulton.

Pennance explained the chain of events and most of his discoveries. Simone's phone, he kept silent about.

"Why here?" asked Fulton when Pennance had finished.

"I've no idea," said Pennance. "Frankly, there's a lot I'm not clear on."

Fulton's phone beeped. "That's one of my team at the hospital. Simone is unconscious but stable."

"Good news. And what about the other victim?"

"A credit card found in his wallet by the paramedics identified him as Alfred Fonseca. Apparently, he's in a coma; critical but stable. We're finding out exactly who he is right now."

An Audi drew up beside Pennance and the door opened. Pennance took the chance to text Fonseca's name to Hoskins. Renfrew made to come over but Pennance held up a hand. "He's with me."

"I got here as quickly as I could," said Kelso, smart in a waistcoat, trousers and bow tie. "Bloody roads."

"You didn't need to," said Pennance.

"Bullshit," said Kelso. "Are you alright?"

"I'm fine," lied Pennance.

Fulton glanced between Pennance and Kelso, said, "Were you and Simone more than just partners, Jonah?"

"We were friends," said Pennance. "I believe that's why she called me." Thankfully, Kelso stayed quiet. Kelso made it an objective to know about the personal lives of his closest officers, even after they'd left his team, so Kelso was well aware of Simone and Rasmussen getting back together, leaving Pennance jogging on the side-lines like an unused substitute.

"And you're okay working this case?" pressed Fulton.

"I want to. Simone and I had become distant since I moved to the NCA, but I need to help her."

Fulton stared at Pennance for a long moment before he said, "Okay, I can live with that. Tell me about these plastic bottles you found."

"Very common design. Could have been bought in any one of thousands of shops. There was some liquid in the bottom of the one beside Simone."

"I'll tell Gough to send the fluid off for immediate analysis. There's nothing more you can do for now. Why don't you go home?"

"With all due respect, I don't work for you, sir."

Kelso chuckled.

"I'm well aware of that and it was a request, not an order," said Fulton. "CSI have barely started and, knowing Gough, it'll be another couple of hours before she provides an update. There's not much more any of us can do right now."

"He's right," said Kelso. "I'll drive you home. I'm surplus to requirements here, too." He held out his hand for Fulton. "Nice to have met you." They shook. Then Kelso placed the same hand on Pennance's shoulder. "Come on, get in the car."

Pennance did as his ex-boss suggested and slid into the passenger seat. Moments later, Kelso was beside him, starting the engine and swinging across Whitehall, the same as the ambulance had earlier. "You can drop me off anywhere when we're away from Fulton."

"No need," said Kelso. "I knew you'd go to Simone anyway, so I'm taking you there."

Eighteen

The traffic was relatively light at this time of evening. However, central London had its fair share of stop lights, so any journey felt like a fitful process. Which was one of the reasons Pennance didn't own a car. The other was the cost – of parking and the central London congestion charge. It all ate into his wages.

"How's it going at the NCA?" asked Kelso. It was Kelso who'd suggested Pennance transfer and Kelso who'd arranged an interview with Meacham.

"Okay, I think," said Pennance. "I'm still finding my feet."

"Having your first proper case will help settle you, you'll see."

"I've moved divisions before, Devon."

"True enough," accepted Kelso.

"Thanks for the glowing reference, by the way," said Pennance. "It made all the difference."

"You were my best investigator, Jonah. And you got the job on your own merits; remember that. Meacham wouldn't employ someone simply on the basis of a testimonial. I know you weren't sure about the shift, but it was the right thing to do. There are changes coming now my retirement is out in the open."

"I guess. I'm just not convinced the NCA is the right home for me."

"Give it time, son."

Both men fell silent until eventually Kelso drew up outside the Accident and Emergency entrance of the University College Hospital which sat on the busy junction of Euston Road and Gower Street and braced by two tube stations – Warren Street and Euston Square. "I can come in, if you want?" Kelso left the engine running.

"I'll be fine, thanks."

"I thought you'd say that." Kelso gave a weak grin. "She'll be alright and so will you."

"I know." But Pennance didn't.

"Why do you think she called you and not Rasmussen?"

"I've no idea."

"Must mean something good, right?"

Pennance shrugged, said, "I'd better go, Devon. Thanks for being here. I appreciate it."

"Simone was one of my best officers, too." Pennance reached out for the handle, tugged on it. As he was part-way out the door Kelso grabbed hold of his arm. "Call me if you need anything, okay?"

"Sure."

Kelso briefly maintained his grip before releasing. Pennance slammed the door shut and watched while Kelso drove off. Neither man waved goodbye. It wasn't that kind of parting. Nor were they that kind of people. When Kelso had gone Pennance dialled Hoskins.

"I'm outside," said Pennance when Hoskins answered. "Where are you?"

"Fourth floor," said Hoskins. "She's got her own room near the Weaver Suite and she's doing okay."

Pennance disconnected, went through the sliding doors into A&E, asked a nurse the way and got walking as fast as he could without breaking into a run.

**

When Pennance rounded the corner, he knew he was in the right place because of Lars Rasmussen's hulking presence. Rasmussen paced the corridor, heading away from Pennance, passing a uniform cop outside a door. He reached an imaginary end point, turned, spotted the interloping Pennance, and then stomped over with purpose.

"I've been trying to see Simone." Rasmussen's mouth worked like a cow angrily chewing cud, an obvious piece of gum on the go. "But *he* won't let me in." Rasmussen hiked a thumb. The cop made no sign he was the objective of Rasmussen's vitriol and carried on performing his training-ground-honed, nine-yard stare. Pennance could employ one too, when he wanted. So could every graduate of every uniformed service.

"There will be a good reason, I'm sure," said Pennance. "Right, constable?"

"Pruitt, sir," said the cop. "And yes, sir." One sharp nod. "Very good reason."

"Well, it would be preferable if they actually informed the patient's family." Rasmussen raised his voice so Pruitt couldn't fail but hear. Which was pointless as Pruitt would just be doing as ordered.

"Where's Natalie?" Pennance meant Simone and Rasmussen's teenage daughter. "Is she okay?" Pennance got on well with Natalie, he liked her. She could fly into a fury, just like her mother, which blew out as fast as it started, but Simone had raised her well.

"*Astrid*, is absolutely fine." Rasmussen's mouth tightened, daring Pennance to correct him. Pennance clenched his fists tight enough for nails to bite into flesh while a near overwhelming desire to smack Rasmussen in the mouth coursed through him, until Pennance caught the flicker of a sneer across Rasmussen's lips and he managed to tamp the urge down.

"I'll check on Simone," said Pennance through a tight jaw.

"If he lets you in," said Rasmussen.

Pennance showed Pruitt his ID who, with a carefully restrained smirk, opened the door for Pennance. "After you, inspector." Pennance almost bumped into a clipboard-carrying woman wearing a lab coat. Her striking deeply ginger hair was cropped short, shorter than Pennance's, even. Her skin had that kind of yellow-ish hue which redheads possessed, making the freckles on her cheeks stand out even more, and she wore bright red lipstick. "Sorry, I'M DI Jonah Pennance."

"My fault, I wasn't paying attention. Dr Alice Conryn, I'm treating Miss Smithson."

"It's Mrs Rasmussen," said Rasmussen from the corridor. "She's married to me."

Conryn sighed. "Perhaps we should talk inside?" She shuffled a couple of steps back, and Pennance followed. As the cop shut the door Rasmussen scowled, before spitting his gum into a bin.

Simone lay in bed, propped up at a shallow angle by a tilted mattress. Her unnaturally blonde hair was matted. A new, Scandinavian style to please Rasmussen. She wore a standard hospital-issue white gown. The sheets were white too. Her face was washed out. It was as if she had been absorbed by the bedding. On this side of the bed stood a drip and a machine which beeped repetitively, marking the pulse of Simone's slow and steady heartbeat. Only the rhythmic bleat of the machine, and the steady rise and fall of her chest, indicated there was life within her body.

"She's fine, Jonah." On the other side of the bed, slumped in a chair, sat Hoskins, like a scruffy stick insect. Hoskins's porkpie hat sat on the covers near Simone's feet. A greasy, tear-shaped stain marked his raincoat, as if some filling had fallen out of a sandwich and scuffed the fabric before hitting the floor. Normally, Pennance would be grinding his molars at Hoskins, but now he was just grateful he'd dropped everything and come.

"Your friend isn't quite correct," said Conryn. Hoskins grinned at 'friend'. Conryn continued, "And we had words when he first arrived. Using any electronic devices in the same room as sensitive medical equipment is forbidden."

"It's an exaggeration that Wi-Fi affects nearby apparatus. Like using a phone on a plane in flight," protested Hoskins.

"Nevertheless, I'm in charge here." Conryn arched a fine, pencilled eyebrow. "Not you."

"Yes, ma'am." Hoskins lifted his hands in surrender. "You win."

"I'd prefer to say that good sense has prevailed. Let's focus on the patient instead, shall we?"

"Please," said Pennance.

"Miss Smithson was very ill when she was brought in," said Conryn. "The paramedics believed she'd ingested something, so we pumped her stomach and gave her some *Midazolam* to keep her sedated. Don't worry." Conryn raised a palm like a cop directing traffic as Pennance made to ask a question. "It's perfectly safe, we're monitoring her closely as you can see and, given the circumstances, this is the best medical option. We're running a battery of tests, including a blood sample which is being analysed to determine what she ingested."

"Could a high concentration of salt do this to her?" asked Pennance.

Conryn thought for a moment. "It's unusual, but maybe. The content would have to be extreme, though." Conryn made a note on her pad. "Believe me when I say we're giving your colleague the best treatment possible. You should be encouraged. Her vital signs are strong and stable. Unlike Mr Fonseca."

"Can I see him?"

"Absolutely not. Mr Fonseca is on the intensive care ward receiving acute medical care. He's currently in a coma and unresponsive."

"Why is he in a worse state than Simone?"

"I suspect Miss Smithson ingested less of the material than Mr Fonseca." Pennance thought back to the bottles. Fonseca's had been empty, Simone's part full. Conryn said, "I understand she vomited several times?"

"She did."

"Then that could have helped her condition. However, inspector, let's take one step at a time." Conryn flicked a glanced at her watch. "I really must go."

"One more question, doctor."

Conryn sighed. "Okay."

"Did you find marks on either Mr Fonseca or Miss Smithson? Pinpricks, about here." Pennance tapped two fingers in a V just above his heart.

"I can't recall seeing any, but I was more interested in stabilising both of them than checking them over."

"I'd appreciate it if you can look into it and let me know, please?"

Conryn nodded then was gone, leaving Pennance and Hoskins alone.

"I'm considering asking that doctor out on a date," said Hoskins. "What do you reckon?"

"I think she'd eat you for breakfast."

Pennance realised he'd made a food related statement when Hoskins produced a broad grin. However, Hoskins' expression quickly morphed into one of seriousness. "She'll be okay."

"Everyone keeps telling me that. But it's not me lying there, Vance." Pennance glanced at Simone, who hadn't moved a millimetre. The machine continued to rhythmically beep.

"Where did you get the idea of salt from?" asked Hoskins.

"There were bottles lying next to Simone and Fonseca, I tasted what was inside," admitted Pennance.

"Huh." Hoskins gave an appreciative nod.

"Keep that to yourself," said Pennance.

Hoskins winked then said, "Risky, though."

"Had to be done. It was for Simone."

"Your funeral."

"What have you learnt about Fonseca?"

"Not a great deal so far." Hoskins bent down, pulled a laptop out from under Simone's covers and flipped open the lid.

"You sneaky sod."

Hoskins grinned while he tapped in a password. A photo came up on-screen of a young man wearing a black gown and a mortarboard hat at a rakish angle. He held a roll of paper, bound by a red ribbon. His expression was one of mild surprise, despite this clearly being a staged photo. "Alfred Fonseca, recently graduated from the London School of Economics with a PhD before joining Her Majesty's Treasury. That's the government ministry responsible for setting financial policy, taxes and financial services."

"He's a civil servant?"

"Apparently so. I'd assume he's very junior as it takes years to wend through the ranks; one precise step at a time on a time served basis. My father worked in the department of agriculture, his entire career. Eventually he reached the top job – Parliamentary Under Secretary. Various Cabinet level secretaries of state came and went, but my father remained until the day he retired on his 65th birthday. He had the same haircut and wore the same suit and tie every day. No bowler hat or umbrella, thank God."

"You didn't want to follow him into politics?"

"Actually, it was my father who suggested I join the police. He said I wasn't made for the back biting and scheming. Anyway, I've asked him to put some feelers out on my behalf. He still retains a lot of contacts and influence."

"Plenty of skeletons in closets?"

"Something like that, I'm sure. I also cross-referenced all of Simone's past cases and there's no mention of Fonseca. He doesn't have a criminal record, no DNA on file, no sign of any previous complaints. As far as the police is concerned, Fonseca is a model citizen. I also checked on social media. Fonseca doesn't have a profile on any of the platforms. I only picked up what I just told you from the LSE website and a brief newspaper article in *The London Evening Standard* listing university graduate results."

"So, how could they possibly know each other?"

"From what I see, they can't." Hoskins paused briefly, the machine beeping several times before he said, "She'll come back, Jonah."

"I know."

"I meant to you." Pennance just stared at Hoskins who tapped his temple. "I understand people. It's my primary ability. Forget that Rasmussen guy, he's a dick. It's you she wants."

"How could you possibly be so sure? This is the first time you've seen her."

"I've watched interview footage of you two questioning suspects together. I've spoken to your ex-boss, Kelso. You've talked about her on multiple occasions. It's obvious. You're her man." Hoskins paused for a moment while Pennance thought.

"There's something else I need you to look into, Vance."

"Okay." Hoskins opened up his laptop.

"Anything you can find on 15A Whitehall. That's where I found her. It seems to be a kind of serviced office. There were postal boxes in the hallway. One was labelled Blackthorn."

Hoskins tapped away at the keyboard for a few moments before leaning into the screen and narrowing his eyes. He said, "I'm on the Companies House website. 15A Whitehall is the registered address of 3,327 companies using that very location."

"How is that possible?" asked Pennance. "They couldn't all fit in there."

"It's just a detail on an application, Jonah. These guys could be anywhere in the world. It takes a matter of minutes to set up a UK registered company and a £12 fee. Whoever owns these companies are using the Whitehall address for prestige."

"It's a crappy building between a pub and a phone shop."

"So? Who's going to check?"

"What about Blackthorn?"

Hoskins tapped away again. "There are several businesses called Blackthorn." Hoskins sat back. "And one of them is registered at 15A Whitehall. They're owned by another company, based in the British Virgin Islands, a tax avoidance haven. Which more than likely means it'll be a shell corporation hiding the true titleholders. I'll need some time to look into all of this, cross-referencing the details of each organisation."

"I've one more request," said Pennance.

"Shoot."

"Can you access this?" Pennance held out a mobile. "I found it at the crime scene. It's Simone's."

"And you took it?" asked Hoskins.

"As I was told earlier today – go big, or go home, Vance."

Hoskins gave Simone a long, meaningful glance and then reached out, accepted the handset from Pennance's grasp. "I want a favour in return." Hoskins wagged the mobile at Pennance. "Have a talk with Rasmussen because he's doing my head in. Tell him what's happening, then maybe he'll clear off."

Pennance's phone rang. Meacham.

"Alright," said Pennance as he answered the call.

"Where are you, Jonah?" asked Meacham.

"At UCH, checking on Simone and Fonseca."

"How are they?"

"Both unconscious. The doctor couldn't tell me when I'll be able to talk with them."

"I know it's late, but can you get back here and come up to my office? I'll explain when you're here."

"Yes, ma'am."

"Be as quick as you can," said Meacham, then she was gone.

"Meacham wants me at the NCA," said Pennance.

"I'll keep an eye on Simone. I can operate here just as easily as in the office and this chair is way more comfortable. I'm sure I can get a pillow from somewhere. Remember to talk to Rasmussen before you go."

Pennance took one last, reluctant look at Simone before stepping back out into the corridor.

Rasmussen stood directly opposite the entrance, arms crossed, staring at the floor. His head snapped up as Pennance closed the door. "Well?" Rasmussen pushed off the wall, faced Pennance, hands clenched. "Are you going to tell me how Simone is? That fucking quack barely said a damned word."

"Doctor Conryn is working hard to save Simone's life. You should give her more credit."

"It's what she's paid to do," mumbled Rasmussen.

"Simone is doing fine, she's been given a drug so she sleeps while the doctor runs some tests."

"Can I see her?"

"Not yet."

"Why?"

"Doctor's orders."

"You were in there a long time after she left."

"I was talking to my colleague." Rasmussen grunted. Pennance continued, "Has Simone ever mentioned an Alfred Fonseca?"

"Who's he?"

"Another person found nearby."

"Why don't you just ask him?"

"I would, but he's in a coma."

"That's poor of him," said Rasmussen. Pennance waited. "No, I've never heard of anyone called Fonseca."

"What about 15A Whitehall?" asked Pennance.

Rasmussen shrugged. "Which is?"

"Where Simone and Fonseca were found."

"Don't know."

"And where were you earlier?" asked Pennance. "Say in the last two hours."

"Having dinner with a client."

"Who?"

Rasmussen frowned. "Are you accusing me of something?"

"Standard procedure to determine the whereabouts of anyone close to the victim."

"So, what about you, Inspector? What were you doing? Oh, wait." Rasmussen snapped his fingers. "You and Simone aren't exactly *tight* these days. You need to find whoever did this to me, do you understand?" Rasmussen grabbed hold of Pennance's arm.

"To you?" Pennance tried to shake off Rasmussen's grip, but he held fast. "It's Simone lying unconscious."

"I love her, she's *my* wife." Rasmussen got in close, his hot breath basting Pennance's face.

"Get your hand off me." Pennance spoke quietly. Rasmussen returned Pennance's glare, breathing deeply.

"Sir, do as he says." Pruitt had moved away from Simone's door and was there, about to insert himself between them if need be. "Or I'll take great pleasure in arresting you for assault."

Rasmussen stared into Pennance's eyes before he gave a final squeeze and released. Pennance resisted rubbing his arm where it tingled from Rasmussen's grasp.

"Sir?" asked Pruitt.

"It's okay," said Pennance, eyes still locked with Rasmussen. "Mr Rasmussen is just exhibiting a degree of grief. He's not quite in command of himself. Isn't that's right?"

"If you do actually want to know where I was, feel free to contact Hillary. You remember her? My PA? She'll tell you."

"I will," said Pennance. "I appreciate all your help. Go home now."

"Come on, sir," said Pruitt. "Let's get you downstairs."

Rasmussen reluctantly allowed Pruitt to lead him away. Then he turned and shouted back at Pennance, "She'll be coming home to me." Pruitt pushed his way through double doors dragging Rasmussen after him. "Nothing is more important than family!"

Pruitt let the doors shut behind him, closing off Rasmussen's rant.

Nineteen

Only one room along the corridor had light spilling out from the door. Pennance paused outside Meacham's office and glanced through the glass strip. She was focused on her monitor, tapping away on the keyboard. Pennance knocked and Meacham waved him in.

Once Pennance entered he realised Meacham wasn't alone. A man leant against a wall. His style screamed government: plain dark grey suit, white shirt, dark blue tie with a crest on it. A three-button jacket, the top two done up. Pennance would bet on a public school education and connections to match, both privileges which got Pennance's back up.

Meacham's guest held out a hand for Pennance. "Leo Raskin, pleased to meet you."

"Uh-huh," said Pennance. He switched his attention to Meacham to see what she had to say.

She emerged from behind her desk, and indicated the meeting table. "Why don't we all sit?" When they were settled Meacham said, "Perhaps we can start by repeating why you're here, Mr Raskin?"

"Excellent notion," said Raskin. "My presence is as a result of my charge, Alfred Fonseca."

"Charge?" Pennance thought it an unusual word to use.

"Alfred is the son of a friend, so I keep an eye on him." Fonseca paused briefly. "Not too well, clearly."

"Who's Alfred's father?"

"Sir Hugh Fonseca. He works with the EU in a kind of senior diplomatic role."

"Kind of?"

"That's all I know."

"And what's your relationship to Alfred?"

"Relationship?" Raskin laughed briefly. "There is none. He works for me, Inspector."

"Where?"

"Whitehall. Not the street between Charing Cross and Parliament of course." Raskin gave a self-deprecating grin.

Pennance blinked. Had Meacham known this when she'd asked him here?

"Or the original palace where King Charles the First was executed," said Meacham. "As that burned down in 1698." Raskin's smile narrowed to a thin line. "So," continued Meacham, "I assume you mean government?"

"Correct," said Raskin. Pennance had been right. "Specifically the bureaucracy."

"HM Treasury," said Pennance.

Raskin looked Pennance up and down through narrowed eyes. "You've done your homework."

"How long has Mr Fonseca worked for you?" asked Pennance.

"A couple of months. And he appears to have hated every minute."

"Why?"

Raskin wrinkled his forehead. "I'm truly unclear on the root cause. We don't have that kind of association. I'll let you into a little secret, Inspector." Raskin leaned across the table. "I owed his father a favour. We used to go to school together,

Eton, you know." Pennance groaned inside. That was a pair. "Alfred had run up quite debt as a student at the LSE. His father wanted Alfred to get a job and start paying his way. I had a space and took Alfred on under a short term contract."

"What favour?"

"A professional one." Raskin sat back. "That's how the world turns, after all."

"What do you think of Mr Fonseca?"

"Which one? Alfred or Hugh?"

"Alfred."

"Clearly very bright, his work was good and his PhD was a benefit. However, his real-life experience was highly limited. Like he'd kept his nose in a book while growing up. He could be very naïve so I quickly learned to keep him out of any meetings that possessed a serious tinge."

"And you were there to raise his eyes to educate him further?" asked Pennance.

"Hardly." Raskin chuckled. "I just gave him employment and therefore an income. Whatever he did with his free time was up to him."

"Do either of you operate out of 15A Whitehall?" asked Pennance.

"No, why?" Raskin's eyebrows drooped to a steep V.

"Is it a building where you store supplies, for example?"

"What are you getting at?"

Pennance changed tack. "Do you usually keep your staff working late?"

"Sometimes, why?"

"What about tonight? It appeared like Alfred had come straight from work."

"I've no idea what time he left. I was at a meeting in Downing Street, no. 11 to be precise. And Alfred wasn't a direct report. As I said, he was very junior to me."

"So, why are you here and not his actual boss?"

Raskin pressed his hands together between his legs. "To demonstrate to his father I'm doing all I can."

"Because that's what makes the world turn?" asked Pennance. Raskin glanced away and didn't answer. "Can you find out and let me know what time Alfred left your office?"

"Of course."

"Does Blackthorn mean anything to you, Mr Raskin?"

"Blackthorn?" Raskin blinked fast, several times. "It's not a cryptonym I recognise."

"It's a company. Based out of 15A Whitehall."

"I'm sorry, I've just realised I'm late for a meeting." Raskin stood. "I'd appreciate it if you can keep me appraised of developments and I'll endeavour to answer any outstanding questions on Alfred in due course. I'll see myself out."

"Wait, Mr Raskin," said Pennance. Raskin froze, half out of his seat. "You'll need my business card to get in touch." Pennance held one between his fingers.

"Of course." Raskin flashed his teeth, and took the offering.

"Don't forget your umbrella," said Meacham.

"Thank you." Raskin collected the brolly from where it leaned in the corner by the door. "Good evening to you both." Then he was gone.

"Bloody Whitehall," said Meacham. "Smart arse."

"You put him in his place, though."

"At least my art history degree hasn't gone completely to waste." For a few moments neither Pennance nor Meacham spoke. "What the hell is Blackthorn?" asked Meacham.

"Sorry ma'am, things have been moving so fast I've not had chance to update you. I found a post-it note behind Thewlis' desk – Blackthorn was written on it. 15A Whitehall appears to be a location where multiple businesses are registered. Blackthorn, probably a shell company, is one of them. I just threw it at Raskin to see how he'd react."

"He looked like you were driving a big truck at him with your headlights on full beam." Meacham grinned. "What did you think of him?"

"Transparent as milk," replied Pennance. "He's pretty used to getting his own way."

"That's public school boys for you. They're built like that," said Meacham. "I've had the misfortune to be around civil servants for years and there was something off about our Mr Raskin. I just can't put my finger on what."

"I assume Raskin knew I'd just come from the hospital?" asked Pennance.

"He was in the room when I called you."

"You know what's interesting?" said Pennance. "He never once asked how Alfred Fonseca was actually doing."

"Take a look into him, Jonah. I want to everything. Talk to Hoskins, our little secret agent can help."

"Secret agent, ma'am?"

"Dismissed, inspector." Meacham smiled. "And don't leave it so long to give me an update next time."

DEAD MONEY

In the corridor outside Meacham's office Pennance pulled out his mobile, dialled Hoskins, got walking. Hoskins picked up within a few rings.

"She's still unconscious," said Hoskins, his voice low.

"I need even more help from you."

"Slave driver."

"Strictly, this one's from Meacham." Pennance reached the stairs, began to descend. "I just met a guy by the name of Raskin in her office. Apparently Alfred Fonseca works for Raskin in Treasury. Meacham reckons there's something off about him."

"Sounds like Meacham," said Hoskins. "She's almost as untrusting of people as I am. I'll access the NCA's CCTV system and grab an image of this Raskin."

"I'm heading for the hospital now."

"There's no need, Jonah. Simone is still unconscious and Conryn threw me out of her room. I'm currently in a waiting area just along the corridor. Pruitt is on the door, so between us we'll ensure she's okay. Frankly, there's nothing you can do here and you'd just be in the way. Go home, get some sleep."

"Where's Rasmussen?"

"No idea. Not here, that's for sure. After Pruitt tossed him out, he must have given up and left."

"What about you?"

"I don't need much rest, a couple of hours and I'm as fresh as a dew kissed daisy."

"I can't let you do that, Vance."

"I've news for you, matey. I don't report to you. Get going. By the time you're home, I'll have some information ready."

"You don't know my address." Pennance stepped outside onto the pavement.

"Are you sure about that?" Then, with a chuckle, Hoskins cut the call.

Twenty

Pennance actually lived off Clapham High Street. The entrance to his upstairs flat was along a route which was more alley-like than road. The accommodation was spread over two floors – arranged traditionally into living area below and sleeping area above. He also had access to the roof space where he'd put a few hardy plants into pots around a table and chairs; about as green-fingered as he got.

He appreciated natural materials so there was as much wood visible as possible – no carpets or rugs, just stripped floorboards. And the walls were exposed brickwork, Pennance had smashed all the plaster off when he moved in before sealing it to eliminate dust. The kitchen was steel and brass, with a few pieces of expensive equipment. A large sofa dominated the living area although the television was small and in one corner of the room, instead of fixed to the wall. TV wasn't important to him. The recessed floor-to-ceiling shelves either side of a fireplace were his thing. Pennance collected first editions, usually picked up cheaply from charity shops – the thrill of the find. Maybe, if the author was a favourite and the book was a limited print run, he paid full price online or from a small shop he knew tucked out the back of Covent Garden.

A large glass tank (though nothing like the size of that in the Heron Tower) sat on a low table beside the kitchen doorway. Pennance squatted, tapped on the outside. As usual, Lars the beady-eyed iguana paid him no consideration. He wished the iguana's namesake were the same. Pennance grabbed a plastic box from the kitchen, slid back the tank lid and dropped a couple of live crickets inside. Now he had Lars' attention, or, more specifically, his dinner did. Lars' eyes swivelled in their sockets to where the feast hunched.

"I'll leave you to it," said Pennance. He headed into the kitchen, put the kettle on, deposited a teabag into a mug with the picture of a sheep on the front and 'You're ewe-nique' on the back. Simone had bought him an identical design as a peace offering the previous time they'd fallen out. However, it was knocked off Pennance's desk and broke on Simone's last day at Sapphire. Some sort of omen. Unknown to Simone he'd bought a replacement and kept it at home as his go-to cup.

His phone dinged. A message from Hoskins, 'Check your email'.

There, waiting for him, was a screengrab of Raskin leaving the NCA.

Hoskins called. "Got it?"

"Just now. You were slower than I expected." Pennance grinned.

"Not even I'm perfect. I've done some initial digging but there's very little information on the man. Like none. It's as if he's a ghost. But nobody stays hidden from Vance Hoskins for long. I'll keep working, buddy." Hoskins disconnected.

Pennance went back to the kitchen, re-boiled the kettle, poured the hot water onto a teabag. He was just fishing out the paper pyramid containing the leaves when he received a text which read, 'Inspector Pennance, this is Damian Mulcahy at Sting. We were due to meet earlier, but you didn't turn up. Can we re-arrange?'

Pennance swore; he'd forgotten their arrangement. He dropped the teabag in the sink then dialled Mulcahy, said, "I'm sorry about missing you, I've had a hell of a day."

"No problem!" replied Mulcahy, "One of our clients got hacked so I've been up to my eyeballs, too. I'm just nursing a lager right now."

"Do you mind if I come over tomorrow?"

"Sure, first thing?"

"8am?"

Mulcahy sucked air through his teeth. "Bit early, that. I'd prefer 10?"

"Let's split the difference, Mr Mulcahy, and make it 9, okay?"

"If you must. See you then. Ciao." Mulcahy rang off.

Pennance took his drink to the roof where the table and chairs nestled against the brickwork block of a chimney stack, positioned to keep him out of the prevailing wind carrying its burden of smog across London.

Five floors up, Pennance had a reasonable view over the nearby roofs and TV aerials of Clapham High Street. The sound of trains passing through the busy train junction easily reached him.

Pennance wouldn't be able to pick out his next-door neighbour in a line-up but he did know they made honey because they had two hives on their roof from which the bees buzzed back and forth and sold jars out of an honesty box fixed on the wall beside their front door, just below a video doorbell.

More than once he and Simone had sat here. He remembered the last time; Simone had come for dinner. He'd gone to a lot of effort cooking a three course meal from scratch and investing in a very decent Argentinian Malbec recommended by a know-it-all shop assistant. Simone had proven uncharacteristically quiet throughout, toying with her food, though drinking plenty of alcohol, even opening a second bottle, which she'd brought. She'd barely made eye contact with him.

"What's going on, Simone?" asked Pennance.

"Have you noticed it smells less up here?" said Simone. She held a half-drunk glass of red in her hand, the rim stained with a smear of lipstick, some dark russet colour which doubtless had a name like Autumn Sunset.

Pennance frowned. "What's that supposed to mean?"

"I mean the air's a bit cleaner; it doesn't stink of car so much." Simone faced out towards the twinkling lights of Clapham.

"Is everything okay?"

"Honestly? No, not really." Simone sighed heavily. "There's no easy way of telling you this."

She gulped down the rest of her wine and reached for the bottle, pouring some for herself before aiming for Pennance's glass but he blocked her with a hand. She lifted her glass, held it in front of her face, arms loosely folded, like a barrier. "I'm getting back together with Lars."

Pennance couldn't speak for a few moments. If he'd written a list of likely comments by Simone he doubted 'going back to Lars' would have made it to even the third page. "Rasmussen? Your ex?"

"He's the only Lars I know." She gulped half the wine down.

"Jesus." Pennance tried to swallow the huge lump that had appeared in his throat. "Why?"

"He's the father of my child."

"So? He's also the guy who treated you like crap."

"Natalie needs two parents, particularly now she's a teenager. They're formative years and I can hardly do it by myself."

"You've got me."

"I know that, but does Natalie have you?"

"Of course!" Pennance felt like his ribs were squeezing together, constricting his lungs. "I don't get this. You've spent the last year breaking away from Lars and been in bits most of that time. Finally you're putting yourself back together and now you're considering returning to him so he can smash you to pieces all over again?"

"That's not how it was, Jonah."

"So all the times you complained about Rasmussen right there in that seat were lies?" Simone seemed not to have an answer. Pennance continued, "And what about all this?" Pennance passed a hand over the rapidly cooling meal. "One last blowout?"

"That's out of order, Jonah." A flash of fury crossed Simone's features.

"Jesus." Pennance passed a hand over his face. He'd shaved before Simone had arrived, even put on some cologne. What had he been thinking would happen?

"As I said, Natalie needs two parents and one of them can't be you."

"Why the hell not?"

"You're hardly the domestic type and the crazy jobs we both have..." Simone shook her head. "Where would the stability be for her?"

"I remember you complaining that the life of a successful financier wasn't ideal for family life, either."

"He's changed."

"But his money hasn't."

"That's not fair."

Simone was right, though Pennance wasn't in the mood for sympathy. "I just say it how I see it."

"I'm not going to apologise." Simone crossed her arms tight across her chest now. "I need to do what's best for me and Natalie."

"I didn't realise I was that terrible a person."

Simone turned to Pennance, put a hand on his arm. "You're not, it's just..."

"Go on," said Pennance.

But she dropped her hand, shook her head once more and turned her focus back onto Clapham's lights. "I'm sorry," she said, so quietly Pennance barely heard the meaningless apology.

"How long has this been going on? You and Rasmussen?"

Simone clasped her hands between her thighs, her shoulders hunched. "A few months."

"So you've been seeing him and me at the same time?"

"Lars and I had to discuss Natalie and we kept meeting, just as friends."

"Until he asked you back."

"I'm staying in my house. I'm not moving Natalie. She's settled at school."

"Pull the other one, Simone. I'm no idiot." Pennance knew he sounded childish and petulant, he just couldn't help himself. "Anyway, I've something to tell you, too. I'll be leaving Sapphire." Which wasn't entirely true – Pennance hadn't even been for the final interview at the NCA yet, although Kelso had told him it was a done deal.

"What?" Simone spun back around. Her expression was one of total surprise. "When?"

"The dates aren't decided. Weeks, I expect. Hopefully faster now if I can manage it." Actually, Pennance had been going to turn the opportunity down and stay in Sapphire with Simone, but now he just wanted to get away from her as fast as he possibly could.

Simone's features hardened then. "It's probably for the best. I'm pleased for you."

"Likewise," lied Pennance.

"I'd better go." Simone rose.

"Don't come running back when it all turns to dust."

Simone stood in front of Pennance, clenching and unclenching her fists, her jaw working. She eventually ground out, "I'll find my own way down." Her feet rattled on the ladder behind him. She paused, perhaps to say something else, maybe a rebuke, but Pennance didn't turn around and after a few moments she carried on her descent.

Pennance rose, went to the edge of the roof, careful to stay back a short distance. Gingerly he leaned over. Half a minute later the door slammed and Simone emerged into the alleyway, yanking on her coat and carrying her bag. She stalked off, not looking around, until she turned onto Clapham High Street and was lost from view. Pennance left the dishes, took himself to bed and sulked.

The following day Simone, who'd occupied a desk opposite Pennance, moved across the office and they avoided each other until just over a week later he came into work and she'd gone, desk cleared. Pennance later found out from a colleague that Simone had taken a temporary transfer to City of London Police. She'd never returned to his house since and, as far as he'd known, Simone and Rasmussen were happy.

More than once he'd sat here and remembered how he'd felt when Simone told him about Rasmussen. As if she'd taken his heart in her soft palm and crushed it like a paper cup. And now it was happening all over again.

Twenty One

Pennance rose at just before 6am and rang Dr Conryn while the kettle boiled.

"How's Simone doing?" he asked when Conryn answered.

"No change, Inspector. She's still unconscious. However, Mr Fonseca suffered a seizure overnight. At this stage, I don't know why. He's going for a brain scan shortly. Between this and the blood sample analysis that's due any moment, I'm hopeful the data will point me in the right direction."

"I'll be popping in on my way to the office."

"I strongly suggest you leave it until at least late morning, inspector. Perhaps even early afternoon. I'll be certain to have the information by then."

"Okay."

"I can hear the reluctance in your voice, but you'll be wasting your time otherwise. I sent your friend away earlier for the same reason."

"Hoskins? He's hardly my friend."

"That's what I'd call someone who sat by a stranger's bed all night, looking out for them, when there was absolutely no need."

"Maybe." Pennance didn't make friends easily.

"Come find me later and I'll tell you the latest," said Conryn. "Provided I'm not slumped in a chair somewhere." She rang off.

Pennance rang Hoskins. The call diverted straight through to voicemail. Hoskins was probably getting his two hours of sleep right now.

While Pennance made himself a coffee his phone vibrated on the work surface. A text from Fulton: 'I'll be at Fonseca's flat later, let me know if you want to be there.' Pennance replied with, 'Yes' and Fulton sent Fonseca's address by return before Pennance took his coffee upstairs to get ready for the day ahead.

***

Clerkenwell Close in Farringdon, just off King's Cross Road, was a collection of terraced Georgian-style houses and new-build commercial properties mixed together, the thoroughfare narrow enough to need a one-way route for traffic along with double yellow lines and no waiting signs throughout.

Farringdon, in the borough of Islington, was an upmarket area which typically attracted a younger demographic than either Pennance or Fulton. Heron Tower was just over 1.5 miles away, while 15A Westminster was only a handful of underground stops south-west and three miles distant.

Fulton was there already, propping up the external brick wall of the house, thumb scrolling down his phone screen. He glanced up at Pennance's approaching footsteps, and slid the mobile into a pocket.

"Where's CSI?" asked Pennance. He'd expected to see a uniform cops and suited up technicians milling around the property.

"I handed the investigation over to the Central West BCU which covers Westminster – remember it's outside of my jurisdiction – their detectives went into Fonseca's flat last night."

"So, what are we doing here now?"

"I called in a favour." Fulton held up a set of keys and jangled them. "I thought we could have our own nosey around." He grinned and Pennance joined in.

Fulton unlocked the front door, held it for Pennance. The narrow hallway contained two bikes, the entrance to a couple of the apartments and a set of stairs. "Fonseca's is the loft flat."

"Of course it is," said Pennance.

Four floors later, Fulton paused on the tiny landing area outside Fonseca's flat. Pennance remained two steps below. Fulton unlocked the door, entered, leaving the way clear for Pennance. He made it no further than a couple of feet inside. Fulton flicked on the light as the curtains were drawn.

"Jesus." Pennance stood, hands on hips, surveying the wreckage in the living room. "It's like a tornado went through here." Chairs had been turned upside down, the fabric sliced with a sharp blade. All the books had been pulled off the shelves and lay spread eagled across the floor. Carpets were yanked up, and a couple of floorboards too.

"This wasn't CSI," said Fulton. "Somebody tossed it before they arrived." Many of the exposed surfaces were covered in a white dust. "Apparently the only fingerprints CSI discovered were Fonseca's." Meaning the intruder came prepared and wore gloves.

"I assume all the rooms are the same?" asked Pennance.

"Take a look for yourself." Fulton waved an arm like a concierge welcoming a guest to a hotel suite.

Pennance wandered the flat, watching where he stepped. The bathroom, kitchen and both bedrooms had been thoroughly searched – mattresses slashed open, exposing stuffing and springs, every drawer stuck out like thick wooden tongues, the contents of each cupboard lay in a jumbled mess directly in front of the doors like the furniture had vomited. The curtains were drawn across every window. Pennance parted the pair in the main bedroom and got a view of a graveyard behind.

When Pennance returned he found Fulton standing in the same spot in the living room. "My contact at CWBCU said she reckoned the search was professional," said Fulton.

Pennance squatted down, picked up a treatise on mathematics, flicked through some of the pages, understood nothing. "What about downstairs, did they hear anything?"

"The residents on the lower floor were at work and didn't return until after 6pm, so we can assume the flat got turned over earlier in the day while they were out."

"Any signs of a forced entry?"

"Some scratches on the lock, meaning it was probably picked, but nothing else."

"I wonder if they found what they were looking for?" asked Pennance.

"Maybe they got it out of Fonseca later in the evening," said Fulton.

Twenty Two

Shoreditch was hipster central in London and exuded a slightly fake down-to-earth vibe. Located in London's East end in the borough of Hackney, Shoreditch, and its next-door neighbour Hoxton, was where the comfortably fashionable set lived.

Originally, the area was known as Soersditch, which translated as sewer's ditch. Centuries ago this had been a marshy, diseased area. Over recent years Shoreditch had transformed into one of the most expensive and sought-after boroughs where once it had ranked among the worst and least desirable; full of squats, run-down pubs and boarded up shops – somewhere not to be after dark unless drugs or prostitution piqued your interest.

Now this was a creative district – Brick Lane, an artist's enclave, sat within the municipality boundary. Throw a partially ripened avocado and the chances of it hitting a guy with a well-trimmed beard were pretty high. There were plenty of specialised bars, boutique and artisanal shops selling handmade goods and enough vegan and vegetarian restaurants to make even the most apprehensive of cows feel welcome.

Even the rare sunny weather was appropriate; so the vintage sunglasses and wide brimmed hat brigade were out in full force. One thing the casual visitor definitely wouldn't find anymore was the sewer's ditch.

Sting, the company employed by Hussle, was located within one of Shoreditch's more well-known landmarks –

four disused underground train carriages. All were painted; colourful murals masked the original dull gunmetal grey, like the rest of Shoreditch – every inch of wall space in the borough was covered in graffiti and murals.

A pair of carriages were located high up on a disused viaduct. The central span had been removed years ago and the coaches placed right at the edge, partially overhanging, so it appeared they might plunge off at any moment. The remaining two were at ground level and bordered by a small garden. Pennance had walked within sight of them several times but never had cause to go inside.

Today was a day for climbing because the one Pennance wanted was on the viaduct. A narrow spiral staircase hulked beside the garden. Pennance wound his way up. He poked his head inside the nearest coach. The usual seats along either side of the interior had been removed and replaced with tables, bolted to the floor, and chairs. It felt like a greenhouse, hot and arid from the sun which beat down onto the metal exterior and blasted through the glass, more suited for growing tomatoes or chillies, rather than as a workspace.

A man occupied a nearby table, laptop open, coffee cup by his elbow. Unsurprisingly, he had a beard – a goatee shaped to a point below the chin, Elizabethan style, and hair in a topknot. He sensibly wore shorts and a t-shirt.

"Excuse me," said Pennance.

The man glanced up absently, his attention clearly elsewhere. "Uh-huh?"

"I'm looking for Mr Mulcahy."

"That's me."

"DI Pennance, we spoke last night."

"Sure, sorry. I was up to my metaphorical elbows in code." Mulcahy stood quickly, banged his head on the low ceiling. "Bloody hell, you'd think I'd know better by now." He rubbed his skull. "Come in." Ducking down, Pennance entered. Even just a few feet inside, the temperature lifted and Pennance shrugged off his jacket. "Take a pew, I'd recommend one in the shade."

"Thanks." Pennance parked himself next to Mulcahy. "Interesting place to work."

"You'd think so, right? Although autumn and winter they're freezing, then spring and summer they're bloody boiling. When it rains it's like sitting inside a snare drum." Mulcahy grinned. "But they're cool, right? There's even the driver's cab with all the gear, if you want to see it?" Mulcahy hiked a thumb over his shoulder. "Kids love it; big and small."

"Maybe next time. I'd prefer to discuss your work for Hussle."

"Sure, however, I'll have to be careful what information I disclose. Metzler called to remind me of the non-disclosure clause in our contract, not that he needed to."

"Let's see how we go, okay?"

"Got to keep the client happy." Mulcahy shrugged.

"What does your company do?" asked Pennance.

Mulcahy settled back into his chair, dropped his hands into his lap. "Electronic data, something you can't touch and can't hold, surpassed oil as the world's most valuable commodity in 2017. I'm sure you appreciate that where there's money there are criminals. So, cybercrime has been expanding exponentially, it's not far off being a $6 trillion business, inspector – as profitable as the global trade in illegal drugs. Yet nobody has to pass through airline security with narcotic filled condoms in their stomach or hide them in shipping containers. All you need is a laptop, internet access, some tools from the dark web and a suitably inventive brain."

"Sounds like a sales pitch," said Pennance.

"It kind of is." Mulcahy held his hands out beside him in a non-apology. "The problem we find is that people only properly think about online security once they've been hit. Somewhat like having your car stolen, *then* fitting a car alarm. That's what we most often do at Sting; come in after the hacker's partied in the client's system, stolen all the booze and backed up the toilets. We sweep up the mess they've left behind and make sure there's no-one hiding in the roof space to pop out later and repeat the whole smash-and-grab. The use of metaphors is deliberate, by the way. It helps clients picture what's happening to them. The vast majority of people haven't a clue what goes on behind the keyboard." Mulcahy double tapped his laptop.

"Which clearly includes me," said Pennance.

"Don't beat yourself up about it." Pennance wasn't. Mulcahy continued, "We set up intrusion detectors, like burglar alarms, watching specific sections of a clients' system, like where the data is stored. If a hacker sets off the trip wire then we step in. Ideally a company should have their own response team, but some are so small they can't; so Sting does so on their behalf.

"There's just three of us here. We work remotely. There's no need to be together in the same space or go to the client for anything other than the first introductory meeting.

Everything else we do is online, which means we're unobtrusive; and that's particularly important to some of our clients. Typically, companies don't want their customers to know they've been hit. It creates doubt in people's minds about the rest of the business.

"We're very specific about the product we offer. Much larger competitors than us provide all round security, however we can be extremely responsive and flexible. We run a relatively select client list, which means we keep an eye on them all for any breaches."

"I was at Hussle when you called."

"There you go." Mulcahy wagged a finger, like Pennance had made his point for him. "On average companies take nearly 200 days to even identify a data breach, then half as much time again to fix the problem. Recently, the American government accidentally fell over evidence of a Russian attack that had been going on for *months*. Trojan software had found its way into all kinds of agencies."

"I assume that's like the Trojan Horse fable? Looks innocent from the outside, but there's a nasty gift hidden away inside?"

"It's just one of the tactics hackers use. We're hackers ourselves, obviously." Pennance always found it puzzling (and annoying) when people declared something obvious when it only was to them. "White hats, that is. On the side, not part of the day job."

"I don't understand," said Pennance.

"Sorry, awful habit of mine." Mulcahy grinned sheepishly. "In movies the bad guys wear black and the good guys don white, right? Like the Devil and God. So, a black hat is a hacker who operates with malicious intent – to damage systems or steal money. A white hat, like me, uses their skills to damage an organisation, but only theoretically. We look for vulnerabilities in systems under the client's direction and make proposals. We function more in teams."

"So grey hats are something in between?"

"They too look for system issues, but don't cause malicious damage. They're not doing so at the invitation of the organisation, though, and also tend to operate individually."

"They're like whistle blowers, then?"

"That's a good way of describing them." Mulcahy nodded. "My colleagues and I liaise with other white hats around the world to track down cyber criminals."

"Do these people ever get caught?"

"It's extremely difficult to track them down, but not impossible if you're talented." Mulcahy smirked. "Most decent hackers are capable of hiding their identities by faking their web address, using self-erasing code, operating through Virtual Private Networks or even routing their attacks via the computers of innocent victims. As a result, even finding the country location of a hacker can be tough.

"However, just like police, cyber-investigators use past hacks to build up knowledge, comparing the specifics of the crime, the M.O. and so on. Hackers use custom designed code to access systems and that code has a style about it, like an author's voice in a novel. Over time we can attribute attacks to a specific hacker. And as we white hats operate in a community, the information we share is huge. There may only be three of us in Sting, but we have the advantage of social scale."

"Is the hacker typically just one person?"

"Often, yes. However, there are certain sponsor governments around the world – Russia, North Korea and China in particular. An example is the Russian attack on the 2016 Presidential election, which was coordinated across multiple platforms and incorporated artful social engineering. The Russians were playing with the American consciousness to cause massive change. Individuals just aren't capable of that."

"Mr Neumann told me the Hussle hit was initially negative information posted online."

"That's right. SEO optimisation is another service we offer, also a post-attack provision. Most of the comments appeared to come from the wider financial community about Hussle's ability to manage client's money and keep it safe. We buried them in an avalanche of positive news, and we had some sites remove statements or articles which were clearly speculation."

"You can do that?"

"Sure, depending on how far the client wants to go to. Take a restaurant who suffers a deluge of one-star ratings and negative statements. Their trade can be impacted really quickly. They could even be forced to close down. Several of the review sites refuse to remove the most obvious of fakes, even ones that clearly breach their policies, unless someone like Hussle goes to an official body and obliges a change."

"And then came the actual hack."

"Right, the critical comments were possibly unrelated. The hackers accessed Hussle's system via a zero day, that's a previously unknown software weakness. It was actually through Mr Carnegie's WhatsApp account. They inserted some ransomware which subsequently spread through their system, locking them out of certain key areas."

"Like a virus?"

"Absolutely, Inspector. To take the parallel one step further, Sting's objective is to find the source and wipe out an infection before it becomes a pandemic and the company is so paralysed it shuts down."

"It sounds like a complex role, Mr Mulcahy."

"There's always more work for us than we can possibly undertake. $6 trillion segment, remember."

"If companies protected themselves better, you'd be out of a job."

"For sure. But as I said, most people don't know what truly goes on behind their laptop and Hussle was one of them."

"Mr Neumann told me that Hussle chose to pay the ransom to recover their data."

"Correct. Carnegie was relatively calm at first. He told me that the majority of their assets, stocks and shares, fund wrappers and so on, weren't traded very often – maybe once a quarter during a rebalance, or when a new client joined or an existing client wanted to move funds. So he was happy to hold tight. He reckoned he could fudge his way through while we worked to regain access to his data. But that didn't last long. Within a couple of days Neumann was on my case telling me Carnegie was underestimating the challenge they faced because of several higher risk investments."

"Blockchain technology, right?"

"Right again." Mulcahy nodded, eyebrows raised. "As a guy working in the industry, I'd personally stay well away from products like that. The blockchain network itself is next to impossible to penetrate, but there have been instances of digital wallets — that's where the owner stores the bitcoin — being accessed by outside agents. And there are risks inherent in the actual trading process, too."

"Such as?"

"I assume you feel safe having your wages paid into a bank?"

"Of course."

"Why?"

Pennance thought for a moment. "Because I trust them."

"And that's the key: validation. The banking sector has been around for hundreds of years. It's relatively well structured and there are laws and rules which affect how and where money is transferred. Cryptocurrency, though, is a completely different matter. It's a huge disruptor. The existing cash transfer processes are gone – anyone can move bitcoin or trade, there's no legal oversight or governing body. Hell, there isn't even any real legislation in place!

"Think of it like Facebook. Thirty odd years ago it was set-up to be a site for social contact within a US college. These days' critics argue it's effectively an unregulated news site – Facebook competes with the BBC, or CNN, or the Murdoch empire in how a consumer gets their information, right? Yet, unlike the news corporations, there are very few, if any, methods of holding Facebook accountable. That's where we are with cryptocurrency. It's a gold rush – a few people will make lots of money, the majority will get very badly burned. Bitcoin has suffered some pretty wild swings in price. Back in the early days – 2015 – Bitcoin cost maybe £200. Now it's over £40,000."

"*Each?*"

"That's right. Some days it can rise or drop in value to the tune of thousands. And that was Hussle's problem. A couple of days into the intrusion there was some turmoil in the cryptocurrency market."

"The price went down?"

"Just the opposite. Up, and fast. A well-known tech entrepreneur made a big purchase and the value skyrocketed."

"Surely that was okay?"

"Ordinarily, but Neumann wanted to crystallise those gains and sell before the value sank. He then planned to buy back in later. He was chafing, big time. So, he went against my advice and told Carnegie to pay the ransom."

"How did you feel about that?"

"My emotions are irrelevant. Ultimately, the client can choose to do as they wish. As Neumann got his data back, he believed he was vindicated in making the decision. Though, I reckon it was more than the financial cost affecting Carnegie's thinking and why Carnegie blinked."

"How so?"

"Carnegie had a reputation as a solid pair of hands, right? I wouldn't be surprised if being locked out of his own business would have been extremely embarrassing."

Pennance thought about that for a moment. It made sense. He recalled what Neumann had said yesterday about markets being based on sentiment, not reality. "Are you aware of other businesses having been hit in a similar fashion to Hussle? Before or after?"

"There's no question, inspector. There are 2,200 individual frauds *every day* in the UK. I've been working with my colleagues to track down who struck Hussle. It's a work in progress."

"Would you be able to give me a list?"

"As I mentioned already, the majority of victims try to keep attacks out of the public eye; they simply don't want the negative publicity so this kind of information needs to be kept confidential."

"I think I can manage that." Pennance handed Mulcahy his business card.

Mulcahy focused on his laptop, fingers tapping on keys. "The details are on the way to you," he said.

"Thanks," said Pennance. "And if you make any progress on determining the source of the Hussle hack you'll let me know?"

"You can count on me, Inspector. And, when you stand," grinned Mulcahy, "Duck."

Pennance took Mulcahy's advice and avoided banging his head on the low ceiling. He was halfway down the narrow spiral stairs when Mulcahy's note hit his inbox. At the bottom Pennance made a call. "Vance, its Jonah. I need a favour."

Hoskins' sigh was audible all the way from the NCA.

Twenty Three

Hoskins was at his desk, eating as usual, when Pennance entered his office at the NCA in the late morning.

"Hey, Vance," said Pennance. "I just wanted to say thanks for being with Simone yesterday."

"Sorry I couldn't stay through the night, Conryn wouldn't have it." Hoskins kept his attention on the monitor. "And it's no problem, I can tell she's important to you."

"She's a good friend."

Hoskins's eyes flicked briefly at Pennance then back to his screen. "Sure." A slight smile flickered across his lips.

"Next time I go to the café I'll get you your food of choice."

"Now you're talking." Hoskins' smile morphed into a wide grin. "By the way, someone's been keen to get hold of you. And not Meacham." He pointed with the mangled end of a baguette at a note on Pennance's desk. "A guy named Hicks. Left several messages. Sounded like an old duffer."

"Never heard of him," said Pennance.

Hoskins shrugged and returned his attention to his monitor. He shoved the baguette into his mouth and tore off another strip, chewed like a wildebeest. "Anyway, a couple of things. First, I've gone over that inventory of hacks that white hat bloke sent and then you dumped on me."

"Mulcahy at Sting?"

"Him. I've got the list up here." Hoskins nudged his chin at the left hand of his three monitors. "Then I've been looking through each of the websites to understand their business type." The internet browser was open on the central screen. "And I'm collating any relevant information in a searchable database." On Hoskins's third screen. "I'm also cross-referencing with HOLMES to determine if there have been any police investigations. So far, with surprisingly few hits." HOLMES, the Home Office Large Major Enquiry System, was a piece of software, custom-built for the police, originally introduced in the mid-1980s, designed to support investigations. All case data developed by the otherwise independently operating police forces around the UK was loaded onto HOLMES, allowing an investigating officer to search existing data and potentially develop new lines of enquiry.

"Mulcahy did say the majority of businesses wouldn't be keen on having the negative publicity." Pennance shrugged. "It seems the companies root out the malware, then boost their protection and hope it never happens again."

"Arse backwards," said Hoskins. Pennance didn't have a suitable counter argument. Hoskins continued, "At the moment I can't find a clear overlap. They're engaged in all kinds of sectors. Some are agricultural, some financial, others are charities. I'll keep going, hopefully I'll be able to group them at some point."

"Alright."

"However, I've had a lot more success digging into 15A Whitehall. I spoke to a friend, it doesn't matter who, about the companies registered there. So, I assume you've heard of offshore tax havens, like The Caymans and Bermuda?"

"Sure."

"What about Britain?"

"Seriously?"

"I didn't realise you were so naïve, Jonah. Of course, Britain. Our country is a vast facilitator of corporate money laundering. That's the process where dirty cash is washed."

"I know what money laundering is, Vance."

"You could set up your own cleaning business from the comfort of your armchair and, if you did it right, with very little chance of getting caught."

"I don't believe it," said Pennance.

"Then settle down, Inspector. You're about to get a lesson. Say you want to commit a fraud, the first thing you need is a bank account. But it can't be one with your name on it, otherwise authorities like us come knocking on your door. The way around that problem is to have an organisation owning the bank account. Since a law change in 2011 it's easy to open up a new company in the UK – for a small fee, online, and in just a matter of minutes from anywhere in the world."

"There must be information recorded on the application forms?"

"Of course. Each company has to have one Person of Significant Control listed. But my friend told me nobody checks. Ever. You can literally make up any name you like, Daffy Duck or James Bond or Jonah Pennance, and no-one at Companies House reads it. A fraud group carried out an analysis of PSCs a few years ago and they found 4,000 people registered under two years of age. Some birth dates showed the PSC hadn't even been born when the company was created. All because Companies House don't look. Management there has actually gone into writing saying they won't do so."

"But that's against the law."

"Agreed. However, only one person has ever been prosecuted for creating a false identity at Companies House. Guy by the name of Kevin Brewer, a businessman in Warwickshire, who deliberately set up a fake company and told the government he'd done it to demonstrate how easy fraud would be. They ignored him so a few years later he set up a second bogus company and told the government yet again. This time the government prosecuted him. Brewer was found guilty and fined."

"He's a whistle-blower," said Pennance.

"Right, and he got punished for it."

"Why? What's in it for the UK?"

"Profit." Hoskins shrugged. "Billions, maybe trillions, of pounds of fraudulent money flow through the UK every year, all handled by banks and institutions based here. That generates cash for the banks who employ people – they and the banks pay taxes to the government." Hoskins shook his head. "The smart fraudsters lie, but lie cleverly. They steal an actual person's identity and register that as the PSC. Each year they submit legal-looking financial accounts, completely fabricated of course, but that's not the point. They put the name of an existing accountant down as the auditor, although that never happened. Finally, they use a rented service office as an address – like 15A Whitehall. Owners hide their identities behind UK registered corporate structures all the time."

"Jesus," said Pennance.

"And that's precisely the problem with Blackthorn. The company is listed here, but owned by a company in the British Virgin Islands. The only aspect I can determine on Blackthorn's business is their function – 'corporate services'. Which could mean anything, frankly."

"So it's a dead end?"

"Unless you can get the UK government involved, there's no way to find out who really holds the shares, yes."

Pennance ran a hand over his face. "What about Simone's mobile?"

"Nothing yet, I'll likely ask McAleney to help me."

"Can you trust her?"

"Of course."

"Whatever you think, Vance. And thanks."

"No problem, I'll keep going."

Pennance sat back for a few moments, before regressing to familiarity – email. He fired up his laptop and found several unread notes awaiting his attention. Two caught his eye. The first came from Proudfoot. He'd sent the analytical reports on Carnegie and Thewlis' blood work. Proudfoot had also summarised a conclusion in the note: high levels of carbon dioxide, red blood cells and lactic acid, as he'd expected, and further conclusive evidence of the men being asphyxiated.

The other missive was from the Crime Scene Manager, Gough, containing another analysis, this time into the liquid found in the plastic bottle at the factory crime scene. The note was only a few paragraphs long and didn't take much reading. Pennance picked up the phone and rang Gough on the number in the footer.

"This is DI Pennance, I just read your report. The liquid was normal old London tap water with common garden salt mixed in."

"But in an extremely high concentration," said Gough. "I don't know how anyone could stomach it."

"Simone threw up."

"I'm not surprised," said Gough.

"Fonseca didn't vomit, though."

"Maybe he wasn't capable of doing so."

"Wouldn't the body act subconsciously? Try and rid itself of a poison?"

"I don't know, you'd need to ask a doctor."

Pennance thought of Conryn. "I'll do that."

"I'm just writing up the fingerprint evidence found at the address," said Gough. "You're not going to like it." She paused briefly. "I found the same set of patterns. They belong to Simone."

Pennance dry swallowed. "You're sure?"

"Absolutely. They were very clear and I got a hit almost immediately. I ran the tests three times, just to be certain. She held the bottles in both hands about halfway down. As if she poured the liquid into Fonseca's mouth and then her own. Like a murder-suicide. I'll email my conclusions out in a few minutes."

"Is there any chance you could hold the report? Just for twenty four hours?"

"Not a chance," said Gough. "I'd get into deep shit. There's eyes all over this investigation. Sorry, Jonah."

"I understand." Pennance put the phone down, leaned back in his chair and thought through what he'd just heard.

The facts didn't fit at all with what he knew of Simone. She wasn't a killer. Or someone who'd contemplate suicide, either.

Hoskins was peering at Pennance closely. "You look like someone pissed on your chips."

"I'm just worried about Simone, is all."

"Right." From Hoskins' tone it was clear he didn't believe him. Pennance's phone rang. He picked up the handset. "That'll be Hicks again, I bet."

"DI Pennance."

"Ah, the elusive inspector! I'm Doctor Hicks."

"Are you calling from the hospital?"

"No, should I be?" Hicks sounded confused. "I'm nothing to do with the medical profession, I'm a historian." Hicks dissolved into a coughing fit. Pennance moved the phone away from his ear.

"Is it him?" asked Hoskins. "Sounds like he's dying, right?"

Pennance nodded, listened again but Hicks was still coughing. Moments later he was back. "I think I can help you, Inspector. I've seen all the stuff in the papers about the two deaths. They had bread in their mouths, I understand?"

"I can't confirm anything the press may have printed, Dr Hicks."

"What about salt?"

"Excuse me?"

"Did you find salt on either of the corpses?"

"Not on them, no."

"What about somebody else connected to the victims?"

"Is there a significance to all of this, Dr Hicks?"

"Have you ever heard of sin eating?"

***

Hicks had suggested they meet in a pub called the Lamb and Flag, the other side of Covent Garden to Pennance's bookshop, a shopping and entertainment hub in the West End popular with tourists and Londoners alike, situated near to Leicester Square underground station. The pub was hidden away down a constricted flagstone alley barely wide enough for one person, off a narrow, cobbled street that connected Floral Street and Garrick Street – the latter one of six roads which all intersected at Covent Garden itself.

Pennance had never previously been inside and he paused to glance around, silhouetted in the entrance. The lighting was low, not helped by the ample amount of dark wood – stripped floorboards, a panelled bar which dominated one length of the pub, and more sections on the walls above which was plenty of brass paraphernalia and framed pictures. A multitude of closely packed tables and chairs, organised cheek by jowl, made the interior feel tight. He imagined this would be a noisy place on a busy evening after work.

Hicks was easy to spot, particularly as the pub had only just opened and hardly anyone was seated. Hicks had described himself to Pennance on the phone and he'd been accurate. "Large of belly and wealthy of hair," boomed Hicks down the phone. And Pennance couldn't miss Hicks' bright red jacket, which looked like an old army uniform. Pennance let the door shut behind him and made his way over to the doctor perched on a high stool pushed up against a wall.

The historian rose when Pennance reached him; Hicks had insisted Pennance describe his own looks, something he'd not found easy. In the end he'd simply just said, 'Tall'. Hicks put out a liver-spotted hand as dry as parchment in Pennance's grip. Hicks said, "Bloody hell, you weren't exaggerating, were you, inspector? Do you play basketball?"

"Too short."

Hicks release his grip, used the same hand to wave at the bar then patted an empty stool beside him. "Saved you a seat. It can get rammed in here as lunchtime approaches. Like being on the tube, but with booze." Hicks nursed a pint of something dark, almost black, the pint glass sitting on a narrow shelf fixed to the wall at a height where Hicks just had to stretch out an arm. "They know me here." Hicks tapped the side of his nose. "So, I get special treatment."

"Your local?" asked Pennance.

"One of them, sure." Hicks laughed. "I prefer not to be tied down to a single location. Like my women. When there's such choice there's no need to get stuck with a solitary example. And I tend to wear out my welcome. My three ex-wives could tell you that." Hicks chuckled, deep from the belly.

"Here you go." A barmaid put down a pint which appeared identical to Hicks'. There was a second for the historian, too.

"Thanks, Ruth. I'll settle up my tab before I go."

"Roger said you weren't getting out of that door until you do," said Ruth, "Or he'd break your other arm."

DEAD MONEY

Hicks chuckled again, pointed at Pennance, said, "My friend here is a cop."

"And I'm an international jewel thief." Then Ruth was stalking back to the bar.

"Roger is the landlord," said Hicks. "I got you a plum porter – a very strong, very dark and entirely traditional British beer. None of that bloody lager."

"I'm on duty, Dr Hicks," said Pennance.

"I won't tell anyone if you don't." Hicks tapped the side of his nose, lifted his pint, had a long draft. "Good stuff, that." He put the glass back down. "Did you know this place used to be known as the Bucket of Blood?"

"I didn't."

"In the 19th Century the landlord at the time used to hold bare knuckle fights in the back bar. It wouldn't surprise me if Roger looked after the place back then, too. Old bastard. The pub sign, if you noticed, is a lamb bearing a holy cross. Are you aware what that means?

"I've no idea." Pennance took a sip of the beer. It was like drinking slightly sweet and fruity cold tar.

"The Knights Templar, the crusading military order. They still exist, you know, hidden away in society."

"I read the book," said Pennance.

"Dan Brown? That's just fiction, I'm speaking truth. Charles Dickens used to frequent here too. And the alley you came down – the lyricist John Dryden was attacked there by soldiers sent by Charles the Second after Dryden penned a satirical verse about Charles' mistress." Hicks paused briefly. "I can see I'm losing you. My field is social history in the urban environment. I lecture History and Sociology at The

University of Westminster and I teach modules with The Open University. My point is I believe that as an historian it's important to live your subject, so I regularly walk London's streets, seeking out antiquity. It helps me imagine how life must have been and then reflect that to my students. And if part of that past happens to be in a pub, it's a happy coincidence!"

"You mentioned sin eating on the phone. I've never heard of it."

"You're right, Inspector. Let's stick to the subject at hand." Hicks supped some more of his pint before shifting on his stool. "Sin eating is a very old tradition, one that died out in the UK in 1906 with the last practitioner, one Richard Munslow. He's buried in Ratlinghope, near Shrewsbury. I went to his grave once.

"Hundreds of years ago practically every village and town had their own resident sin eater. They were always men and employed by the family of the recently passed. The sin eater would enter the house where the corpse rested, place a piece of bread and a small pile of salt on the corpse's chest and leave before returning the following day. It was believed that the bread and salt soaked up the deceased's iniquities overnight. The sin eater consumed the now contaminated foodstuffs, thus allowing the dead to go to the afterlife free of wickedness."

"So, the sin eater comes to possess the person's immorality?" asked Pennance.

"That's right. It's important to remember this was a transactional process – the sin eaters were paid for their efforts. Sin eaters were usually life's outcasts already, finding work for people like that was quite difficult. They had to take whatever employment they could. Absorbing so many sins meant they were generally shunned by their pious neighbours. A real catch-22. It would have been a hard life, I suspect."

Pennance thought of Thewlis, doing what he could to make ends meet. He said, "Did the bodies effectively lie in state?" Carnegie, Thewlis and Fonseca had all lain on their backs, arms crossed. Only Simone had not.

"Yes." Hicks nodded. "This was in the time before funeral parlours were accessible to anyone but the super-rich." Pennance took the merest sip of his pint instead. His second try did nothing to improve his lowly impression of it. Hicks asked, "The bread was in the mouth, I understand? And what about the salt?"

"I can't really comment."

Hicks thought for a moment. "Okay, I'll assume the additional victims consumed the salt somehow, and give you three scenarios for you to select which you think fits best. First," Hicks flicked a thumb up from a fist, "the bread and salt lay on the victim's chest, even for a short period before it was consumed."

"Which would mean the victim was eating his own sin," said Pennance.

Hicks nodded. "Second." Hicks' index finger joined the thumb. "The bread or salt lay on the killer's chest for a period before the victim consumed it."

"The victim soaks up the killer's sin."

"And finally." Up popped Hicks' middle finger. "The bread and salt just went straight into our victims." Hicks lowered his hand.

"No sins absorbed," said Pennance. "There's a fourth scenario, doctor. The bread and salt lay on the chest of one of the other victims first."

"Therefore the sins of one person are being passed to another." Hicks nodded.

Pennance leaned on the shelf, rested his cheek on a fist while he considered each of the options.

"Are you going to drink that?" Hicks pointed at Pennance's barely touched pint.

"Feel free."

Hicks pulled the beer towards him. The glass was half empty by the time Pennance spoke again. "None of it makes complete sense."

"Why?" Hicks rotated on his stool to face Pennance, pressed his hands together in his lap, like he was Pennance's tutor.

"As you describe it, sin eaters absorb other people's evils as their own, making them outcasts. Only the most desperate of people choose this kind of life."

"I said that, yes."

"The victim absorbing their own sin appears pointless because nothing changes. Likewise if the bread and salt simply went straight into the victim – no sin absolved. If the victims were absorbing the killer's sin then the deceased becomes the pariah."

"And cleansing the murderer in the process," said Hicks.

Pennance recalled what Gough had told him; that Simone appeared to have poured the salty water into Fonseca's mouth before her own. "It still doesn't quite fit." Pennance ran fingers though his hair.

"Then there's a fifth option." Hicks eyed Pennance. "That all this is smoke and mirrors, a blind to throw you off, waste your time. Have you heard of Laplace's demon?"

"No, but I guess I'm about to."

"I am a lecturer, after all." Hicks opened his arms and bore a grin almost as wide. "More and more philosophers and thinkers are suggesting that free will, that we choose our own path in life, is a myth – a valuable tool in history for leaders to motivate their people to die on their behalf to fight one's enemies. One of my colleagues at the university is a neuroscientist. He's been mapping physical brain activities for some years. His analysis shows our 'free choice,'" Hicks made air quotes, "originates in our brains from milliseconds to ten seconds before we're actually aware of them. The moment of supposed selection was caused by what happened previously, from the neuron pattern in your brain, back to your parents meeting, their parents and all the way to The Big Bang. In other words, I didn't pick your beer, it was predetermined."

"And Laplace?"

"A little more history – Pierre-Simon Laplace was a French polymath who asked in 1814 how there could be free will in a world which moves forward like a clock. His demon was a super-being able to predict the future because he knew the past."

"What does all of this mean, Doctor Hicks?"

"To you, as a lawman, a huge amount. If there were no free will and everyone is a puppet then nobody could be truly responsible for their actions, which means no police to investigate cases, no courts to find anyone guilty with no rules to break. Hate disappears, love evaporates because neither actually exists. In other words, we have total anarchy."

"This is all fascinating, but I struggle to see what bearing it has."

"I'm trying to say that the logic of free will is as cold as it is inevitable. The crime you are investigating right now is caused by prior events and so on in an unbroken chain according to the laws of nature. So, determine these causes and you find your criminal."

Pennance's phone rang before he could answer the doctor and Pennance took his chance. "Excuse me, Dr Hicks. I've got to take this."

Pennance headed quickly into the alley and answered. However, the signal was poor and Pennance could only pick up every third word. "Hang on a second," said Pennance. He went onto Floral Street.

"Is that better?" asked Conryn.

"I can hear you fine now," said Pennance.

"I'm calling to let you know that Miss Smithson is conscious."

"That's great news."

"And I looked into what you asked, inspector. Whether either patient had marks in their skin above the heart. Fonseca has them, Sergeant Smithson does not."

"You're sure?"

"Absolutely. I checked myself."

Pennance disconnected, his head spinning. He had to lean against a wall to keep himself upright.

Fonseca, like Carnegie and Thewlis, had been tasered and therefore incapacitated. But not Simone...

Twenty Four

When Pennance arrived at University College Hospital, Pruitt, the uniform cop, was on duty again outside Simone's door. Pruitt nodded at Pennance in recognition.

Pennance called Conryn, but it rang out before she answered and leaving a voicemail wasn't an option.

"Have you seen Dr Conryn recently?" asked Pennance.

"Not for at least fifteen minutes, sir," replied Pruitt. "The husband has been here regularly."

"Ex-husband," said Pennance. "Simone and Rasmussen are divorced."

Pruitt shrugged. "I get why."

"Has Rasmussen spent time in her room?"

"He was with her when she awoke, sir."

"Where is Rasmussen now?"

"I don't know, he left earlier without a word. I suspect he doesn't like me." Pruitt's flat expression told Pennance he couldn't care less either way.

"I'm going to see how she is for myself."

"Whatever you want, sir."

Pennance softly turned the handle, opened the door halfway.

Simone was propped up in bed, a drip still connected to her arm. "I thought I heard your voice outside." Briefly she stared straight at Pennance before shaking her head and turning away to face the wall. "You can't be here." Simone's voice was different, deeper and harsher than usual. Like she'd been smoking a pack of cigarettes a day for years.

Pennance moved around the bed yet still Simone avoided his eyes. "Why?" Simone didn't answer. "It's Lars, isn't it?" Simone's eyes flickered towards Pennance, then away again. "I know I've not been here, but I've been working, trying to find out who attacked you."

"There's nothing you can do, Jonah. It's best you stay away. Natalie..." Simone stopped mid-sentence, frozen. Then her head jerked, and her arms straightened like her limbs had become branches.

"Simone?" Pennance had no idea what was going on.

Simone had gone totally rigid, her neck muscles straining, hands balled into tight fists and her teeth bared. Then she began to jerk and thrash, legs and arms kicking wildly. The drip stand hit the floor with a clatter. She was having a seizure.

Pennance tried to hold her down as Simone bucked and writhed. "Help!" shouted Pennance. "Somebody help!"

Pruitt burst in, took a second to assess what was happening and ran over. He slammed a palm into a red button on a panel near Pennance's head. An alarm began to blare outside in the corridor. Pruitt got his hands on Simone and between them they did as much as they could to hold Simone down.

Within seconds several nurses arrived and suddenly the room was filled with people and calm but hurried activity. "Out of the way." A nurse pulled Pennance's shoulder. "We can help, so move." Pennance shook her off.

"Sir," said Pruitt. "Let them work."

Reluctantly, stepped back and the nurses attended to Simone. A second nurse got between Pennance and the bed. "You need to leave the room, please." A polite yet firm order with no possibility of doubt. Pennance slowly backed away as a nurse filled a syringe from a vial with a clear liquid. Then Pennance and Pruitt were in the corridor and the door closed. Pennance leant against a wall and sank to the floor.

"Jesus," said Pruitt, rubbing his forehead with a hand. "That was crap."

"Thanks," said Pennance. "Quick thinking to hit the alarm." His hands were shaking and they wouldn't stop so he crossed his arms over his chest.

"Just seemed the obvious thing to do."

Conryn arrived, trotting down the corridor. She glanced at Pennance before entering Simone's room without a word. Pennance got a brief glimpse of Simone through a gap between the nurses. She was lying flat now, no convulsions, as if all the wind had been knocked out of her.

The nearby double doors burst open. Rasmussen came storming through. "What the hell is going on? How is Simone?"

"She's had a seizure." Pennance pushed himself to his feet. "She's being stabilised right now."

"This is your fault." Rasmussen got in Pennance's face, close enough that Rasmussen's halitosis washed over him, and jabbed a finger hard into his chest. "You caused this."

Pennance didn't have the strength to raise his arms, to defend himself. Maybe Rasmussen was right.

Pruitt, however, had different ideas. "Sir, step back," he said.

"You should have just stayed away." Rasmussen ignored Pruitt. "You only want to keep us apart, so you can slither back into her affections like the worm you are."

"Sir," said Pruitt.

"I'm investigating," said Pennance. "That's all I'm doing."

"Bullshit." Rasmussen snorted. "Before all this happened, Simone was going to tell you to back off. You might think you're untouchable, but I know people who couldn't give a shit that you're a cop. So, this is me *telling* you."

"Sir," warned Pruitt. "I'm asking you one more time to step away from my colleague and withdraw your threats."

Ignoring Pruitt, Rasmussen jabbed with his finger again, hard into Pennance's ribs. "Back the fuck away, Pennance. Permanently."

"Right, that's it." Pruitt grabbed hold of Rasmussen's prodding digit and spun him around before he could react. Rasmussen stretched out a high-pitched shriek as the cop twisted his arm up his spine and started to read him his Miranda Rights while he expertly multi-tasked, unhooking a pair of handcuffs from his utility belt.

"Wait, PC Pruitt," said Pennance when Pruitt had one of the cuffs ratcheted around Rasmussen wrist.

"Sir?" Pruitt glanced over his shoulder. Rasmussen grimaced, teeth bared like he was in real pain. Pennance struggled to have any sympathy for the man.

"Let him go."

"Sir, he assaulted you."

"I'm aware of that." Pennance sighed. "Just get him the hell out of here."

Pruitt paused briefly, giving Pennance one sharp nod of acceptance before propelling Rasmussen forward and through the double doors. Rasmussen looked over his shoulder; lips squeezed together and his neck muscles as tight and prominent as a rope cord before the doors flapped shut.

Pennance leant against the wall outside Simone's room. He clenched his fists several times and forced his breathing under control by taking in a lungful of air, holding it briefly and slowly releasing. The spot where Rasmussen had dug him in the ribs tingled.

Within a few minutes Pruitt was back. "I kicked him out of the hospital and sent him home."

"Good," said Pennance.

"Personally, sir I'd have chucked him in a cell for a few hours. That'd have sorted the arrogant sod out; always does."

"Maybe, but I felt it was better to defuse the situation."

"Unfortunately that didn't work, sir, considering some of the things he said to me once he was outside. He's an entitled..." Pruitt stamped down on what would have obviously been a swear word.

"He'll get over it." Recalling Rasmussen's final glance, Pennance didn't believe his own words.

Then the door to Simone's room opened and one by one the nurses filed out until, right at the rear, Conryn emerged. "We've managed to stabilise her." Conryn's face was flushed, like she'd just run fast round the block.

"What caused the seizure?" asked Pennance.

"At this stage, I don't know." She scratched her scalp with her nails.

"What about Fonseca?"

"He's still in a coma. Look, let's talk about all that in my office rather than here. No offence." Conryn directed this final comment towards Pruitt.

"None taken." Pruitt raised both hands, palms out. "I'll keep an eye on the patient. And, sir," Pruitt fixed Pennance with a firm look. "If Rasmussen returns and makes the slightest fuss then I *will* be taking him down the station."

"Fine by me," said Pennance.

"This way." Conryn led Pennance along the corridor, through several doors and down a set of stairs until she shouldered her way into a room containing a desk, a couple of chairs and a sofa. Pennance eyed the blanket bunched at one end, and a squashed cushion at the other.

"I was sleeping when the alarm came in for Simone," said Conryn. "Sometimes it's just easier than going home." She pointed to a chair opposite her desk.

"No need to explain yourself, doctor." Pennance sat.

Conryn lowered herself into her seat, then pulled over a blue coloured folder lying on her desk and flipped it open, revealing a document with close-typed words which Pennance couldn't read from where he was positioned. "These are the blood tests results on Miss Smithson and Mr Fonseca," she said, tapping the paper. "*Metoclopramide* was found in both of them. The concentration was about 20% higher in Fonseca. *Metoclopramide* is an anti-sickness drug usually prescribed following radio or chemotherapy treatment for cancer," explained Conryn before Pennance could ask. "It can be obtained by prescription or bought over the counter and comes in tablet or liquid form. One of the drugs' side effects is drowsiness."

"Simone was sick, though."

"The amount of *Metoclopramide* in her body was lower. She'd have had less of a tolerance for the salt. Her vomiting would have reduced the poison in her system and more than likely saved her life."

"What about the seizure?"

"That could be a side-effect from the saline ingestion. I've booked her in for a brain scan at the earliest opportunity. We should be able to determine any injury she's sustained and determine the next course of action."

"That's good."

"Not really, Inspector. Frankly, I should have organised the examination yesterday. If I had, I might have been able to avoid Miss Smithson having that convulsion." Conryn closed Simone's folder, huffed some air through pursed lips. Pennance suspected there would be nothing he could say to make Conryn feel better, probably just the opposite, so he stayed quiet. Conryn continued, "Mr Fonseca, however, is in a far, far worse state than your friend." She moved Simone's folder to one side, revealing another of the same colour beneath. "As a result of the salt, Mr Fonseca's brain swelled up and pressed against the skull." She revealed a monochrome image of what looked to be a walnut inside its shell. "See here and here." Conryn placed the tip of her finger over two spots where there was a lot of white. "Mr Fonseca suffered intracerebral haemorrhage, a bleed on the brain, and significant loss of right parietal brain parenchyma – that's the functional brain tissue brain made up of neurons and glial cells."

"I've never heard of glial cells," said Pennance. "Neurons are associated with thought, right?"

"More like subconscious action, such as receiving sensory input from the outside world, sending commands to our muscles and so on. Fundamentally, damage to this section of the brain means a loss of cognitive ability as a minimum. I haven't given up, but if Mr Fonseca survives he could have a rather limited quality of life." Conryn slapped the folder closed. "I've determined that both Miss Smithson and Mr Fonseca suffered *hypernatremia*, a single, massive exposure over a short period of time to sodium chloride. In other words, salt toxicity or poisoning. It's very rare because the body tends to reject salt. I've never come across it before and neither have any of my colleagues, which is why we've taken so long to get the root cause. The few cases on record tended to result from the victim's steady consumption of sodium chloride over a long period of time.

"With *hypernatremia* the cells shrink as fluid is drawn out by osmosis. This is particularly problematic as about two thirds of all the water in your body is found in cells and the brain is particularly at risk. This movement of fluid can cause a shearing force which results in a haemorrhage. To correct the imbalance, the brain cells pump in electrolytes and endogenous osmolytes, which brings brain volume back to roughly normal within a couple of days.

"However, a massive salt ingestion over a very short period is very different because this causes the plasma sodium concentration to escalate in minutes, reaching a peak in hours. So everything I just described happens very quickly and the brain can't adjust fast enough before it is damaged. Four tablespoons of salt is sufficient to be lethal."

"Four, that's all?"

"Try ingesting even one tablespoon."

"I'll pass, thanks."

"Seizures are known to be a side effect of salt poisoning, which is why I'm so annoyed with myself."

"When did you get the analysis back?" asked Pennance.

"I read it just before I fell asleep."

"Then you wouldn't have done anything more."

"Maybe." Conryn didn't sound convinced. "There are AEDs – anti-epileptic drugs – I could use to treat Miss Smithson, but their application in patients who aren't actually epileptic is controversial." Conryn was talking to herself now, like she was figuring out Simone's next treatment. Then she shook herself. "Anyway, Miss Smithson and Mr Fonseca are both having their plasma sodium levels rebalanced by a hypotonic intravenous fluid. That should bring Miss Smithson out of any danger of risk to life. Longer term she may suffer kidney problems and possibly oliguria; that's passing less urine than normal. I just don't know yet." Conryn yawned. "Sorry."

"I'll let you get some more sleep." Pennance stood.

"I can't yet." Conryn picked up her desk phone. "I need to ensure Miss Smithson's brain scan is prioritised. There's some jiggery pokery and arm twisting needed so she gets bumped to the top of the list."

"Thanks," said Pennance. "I appreciate it."

"Just part of the job." Conryn was tapping away on the keypad of her desk phone as Pennance closed the door.

He made his way back to Simone's room – easier than navigating his way around the maze of NCA HQ – and found PC Pruitt still outside her door.

"Any change?" asked Pennance.

"Not that I know of," said Pruitt. "There's a nurse with her. She told me no-one's allowed in under any circumstances."

"Fair enough." Pennance wasn't keen on speaking with Simone just yet anyway but he had wanted to probe into what she'd meant about her daughter immediately before suffering the convulsions. "I'll be back later, and thanks."

"No problem. And, sir. That idiot Rasmussen was talking out of his arse."

"In what way?"

"There's no chance you caused Simone's seizure."

"I hope so."

"I asked the nurse. Whatever Rasmussen or you think, you aren't the cause, sir."

"I appreciate that. And it's Jonah." Pennance held out a hand, which Pruitt shook.

"Kristian."

***

When Pennance stepped onto the pavement outside the hospital a man nearby threw his half-finished cigarette to the floor and pushed off the wall where he'd been leaning. He blew smoke out the side of his mouth as he purposefully strode over, hands in pockets, like some 1950s actor.

"Detective Inspector Pennance," he said, "I'm Nathan Cruikshank reporting for *The Star*."

Pennance knew *The Star*, a red top sensationalist newspaper which specialised in splashy exposes. Pennance kept walking. "Whatever it is, no comment."

Cruikshank fell into step beside Pennance, a small silver voice recorder in his hand now, which he held towards Pennance at chest height. "What's your relationship with Detective Sergeant Smithson?"

Pennance stopped dead. "Excuse me?"

Cruickshank spun on his heel so he was directly in front of Pennance. "How can you be allowed to work on a case which involves her after you left the department in which you both worked because of an office scandal?"

"I don't know what you're talking about."

"According to my sources she rebuffed you and complained to her superiors about your behaviour."

"Total crap." Pennance sidestepped Cruikshank and fast walked. He glanced over his shoulder, looking for a taxi, keen to escape the reporter.

"And now you're investigating a case in which DS Smithson is a murder suspect." Cruikshank was easily keeping pace, trotting alongside Pennance. A passer-by threw a puzzled look in Pennance's direction.

Pennance spotted a black cab, the sign on its roof lit. Pennance stopped, raised a hand. The cab indicated and swung towards the pavement.

"Anything else to say, inspector?" Cruikshank held the recorder under Pennance's chin. "No? Why are you avoiding my questions?" The cab drew up. "I've reported on enough people to know a guilty party when I see one," said Cruikshank as Pennance tugged open the door. He clicked off the recorder.

"Where to?" asked the driver, a pair of eyes in the rear-view mirror.

"Tinworth Street, Vauxhall," said Pennance as he pulled the door shut. Pennance stared over his shoulder while the cabbie waited for a gap in the traffic. Cruikshank stood in the gutter, hands in pockets, staring after the taxi. Pennance was annoyed, allowing himself to be baited like that. So much for 'no comment'.

Pennance settled back in his seat and considered ringing Meacham to tell her about Cruickshank. But if he did and Meacham took him off Simone's case, he'd be unable to fulfil his promise to her. If Cruickshank was fishing then no harm and no foul. But if Cruikshank did publish, then Pennance would just have to ask her forgiveness.

Pennance rang Meacham anyway. "Ma'am, just calling with a quick update."

"Go on. Be quick, though. I've only got a few minutes."

"I had a report from Proudfoot, the pathologist – the bloods confirmed asphyxiation. Then I met a historian called Hicks. He reckoned there's a connection between the bread and salt."

"Oh?"

"An ancient burial rite called sin eating. The foodstuffs are placed on the chest of the dead to absorb their sins."

"Bloody hell. What does it mean?"

"I wish I knew."

"Anything else, Jonah?"

Pennance paused. He had to tell Meacham about Gough's report, too. It would be out soon, if not already. "The CSM who attended the scene at 15A Whitehall got a hit on some fingerprints on the bottles found there. They belong to Sergeant Smithson."

"Come again?"

"Simone seems to have poured the liquid into Fonseca's throat, then her own."

Meacham paused a beat. "You know Simone well, Jonah. What do you think?"

"I don't believe the evidence."

"But that's what it is, right?"

"Yes."

"I have to go, unless there's more?"

Pennance thought of Cruickshank. "No, ma'am. That's it."

"Plenty though. Good work, Jonah."

No sooner had Meacham rung off than Pennance's mobile went again. "Jonah, its Vance. When can you get back here?"

"Already on the way." Pennance grabbed hold of a strap above his head as the taxi took a tight corner too fast.

"Good, because you're not going to believe your eyes."

Pennance clung on, wondering what he was being swept into this time.

Twenty Five

They were three of them – Pennance, Hoskins and McAleney – in a small, windowless meeting room in the basement of the NCA, just off the main IT office. A round wooden table and four matching chairs were the only furniture.

Hoskins wiped a finger along the top of a TV screen fixed to the wall. "Does nobody clean in here?" His finger was covered in a thick layer of grey dust.

"No-one ever comes in, full stop, Vance," said McAleney as she put her laptop down on the table. "That lot outside," she pointed through the wall, "are all anti-social types. When they're not working, they're playing games. When they're not playing games, they're sleeping. There's zero time to sit around in a space like this and actually *talk*. So, this is the safest room in the building. Nobody will find us." McAleney twisted a knob on the door handle and a lock clicked into place.

"I thought you said this was the safest room in the building?" asked Hoskins.

"Doesn't hurt to be careful." McAleney sat, opened up her laptop. Hoskins settled beside her while Pennance leant a shoulder against the wall, arms crossed; he tapped his foot on the floor.

"You alright?" asked Hoskins.

"Perfectly fine," lied Pennance.

McAleney picked up a remote control, pressed a button and the TV flickered on. McAleney paired the screen with her laptop and opened a media player app.

"What are we looking at here?" asked Pennance.

"It's best you just watch. Then you'll understand." McAleney pressed play, steepled her fingers. She and Hoskins glanced at each other briefly, some unsaid comment passing between them.

The screen remained dark for a few more moments. A rustling, scratching sound emerged from the speakers. Some light appeared at the edges of the picture which widened into the outline of a person as they stepped back from the lens. However, they were just a black shape, their features lost in the camera flare. The person staggered a little, as if they'd almost tripped over something. The person came close again, shifted the angle once more; ensuring the perspective was right. Then camera balanced out the bright light and the person came into relief.

Simone.

Pennance pushed off the wall as Simone walked off-screen revealing a small room with boxes piled up either side of the perspective. He recognised it immediately as 15A Whitehall. "What the hell?"

"Keep watching," said McAleney, her attention firmly fixed on the footage. "It gets worse. Much worse."

Pennance's attention shifted to a form lying prone on the floor.

"Is that Fonseca?" asked Pennance. McAleney pursed her lips, clenched her jaw.

Simone returned holding a large plastic bottle by the neck, swinging the container casually, like a shopping bag. Then she straddled Fonseca, one knee either side of his waist. Simone behaved as if drunk, a giddy nonchalance about her which jarred with Pennance.

She ground her hips on Fonseca briefly, making the small man open his mouth wide and groan. Pennance grimaced, wanting to turn away from what he was seeing, but unable to. Then Simone put the bottle under her arm, the neck tilted upwards, unscrewed the cap and tossed it to one side before she reached out, grabbed a fistful of clothing and pulled Fonseca upright. Fonseca's head lolled but Simone leaned over, directing the neck of the bottle towards his mouth and poured. Fonseca gagged and Simone paused until Fonseca's natural reaction kicked in and he swallowed.

A siren passed somewhere nearby. Simone paused, twisted her head. As the sound retreated. Simone started over but slower this time, steadily forcing more of the fluid into Fonseca over several minutes. He coughed once, spraying Simone with a mouthful of the brine, but she didn't even wipe her face clean.

Eventually she shifted the bottle into one hand, holding the lip in Fonseca's mouth, his Adam's apple bobbing as he drank. Simone continued her grisly task until the contents were finished. She held the bottle out to one side and dropped it, the snick of plastic on wood unmissable.

Finally, Simone pulled Fonseca towards her and kissed his unresponsive lips before lowering him back down onto the floor, releasing her grip and standing. Simone leaned into the camera and the screen turned black once more.

Pennance dropped into one of the chairs. For a few moments nobody in the room spoke until Pennance said, "This can't be real."

"It's genuine, Jonah." McAleney stretched out a hand, clicked the mouse and minimised the video app. "I checked, more than once."

"No, it has to be a fake."

"I wish it was. I analysed the footage down to the pixel level. It's unaltered. Sergeant Smithson starred in and directed this movie. I'm truly sorry, but that's my expert opinion."

"There's another one," said Hoskins. "Carnegie is the star."

"Put it up," said Pennance.

"You really don't want to watch."

"Ava, play the file. That's an order."

"I'm a civilian," mumbled McAleney but she called up the footage onto the monitor anyway. Beneath the lens Carnegie lay on the floor, only his shoulders and head visible. His head lolled over partly and his eyes were obviously dilated. The perspective was from overhead, like looking through the killer's eyes. An arm stretched out, pushed a piece of bread into Carnegie's mouth. He groaned.

"They're a wearing an evidence suit and gloves," said Pennance. The kind everyone adopted at a crime scene.

Several more chunks followed in quick succession. Carnegie gagged now, tried to oust the blockage, tried to swallow, wasn't successful in either. More bread, the killer dipping their hand below the shot each time, and Carnegie began to struggle for air, body working hard to draw oxygen into rapidly depleting lungs. Another attempt at an expulsion, Carnegie's body heaving, but the killer reached out, put their hand over Carnegie's mouth and nose until the jerking stopped and Carnegie lay still, eyes open and staring sightlessly at the ceiling. The killer kept pushing bread in until there was room for no more.

"Jesus," said Pennance.

"I told you it wasn't pleasant," said Hoskins.

"It seemed like the killer was reaching down beneath them for the bread, maybe taking it from Carnegie's chest." Pennance thought back to what Hicks had told him.

"Is that significant?"

"I don't know."

"Or it was out of a bag," said McAleney.

"What about Thewlis?" asked Pennance. "Is there any video of him?"

"No, those are the only two," said McAleney.

"Surely that's enough?" asked Hoskins.

Pennance leaned forward, forearms on thighs, tempted to put his head between his knees in the crash position because that's what he felt was happening here. "Which means Simone murdered at least one person and tried to kill a second."

"And then attempted to commit suicide," said Hoskins.

Pennance wanted to throw up. He squeezed the bridge of his nose between two fingers. "None of this makes sense. This isn't my Simone."

"I'm sure this is difficult, Jonah."

"It's not difficult, it's *impossible*."

"For what it's worth, I don't believe her to be capable, either."

"You barely know her," said Pennance.

"So?" Hoskins shrugged. "I can have an opinion."

Pennance held out his hand. "I'll take the phone."

"But its evidence," said McAleney.

"I'll make sure the footage gets submitted."

"Hand the mobile over," said Hoskins. "Let's trust the inspector."

McAleney gave Hoskins a long stare before reaching out, picking up the handset and passing it to Pennance.

***

Pennance's feet felt like they weighed 100 kilos each as he climbed the stairs, Hoskins following close behind. Maybe Simone *was* a killer. If so, everything he'd believed about her over the years had been wrong. Completely and utterly *wrong*. Her phone was a large, physical presence in his pocket. He entered the MCIS office and paused. Meacham was standing there, waiting for him.

"Ma'am?" asked Pennance.

"I'll make myself scarce." Hoskins backed out. "I could do with something to eat anyway."

"I was just leaving you a note," said Meacham once Hoskins disappeared. "To let you know that DS Smithson will be interviewed shortly about the events surrounding her and Alfred Fonseca's status now she's conscious. I've informed DCI Fulton."

"I'd like to be there when you speak with her."

"That's not possible." Meacham shook her head. "I'll be asking the DS some difficult questions. Like how her fingerprints got onto the plastic bottles found at the scene."

"I can be objective."

"Maybe, inspector," said Meacham. "But regardless, you're too close to her. Be honest with yourself." Pennance didn't answer. Meacham shook her head. "Didn't think so."

"When will you talk to her?"

"Soon as I can. Now, don't you have a case to pursue?" Meacham walked out of the office.

The moment the door closed Pennance rang Fulton.

"I've already heard," said Fulton. "Meacham called me a few minutes ago."

"Its bullshit," said Pennance.

"I couldn't agree more. I haven't worked with her for long but this isn't Simone."

"Will you be attending?"

"No, I'll be kept out for impartiality's sake."

"Me too," said Pennance.

"She'll need someone independent, someone senior."

"I know who – Kelso."

"Your ex-boss. Great idea."

"I'll get in touch with him now," said Pennance.

"Good man; stay in touch." Fulton disconnected.

Kelso's number was in Pennance's favourites list, near the top of his contacts. Kelso answered immediately.

"I assume you're calling about Simone," said Kelso.

"News travels fast," said Pennance.

"I don't accept she had anything to do with the lad's attempted murder."

"That's three of us. Simone is going to need some form of representation, Devon. I was hoping that could be you."

"I'll ring Meacham in a moment and offer my services."

"Keep an eye out for her."

"Of course. She's important to both of us."

"Thanks."

"Don't mention it." Kelso disconnected and Pennance sat. He removed Simone's phone from an inside pocket, spun it around in his hands. Then he picked up his own mobile once more and made another call.

"This is Damian Mulcahy." He sounded like he was focused on something else.

"Mr Mulcahy, its DI Pennance."

"Oh, inspector, apologies. Was the list of hacked companies any use?"

"We're working on it. However, I'm not ringing about that."

"Oh?"

"I've got some video footage I could do with you looking at. It's part of a case and highly confidential, so needs to be treated as such."

"I can be trusted. I handle sensitive data all the time. I can send you a non-disclosure agreement, if you wish."

"That won't be necessary."

"What do you want me to do?"

"I've no idea. If I'm honest, I'm reaching."

"Where's the file?"

"On a phone."

"If you can courier the handset over, I'll have a general sniff around and examine the root data, too."

DEAD MONEY

"Where are you?" asked Pennance.

"Ennismore Gardens in Knightsbridge."

"I'll have a bike bring it over within the next half hour."

"I'll take a look soon as I can."

"Thanks."

"No problem." Mulcahy disconnected.

Pennance lay back in his chair and stared at the ceiling for a few moments. He realised he needed to be doing something. Maybe a train journey would help...

Twenty Six

Hugh Fonseca, Lord High Commissioner of Blean, resided in the commuter town of Canterbury, Kent. Blean itself was the remnants of an ancient woodland beyond the outskirts of the city. Pennance knew this only because an internet search engine had told him so.

The fastest route to the city was via train. By car it could have taken Pennance the same amount of time just to reach the capital's outskirts. In true London style, Pennance stepped down from the carriage the moment the doors opened and headed out of the small station, carrying only his phone. A map app delivered directions to St. John's Place. Apparently, it was 0.6 of a mile distant.

The houses around the train station were a mix of new and old, the most recent styled by architects and planners to resemble the originals – narrow terraces, working family houses placed near the smog from the train yards over a hundred years ago.

Pennance cut along a narrow footpath before crossing the River Stour – maybe it had once been a torrent meeting Canterbury's needs; now it was simply a stream. He paused at the junction with Northgate – in Roman times Canterbury had been a walled city with fortified entrances at each point of the compass. Now this was a holy city. The spire of the world famous Canterbury Cathedral, burial place of The Black Prince and seat of the church's power, was a visible marker ahead.

Dismissing religion, Pennance turned into St. John's Place, a dead end thoroughfare even more constricted than Northgate, with a brick-built primary school on one side and a modern hospital at the far end. The sound of heavy duty drilling reverberated along the street, like concrete was being smashed up, someone else's work being torn apart and regenerated.

Fonseca's house proved to be a converted boarding school – a huge stone sign on the wall under the apex of the roof said so, along with its date of construction; 1876. On the upper floor three impressively sized arch windows surveyed the building opposite. The ground floor adopted more austere sash windows. Beyond an electric wrought iron gate, painted a glossy black, were two parking spaces. The rear of St. John's hospital was yards away and was from where the sounds of construction work issued. Pennance pushed open a low metal gate into a narrow garden just feet wide, lifted the knocker set into an equally glossy black door and dropped it a couple of times as the drilling halted. Pennance doubted the two events were related.

The door was opened by a dapper man in his 60s. He sported tartan checked trousers, a white shirt partnered with a colourful cravat at his neck and a pale woollen jumper. "Inspector Pennance?" Hugh Fonseca's accent was the kind most Americans assume every Brit possesses.

"Thanks for seeing me, sir." Pennance showed his ID and Fonseca stepped back, allowing Pennance room to enter with a sweep of a bony hand which clutched rimless glasses. The interior was not at all how Pennance expected – open plan and expensively furnished; parquet floor, thick rugs, an

Ottoman sofa and highly polished tables with spindly legs. It felt large and spacious, so different to the street outside.

"Come out to the back," said Fonseca. "How was the journey?"

"Straightforward," said Pennance. Fonseca led him through the living room, past a spiral staircase giving access to the top floor, and the obvious focal point: a pair of ruby red lips maybe four feet across and two feet high fixed to the wall. It took Pennance a few moments to realise it was a fireplace.

"My wife likes it," said Fonseca, noticing Pennance's stare. "It's an ice breaker, I suppose." He shrugged.

Fonseca passed through a large set of sliding glass doors into a courtyard garden which ran the width of the house. It wasn't overlooked at all, with high walls, yet appeared to be a sun trap because a sail-shaped piece of fabric stretched across part of the garden beneath which stood a table and chairs and, nearby, a jacuzzi, covered by a wooden lid to keep the heat in.

"Your arrival is timely," said Fonseca. He pointed to the metal table and chairs. "The damned workmen at the hospital take a break about now, so we'll get brief respite from the bloody racket. Sometimes they pause for ten minutes, other's it's twenty. Only another two months to go." Fonseca gave Pennance a weak, toothy grin and sat. "I have coffee. But I can easily get you tea if you prefer." A tray with a pair of cup and saucers and a tall silver pot stood in the centre of the table. "It's a bit late in the day for English Breakfast, but I have Early Grey and my wife likes green tea. And chamomile, and peppermint. The list goes on." Fonseca blew

DEAD MONEY

air through pursed lips; their taste in beverages as divergent as heat sources.

"Coffee is absolutely fine, thanks," said Pennance. "I'm here about Alfred."

"So you said on the phone." Fonseca poured coffee into a cup for Pennance. "There's milk and sugar, if you want." Fonseca's was black.

"You're aware of your son's condition?" asked Pennance as he poured the milk.

"Stepson to be precise, and of course. My wife keeps me well informed via regular updates."

"You're here, though, not in London."

Fonseca frowned. "My wife is with her son and he's in a coma. There's little I can do for him and I have my work, which keeps me busy."

"In London?"

"Sometimes, usually in Brussels."

"What is your job?"

Fonseca flashed a humourless smile. "It's not a *job* in the common sense, inspector. I'm a senior liaison to the European Union. Canterbury is a good jumping off point to reach the continent. There's the Eurostar into Brussels or Paris and the Eurotunnel out of Folkestone if I want to be driven. It's very convenient."

"Surely post-Brexit, any need to align with the EU is irrelevant now?"

"Relations will continue." Fonseca sipped his coffee. "And hopefully flourish once more."

"And when you're in London, where do you work?"

"It depends who I'm meeting."

"Whitehall?"

"That is, of course, possible. As government operates from there."

Pennance almost sighed. Fonseca was at heart a politician and Pennance had expected him to be guarded on the key topics where damage control was required yet expansive on the irrelevance. Pennance needed to remain sharp, listening hard for any cues.

"You said, *her* son, Mr Fonseca," said Pennance. "I take it Alfred isn't your child?"

"Obviously, when I describe Alfred as my stepson, I mean he is not of my blood. Fenella and Alfred came as a take it or leave it deal."

"How close was the choice?"

"Not at all; a straightforward selection. They came from a poor background."

"I meant for you."

"I wouldn't have asked Fenella if the reasoning wasn't clear."

"Alfred was found at 15A Whitehall, that's near where he works. Do you have any idea why he would have been there?"

"My stepson is often a mystery to me." Which wasn't an answer. Pennance waited. "Alfred and I have divergent views on some matters."

"Such as?"

"Well, personal wealth for one. And politics."

"How so?"

"Which are you asking about?"

"Both."

"Generally Alfred has a socialist, left leaning attitude. Some may even say a communist approach; all people are equal and money should be shared equally. Whereas I take the view that social order and hierarchy are perfectly natural and desirable."

"Survival of the fittest?"

"Quite."

"So, how does that apply to Alfred right now?"

"That's a highly distasteful question, inspector. And beneath me to answer."

Pennance said, "One of your colleagues came to the NCA a few days ago." Fonseca eyed Pennance. "Called himself Leo Raskin."

"I don't believe I've heard that name before, but I meet many people." Fonseca shifted slightly then crossed one leg over the other. They were small movements but immediately Pennance had the impression Fonseca was uncomfortable with Raskin being raised.

"He's in the civil service, too," said Pennance.

"So?" Fonseca scoffed. "That's like asking if I know everyone in Canterbury. Are you aware how many people are in the government's employ, inspector? It's thousands."

"Over 450,000 civil servants, more than 8,000 are in government," said Pennance. "I looked it up."

Fonseca sniffed. "I'm pleased for your fingers."

"So you don't know Raskin?" asked Pennance. Fonseca merely shrugged. Pennance continued, "That's distinctly odd because Raskin definitely mentioned you."

Fonseca tilted his head, giving the impression he was searching through his memory.

"Apparently, you and he are friends," said Pennance. "Close friends."

"I count very few people in that latter selection."

Pennance believed him. "But friends do favours for each other, right?"

"What could you possibly mean?"

"You asked Raskin to find your son a job."

"Stepson," corrected Fonseca, and poured himself more coffee. Pennance let him think. "Perhaps I am familiar with Mr Raskin, but only vaguely. He's well below my station."

"He works at HM Treasury."

"Exactly." Fonseca fixed Pennance with a beady eye. "It wasn't I who approached Leo Raskin. The whole situation is volte-face. I had a call from an associate, enquiring if a mutual contact could come and see me – it turned out to be Raskin. He'd heard through the grapevine that I was attempting to secure a role for Alfred. It was *Raskin* who told *me* there was a position in his department which he'd like Alfred to apply for."

"That's not how Raskin put it."

"Clearly Raskin and I possess differing recollections. The only recourse would be to ask Alfred for an unbiased opinion."

"He's in a coma."

"I can't help that." Fonseca lifted the cup, took a drink.

"Why did Raskin want your stepson?"

"I have no idea, Inspector." Fonseca carefully lowered the cup back into the saucer. "Frankly, I wasn't interested in enquiring because having Alfred in gainful employ meant he was out from under my feet. Alfred was monopolising his mother's time to the detriment of our marital position. After completing his PhD, he was bored and disrupting our routine here, dragging Fenella to some bloody historical site or another or regaling us with dull tales of yore. I didn't enjoy or appreciate it. Alfred wasn't keen on the job but I can be very persuasive when I choose to be. I told him he could join a society or something, explore the city. It wasn't long before Alfred was packing his bags. I even helped him."

"In my experience," said Pennance, "When a person does someone a courtesy, they usually expect a payback at some point in the future. I assume that's the case in political circles, too?"

"So?" Fonseca gave a slight shrug with one shoulder.

"So, what did you want from Raskin?"

"I haven't decided yet." Fonseca made an obvious gesture to check his watch. "Look, time is moving on and the workmen will be back soon making their frightful clatter. I think we should finish now."

"We could talk inside."

"Believe me, actual walls make very little difference."

"Just a couple more questions, sir. Then we're done." Pennance had asked all he wanted, but Fonseca's superiority irritated him, so if he could disrupt him even just a little, he would.

"If you must." Fonseca rolled his eyes. "And a couple means two, Inspector."

"What is Alfred's PhD in?"

"How the hell would I know?" Fonseca waved an expansive arm. "Something to do with economics. Ask Fenella. Alfred sent her a copy of his thesis. I never bothered to read it.

And I've no idea if there's a copy in the house, which is your second question." Just then the drilling began again and Fonseca raised his arms in a non-apology. "Now we're finished, inspector." Fonseca had to shout.

Pennance slowly stood. Fonseca led Pennance through the house, opened the door wide for him to step through then shut it, all without another word. Pennance paused on the threshold for a few moments, wanting to knock, but well aware Fonseca would just ignore him. He got walking back to the station. Trains ran frequently in and out of the capital, so he wouldn't be waiting long.

***

While Pennance was being carried back to London by the train he called Hoskins.

"What's up?" asked Hoskins.

"I interviewed Fonseca Senior earlier. "He disagreed with Raskin's depiction of events. Apparently, Raskin asked Fonseca to persuade Alfred to work in government."

"Bloody odd."

"The only person who can confirm if this is true is Alfred himself, and he's in no state to do so. Has your father found anything on Raskin?"

"I've not heard back from him yet. He's quite a secretive little tyke when he wants to be."

"Why is it taking so long?"

"You've got two choices when you enter a lake full of barracuda. A straight dive or lowering yourself in slowly.

One creates an almighty splash and attracts all comers, the other is barely noticed."

"I'd have thought cess pit would be more applicable than lake."

"I don't think a cess pit is the natural habitat of a barracuda." Hoskins chuckled. "Although who willingly throws themselves into a hole full of everyone else's crap?"

"Us, every day when we do our job."

Hoskins grunted. "The point is to keep Raskin unaware we're asking after him, otherwise he'll be swimming away and gone before we know it."

Pennance said, "There's something I don't get, though. I'd bet there are hundreds, maybe thousands, of Alfred's in the UK. Why him?"

"Well, that's what you need to find out, Jonah."

Twenty Seven

When Pennance alighted from the train at St. Pancras Station fifty seven minutes after departing Canterbury, thanks to a delay at Ashford, he walked to University College Hospital less than a mile away and straight along Euston Road. However, he wasn't here for Simone.

Alfred Fonseca had his own room in the intensive care unit, one floor below Simone. It was the first time Pennance had seen Alfred since he'd been loaded into the ambulance outside 15A Whitehall and his condition appeared unchanged. He lay on his back, arms on the covers, hooked up to a drip and monitors. A tube taped to his cheek entered his mouth. Alfred's eyes were closed, hair neatly brushed, but stubble was emerging on his chin and jawline.

"Excuse me?"

Pennance turned. In the doorway stood an imposing woman, hands on hips and eyes narrowed. She wore jeans, flat shoes without socks, a pristine white shirt and a colourful silk scarf over her shoulders. She held a plastic cup, a milky liquid within, and an e-reader.

"Mrs Fonseca?" asked Pennance.

"Yes, what do you want with my son?" She entered the room, stood next to Alfred, and carefully placed the cup and reader on a bedside cabinet.

"DI Jonah Pennance." He showed his ID. "I'm investigating Alfred's case."

Mrs Fonseca visibly relaxed. "You can call me Fenella. Dr Conryn has told me about you." Fenella sat down, picked up her son's limp hand, clasped it between her own. "He's such a pleasant boy. He wouldn't hurt anyone. Why would someone do this to him?"

"How is he?"

"Dr Conryn has proven very forthright. She told me in no uncertain terms that Alfred's brain is damaged beyond repair. If, by some miracle, he survives, he'll never be exactly himself again, but I don't care, he's my son and he'll be coming home with me."

"What will your husband think of that?"

"I'm not interested in Hugh's considerations. He'll put up with it. A divorce would be a stain on his career prospects, and he knows it. I hold all the cards in the deck, inspector."

"I met him earlier. In Canterbury."

"Hugh wasn't working for once?"

"Not while I was there."

"Usually he's at some dusty gathering making dusty small talk."

"Have you heard of Leo Raskin?"

Fenella thought for a few moments. "No. I assume he's one of my husband's connections?"

"Seemingly."

"Hugh keeps me completely out of that part of his life, which I readily agree with. Unfortunately it happens to be most of his life." Fenella pursed her lips. "I'm afraid I would be no help at all if that's what you're looking to probe into."

"Alfred was working for Raskin, here in London, apparently thanks to your husband."

"He never mentioned any names but it would make sense if Hugh used his network to secure a position for Alfred."

"Did Alfred tell you anything about his job?"

"Very little beyond the fact he was at HM Treasury, although it was obvious he was bored to tears, inspector. He's an extremely bright boy and could've had his pick of employment, if he'd have just had the time to choose." Fenella gently patted the back of Alfred's hand. "But Hugh wanted him packed up and out of the way at the earliest opportunity."

"What about the names Carnegie, Simone, or Thewlis?"

"Carnegie I've seen on the news, he died. But the other two?" Fenella shook her head. "I'm sorry. My focus has been entirely on Alfred."

"Was there any change in Alfred's behaviour in recent days or weeks?"

"Only that he wasn't calling me as much. At first, we spoke every day. Then it was every other day. He hadn't been in touch for almost a week when the phone went two days ago. He sounded enthusiastic and maybe just a little afraid, where before he'd been listless."

"What was he excited about?"

"I asked but he wouldn't be specific. Only that I'd be proud of him."

"Alfred was attacked in an abandoned serviced office not far from here. Would you have any idea why he'd be there? I asked your husband but he couldn't give me a single reason."

"Of course not." Fenella raised her eyes to the heavens before she looked at Pennance once more. "I wish I could help."

"I understand Alfred studied at Cambridge."

"That's right." Fenella brightened slightly, perhaps recalling a memory of better times. "He was an undergrad and postgrad at King's. I was extremely proud of him. The first in my family to make it to one of the Oxbridge Universities. Hugh says it's because he paid for Alfred's education but I believe it took Alfred a lot of hard work and sacrifice."

"What was his PhD in?"

"Economics, something to do with cryptocurrency and hive theory. Alfred explained it to me in a tea shop on the King's Parade, opposite the college. I nodded a lot, but most of it went over my head. I'm reasonably intelligent, but Alfred is a whole level above me, maybe two levels. He's brighter than Hugh too, which of course Hugh hates."

"Your husband told me you had a copy of Alfred's thesis?"

"I had it printed and professionally bound. Vanity, Hugh called it. The book is on a shelf in the study of our house."

"Could I get a copy?"

"Will it help?"

"Honestly, I don't know."

"I have the digital version I sent to the publisher. I'll forward it on. I can't do that now, of course. No electronic equipment allowed."

"Is there anything else you can tell me about Alfred?"

"Do you have all day, Inspector? I've lots of stories. Maybe not all relevant." Fenella gave a weak smile.

"What did he do in his spare time?"

"Not much, he liked to play chess online with friends. And he had a taste for history. In fact, some friend of his came by yesterday, enquiring after him."

"What was his name?"

"He didn't tell me and I didn't ask. I've been so worried about Alfred that I forget social niceties although I do recall the society he was from because the name was a bit silly. SoHO – upper case S, lower case o, upper case H and O. Stands for Soho Historical Organisation."

"These are my contact details, Mrs Fonseca, for the thesis." Pennance gave Fenella his NCA business card. "I'll leave you alone with Alfred."

"Thank you for trying to find who hurt him, Inspector."

"You're more than welcome." Pennance left Alfred's room, pulled out his phone and tapped SoHO into a search engine as he slowly walked along the corridor. He got back a stack of articles on the London borough so he typed in Soho Historical Organisation.

"Excuse me. Inspector?" Pennance stopped, looked up from his screen. Dr Conryn was a few feet along.

"Sorry," said Pennance. "I wasn't looking where I was going." He put his phone away. "I just met Mrs Fonseca."

"She's a tough lady. No sugar coating needed with her. I'm glad you and I bumped into each other because I've had the results back on Miss Smithson's brain scan. There's some shading on the temporal lobe which led to her focal seizure; that's when the spasm is limited to one brain hemisphere. Thankfully, the colouration is fairly light so I don't foresee any permanent damage. We'll need to be careful of any further events and as a result I've started a course of an AED.

But otherwise I think she's fine. I'm about to inform your colleague. Meacham, right?"

"That's her. Good news, doctor."

"You don't sound particularly enthusiastic."

Conryn's diagnosis meant Meacham would have the all clear to interview Simone. "No, I am, really. You've done a fantastic job."

"It's what I signed up for." Conryn smiled. "I'd better check on Alfred, if you'll excuse me."

"Of course." Pennance shifted to one side and Conryn passed by. Pennance rang Meacham.

"Ah, Jonah," she said.

"I'm at the hospital, ma'am. DS Smithson has been given the all clear by Dr Conryn."

"Excellent. I have a team on standby to interview Simone. We'll be leaving shortly."

"I'm at the hospital already, ma'am."

"We've had this discussion, Jonah. You will not be present."

"Ma'am..."

"Detective inspector." Meacham cut across Pennance. "The interview will be recorded, you can watch it afterwards and give me your impressions then."

"It's not the same as attending. And I know her better than any of you. I can be an asset."

"Or a liability."

"I know my job, ma'am."

"I'm not doubting that. However, DS Smithson agreed to the interview under the condition that you *not* be there."

"Excuse me?"

"You heard. Perhaps she'll be more willing to open up without you?" Meacham sighed. "Look, I understand how difficult this must be, but I can't allow the feelings of one of my officers to compromise an investigation. Do you understand me?"

Pennance gripped the phone tightly and forced calmness into his tone. "I absolutely do, ma'am."

"Good. The interview team includes Superintendent Kelso. We'll talk afterwards, okay?" Meacham disconnected before Pennance could answer.

He didn't blame Meacham, she was following procedure. Pennance got walking. He needed to hear what Simone had to say. Pennance dialled Hoskins, said, "If I asked you to help me with something against the rules, what would be your reaction?"

"Could it get me fired?" asked Hoskins.

"Maybe."

"I like breaking windows in the big house, Jonah." Hoskins chuckled. "I'm in."

Twenty Eight

"I could get fired for this." A scowling Ava McAleney sat on the other side of the table. She rattled away at the keys of her laptop, her tongue sticking out from the side of her mouth as she concentrated. There were three of them in the basement meeting room they'd used earlier to watch the footage on Simone's phone.

"You're telling me you've never gone against regulations?" asked Hoskins. He sat on the edge of the table beside her, feet on the floor, picked up a baguette, bit into it and began to chew. "Your father did."

McAleney paused briefly, mouth half open to say something, then clearly decided not to as she carried on working.

Hoskins waved the sandwich that Pennance had bought as recompense (along with a cream cake and coffee) and said, "All interviews are uploaded onto the NCA's storage system. We just needed someone suitably proficient and with the right passwords to gain entry."

"It's accessing the live feed that could get me into trouble," said McAleney.

"It won't. I'll make sure of that." Hoskins pushed over the cake, still wrapped in its plastic, towards McAleney. "Have your bribe."

"I'm dairy intolerant, Vance."

"Oh."

"I'll take full responsibility, Ava," said Pennance.

"For the dairy intolerance?" asked Hoskins.

"No," said Pennance. "Any fallout from accessing the feed."

McAleney glanced away from the screen to Pennance before returning her attention to her task again. "Stuff like that only happens in the movies, Jonah."

"Sometimes on TV, too," said Hoskins. McAleney sniggered, earlier irritation apparently forgotten. Pennance felt like he was on the outside of a joke. Hoskins continued, "You've no reason to be so chivalrous, Jonah. Meacham needs me for an upcoming investigation. If I don't agree, no case." Hoskins spread his hands wide, palms up, and grinned like he was a magician revealing the secrets of his trade.

McAleney said, "I'm in."

"I knew you'd do it." Hoskins placed a hand on McAleney's shoulder, kissed her on the cheek, then realised what he'd done and snatched his hand away like her skin was scalding. McAleney's face turned a deep scarlet.

Pennance dragged his chair around next to McAleney while Hoskins slid off the table and took the space the other side of McAleney as she picked up the TV remote.

"Leave it on the laptop, just in case," said Pennance.

"The door's locked," said McAleney.

"Even so."

"Alright." McAleney shrugged, put down the remote again and the laptop became the focus of their attention.

The perspective was obviously Simone's hospital room. Simone, placed centrally in the viewpoint, sat up in bed, with Meacham and Kelso to the right hand side of the lens. Both were seated. Kelso leaned back in his chair, while Meacham had a notebook on her lap and pen in her hand.

Her position appeared awkward and she shifted, as if trying to get more comfortable.

Meacham spoke but no sound came out of the speaker. McAleney leaned over and increased the volume until they could hear. "... present during this interview."

"You're sure this is live?" asked Pennance.

McAleney raised an eyebrow at Pennance. "There's a delay of a few seconds between transmission and receipt, but that's it."

"I want to see Natalie." Simone's tone was strong and no-nonsense. Her expression was set tight, lips pursed. Her skin appeared washed out, though maybe that was just the lighting.

"Who?" asked Meacham.

"My daughter. She hasn't been able to visit since I came in, she'll be worried about me."

"Natalie is outside with your husband," said Kelso. "She's fine, by the way."

"They're not married," mumbled Pennance. Hoskins gave him a sideways glance which Pennance ignored.

"I'm confused, he called her Astrid," said Meacham.

"That's her middle name." Simone gave a tiny shake of the head. "Let's start, shall we? Get this over with."

"Just to repeat the question," said Meacham. "Please confirm you do not wish to have a lawyer present during this interview."

"That's correct, ma'am," said Simone.

"We're recording this." Meacham nodded towards the camera, seemingly looking directly at Pennance for a moment.

"I'm well aware of how these things work, ma'am."

"True." Meacham inclined her head. "What can you tell me about the events of yesterday evening DS Smithson?"

"I don't remember anything."

"What's your last memory?"

"When I got home from work. Natalie was with Lars. I called him to make sure she was okay, and that's it. Everything after that is a blank."

"You don't co-habit with your husband?"

"Ex-husband," mumbled Pennance.

"Not at the moment," said Simone. "We split up well over a year ago, we've lived apart since then but we're planning to get back together. Natalie spends separate time with both of us."

"How is your relationship with your husband?"

"What's that got to do with anything?" asked Simone.

"It's just a question," said Meacham.

"We're fine."

"What do you know of 15A Whitehall?"

"Where?"

"It's the address where DI Pennance found you."

"That was Jonah?"

"Correct."

"Nobody told me." Simone blinked.

"How did you get to 15A Whitehall that evening?"

"I don't recall even leaving my home, ma'am."

"Nothing?"

"My mind is a blank."

"Dr Conryn told me she'd found light shadowing on Simone's frontal lobe in a brain scan," said Pennance.

McAleney turned to Pennance. "That's where recall is stored."

"So she could be having difficulty remembering."

"Or she's lying," said Hoskins. Pennance glared at Hoskins who raised his hands, said, "Just being logical, Jonah."

Meacham continued. "Your work phone was recovered from the scene. You took a call an hour prior to DI Pennance finding you. The number was blocked."

Simone tilted her head. "I don't recall that."

"You've no idea who you spoke to?"

"No."

Meacham checked her notebook. "The duration was one minute and twelve seconds." She looked back again at Simone. "More than just a hello, I'd say."

"Have you traced back the number?"

"Of course," said Meacham. "It's a burner. Used once, to contact you."

"I can't help, sorry."

Meacham paused, the seconds stretching. Simone didn't fill in the gap. "Okay." Meacham reached into her notebook and drew out a photo. She placed it on the bed covers next to Simone. "Do you know this man?"

Simone bent forward, glanced at the photo before shaking her head. "Who is he?"

"Alfred Fonseca," said Meacham. "He was found in the room next to you at 15A Whitehall, also by DI Pennance."

"You're the star today," said Hoskins. Pennance ignored him.

"Alfred is currently in a coma one floor above us." Meacham pointed upwards with a finger.

"I've never met him or heard his name until you mentioned it now, ma'am."

"He consumed a large volume of extremely salty water just prior to his discovery. Alfred was poisoned."

"Okay."

"The same as you, sergeant."

"I drank salty water?" Simone rubbed her forehead.

"If she is lying," said McAleney, "she's a very good actress."

"DI Pennance found Mr Fonseca unconscious and you delirious," continued Meacham. "DI Pennance said you apologised to him."

"For what?" Simone furrowed her brow.

"That's something I was hoping you could enlighten me."

"I've no idea what you're talking about." Simone jerked her shoulders sharply upwards. "If I knew I'd tell you!"

"Okay, we'll circle back to that shortly." Meacham turned to Kelso. "Do you want to ask Sergeant Smithson anything?"

"Not right now," said Kelso.

"Do you know these men?" Meacham produced two more photos from her notebook and laid them over Alfred's image.

Simone stretched out a hand and tapped the photo on the left. "This is Grady Carnegie, I attended the crime scene at his apartment. But the other guy I've never seen before."

"He was an investigative reporter by the name of Stanley Thewlis."

"Was?"

"Like Carnegie, Thewlis was found dead in his home with bread rammed down his throat." Meacham took back the photos, knocked them into a neat, small pile like she was dealing with a pack of cards and slid them into her notebook. "Meaning their deaths appear connected."

"And I'm supposed to have something to do with all of this, ma'am?"

"Again, I'm hoping you'd be able to help," said Meacham.

"I don't even know why I'm here!" Simone threw her arms up in the air. She turned to Kelso. "Sir, what the hell is going on?"

"I'd like to know that too, DCI Meacham," said Kelso.

"Fingerprint evidence implies you poured the saline solution down Fonseca's throat," said Meacham.

Simone stared open mouthed at the DCI for a few moments. "You're saying I tried to murder someone?"

"Then you drank from your own bottle." Meacham put another photo down on the bed and tapped it, like Simone had. "This bottle, in fact."

Simone burst out laughing, short and sharp. "That's fucking ridiculous!"

"Fingerprints were found on each container that conclusively prove you held each in your hands."

"Total crap," snorted Simone. "Next you'll be attempting to pin Carnegie and Thewlis on me."

"Have you heard of sin eating?" said Meacham.

"What?" Simone raised frustrated hands at Kelso. "Sir?" Kelso stayed quiet.

Meacham said, "One working theory is the bread and the salt were used to absolve sins after death."

"But I'm not dead!"

"No, and that's kind of the point, Sergeant Smithson."

"Whose ridiculous theory is this? Wait. Let me guess." Simone held up a hand. "Jonah bloody Pennance?"

Pennance ignored Hoskins's obvious glance.

"Inspector Pennance is investigating the murders, as you are aware."

"Jonah regularly comes up with crazy ideas, he's well known for it. Isn't he, sir?" Simone directed her question at Kelso. "But this one? I thought he knew me better." Simone leant towards Meacham and Kelso. "I'll be as plain as I can. I know nothing about any of this. I can't remember a damn thing. And I didn't kill anyone. I apply the law, not break it."

"You wouldn't believe how many times I've heard that phrase from coppers on the wrong side."

"So, that's what I am now?" Simone's eyes flared. "Bent?"

"I don't believe DCI Meacham meant that," said Kelso.

Meacham interlinked her fingers on her lap. "What is your relationship with DI Pennance?"

"Excuse me?" Simone blinked, shook her head. Meacham waited until Simone said, "We're colleagues." Simone caught herself. "Correction, we *were* colleagues."

"What changed?"

"Different jobs." Simone shrugged. "We moved on."

"In the course of your career have you been trained in the use of a taser?"

"Pardon?"

"A taser, used to incapacitate people."

"I know what they are. And yes, I have."

"Do you own one, personally?"

"No, why would I?"

"London can be a dangerous place."

"I don't have a bloody taser, ma'am."

"So, we won't find one in your house when we search it?"

"You're in my house?"

Meacham checked her watch. "As of a few minutes ago, yes. And I have a warrant, before you ask." Another document came out of Meacham's notebook.

"Fuck's sake."

"There's no need to curse, sergeant," said Meacham.

"At the moment, swearing seems like the most apt approach." Simone crossed her arms. "I think we should bring this conversation to a close. If there are any further questions you want to ask me, we'll do so with a lawyer present."

"Are you sure that's how you want to play this, Sergeant Smithson?"

"Up to this point I think I've been more than co-operative. Now I'm simply responding to your style, so this is on you, ma'am. Please turn the camera off."

Meacham turned around and waved at whoever was behind the lens. Moments later the stream was cut and the TV screen turned black. McAleney reached out and shut the laptop lid.

"Did you know Simone's house was being searched?" asked Hoskins.

"No," said Pennance. "Meacham didn't tell me."

"She's keeping secrets from you, then."

"Meacham's a senior officer, of course she hides stuff."

"Are you going to speak with her?" said Hoskins.

"What's the point?" asked Pennance. Hoskins shrugged. Pennance continued, "Thanks for your help, Ava."

"Really, it's nothing."

"What are you going to do now?" asked Hoskins.

"Go home. I've had enough." Pennance stood, flexed his fists. He wanted to punch something.

"Good idea."

"What about you?"

"Ava and I have cake to eat."

"I'm dairy intolerant," said McAleney again.

"Then I've got cake to eat," said Hoskins.

Pennance left them in the meeting room and found his way out of the building. As he walked along Tinworth Street Pennance glanced over his shoulder at NCA headquarters. He'd be back tomorrow. But after that, when this case was closed?

Maybe his time was done.

Twenty Nine

Pennance turned into a narrow alley off Clapham High Street, heading for his flat. A breeze had picked up and the narrow road filtered the wind. Pennance had tried calling Kelso several times, no answer.

Once Pennance was inside he rang Kelso again. He finally picked up. "Sorry I couldn't call sooner to give you an update. Meacham and I had a quick debrief after Simone's interview."

"Devon, you need to know that I watched the whole thing on a live feed." Pennance trotted up his stairs.

"How? No, don't tell me. I'd rather stay unaware," said Kelso. Pennance reckoned he could hear Kelso's eyes roll down the line. "Something wasn't right about Simone. In fact, I didn't like the whole event. Interviewing her in a hospital room, what was that all about?"

"It's been done before."

"I know, but she's one of our own."

"When Simone said she had no memory of getting to Whitehall or the attack on Fonseca, did you believe her?"

"I'm still not sure." Kelso was quiet for a few moments. Pennance paused, put the phone between ear and shoulder and unlocked his flat door. Kelso continued, "I can usually spot bullshit at twenty paces, we're trained to do that, right? But what happens when the person telling you the lies possesses the same skills?"

"Did Meacham share with you that a brain scan on Simone displayed some shadowing which may affect her memory?" Pennance pushed the door to behind him with a foot.

"She did not."

"Maybe Meacham felt it was unimportant."

"Well, she's wrong and just adds to my impression that how Meacham approached Simone was poorly judged. I thought better of her." Kelso briefly paused once more. "There's one moment that sticks in my mind; Simone seemed really scared. Right at the outset; when Meacham said Rasmussen had Natalie. It was only fleeting." Pennance heard Kelso's click of his fingers. "Before Simone squashed the emotion like a bug, fast enough that I doubt Meacham spotted it. If I'd looked away for an instant, or blinked at the wrong time, I'd have missed it, too."

"She's worried about Rasmussen?"

"Or Natalie, maybe. Frankly, I've no idea. One thing's for sure, Simone has something on her mind. You need to find out what."

"That'll be next to impossible as she's not talking to me."

"Well, you'll have to find a way, otherwise this all could end badly for someone. At this rate it'll probably be Simone." Kelso disconnected.

Pennance shrugged off his jacket, threw it over the back of the sofa, checked on Lars the iguana. As usual the beast was lying on a rock underneath the sun lamp. Pennance felt hungry, went to the fridge but there was little inside, other than some milk, cheese and butter. He could make a sandwich; if he had bread. Which he didn't. He opened a nearby drawer where he kept the takeaway menus and took them into the living room. He flopped onto the sofa and riffled through the options from Indian to Thai to burgers. His watch vibrated – an email notification. He'd received a note from Fenella Fonseca, the subject read, 'Alfred's Thesis'.

Putting the menus to one side for now Pennance opened the email on his phone, ignored Fenella's message to him and clicked on the PDF attachment, which took a long few moments to download. The document title was 'The Psychology of High Value Investment and Its Relation to Cryptocurrency'.

Pennance scrolled the page and dropped into a summary section, read several lines and immediately got lost in the text. Alfred mentioned Hive Theory, then Culture-Gene Coevolution and some other stuff Pennance frankly didn't get. It was like a foreign language. He needed help to interpret the information. He closed the document and dialled Tremayne.

"Hi, Alasdair, it's Jonah Pennance."

"How's the case going? Have you got some news for me?" asked Tremayne between breaths. As a jogger himself Pennance recognised the moderated inhalations and pounding of feet on the pavement. Tremayne would be talking into an earpiece.

"Actually, I'm after some help. I've got a PhD thesis here written by one of the victims. It's utter gobbledegook to me. Would you mind reading it over and giving me a simple view please?"

"Sure, when do you need it?"

"Soon as you can."

"When I'm home from my run I'll take a look."

"Thanks." But Tremayne was already gone. Pennance emailed the thesis to him and returned his attention to his stomach. He settled on Chinese, placed an order over an app, then put the kettle on to make himself a cup of tea – at least he had bags in the flat.

As he poured milk into his tea the doorbell went. If that was the takeaway it had been extremely quick. Pennance trotted down the stairs, opened the door. A large man filled the space, silhouetted by a streetlamp so Pennance couldn't see anything of his features. Pennance reached out for the light. However, before his fingers found the switch the guy planted a solid fist in Pennance's stomach. All the breath whooshed out of Pennance and he folded over, gasping for oxygen. He dropped onto the ground, curled up into a ball, eyes scrunched tight. The guy must have bent down because he whispered into Pennance's ear. "Forget Blackthorn."

Pennance lay on the doorstep for a few minutes. First forcing air into his lungs, before he sat up inside the doorway, leant against the wall and rode the waves of pain which surged through his gut until they began to subside.

"Takeaway?" A woman leant over him. She wore a motorbike helmet, the visor up and the concern visible on the exposed section of her face – probably for herself as well as him. Pennance smelt Chinese food. She placed a paper bag beside him.

"Did you see anyone outside?" he asked.

"No, the alley is empty, sorry," she said. Pennance pushed himself to his feet and the agony flared again. He put out a hand to steady himself. "Are you okay?"

"I'm fine," lied Pennance.

The delivery driver picked up the bag and held it out for Pennance. He grabbed the handle, pushed the door closed and slowly climbed the stairs, palm pressed against the wall for support. Inside his flat he leant against the door, turned the lock. He limped over to the sofa and lowered himself down carefully. His mobile rang and he let it go to voicemail. He lay on the sofa for a few minutes, forearm resting on his forehead, allowing the discomfort in his gut to subside. He thought back to what the guy had told him after punching him – not what he'd said, but how he'd said it. An accent, though muffled.

American.

Eventually, Pennance felt like he could move around comfortably and he pushed himself up, carried the takeaway into the kitchen, poured the gloopy food onto a plate – it remained warm enough, but didn't look particularly appetising. He carried his mobile and his food to the table. While he forced his dinner down his throat he checked the call log. He'd missed three attempts to reach him, all from Fulton. And there was voicemail.

Pennance picked up the message, "Jonah, its Leigh Fulton. I had to release Neumann and Metzler earlier. Their lawyers found an excuse for them to walk. Just thought you should know. Call me if you want to talk."

He deleted the message.

Talking was the last thing he wanted to do.

Thirty

Pennance slept badly and when he rose the following morning it was a good half an hour before his alarm was due. A dull ache still throbbed across his stomach. In the bathroom he swallowed a couple of paracetamol and two ibuprofen – for pain and swelling respectively – and sunk them with a glass of water.

He made a coffee, headed for the roof, settled in one of the chairs and turned his phone back on. Once the signal dropped in, he received a text from Tremayne. "Call me when you get this." It had been sent more than an hour ago. Pennance dialled and Tremayne answered, despite the time.

"Up and at them early?" asked Pennance.

"Normal time for me, Jonah. It's the farming genes, to bed at dusk, rise at dawn." Pennance stifled a yawn. Tremayne continued, "And I had a fascinating read, thanks to you. Bright chap, that Alfred Fonseca."

"He was up until he got spiked. He's brain damaged now."

"Oh God, sorry."

"You've no need to apologise to me," said Pennance.

"I know, it's just..." Tremayne trailed off. Other people's bad news.

"The thesis?"

"Yes, of course," said Tremayne. "On a fundamental basis, Alfred wrote about behavioural economics, i.e. the study on the effects of psychology, culture and emotion on decisions made by investors, analysts and institutions. Alfred combined a number of models and then applied it to the cryptocurrency market. Okay so far?"

"Just about."

"I'll carry on then," said Tremayne. "People, and men in particular, are often deemed as individuals competing with each other. In other words, survival of the fittest, a theorem which arose from Darwin's evolutionary studies." Pennance thought back to his conversation with Fonseca Senior. Tremayne continued, "This kind of tussle dates back to the dawn of history. Battling for food, keeping the family alive and so on."

"Cave men vs. dinosaurs?"

"If you wish. Although there's little evidence *homo erectus* and genii actually lived in a cave and humans certainly weren't around at the time of the dinosaurs." Tremayne sounded stiff, and Pennance grinned to himself. "Fundamentally this approach is a pervasive win-lose mentality. So, if you live, someone else doesn't. If you get the promotion, someone else stays at the same rank."

"That one I understand. A zero sum game."

"Quite. However, in comparison, the hive approach describes a situation where organisms deliberately place their individualism to one side for co-operation and with the idea of *group* survival in mind. A win-win mentality."

"Like bees."

"That's the obvious example, yes. However, this can also occur when a family or several families combine. Darwin again made this very point; he postulated that, in the evolutionary struggle for survival, tribes who learned to work together had an advantage over those who did not. He also believed this was instinctive, not learned. Also, people may come together for reasons other than animalistic endurance, but because they seek approval or fear being isolated; much more common in modern society. So, that's Hive Theory, Jonah."

"Okay. I'm still with you."

"Next is Dual Inheritance Theory, also known as gene-culture co-evolution or biocultural evolution. They all assume human behaviour and biology are affected by a cultural and genetic link."

"In other words, nature vs. nurture."

"Absolutely; the genes we receive from our parents, the way we are raised and the environment we grow up in."

"This is all great, Alasdair, but what's it's got to do with my case?"

"I'm getting there. Remember the 1980s – yuppies, greed is good and all that crap?"

"Just about," said Pennance.

"Investors and traders operate in a highly competitive environment; the win-lose survival of the fittest mentality again. It happens that most of these people are men. Cortisone and testosterone affect aggressive behaviour in male traders. Aggressive behaviour is associated with high testosterone and reward. Cortisone, on the other hand, is present during events of heightened uncertainty. Studies found that financial crashes occurred as a result of intensified testosterone in traders while cortisone in these same individuals can delay economic recovery."

"Wow."

"It's all about subconscious emotion and physiology, Jonah. Comparatively, women have a fraction of the testosterone and consequently are much better at managing money. My wife deals with all of our finances. However, there are very few female traders. Then, if we move to groups, like a company, then crowds can be a problem in the investment world – groupthink, bubbles, crashes, irrational pessimism or exuberance are all driven by a negative hive type behaviour."

"Joe Kennedy's shoe shine boy."

"That's right, all the lemmings running towards a precipice. And this attitude is made worse without data to draw upon."

"Surely these days with internet access an information shortage isn't a problem?"

"That's assuming the relevant data is actually being shared. To receive, one has to give."

"What about the cryptocurrency angle?" asked Pennance.

"Ah, interesting also. Alfred appeared focused on the ideology of the minority wealthy ruling elite vs. the masses. He saw the former as politicians and the businesses which support them and the latter as the rest of us who aren't able to participate in this relationship."

"So, a small number of people telling everyone else what to do."

"Correct – queen bee and workers." Tremayne chuckled. "At certain times in history the masses revolted against this kind of control. Such as the English and French civil wars and the American Revolution. However, given enough time and a fading of memory the old status quo re-exerts itself, just under a different guise, always because the people who have the wealth have the power. An example is banks. The UK government owns the Bank of England and all its money. A tiny handful of people make laws, tax us and so on. Imagine if the Bank no longer had control over all the cash."

"Then the government loses a degree of influence."

"Right, and a significant amount at that."

"Someone I interviewed yesterday told me that the availability of cryptocurrency means we no longer have to follow the rules of banks."

"Right, so the masses throw off the control of the elite. However, Alfred saw this as an approach to be treated with caution."

"How so?"

"Money is the foundation of financial stability. There are two forms of cash creation – via the Central bank and commercial bank. So, that's the Bank of England and your high street institution respectively. The BoE establishes sterling as the main currency in the UK, or the Fed for the dollar in the US and literally prints the cash. Commercial bank money is generated by loans – car finance, mortgages and so on – which the bank offers based on the cash it has in its coffers, provided by the Central bank. Now, if something gets in the way of this relationship between credit and cash then there's a risk to the economy."

"Cryptocurrency."

"Correct, because that digital coin has not been manufactured by the Central bank, but some other party. A source outside of the government's control has created and distributed wealth which, if it happens on a large enough scale, disturbs the existing equilibrium and means a party other than the UK government could disrupt or even largely command the British economy – literally where citizens get their cash from."

"Bloody hell."

"The Bank of England and other Central banks around the world have been trying to create their own cryptocurrency, so a digital pound, digital dollar and so on. Then the Central bank is back to governing the money in our pockets and on our phones. However, they're not available yet.

"Now, Alfred went back to his Hive Theory behaviour and flagged that if cryptocurrency became increasingly popular then the group think of male traders hunting profit could force investors towards digital coins faster than the Bank of England were able to create their own. Then we are in a potentially dangerous situation. If there was another crash like in 2008 and many people held unregulated cryptocurrency, then their wealth would *literally* disappear. We could end up in a situation way, way worse."

"Did Alfred offer a solution?"

"No, he simply postulated the risk."

Pennance thought for a few moments. "This is all interesting, but I can't see why Alfred would be attacked and where the connection with Simone is."

"There must be something else," said Tremayne. "Which got me thinking and is why I've been pacing the floor from well before the sun rose. I think I got hit with a long con at Hussle. As a professional gambler, I should have known better."

"You've lost me."

"It's an elaborate confidence trick that develops over several stages and an extended time period to fool someone and gain their trust and then trick them into a big loss."

"A sting."

"Right, although the objective of the scam wasn't to take our cash, it's to hide something more significant."

"Like what?"

"Right now I don't know, Jonah. But I'm going to find out. The warrant for Hussle is still active. I'm back into their system and having another look through the data in case I missed something in my excitement over the Ponzi scheme."

"Call me if you discover anything."

"Absolutely." Then Tremayne was gone.

As was Pennance's habit, he checked the Underground service for any potential delays. He accessed the web browser on his phone and found the results from his previous search still on the page – the SoHO history group – which he'd opened yesterday before being distracted by Conryn. He headed for the 'About' section which told him SoHO had been created to 'bring compatible individuals together who care about preserving London's historical record'.

SoHO claimed to be 'The premier London society for organising site tours and visits to unique locations due to the Chairman's knowledge of the city and many contacts'. Pennance dropped into the blog page and found several articles detailing historical tours. Peppered throughout the text were photographs of members, presumably, maybe guests too, being walked around. Pennance peered at one of the most recently posted images, then he pinched and expanded it until

Alfred Fonseca, standing in the background, was unmistakable.

One man was front and centre in pretty much every shot, pointing something out or making a speech.

And Pennance knew him too.

***

Pennance hammered on the door repeatedly until there were footsteps on the stairs. A couple of menus hung out of the letterbox and, as usual, the alley was filled with the pungent odour of last night's cooking.

"Who is it?" A voice from inside.

"DI Pennance, open up right away."

The lock turned and a dishevelled Scott Langridge stood in the entrance, pulling a dressing gown about himself. He wore one slipper, his other foot bare, and his hair was a thatch. Langridge's eyes widened when he realised it really was Pennance. "Inspector, what are you doing here?"

"We need to talk," said Pennance. "Inside." As Langridge opened his mouth to ask another question Pennance spun him around and pushed him towards the stairs. Langridge stumbled, rescued himself by putting a hand out.

"Hey!" protested Langridge.

Pennance entered the hallway, pushed the door shut and followed Langridge up. "Keep going."

Pausing on the landing outside the kitchen Langridge said, "I was just making a cup of tea…"

"I don't care." Pennance pointed towards Langridge's office. "I'm here about Alfred Fonseca."

Langridge stared at Pennance for a long moment before he followed Pennance's direction. Langridge went to the windows, threw open the curtains, revealing rustled sheets and a pillow on the sofa. The funky odour of sleep hung in the air. He lifted one of the sash windows a crack, allowing in fresh air and the sounds of the street below before dropping into the chair behind his desk like his legs had suddenly run out of strength.

"Poor Alfred," said Langridge.

"Why didn't you tell me you knew him?" Pennance leant on the desk, towered over Langridge who seemed to shrink into his seat even more.

"Alfred hadn't been attacked when you came here," said Langridge in a quiet voice.

"What about after?" asked Pennance. "With Thewlis dead and Alfred seriously ill it didn't cross your mind to contact me?" Langridge only answered with a tiny shrug. Pennance continued, "You went to the hospital to see him."

"They wouldn't let me into his room. I spoke to his mother briefly, nice woman."

"Who's looking for answers about what happened to her son, Mr Langridge. Answers you could help provide but didn't bother."

Langridge looked away then, unable to meet Pennance's glare. He said, "Because I wondered if what happened to them was my fault. The thought has been eating me up."

"You introduced Alfred to Thewlis, right?"

"Yes."

"Why?"

"Alfred had come along to several meetings, but he barely made an impression on me. He always slipped into the society meetings last and left first. He never asked questions, never commented. He came to a couple of tours yet seemed irritated with the ennui. It was as if Alfred had no actual interest in the past. Or at least the past I was discussing. However, if he was willing to pay for the pleasure of boredom, I didn't mind. SoHO is a non-profit organisation and every penny counts."

"What changed?"

"A month or so ago, Alfred stayed behind after a meeting, which was unusual. Once everyone had left, he approached me, said he had a story he needed someone to write and publish. He wouldn't give me any detail beyond the fact that it was to do with his job and could be huge. Like I haven't heard that before." Langridge rolled his eyes.

"He said he didn't want to go to a big newspaper because they were all controlled by the elite. He sounded perfect for Thewlis, Alfred spouting the kind of stuff which turned him on." Langridge grimaced. "Thewlis called me the following day to thank me for giving him the opportunity to work with Alfred. I'd stopped engaging him for work by then you see. He sounded excited, energised in a way I hadn't seen or heard out of him for years. After that he sent me several emails, telling me the article was developing well. The last communication was a WhatsApp note saying he'd be able show me the final version shortly. I never heard from him again."

"When did he last message you?" asked Pennance.

"Two days before he died."

"Did you consider that his murder and the article could be connected?"

"No, why would I? It was only when Alfred was found that I started to think back to some things I'd dismissed as ridiculous that maybe weren't."

"Such as?"

"A man standing outside in Berwick Street, looking up at my window. Calls which went to answer machine and nobody leaving a message. Being followed when I left the office by the same guy. Thewlis had told me something similar, that he was convinced he'd been watched. I just dismissed that as Thewlis being his usual overly paranoid self."

"What did the man look like?"

"Just big. He stayed out of view, but in sight, if you know what I mean?"

"Not really," said Pennance.

"All I got was his size. Not tall, like you, bulky. And I believe he was American."

"Why?"

"I heard him on the phone once. He said, 'See ya.' In a cowboy twang.

"Have you heard the name Blackthorn?"

"Yes, Thewlis mentioned it. But no more."

"You're sure?"

"I have a good memory."

"Except for when it comes to helping your friends, Mr Langridge." Langridge didn't answer. Pennance stood, gave Langridge one last glance. "I'll see myself out."

"I'm sorry," said Langridge.

Pennance ignored him.

Thirty One

As Pennance pulled Langridge's door closed his mobile rang. Pennance moved away from the exhaust vent, towards Berwick Street and the calls of market stallholders advertising their wares, then answered.

"DI Pennance, its Damian Mulcahy at Sting. I've been looking at that phone footage you sent me, and something isn't right."

"How so?"

"Have you come across Deepfake images in your work?"

"Sometimes." All of Pennance's social media photos were Deepfakes. "It's the modern day equivalent of Photoshopping."

"More recently it's been applied to video, rather than image stills. The vast majority of Deepfakes out on the web are pornographic, some celebrity's face mapped onto a previously filmed porno, making it look like some amateur footage."

"Sounds pretty crude."

"In that form, yes. Hollywood is using the technology to bring long dead film stars back to life in new movies. It can be used to fabricate voices, too. The technology is similar to artificial intelligence and is called deep learning. Step one is to run literally thousands of photos of the person you want to imitate into an encoder which detects and learns resemblances between the features, before compressing the two together, eliminating the differences and leaving just the similarities. A second AI system, called a decoder, recovers the face from those compressed and pushes them into the video footage, replacing the original. To be convincing this has to happen on every single frame."

"That sounds like a lot of effort."

"Vast would be a more applicable word. It's next to impossible to achieve to any decent quality on a standard home PC. So, this is typically carried out on specialist equipment, a powerful unit with a serious graphics card or access to a hell of a lot of cloud computing power. That immediately reduces the number of people able to produce something convincing. Even then it would be hours of effort just to get the initial output. After which there's a touching up process which chews up even more time.

"For example, go back a couple of years and the modified subjects in Deepfake videos didn't blink. Then algorithms were developed to deal with that. More software improvements have followed, so it's become increasingly difficult to find these blemishes. Skin tone may be off, or the lighting looks weird, or there's a flicker as the tape rolls."

"What's wrong with this footage, then?" asked Pennance.

"At first I thought this was real. However, once I'd watched it twenty or more times I noticed some issues with the subject's hair. The AI systems struggle with individual strands. I sent the file to one of my white hat hacker friends to run an even more comprehensive review. Their assessment is the video is definitely modified. Whoever attacked the other guy, it wasn't the person in the video. Her face was replaced."

"Jesus," said Pennance. "One of my colleagues in digital forensics told me she'd analysed the footage, right down to pixel level, and deemed it genuine."

"How well do you know her?"

"Not so much, I only met her a few days ago."

"Would you say she's intelligent?"

"Definitely."

"And otherwise competent?"

"She's highly thought of within the NCA."

"Then it's probable your colleague lied to you. Anyone smart and with sufficient experience would detect enough to be at least wary."

"Thanks, Mr Mulcahy," said Pennance.

"If I can do any more, just shout, Inspector." Mulcahy disconnected.

Pennance phone rang almost immediately.

"Vance," said Pennance. "This had better be bloody good."

"No, it's not," said Hoskins. "Terrible, in fact. I've traced a connection between some of the hacked companies."

"Let me guess. Ava McAleney."

"She hit Hussle, Jonah. And plenty of others. I found on Companies House that her father used to be a Director of Hussle. Metzler replaced him."

"Bloody hell."

"What do you want me to do?"

"Nothing. Stay where you are. I'm coming for her."

Thirty Two

Pennance found McAleney in the basement of NCA HQ. She watched him walk across the office to her desk. "Inspector Pennance," she said.

"I need to speak with you." Pennance bent over, rested the knuckles of both hands on the desk, said, "I know everything."

"I promise that you don't."

"We can talk in private or here. But so help me, you'll be straight with me or I'll make it my personal mission to put you away for as long as I possibly can, no matter what it takes."

"It's about time you caught up, inspector." McAleney pushed herself out of her chair, strode towards the meeting room, leaving Pennance in her wake. She was waiting for Pennance when he entered, one hand on the door. She pushed it shut, then perched on the edge of the table, her expression neutral. "The video of Simone or my dad's connection to Hussle?"

"Both. I had the video independently verified and Hoskins made the link to your father."

"Well done, Vance."

"Tell me about your father."

"He used to work at one of Carnegie's many businesses. He was a very good trader, excellent in fact. Somehow, he caught Carnegie's eye and my dad accepted a role at Hussle as the Company Secretary. Carnegie even gave him a shareholding. However, before long the business started to tank and my dad took the blame. Carnegie fired him and ensured he never worked in the industry again."

"What went wrong?"

"My dad reckoned Neumann's algorithm was off. He tried to tell Carnegie but Neumann was having none of it. In the end either Neumann or my dad went."

"And this was enough for you to murder Carnegie?"

"I didn't kill Carnegie or Thewlis. Nor did I attack your girlfriend or Alfred Fonseca. I became a computer analyst to catch lawbreakers, not be one, long before my dad suffered at Carnegie's hands."

"Yet you hit Hussle among others."

"Kind of. I'm a grey hat."

"Looking for loopholes in organisation's systems and exposing them."

McAleney gave an appreciative nod. "That's right. I was in it for moral purposes until a few months ago when I received an email. Someone had tracked me down and found out my identity. Believe me, that's extremely difficult to do because I'm intensely careful. I rotate my passwords regularly, I use VPNs and so on. Whoever found me was very, very good. They threatened to expose my extra-curricular activities to the NCA, unless I helped them. At best I'd have been fired. At worst I'd have been thrown in jail. I couldn't tell anyone as they said they were watching me. If I deviated from their demands they'd go after my dad, my mother and my sister, too."

"So what have you been doing? Accessing police records? Making evidence go missing or doctoring it, like Simone's Deepfake video of Simone?"

"No, nothing like that. I swear to you I've not done anything to compromise the NCA. I have my beliefs, Jonah. I didn't put the footage on Simone's phone. I was told to approve it, though. My rubber stamp should have been enough to have made certain it was entered as evidence against Simone."

"You'd have just let her burn?"

"I deliberately introduced some flaws which would be spotted by anyone with a decent brain. I wanted it to happen in a way that my blackmailers couldn't trace back to me, not until it was too late for them. It was me who planted the idea in your head that it be independently checked. And it was me who let it slip to Hoskins about my dad's predicament."

"Why would someone target Simone?"

"You think whoever's extorting me is going to explain themselves?" McAleney snorted. "I've absolutely no idea."

"You could have talked to anyone here about what was going on."

"Have you not been listening to me? These people are extremely dangerous. My dad had a car accident, he ended up in hospital. They told me next time it would be much worse. You've no idea of the stress and fear I've been living under since they approached me. I've had to be seriously careful how I operated until I could strike back."

"Strike back how?"

"Communication is a two-way street, right? If they were able to find me, I could find them. Ever since that first email I've followed their digital trail back to the source. It's a laborious process."

"You've been tracking them?"

"Of course! Do you think I was just passively going to let them roll over me? Nobody else was going to dig me out of the hole I was in. And they were never going to let me move on."

"What have you found?"

"No actual identities yet, however my personal details were breached from an SSID which I tracked back to a company in Canary Wharf, called American Global Securities."

"Oh, my God." Pennance ran his fingers through his hair. "Lars Rasmussen works there."

McAleney's eyes widened. "Simone's husband!"

"Ex-husband," said Pennance.

"We should take this to Meacham."

Pennance shook his head. "I need actual evidence of Rasmussen's involvement or I'll just be accused of bias."

"I'll look into him, see what I can find."

"Hoskins will help," said Pennance. "We're not letting you out of our sight."

McAleney raised her hands, as if in surrender. "I can live with that."

Pennance's mobile rang.

"Jonah, Alasdair Tremayne. I've found something at Hussle. Meet me at Heron Tower, soon as you can. And bring back-up."

Thirty Three

Tremayne was waiting for Pennance in the corridor outside Hussle's office when the lift doors parted. He came over and said, "You took your time." Tremayne grabbed Pennance by the arm and all but dragged him out of the oversized metal box. "Where's the back-up?"

Pennance motioned back to the lift. "DCI Fulton of City Police."

Tremayne released his grip as Fulton stepped out. "He's it?"

"That's verging on insulting." Fulton raised his eyebrows at Pennance. "I assume you're the forensic accountant?" The lift doors closed.

"I am."

"Figures."

"Numbers, actually," said Tremayne. "Figures are the result of a calculation."

"Jesus," said Fulton. "This is the brightest and best of the NCA?"

"You said that?" asked Tremayne of Pennance. "That's kind but incorrect. I've been such a bloody idiot!" Tremayne stomped along the corridor, talking over his shoulder. "I was too busy celebrating my own cleverness to look deeper, which was exactly the point."

"What is, Alasdair?"

"Ingenious in its simplicity. Insidious, even." Tremayne paused at the office door, gripped the handle. "You'll see." He went inside.

Pennance followed, found the office lighting somewhat dim as the blinds were closed against the morning sun. Neumann rose from behind his monitor. He appeared dishevelled, rumpled shirt, tousled hair, enough facial hair to indicate his chin hadn't seen a razor for at least a day.

"Where's your partner?" asked Pennance. Fulton closed the door like a funeral director.

Neumann eyed Fulton, lips pinched. "I wish I knew." Neumann's tone was the opposite of Tremayne's a moment ago. Like someone had sucked all the life out of him. "We parted outside the police station yesterday and I haven't seen or heard from him since. I've called numerous times, straight to voicemail." He sank into his seat as if someone had cut the tendons in his legs. "I've been dealing with the fallout from the Ponzi scheme, liquidating as much stock as I possibly can to fill the hole. We're just about hanging on. The workload is huge, but I'm nearly there, no thanks to Metzler disappearing on me."

Tremayne stalked over to Neumann's desk. "None of that matters. The Ponzi scheme is irrelevant."

"I'm trying to save my company." Neumann looked beyond Tremayne to Pennance.

"It's the cryptocurrency that matters." Tremayne leant over Neumann. "Did you sell any of that?"

"Not yet."

"Of course you haven't. Because that's the key."

"Alasdair," said Pennance. "You're going to need to let us in on what's happening."

"Carnegie did nothing wrong. The Ponzi I found was all too obvious, I was duped, sucked in by a blind to throw me off the scent. Unfortunately for Hussle, the fraud, so to speak, was all too hastily constructed. Looked good from the outside, start digging a little deeper, though..." Tremayne held out his arms, wiggled his fingers like playing cards falling. "Ponzi schemes are a long con, they take place over years and require extensive investigation because of the numerous decisions that have been made by the players, the cash that gets moved around and redistributed, etc. But not here, there was none of that. The Ponzi was all a front and Carnegie was set-up to be the patsy."

"I'm liking this guy the more he talks," said Fulton.

Neumann blinked. "I've no idea what you're saying."

Tremayne continued, "Cryptocurrency is a danger to the establishment because it's unregulated money which operates outside the standard banking structure. The Bank of England has no claim to it, no influence over it. This is where it's brilliant. Hussle has been actively working on their existing clients to convert their holdings from cash and stocks to Bitcoin, Ethereum and so on. Any new clients who join do so in the understanding their investments will be retained in crypto. None of them really care because of the returns from the so-called algorithm. As a result, Hussle holds a disproportionately high amount of digital coin in its portfolio."

"How much are we talking?" asked Pennance. His mobile rang, but Pennance ignored it.

"Billions," said Tremayne. Fulton whistled. "In the scheme of things that's tiny, chief inspector. The UK's gross domestic product equates to approximately £2 *trillion*. Hussle's holdings are a mere grain of sand on the beach."

"Still, I wouldn't mind," said Fulton.

"What's the point of all this?" asked Pennance.

Tremayne grinned. "I found Hussle had been going through a due diligence process with a third party. That's where another company wanting to purchase the business checks out that everything the seller has been saying is true."

"Someone is going to buy Hussle?"

"Was," said Tremayne. "And with an extremely high multiple, some nineteen times annual profits. Why was the sale shelved, Mr Neumann?"

"I've no idea, Grady was the major shareholder. He would have known."

Pennance's mobile rang once more, he let it go to voicemail again. "But surely he would have discussed the move with you?"

"As I told you the first time you came here, inspector. Grady sometimes did as he wished."

Tremayne grinned. "And this, Jonah, is an example of a hastily constructed short con. I strongly suspect that it was, in fact, Mr Metzler and Mr Neumann driving the sale and Mr Carnegie who was resisting."

"Which would give you, Mr Neumann, a motive to murder Carnegie," said Pennance.

"That's a lie!" Neumann jerked out his seat. "It was Metzler who engineered the sale. He brought it to me and Grady only recently."

"Who proposed the move into crypto?" asked Tremayne.

"That was Metzler, too. A couple of years ago."

"And there," said Tremayne, "is your long con."

"Who was going to purchase the company?"

"Is, Jonah," said Tremayne. "Present tense. The sale is back on to a company called Blackthorn. Carnegie isn't alive to block the process."

"Blackthorn has an opaque ownership," said Pennance. "Who is it really?"

"American Global Services," said Neumann. "It's AGS buying Hussle."

Fulton's phone rang and he answered.

"Which means a US company will control all that unregulated cash," said Tremayne. "What will they be doing with it?"

"I don't know," said Neumann.

"Jonah," said Fulton. He held out his mobile for Pennance. "A PC Pruitt is trying to reach you. Says it's urgent."

"What's up, Kris?" said Pennance.

"We've a problem." Words fast and urgent from Pruitt. "DS Smithson isn't in her room. She's done a runner."

Thirty Four

"When did you last see Simone?" asked Pennance. He caught Fulton's deep frown and raised a finger at the DCI – just give me a moment.

"Fifteen, twenty minutes, maybe?" said Pruitt. "Dr Conryn went in to check on her so I took a bathroom break. Then Conryn came out and said Simone had left and there was nothing she could do to stop her."

"Does anyone else know she's gone?"

"Nobody besides me and the doctor," said Pruitt. "Why?"

"I need some time to find her and bring her back. Best if no-one is the wiser, if you get me."

"I'll stand by, Jonah. I'd better go, I've got a door to stand outside." Pruitt rang off.

"What the hell was all that about?" asked Fulton, hands on hips.

"Simone got away from Pruitt, I think with Dr Conryn's help." Pennance dialled Simone's number. "She's out on the streets."

"Jesus!" Fulton threw his hands out. "I'll have Pruitt's fucking badge for this."

The call went straight to voicemail. Pennance said, "No, you won't."

"Excuse me?" Fulton tilted his head towards Pennance like Lars the lizard eyeing a grasshopper.

"You heard," said Pennance. "Pruitt's a good cop. Simone's up to something specific, I'd bet."

Fulton stared at Pennance for a long, long moment before nodding. "Where would she have gone? You know her better than anyone."

"Not so much recently."

"People don't fundamentally change, Jonah." Fulton paused, then said, "Maybe to get her daughter?"

"Perhaps, but I don't think so. If she was that concerned for Natalie's welfare, she'd have burst her way out days ago, not sneaked off quietly."

"What's changed?"

"Good question, and there's one person we can ask." Pennance placed a call which was picked up immediately.

Conryn said, "Simone told me you'd ring. She just wanted a head start."

"Where's she going?" asked Pennance.

"Not where. Who, Inspector," said Conryn. "Her ex-husband."

***

It took Fulton seven minutes to negotiate the less than four miles from Heron Tower to The Isle of Dogs, heading east through Whitechapel and Limehouse, sirens on and blasting through every red light and weaving around static traffic.

While Fulton drove, Pennance clung on to the hand strap above his head. A mile out from American Global Services his phone rang and almost spun out of his grasp as Fulton took a tight corner, tyres squealing.

"Inspector, this is Hillary. Mr Rasmussen's PA. You need to come, quickly. Mrs Rasmussen is here." Hillary gulped. "She's got a knife."

"We're already on the way," said Pennance, shouting to be heard over the siren and aggressive engine tone. "No more than two minutes."

"I'll be in the lobby, please hurry."

Fulton didn't even glance at Pennance as he swung off Aspen Way, on the corner of the relocated Billingsgate Market. The HSBC building towered above them and, beyond, One Canada Square. A sign told Pennance a security checkpoint was ahead. Fulton braked hard as he reached the barrier, a red and white bar across the lane blocking their progress.

Pennance didn't bother to wait; that would mean guards and questions. He undid his seat belt, popped the door open and slid out with Fulton close behind. Pennance dropped into his middle distance, loping pace. Running again for Simone. He entered a covered walkway, like a tubular bio dome, with glass arching above him, and plants growing either side of the path. Then he was into a narrow shopping precinct, weaving his way through consumers wandering between small shops, before he reached a wide open grassed plaza which he cut straight across. He bounded up the concrete steps and found Strevens waiting for him just outside One Canada Square. Wordlessly, Strevens led Pennance, who'd barely broken into a sweat, into the lobby and to Hillary.

"Where are they?" asked Pennance.

"Upstairs," said Hillary. "In his office. She's got the door closed and Rasmussen trapped."

Fulton arrived then. He bent over at the waist, like he was going to heave his lungs onto the floor.

"Have you called anyone else?" said Pennance.

"Not yet," said Hillary.

"Unless you want us to?" asked Strevens.

"Best we handle it," said Pennance. "Take us there."

Hillary nodded, led Pennance, Fulton and Strevens to the lift, one with a notice stuck to the steel doors, 'Out of Order'. Strevens tugged the sign down, selected a key from a large and jangly chain, placed the key into a lock and twisted. The doors parted.

"No waiting," said Strevens.

Pennance entered, turned, faced the lobby, and briefly watched people moving about their normal lives, unaware of other's troubles, before the doors shut. Fulton and Hillary followed but Strevens remained where he was. "It'll take you straight to the floor," he said. "I'll keep an eye on things down here."

"What about the rest of the office?" asked Pennance as the doors closed.

"They haven't a clue," said Hillary.

"Let's keep it that way."

The elevator rose fast, but not quickly enough for Pennance. He wanted to be there instantly, in case Simone did something stupid. Then he corrected himself – more stupid. The box jerked to a halt and Pennance was through the gap as soon as the doors were wide enough, and striding into the lobby area of American Global Services. He entered the open plan area, heard the same hubbub of unmuted conversation and profiteering.

Pennance turned right, made his way to Rasmussen's office, the one next to the corner space he so craved. The blinds were closed across the glass partition, so Pennance couldn't see in. "I'm entering alone," he said.

"There's no point trying to persuade you otherwise?" asked Fulton. Pennance shook his head. "Thought not."

Hillary hovered a few feet back. "Oh, no. Vallance."

The big Texan was striding across the open plan towards Rasmussen's office.

"I'll deal with him," said Fulton. "Good luck."

'Luck'. Another intangible, like digital data, God and cryptocurrency. Pennance raised a fist, paused briefly before knocking lightly.

"Enter," said Rasmussen, his tone high pitched and stretched.

Pennance twisted the handle, crossed the threshold before he closed the door, blocking out much of the noise. He turned the lock. Rasmussen was behind his desk, Simone in one of the two visitor's chairs, facing him. She didn't turn, didn't react at all when Pennance took the seat next to her. Rasmussen flicked his eyes to Pennance, before refocusing on Simone. His jaw worked, like he was talking to himself. A bright red mark was evident on his cheekbone and some smeared blood marked the edge of his mouth. His normally quaffed hair was squashed to the side and his tie askew. Ordinarily, Pennance would have delighted in Simone smacking Rasmussen, but not when she was clutching a kitchen knife with a six-inch stainless steel blade.

"Are you okay?" asked Pennance.

"I've been better," said Rasmussen.

"I wasn't talking to you."

Pennance glanced Simone over. Tousled hair, as if pushed into shape, and she wore nurse's scrubs, probably stolen from the hospital given the clothing was loose on her. And Crocs, a purple pair which appeared over-sized. "I've been lying in bed for days," said Simone eventually. "Battling with my brain. Trying to pull up short term memories, holding back the ones from years ago. And all of them seemingly related to him." Simone nudged her chin at Rasmussen. "All the things he's done to me; manipulating my habits, the clothes I wore, who I saw, who I was friends with. Even the name I call my daughter by."

"What are you intending to do?"

"There's only one reason I brought this along with me." Simone shifted the blade, one of the overhead lights glinting off the metal.

"That's fine with me," said Pennance. Rasmussen's gulp was audible. "But I'd like to ask him some questions first, okay?"

"Sure."

"You can't do this to me," said Rasmussen. "I'm protected."

"Same old bullshit," said Pennance.

"Always," said Simone.

"No," said Rasmussen. "I mean people who'd snatch your job away in an instant and destroy your lives."

"Even if you were telling the truth, Lars, you wouldn't be here to witness it. I'd let Simone stab you first. Might even have a go myself. Perhaps we can claim self-defence. I mean, where's the witnesses?" Pennance glanced towards the shuttered window. "Tell me what I want to know and maybe you can leave, unpunctured."

"They won't let me walk."

"Neither will Simone, so that's your choice." Pennance shrugged. "Bleed to death here on this rather nice carpet, or take your chances outside." Pennance settled back, crossed one leg over another. "Vallance is waiting."

"There's another way," Simone pointed at the tinted glass. "Straight through the window and down onto the plaza." She shrugged at Pennance, too. "Mere seconds."

"Good point," said Pennance.

Rasmussen's eyes shifted between Pennance and Simone several times. Nobody filled the silence.

"Alright!" said Rasmussen eventually. "Ask me your bloody questions!"

"The corner office has always been your dream, I remember," said Pennance.

"So?"

"Hussle was your route to the top."

"Sure, but not to next door. Hussle would've taken me all the way to HQ in New York, like we talked about, Simone. Move as a family, yes?"

Simone didn't respond.

"You wanted to buy Hussle for their cryptocurrency portfolio, right?" asked Pennance.

"Them and others. We're in a financial cold war. Cryptocurrencies are changing who holds what influence. Central banks have run the show since their inception. Digital coin changes all of that. AGS, under my leadership, is sweeping up companies with significant crypto portfolios but without anyone knowing. The more crypto AGS controlled the more leverage it would give us when the market turned bad, because eventually it always happens."

"That's where Blackthorn comes in?"

"Blackthorn is the holding company AGS is using to purchase Hussle and the rest. Because of the ownership structure nobody would have been aware that AGS actually controlled all the assets. Not until we wanted them to, anyway."

"Why?"

"To protect our business strategy." Rasmussen shrugged, as if it should be obvious. "Like keeping your team sheet a secret until the moment before kick-off."

"Who were you talking to at Hussle regarding the purchase?"

"Metzler at first, then Neumann and finally Carnegie."

"But Metzler is the junior partner and neither of them had a controlling interest."

"The offer we made would have turned Metzler and Neumann into very rich men. Neumann was to retire. Metzler, though, was up for a significant retainer along with a transfer back to New York."

"What about Carnegie?"

"Initially he was keen. Until he learned what AGS was up to, then he changed his mind and backed out. Carnegie wanted the UK banking sector to be maintained as it is. He and I were due to meet the evening he died. I was laying on a show to get him back on track, but he never turned up."

"Because you killed him."

"No!" Rasmussen leaned across his desk, pushed his arms out to their full extent, palms up. "That wasn't me." Rasmussen turned to Simone. "You have to believe me, Simone." She stayed mute.

"Who then?"

Rasmussen dragged a hand down his face, from nose to chin. "Metzler called a few hours after I was due to meet Carnegie, told me he'd sorted Carnegie on my behalf. At first I was delighted, until I realised by 'sorted' he meant murdered."

"Why didn't you contact the police?"

"Because I'd have been charged as an accessory." Rasmussen nodded at Simone. "I lived with a cop for long enough to understand what that means."

"And Thewlis?"

"He got himself killed."

"Thewlis forced the bread into his own mouth? Stop talking crap, Lars."

"About a week ago, Thewlis contacted me at AGS, said he wanted to talk. I refused, until he told me he had direct evidence of AGS' plans for the cryptocurrency market and how it would blow open the British banking sector. We met in a pub, all very covert. He asked for money not to publish."

"How much?"

"A million in sterling."

Pennance whistled. "Nice deal."

"And worth paying to keep everything on track, frankly. I demanded evidence to prove what he knew, which he provided. Obtained via Alfred Fonseca, though I didn't know his name at that point."

"So, why kill him? And attack Alfred?" asked Pennance.

"And me," said Simone.

"Thewlis told me a couple of days later that his partner didn't want to deal, that he would be taking the story elsewhere. Metzler decided Thewlis and Alfred needed to be dealt with. Both knew too much, and blackmailers like Thewlis always come back for more."

"What about the sin eating?"

"All Metzler's idea, he reckoned it would confuse the investigation. Metzler has a tendency to over-complicate matters."

"Which brings us to Simone."

"Who's sitting right here, so stop talking about me like I'm chattel," said Simone.

"Sorry," said Pennance.

Rasmussen forced an apologetic grin. "Bringing in Simone was another decision by Metzler. I knew nothing about it until I received the next of kin call from the hospital. I was beside myself with worry."

"Big of you," said Simone.

Rasmussen shifted in his seat. "I blame you for all this, Jonah. You got in our way, mine and Simone's. We were happy until you showed up."

"That's untrue," said Simone. "Except for the early years, we were miserable."

"You might have been forlorn, I wasn't."

"Which says it all, Lars." Simone stared at Rasmussen for a long moment until she turned to Pennance. "He wanted my daughter."

"Our daughter," said Rasmussen.

"Not anymore. Earlier I remembered what happened before you found me, Jonah. I had a call from you, as Meacham said. Asking me to go to 15A Whitehall. It was related to Carnegie's murder."

"That wasn't me."

"It sounded like you."

Pennance remembered what Mulcahy had told him earlier. "Most likely a Deepfake."

"Anyway, when I arrived I found the place empty. I searched around and tripped over a body in an upstairs office."

"Alfred."

"Yes, though I didn't know it at the time. When I was bending over to check his pulse someone hit me on the back of the head. Then I was waking up in hospital with no recollection of how I'd got there. Or the previous half a day."

"That was a result of the salt poisoning."

"So Conryn told me."

"Metzler said later that that was him, too," said Rasmussen. "Alfred was sniffing around the building. He decided he'd do me a favour and deal with Simone, too."

"Deal with?" asked Simone.

"His words."

Simone stood, then slammed the tip of the knife into the desk, making Rasmussen jerk back out of the way. "We're done and so's he."

"Almost," said Pennance. "I got attacked outside my flat. I think by Vallance."

"He was out of control, I told him going after you was a mistake."

Simone stood.

"What are you going to do?" asked Rasmussen.

"Same as always. Let the law decide." Simone yanked open the door, revealing Fulton and a handcuffed Vallance pushed face first into the wall. "All yours," said Simone as she passed her DCI.

"We need to put an APB out for Metzler," said Pennance.

"Okay." Fulton nodded at Vallance. "What about this one?" He hiked a thumb at Vallance.

"Book him for assault." Simone was striding away across the open plan. "I'll get Simone back to the hospital."

"Leaving me to clear up your mess." Fulton grinned.

Pennance caught up with Simone in the AGS lobby area where Hillary was waiting. "You alright?" asked Pennance.

"What do you think?" said Simone.

Nobody spoke while they rode the elevator down or as they crossed the lobby, Strevens joining them. Pennance pushed the door open, held it for Simone. He cocked his head at the far off continuous scream which seemed to be getting louder. Outside, a couple of people were looking up, hands over mouths.

"What is that?" asked Simone.

Pennance leapt back at the loud crack just feet away. Blood splattered up the door. Shrieks now, shrill and loud. A body had hit the steps only feet away from them. Pennance went out as other bystanders backed away.

A man in a suit lay crumpled, bent and conformed to the steps. Blood had sprayed in all directions. An arm had broken off and skidded several feet away. A leg was twisted up under the torso. The skull had split open, revealing grey brain matter, the eyes protruded from their sockets. Despite the damage there was no mistaking this was Lars Rasmussen.

Hillary came out briefly, saw Rasmussen's corpse before she vomited. Strevens, a phone to his ear, led her back inside.

Simone came up to stand beside Pennance. She regarded Rasmussen like he was an irrelevance. "I suppose I did tell him to jump," she said.

***

Later, the entrance to One Canada Square was taped off and the clean-up was in progress. The plaza was empty of anyone unofficial and had been for an hour. After giving a statement Simone had left, not giving Pennance a backward glance.

Rasmussen's body had finally been removed and an ambulance was in the progress of taking him to a nearby morgue, watched by Fulton who stood a few yards away.

Pennance sat at a table outside one of the plaza restaurants. He felt utterly drained and in need of a serious caffeine hit. His phone rang. Hoskins. What now? Pennance answered.

"How you doing, buddy?" asked Hoskins.

"There have been better days."

"Well, maybe this will help. I've got Raskin for you."

"Where?" asked Pennance. Hoskins told him.

Pennance beckoned to Fulton across the plaza.

Thirty Five

Leo Raskin was sitting on a bench in St. James' park, a cone-shaped green space surrounding a substantial lake. Buckingham Palace lay at one end of the park, 10 Downing Street the other, with Whitehall just beyond. Power was everywhere, if you knew where to look.

Pennance approached Raskin from the rear, crossing a strip of grass before settling on the other end of the seat. If Raskin were on a see-saw, Pennance would be his counterbalancing partner.

"Ah, Inspector Pennance." Raskin bent slightly at the waist and dropped some crumbs for the pigeons which flocked about Raskin's feet and began to squabble over the morsels.

"Is that how you like it?" asked Pennance, nodding at the bickering birds, who'd begun flapping their wings and leaping at each other. "Doling out scraps from on high for the rest of us to pick over?"

Raskin gave Pennance a sideways glance, one eyebrow raised. "That's an interesting metaphor." Raskin then looked up when a shadow fell across him.

"Excuse me," said Fulton as he turned and made to sit down where Raskin was seated. The civil servant shuffled along and found himself braced by the two detectives. Fulton settled back, one arm across the rear of the bench, as if he were sunning himself.

DEAD MONEY

"This is my colleague, DCI Fulton," said Pennance. Fulton raised a nonchalant hand in response. "He isn't a very nice man."

"I'm really not," said Fulton.

"And I don't like him very much."

"Me either."

"What do you want?" Raskin's head twisted between Pennance and Fulton, like a spectator at a tennis match.

"Answers," said Pennance.

"I'll help where I can, but I doubt that will be much," said Raskin.

Fulton leant forward, said to Pennance, "Told you." He held his palm out.

Pennance sighed, handed over a ten-pound note which a grinning Fulton tucked away in a pocket. "You lost me the bet, Mr Raskin. I thought you'd be more honourable, whereas DCI Fulton believed you'd attempt to deceive me."

"I..." Raskin started to speak but Pennance cut him off.

"However, where DCI Fulton and are agreed is we loathe self-serving careerists." Pennance pointed at Raskin. "Such as you."

"How dare you!" Raskin started to rise until Fulton placed a hand on his shoulder and forced him back down.

"I'd wait around for another few minutes, if I was in your place," said Fulton. "Maybe try and keep out of jail."

"Jail?" Raskin's voice was barely a squeak.

"Accessory to murder," said Pennance.

"Murder?"

Fulton glanced past Raskin to Pennance once more. "He likes to repeat stuff."

Raskin blinked rapidly several times.

"I was talking to a friend earlier," said Pennance. "His father recently retired from government. He was Undersecretary in the Department of Agriculture."

"Adam Hoskins," said Raskin.

"That's correct. He didn't know you, though. Not at first. Apparently, in the scheme of things, you're quite a small person, despite the impression you like to give. Mr Hoskins had to do some asking around. My friend, Mr Hoskins' son, called me earlier with some information." Raskin sat, mouth slightly agape. "I was told that you're someone whose ambition far outweighs actual ability. However, unlike many people in your situation, you recognise that for a fact. So, you use underhand tactics such as guile and coercion to get on."

"Everyone does in government," said Raskin.

"That's your defence? Jesus." Fulton put a palm across his forehead. "He's going to prison, Jonah."

"You also have a tendency to overshare when you've been drinking tax-payer funded brandy," said Pennance.

The colour fled from Raskin's cheeks. "Mr Hoskins told me he'd been speaking with Hugh Fonseca. That's why I opened up to him."

"He lied," said Pennance. "Mr Hoskins only knew what I told him."

"Oh my God." Raskin buried his face in his hands for a few moments. Eventually he raised his eyes. "I was helping the country."

"Primarily, your interest was in yourself. You made a deal for your career."

"When an influential person asks for your help," said Raskin, "It's foolish to decline."

"That person being Hugh Fonseca," said Pennance. Raskin didn't reply, turned away to focus on the restless pigeons. Pennance continued, "I spoke with Fonseca yesterday. He said you'd approached him requesting Alfred to join your department." Raskin's head whipped around. He peered at Pennance through narrowed eyes.

"Sounds to me like the beginning of blame shifting," said Fulton. "Another government thing, perhaps?"

"Yep, throw someone junior under the bus," agreed Pennance. "That's why you went to Meacham, wasn't it, Leo? To cover yourself, just in case. But you didn't tell us everything. If I was you, I'd get talking right now."

Raskin nodded to himself. "My sub-department has been assessing the pros and cons of developing a sterling-tied cryptocurrency."

"A digital version of the pound."

"It's all been extremely secretive," said Raskin. "The last thing the prime minister wanted was for anyone outside government to hear about it. A rumour such as this could weaken the sterling's strength and, ultimately, affect the economy. On the other hand, Britain couldn't stand by while bad actors like China and Russia developed their own."

"Which is where Hugh Fonseca came in."

"He requested Alfred join my team, I wasn't lying about that. At first I was extremely wary, because I knew where Fonseca's loyalties lay – towards the European Union. The PM views the EU as the enemy, also. So, I said no to Fonseca."

"However, you saw an opportunity."

"A favour now for a favour in the future," said Fulton.

"Quite," said Raskin. "It's how the world works."

"Fonseca told me the same thing," said Pennance.

"Anyway, I informed the PM that everything with Alfred would be alright and his skills were entirely necessary. So, Alfred started working for me a few days later," said Raskin. "Right from the beginning I could see he wasn't cut out for the civil service. He was withdrawn and negative, difficult to engage with. He clearly didn't understand working for government is a sacrifice and that we have to put our own personalities aside for the UK. But, for his father, I took Alfred under my wing and gradually he bent into a useful sort of shape. I thought he was doing okay until Hugh Fonseca called me." Raskin pressed his hands together. "We met right here. He was where you are now, inspector. Fonseca was furious, said Alfred was giving him nothing useful and what the hell was I up to? I had no idea what Fonseca was on about. I was holding up my end of the deal. He told me I was lying and I'd regret misleading him. Then he stormed away. That was two days before you found Alfred."

"Alfred was working with Thewlis instead."

"The reporter." Raskin pursed his lips. "Seemingly so." Holding his hands wide, Raskin said, "That's all I can tell you. I've been scrupulously honest." Fulton snorted, raising a brief frown on Raskin's forehead in response. "What's next?"

"I don't think you've committed any crime I can arrest you for," said Pennance.

"Thank God." Raskin sagged back.

"But I have influential friends, too." Pennance stood. "When you get back to your office, you'll find a letter terminating your employment with immediate effect."

Patting Raskin on the shoulder Fulton said, "Enjoy your day."

Fulton fell into step with Pennance as they headed across St James' park and back to the squad car. "I quite enjoyed that," said Fulton. "What's next?"

"I'm going to hospital. Then a holiday. And afterwards, who knows?"

Fulton raised a quizzical eyebrow but said nothing.

***

When Pennance entered Alfred's ward at University College Hospital he found only a mattress on the bed. The sheets had been removed and taken away, as had Alfred himself. A handbag sat atop the bedside cabinet. The sound of flushing water came from the bathroom and, moments later, Fenella Fonseca stepped into the bedroom. She started when she caught sight of Pennance, put a hand over her heart.

"Inspector, I didn't see you there."

"Sorry," said Pennance. "Where's Alfred?"

"He's being put in an ambulance. I'm taking him home, at last."

"That's good."

"Not really, Inspector. He won't have any quality of life, but I'll be there to look after him until the end, whenever that is."

"I promised I'd find out why this happened," said Pennance. "And I have." Fenella clasped her hands together like she was praying and pressed them against her lips. "He was attacked by Casey Metzler, who was trying to sell his company to an American business and Alfred was threatening to expose him via Stan Thewlis, the reporter."

"Have you arrested this Metzler?"

"He boarded a plane yesterday and flew back to the US. The NCA has connections with Interpol so some colleagues pulled a few strings at the FBI and Metzler is currently in custody pending an extradition petition. It'll take a few weeks, maybe more, but before too long Metzler will be on his way back to the UK to be prosecuted."

"Thank God." Fenella covered her face with a hand. Pennance let her gather herself. Eventually she said, "Why did Alfred get embroiled in all of this?"

"Metzler and another man, Lars Rasmussen, were working together to undermine the UK Central Bank for their own profit. Alfred played a large part in stopping them. He's a hero, Mrs Fonseca."

"That doesn't explain the how, though." Fenella peered closely at Pennance for several moments. "There's something you're not telling me, right, inspector? Just rip off the plaster. The sooner you do it, the sooner the pain is over."

Pennance sighed. "Alfred became involved because of your husband. From what I've heard via a civil service contact, your husband has been working with the European Central Bank on a currency deal. He wanted to have knowledge of the UK's plans, perhaps even derail them, in order to tie our government into Europe. Maybe he thought this could be the start of reversing Brexit in some form. Alfred went to Thewlis to break the story, rather than your husband. As a result, Thewlis died, too."

"It seems Hugh has had a hand in a lot of misery."

"This is all hearsay, Mrs Fonseca. I've no definitive proof."

"You've given me enough, inspector. I can make him pay." Fenella nodded, her eyes narrowed to paper slits. "And I will."

***

Pennance did as he'd said to Fulton and took some holiday. He spent the majority of his time rifling through charity stores and second hand shops across London, deliberately avoiding The City and skirting around Greenwich. He wasn't in a rush to return to either district.

After returning home one day with a reasonable haul, including a signed Bryant & May novel, Pennance was feeding Lars and her offspring (overnight she'd delivered three baby iguanas) when his mobile rang.

He recognised Simone's number. He hadn't heard from her at all since he'd left her outside One Canada Square.

"Jonah, its Simone."

"How are you doing?"

"There's stuff I still can't remember but otherwise I'm fine, thanks. I'm currently standing outside your place."

"My flat?"

"That's what 'your place' means. And get a move on, it's raining and I'm wet."

"I'm coming." Pennance trotted downstairs and pulled the door open, revealing Simone, her hands jammed into jean pockets. She'd got rid of the blonde hair, dying it black instead, and she had dark circles under her eyes.

"It really is you," said Pennance.

"Who else would it be?"

"How's Natalie?"

"Doing surprisingly well, thanks for asking."

"Come on in," said Pennance.

"I'm not staying. I only came to tell you not to give up on the NCA. You'll do great there." Simone reached inside her waterproof jacket and pulled out a cube-shaped packet clad in wrapping paper. "And to give you this." When he took it, Simone turned, glanced over her shoulder. "See you around, maybe."

Pennance slowly closed the door, then, in the gloom of the hallway, tore the paper off Simone's gift. He hit the light switch and found it was a mug, with a cartoon rendition of a sheep doing what seemed to be a Michael Jackson dance move and a statement, 'You're baa-aad'.

He laughed, went back into the alley as Simone took the corner onto Clapham High Street and disappeared out of sight. Pennance stood in the rain, felt the drops splash onto his upturned face.

Everything was going to be alright.

THE END.

Other Novels by Keith Nixon

The Solomon Gray Series
Dig Two Graves
Burn The Evidence
Beg For Mercy
Bury The Bodies
Pity The Dead
The Silent Dead
Betray Them All
The Jonah Pennance Series
Blood Sentence
Dead Money
The Konstantin Series
Russian Roulette
I'm Dead Again
Dark Heart, Heavy Soul
The Fix
The Harry Vaughan Series
The Nudge Man
The DI Granger Series
The Corpse Role
The Caradoc Series
The Eagle's Shadow
The Eagle's Blood

About The Author

Keith Nixon is a British born writer of crime and historical fiction novels. Originally, he trained as a chemist, but Keith is now in a senior sales role for a high-tech business.

Keith currently lives with his family in the North West of England and writes something every day.

Readers can connect with Keith on various social media platforms:

Web: http://www.keithnixon.co.uk
Twitter: @knntom
Facebook: Keithnixonauthor
Blog: www.keithnixon.co.uk/blog

Printed in Great Britain
by Amazon